PRAISE FOR DAVID BLACK

In his hero Harry Gilmour, David Black has created a Jack Aubrey for the modern age. And set him at the heart of a tale as epic as those of O'Brian and Forester; a tale that encompasses not only the same thrill of action, but also the same compassion and understanding for the true heroes of our nation's seafaring traditions – the fighting sailors then, as now.

– Admiral of the Fleet, Lord Boyce KG GCB OBE;
former First Sea Lord and the Royal Navy's senior submariner

It's a wonderful book and . . . the evocation of naval life, submarines, and even the feel of wartime itself are all beautifully done. The characters and the description of 'the Trade' and how it worked reminded me rather of what my old 'Tankies' told me about their lives crammed into those other metal boxes with death often over the next ridge.

– Mark Urban, Diplomatic Editor of BBC2's *Newsnight* and
author of *Rifles* and *The Tank War: The Men, the Machines and
the Long Road to Victory*

TURN
LEFT FOR
GIBRALTAR

ALSO BY DAVID BLACK

The Harry Gilmour Series

Gone to Sea in a Bucket

The Skipper's Dog's Called Stalin

DAVID BLACK

TURN LEFT FOR GIBRALTAR

A Harry Gilmour Novel

Text copyright © 2017 David Black

Published by Thomas & Mercer, Seattle

www.apub.com

Amazon, the Amazon logo, and Thomas & Mercer are trademarks of Amazon.com, Inc., or its affiliates.

ISBN-13: 9781477819494
ISBN-10: 1477819495

Cover design by Lisa Horton

Printed in the United States of America

To Alison, my first muse

*We should have taken Alexandria and reached the Suez
Canal had it not been for the work of your submarines.*

*— Generalleutnant Fritz Bayerlein, Chief of Staff,
Deutsches Afrikakorps*

Preface

This is a work of fiction, but because it takes place in a real place and time in history, it deals with real events and real people. Characters such as Shrimp Simpson, Hubert Marsham and Max Horton were real people, doing the very real jobs I describe throughout the siege of Malta. I have attributed words and deeds to them I could not ever know about, and so neither can be mistaken for fact. The picture I have portrayed of them, however: the cool, calculated valour, tirelessness, tactical skills, the dedication to duty and the care they showed to their men – in fact, all the necessary attributes a man must possess to command in wartime – I believe to be completely true. And I hope and trust that their surviving friends and relatives will forgive my presumption.

Where I name a ship and place her in significant action, I have tried to use a fictional name out of respect for the families of those who actually served in the Royal Navy during the Second World War.

As for the N-class submarine, such as HMS *Nicobar*, there never was such a class in service with the Royal Navy during the Second World War – I invented her because I needed a better U-Class boat.

Finally, when it comes to the action, it is all as true as I could make it.

British, Italian and German officers, mostly from their respective air forces, were indeed interned on Majorca, and they did indeed live hugger-mugger and carry on much as I have described. Although I did not encounter any incident in which any of them tried to escape, certainly not British or Italian officers.

The siege of Malta, too, progressed much as described, as did the losses among the submariners of the Tenth Flotilla.

Anyone interested in delving deeper into the full epic of the siege of Malta should look no further than James Holland's excellent history of the campaign, *Fortress Malta*. And for a blow-by-blow account of Royal Navy's Tenth Flotilla in the central Mediterranean between 1940 and 1944, there is *The Fighting Tenth* by John Wingate.

Chapter One

'You hit the main mast of HMS *Renown* – and you're still alive?' asked Harry, in English.

They'd been speaking Italian up until this point, so Fabrizio frowned, not exactly sure of the precise meaning of what had just been said to him, but from Harry's incredulous stare getting the drift. He gave his Italian shrug.

'You were so low, your wing clipped the mast of a British battlecruiser?' Harry repeated.

But Harry couldn't wait for the answer. He began rolling around on his lounger, helpless with laughter.

Fabrizio's frown deepened. He took another belt of his tumbler full of gin and vermouth, topped off with soda water. 'They weren't interested in me in my single-seat, single-engine, popgun-armed Folgore,' he said, surly, in Italian. 'They were shooting at the Savoia-Marchetti torpedo bombers.'

If you were up on one of the hotel balconies and out of earshot, you'd have thought they were just two ordinary young men, admittedly rather handsome ones, with nothing better to do than sprawl on loungers and tell jokes. They were both wearing light-coloured Oxford bags and open-necked shirts; Harry in a dark-blue sweater, and Fabrizio with his fawn one draped over his shoulders. They were out sunning themselves on the pool terrace, on a still-warm Mediterranean autumn afternoon, not a care in the world. Nothing here to tell you it was 1941 and there was a war on, out there beyond the horizon, and not a hint from these two young men that they fought on opposing sides.

Someone was watching: a tall man in a light-blue summer uniform. The two small golden starbursts below the chevron on his sleeve said he was a Teniente Coronel, a Lieutenant Colonel, of the Ejército del Aire, the Spanish air force, EdA for short. He was bare-headed, so you could see his silky, light-brown hair was already starting to recede, a fact emphasised by the way he wore it swept straight back. He was still young, almost impossibly young. And he was the absolute spitting image of the actor David Niven, right down to the pencil moustache and the crinkles when he smiled. He was smiling now. His name was Eurico de la Peña, and he was very pleased with the way the young Italian seemed to be cheering up these days. The fact that the young British naval officer could speak Italian, and the fact that the circumstances of his arrival here had been even more inglorious, seemed to be doing the trick. Because, for a while, Eurico had feared for Signor Fabrizio's state of mind.

Meanwhile, back in his serviceable Italian, Harry was saying, '. . . and the torpedo bombers. They shot them down? *Renown* shot them down?'

Fabrizio's answer was a sullen stare.

'*Renown* shot them all down,' said Harry, 'and now you feel guilty because you're still alive and they're not.'

His words met with the same stare.

Eurico, eavesdropping from above, nodded. He considered himself a student of the human condition, and not just as a passing fancy. He was fascinated by it. And after all this silliness was over, he intended to take up the study of psychoanalysis as a profession, so this little Petri dish of a command over which he presided had, in the course of the preceding months, turned out to be a most excellent foundation course.

He observed the two young men below more closely. Harry had stopped laughing, and had sat up and swung his legs round. He was looking down at Fabrizio, all serious now.

'Well, that's not your fault,' he heard Harry say.

Eurico couldn't know, however, what Harry was thinking right then. That he was imagining the sheer size and imposing presence of HMS *Renown*; trying to see her as this young Italian airman must have seen her – all 750 battleship-grey feet of her; and her six fifteen-inch guns; and her four-inch and three-inch secondary batteries; and all the light anti-aircraft guns, the whole thirty-two thousand tons of her bristling with them – all blazing away as she pounded through the waves, her four giant props driving her at over thirty-two knots! And he was wondering at the courage that must have driven this fellow.

'It's called fire control,' Harry pointed out patiently to Fabrizio, in Italian. 'You didn't *fail* to draw *Renown*'s fire. They just weren't shooting at you, you daft lump. You were in a fighter plane. The most damage you could do to *Renown* was chip her paintwork. But the torpedo bombers could sink her. The bloke in the gunnery control tower directing her anti-aircraft fire would have been ordering all the AA gunners to ignore you. Good grief, he probably wouldn't even have had to. These were Royal Navy gun crews you were flying against . . . *battle*-hardened Royal Navy gun crews. Those boys wouldn't have needed telling who they should be shooting at.'

And at that, Harry smiled to himself. He was remembering something said to him by an older, more senior officer a long time ago, after he had survived his first close-run thing with death: 'You're not going to be a girl about this, are you?'

'So stop being a girl,' said Harry, all gruff and dismissive, as he reached to top up Fabrizio's glass from the pitcher. 'And have another drink.' Only then did he let his face break into a smile. 'Bet you smashed up their masthead light good and proper, though. Your name will've been mud in the Bosun's mess. And anyway, you haven't heard yet how I ended up here.'

Watching the two men, Eurico was smiling too. After all, his experiment appeared to be working. For Teniente Coronel Eurico de la Peña had a kind heart – he genuinely had not wanted to wake up one morning and find Fabrizio dangling from a home-made noose, especially after he had survived so much. It was not that Eurico had anything such as a formal duty towards him. Neither Fabrizio nor the other young man were under his command, far from it. But as senior air force officer on the Balearic Islands, he was responsible for them, and for the thirty or so others who had managed to fall out of the sky or wash up on the beaches of these Spanish islands – these neutral Spanish islands. Interned belligerents. That was their official designation under international law. Officers of the German Luftwaffe, and the Italian Regia Aeronautica, and from the other side too: the RAF boys and Royal Navy Fleet Air Arm. All here because their war had been cut short somewhere over the western Mediterranean. Mechanical failure or enemy fire, it didn't matter – they'd all faced a pretty simple choice: they could either end up in the drink, as the British called it, with precious little chance of ever being picked up; or bail out, crash-land or otherwise deposit themselves on neutral Spain. So here they were. Not quite prisoners of war, because Spain wasn't at war, yet not quite free to roam around like tourists causing mischief, because no one had invited them in. It was more like being on parole while they waited for their respective consular officials to arrange their repatriation, and then they could get back to their squadrons, and get on with killing each other.

And since they were nearly all aircrew, it fell to the Ejército del Aire, the EdA, to look after them. And that was why Eurico had them all holed up here, together, in the same place – the Hotel El Real, built into the huge fourteenth-century fortress that surrounded the Palacio Real de La Almudaina, overlooking the old port of Palma de Mallorca. No segregation. All bundled together. From the beginning, Eurico had accepted that it was a measure that could lead to complications, but so far it had generated more amusement than conflict, and at least it kept them out of the way of the Army.

The young Italian lad, Fabrizio di Savelli, was Regia Aeronautica; a Sottotenente – or what the British called a Second Lieutenant. He had arrived in a single-engine Folgore fighter that had barely managed to claw its way over the airfield perimeter fence at the Son Bonet Aerodrome before pancaking in a heap on the runway. That had been almost two months ago. Even Eurico had to admit, it had taken some fancy flying on Fabrizio's part to keep his Folgore in the air at all, let alone nurse it back over however many miles of Mediterranean. He had actually watched young Fabrizio bring it in, and had been slack-jawed. Depending on the angle you looked at the Italian fighter, it had at first appeared immaculately unscathed, with no apparent cause for the engine to be racing and screaming as if it were being tortured. It was only when the pilot's efforts flickered and one wing came up and the other dipped, that you could see the aircraft was missing a substantial bit of wing tip – snapped right off, with two sheared spar ends left rattling in the slipstream. How the pilot still had the brute strength to continue holding her from flipping right over into a spin after God knows how many hours in the air defied all logic. So, when the pilot actually stood up from the wreckage – there had been no fire because there had been damn all fuel left to burn – Eurico was already striding across the airfield to meet him and shake his hand, one pilot to another.

He remembered being especially pleased to see that the young Italian appeared to have suffered no injury; in fact, he had risen as you might from a good meal. But Eurico had been wrong about there being no injury.

Despite his dramatic entrance, since he had arrived, Fabrizio had refused to admit to anyone how he had come to lose part of his wing and end up in Eurico's internment camp – *luxury* internment camp. Not to Eurico, not to his fellow Regia pilots, not even to the Maggiore

– the Regia Aeronautica Major – who commanded the extended bunch of Italian aircrew currently languishing under Eurico's hospitality. Fabrizio had brooded. His fellow pilots had tried to josh him out of it – and then given up. The Maggiore had just shrugged and said things like, 'Ah well, you see . . .' and made calming, let-it-be gestures. Eurico, however, couldn't help but suspect that the young pilot was ashamed about something, although after that exhibition of airmanship that had got him here, he couldn't imagine what.

Meanwhile, Fabrizio was quietly shutting himself off; or, as Eurico's RAF guests would say, 'getting himself into a right old tizzy'.

Two months later and Sub-Lieutenant Gilmour had been deposited on the quay at Puerto de Sóller by fishermen, wet, salt-encrusted and exhausted, stepping gratefully off a smelly tuna boat. When he had been hosed down and relieved of the rancid blanket he was wearing, he'd been delivered to Eurico, as all officers from belligerent nations were supposed to be. Eurico had welcomed him, and inquired as to how he had come to be in need of Spanish hospitality.

Harry, apparently, had been picked up from a lifeboat that had been bobbing around for some time on the northern edge of the British main convoy route down the Mediterranean. Except, when the fishermen found them, the British naval officer was looking positively spritely compared to the half-dozen or more half-starved and half-delirious middle-aged merchant seamen from some bombed British tramp steamer whose lifeboat it was. To the fishermen's experienced eyes, the merchant seamen had obviously been in the lifeboat a lot longer than Sub-Lieutenant Gilmour.

So Eurico was keen to hear Harry's story and, when he had, he realised he had a young man whose arrival on Spanish territory must be even more questionable than Fabrizio di Savelli's. And not only that, but a young man who, like Fabrizio, was also a junior officer, and . . . and Eurico could hardly believe his good fortune when he discovered it . . . In fact, if he had been a religious man, which, surprisingly for a Spaniard, he wasn't, he would have regarded it as a sign from God, a divine blessing on his plan: the young British officer could actually speak Italian. Well, Italian after a fashion.

That was what gave Eurico his idea: he would put them together, get them to talk and maybe, just maybe, Fabrizio would see that if this shambling, amiable, laconic youth could live with himself after *his* escapade, then so could he. And there they were, both laughing now. It appeared to be working. Indeed, the pair looked as though they might even become friends. Not that surprising, really. Very few of the British and none of the Italian officers here had seemed to take the war or politics that seriously. Especially when there was carousing to be done. There'd been a lot of friendships. Of course, that would only last until their papers could be processed. Then, he supposed, it would be back to business as usual. That thought pushed the smile from Eurico's face.

It was now late afternoon and shortly they would no longer be alone at the hotel. The British and the Italians had already missed 'afternoon tea' and would be determined not to miss 'sundowners'. It being Thursday, the day the English taught the Italians cricket, one or the other side would be arriving back in particularly high spirits, alas.

And the Germans: they would be due back from their afternoon route march. Eurico found himself hoping the Anglo-Italian throng and the German column would not meet on the drive. For the Germans disapproved of their fellow internees mightily. It was a feeling that was mutual. The Germans disapproved of the British because they were the enemy, and of the Italians because they didn't seem to care, and of both because neither seemed to be treating the war with the gravity it demanded, or to be in the slightest bit eager to return to it. As for the British and the Italians, they disapproved of the Germans for the exact opposite of all the reasons the Germans disapproved of them – and also because they thought the Germans were all arrogant arses who had their Nazi salutes up each other's bums, an achievement that was commented on often and loudly. So, on the odd occasion when their paths did cross, en masse, it invariably ended in a full-throated rendering of obscene songs and a truly childish amount of buttock-baring and rude gestures. And, of course, there was then the ensuing avalanche of letters of complaint from every shocked local who'd managed to crane their neck sufficiently far to be disgusted by the spectacle. Eurico decided not to wait and see. He turned on his heels and marched purposefully back to his office in the hotel.

Chapter Two

Harry wasn't in the mood to see the cricket teams return either. He let Fabrizio head up to the bar, and then went and got his swimming stuff, intending to head off for the pool. The drinking would begin with 'sundowners', then progress to 'aperitifs' before the Italians and the British – English, really, since they made up the entire contingent, bar one – went into the mess for dinner, which was a dress-up affair with candles and waiters and lots and lots of wine. As for the Germans, they made a point of never joining them for dinner – or for anything, for that matter.

Harry had been on the island a few days now, and wasn't enjoying himself, unlike the Italian and English airmen. He supposed he was still in a bit of shock at the events that had brought him here. The bloody war: you never knew what was going to happen next. He should have been on Malta right now, joining his new submarine. Instead he was on another Mediterranean island, in the midst of what he could only describe as a bacchanalian revel, presided over by their own minor deity in the shape of Teniente Coronel Eurico de la Peña, who appeared to be behaving as if it were, in true Greek tragedy-style, all being played out purely for his own amusement. There was even a Greek tragedy-style chorus off to the side, courtesy of the Luftwaffe boys, providing commentary and moral disapproval.

These dinners were rough affairs, especially after the remove. Which was the point at which Harry would eventually be allowed in. Up until then he was barred, because the local British consul had yet to approve his visit to the local tailor. Which meant all that Harry had to wear right now was borrowed stuff, which didn't include white mess Number Twos.

And, as he was informed by several of the RAF johnnies, seeing as he had not yet been kitted out with the proper mess kit, it was quite impossible for him to dine with the gentlemen. 'Standards, old boy,' they had explained. 'Can't let the side down.'

However, he was always admitted in time for the 'digestifs' and then the 'nightcaps', and what that meant was, he was always in time for the 'entertainment'. Mostly that seemed to centre around games of indoor rugby and a form of human steeplechase that involved a course with jumps made from sofas and soft furnishings, where the 'jockeys' had their wrists tied to their ankles and were expected to roll and tumble their way from starting whistle to finish.

Harry, on his first night witnessing these events, had sought out another RNVR Sub-Lieutenant who was also a guest of the Spanish air force. The young man had sported the pilot's wings of the Fleet Air Arm on his crisp, starched-to-a-blade mess whites, and was called Terry Oswald.

They were all standing around the walls of the hotel's beauti-ful, high-ceilinged, faux rococo dance hall. 'Jesus Christ!' Harry had observed as a field of steeplechasers had set off tumbling and rolling down the sprung floor and over the arrayed furniture to much whoop-ing and yelling, and a never-ending, piercing commentary on the changing odds from some Italian flyer perched on a huge dresser.

The young, chubby, curly-haired and deeply tanned pilot had nod-ded in solemn agreement. 'Know what you mean, old man.' Harry hadn't noticed at first how much he was swaying. 'Bloody crabfats!'

Harry had recognised Jack's ancient slang for the Royal Air Force, coined, legend had it, all the way back to the RAF's origins in 1918, when the colour of their new uniforms coincided with the then treatment for pubic lice: a bluey-grey jelly called crabfat.

'A complete amoral shower, the lot of them,' Terry had continued. 'Officers? Ha! I say. Not a scrap of moral decency, moral fibre or moral rectit . . . rectity . . . Ha! Did I say titty? Eh? . . . Not one of 'em . . . what's . . . er . . . you know . . . being upstanding? The word? Anyway, not one, among them! Drunk, they are. And in the King's uniform too! Drunk, I say!'

'So are you,' Harry had observed mildly.

'Quite. You noticed. Yes, well, we've been corrupted, haven't we? Me and Tyrell and Uncle Byron over there,' Terry had said, gesturing to the other Fleet Air Arm boys. 'It's a bloody business!' And then Terry had given him a bleary smile as he looked down at Harry's empty glass and then back to his face. 'Drink?'

And then there had been the senior Royal Air Force officer, Group Captain Jock Mahaddie. A Jock by name, and as Harry had quickly discovered a 'Jock' by profession. That was something Harry was allowed to say, seeing as Harry was a Scot himself. He knew the type.

'So. Another Jock, eh?' Mahaddie had said, looking down his nose at him, rolling his 'rrr's and drawing out his nasal twang. 'You don't sound like one. No' a proper one, oany-wise. Where from?'

'Argyll, Sir,' Harry had replied respectfully.

'Argyll, eh? And what d'ye do when yer no' knittin' socks then, eh, laddie?'

Again, respectfully, Harry had replied, 'I am a submariner, Sir.'

'Submariner, eh? Where's yer submarine then? Eh?'

'It dived, Sir.'

'Don't come the smart alec wi' me, laddie!'

'I was upstairs, I fell off, it dived. That's how I'm here, Sir.'

13

Mahaddie had thrust his face into Harry's, so close Harry could see the individual thinning hairs on his porridgy brow and the little ripples of skin, already sagging to jowl, predicting how that face would look in future. He could even see blackheads.

'. . . Is that right, laddie?' he had hissed.

'Sir,' Harry had interrupted before Mahaddie could launch, 'you know I can't say anything to you about submarine operations. It's regulations, Sir. I just can't. I'm not being smart.'

Mahaddie had slowly withdrawn his face, his watery eyes drinking in every one of Harry's features for storage against the grudge he was going to bear. Of course Mahaddie knew; that was the trouble.

'You could be anybody,' he had said at length, and from that moment on had regarded him as such.

Harry didn't snap out of his reveries until he was already standing at the pool's edge. To all the other internees, it would have been far too cold for a swim; but for Harry, now in his trunks, the Mediterranean autumn was positively balmy compared to the weather back in Blighty, where he'd been mere days before. He looked around, taking in the bleached medieval stone of the surrounding citadel's walls, now brushed golden by the sinking sun, and the deep, dappled turquoise of the pool's water, and for a moment considered how preposterous it was that it had taken a world war to actually get him from his rainy home to this travel-brochure paradise. Then he dived in. And right away, he was back, rehearsing in his head again the final stages of his journey from there to here.

Chapter Three

Had it all started a week earlier, or was it less?

Harry had been lying stretched out on the wardroom's banquette aboard His Majesty's Submarine *P413*, keeping out of the way, as she crept along beneath a pristine turquoise Mediterranean sea at a sedentary three knots, the crew at 'Watch, Dived'.

The *P413* was a Grampus-class minelaying boat, one of many Royal Navy submarines to be denied the dignity of an actual name as a result of some never-announced, obscure Admiralty policy. Some speculated their Lordships had believed that by merely numbering their submarines, the service might somehow appear more efficient, faceless and deadly. Others, indeed most, assumed it was one more slight handed down to an unloved arm. After all, the Senior Service was a gentleman's service, and these johnny-come-latelies in submarines weren't known as 'the Trade' for nothing.

P413 had sailed from Gibraltar the previous evening and this was their first day submerged. If Harry, half-dozing, had been counting the hours, he'd have guessed the crew of *P413* were most of the way through the forenoon watch by then – but he wasn't.

Harry Gilmour, the son of a schoolteacher, from a small seaside resort on the shores of the Firth of Clyde. It had been almost two years now since that Sunday morning when Prime Minister Chamberlain had made his speech announcing that 'this country is at war with Germany.'

On the Tuesday, he'd walked into a Royal Navy recruiting office in Glasgow and signed up, when he should have been getting ready to begin his third year at Glasgow University instead. Two years ago, he'd been an undergraduate reading for an MA in Romance Languages – French and Italian. Now he was a Sub-Lieutenant in the Royal Navy Volunteer Reserve. A lot had happened in those two years: to him, and to the whole world. And the biggest thing to him was that he was now a submariner, on his way back to war again, to Malta to join a new boat, His Majesty's Submarine *Nimuae*. Newly appointed Number Three, the boat's Navigator, and now heading right slap bang into the middle of Britain's bitterest fight of the war so far – the battle for the Mediterranean. Harry – the boy who'd loved messing about on boats, who'd hung around the Royal Northern Yacht Squadron's clubhouse and boatyards at the end of his road, scrubbing and polishing anything for free, just to get a shot at crewing on rich men's yachts. He used to dream of being a ship's Navigator in those days, sailing upon exotic foreign seas. And now he was.

'Isn't it wonderful,' Harry had been muttering to himself, 'when dreams come true', when a rating's head popped around the edge of the wardroom cubby, and caught him. The young sailor's scrubbed, bland face hadn't even twitched a muscle. Officers talking to themselves? Nothing surprised the boy any more. Of course, he'd completely missed the heavy irony.

'Mr Gilmour, Sir,' he had said, 'Cap'n would like to see you in the control room.'

Harry would reflect later, when he had all the time in the world to do so, how even the most shattering of events often began in the most matter-of-fact fashion. He had prised himself off the banquette and headed along a passageway floored with slabs of tinned foods, following the rating, both men moving crouched because the deckhead above them was one long festoon of net garlands, strung end to end and stuffed with sacks of flour. The whole boat was like this; packed to the gills with supplies for beleaguered Malta – Britain's tiny island fortress in the middle of a hostile sea, standing in the way of the lines of communication between the Axis armies in North Africa and the Italian mainland, under constant bombardment by the Luftwaffe and Regia Aeronautica and threat of imminent invasion.

Which was why the minelaying HMS *P413* was currently shipping over 120 tons of aviation spirit in long, specially welded tanks on her mine racks, for the island's few remaining aircraft, and why her ballast tanks were full of diesel for the island's generators and few remaining vehicles. Even the boat's torpedo reload spaces were filled with boxes of ammunition for the besieged island – .303 for the fighter planes, and 20mm for the anti-aircraft guns. There were even other passengers on board, apart from Harry. Several soldiers of officer rank had muscled in on the senior rates' space and there was also a civilian bound for the office of the island's British Governor, who messed with *P413*'s officers. For *P413*, being a minelayer and therefore considerably bigger than most Royal Navy operational submarines, was on more or less permanent 'Magic Carpet' duty – the 'Magic Carpet' runs being one of the few ways left these days to keep Malta hanging on by her fingertips.

Harry emerged into the control room. He'd passed through it on coming aboard, on his way to his allotted banquette, but this was the first time he'd set foot in it since leaving Gib. Coming aboard, he'd seen the other passengers' gawp-faced, sick-looking expressions as they threaded their way through with their respective kits: the soldiers and the civilian all showing the mixture of fear, nausea and incredulity that normally overtakes non-submariners when they first clap eyes on the cat's cradle of pipes, valves, gauges, telegraphs and cable runs – as they try to grapple with how any human could ever understand it all, let alone control and direct it – that, and the knowledge that all their lives depended on someone being able to do just that. And then, of course, there was how small it was. To Harry's eye, however, *P413*'s control room was quite big, and with her First Lieutenant on the trim board and the Outside ERA standing by, and the senior rate on the helm and the ratings on the dive planes, all looked as it should be. *P413*'s Captain had just been stepping back and sending down the attack periscope when Harry had straightened up and announced himself.

'Ah, Mr Gilmour,' said Captain Clasp. Clasp wasn't actually a four-ringer Captain, but a three-ringer Commander – but since he commanded *P413* he was entitled to the honorary title; and from those solid rings on his shirt epaulettes, he was most definitely RN. He gestured as if to say, *one minute*, and then said to the First Lieutenant, 'Right, she's about fifty yards off the port bow now, and there is nothing about, so take us up, Number One. No rush; wouldn't want to topple the poor buggers.' Then he turned back to Harry, giving him his full attention.

Commander Edgar Clasp was a short, fastidious man of indeterminate age – he could've been anything from twenty-five to fifty-five years old – with slick, brilliantined blond hair that was probably curly underneath, and a perfectly smooth, oval face set permanently in an expression of benign complacency. Together, these were features that should have yelled to the world, 'Idiot!' But they didn't. Harry had liked Commander Clasp right from the minute he set eyes on him. And right after Clasp had first spoken to him, he'd liked him even more.

'You were on *Pelorus* when she was lost,' Clasp had said after they'd been introduced in *P413*'s wardroom, just before she'd slipped from Gibraltar. 'Yes. I remember that name. Gilmour. It was you who hauled that disreputable rogue Padgett out of her, wasn't it?'

Pelorus had been Harry's first boat and Ted Padgett her Warrant Engineer. They'd been rammed after straying into a British North Sea convoy in the dark, and *Pelorus* had gone to the bottom. That had been a long time ago. The winter of 1939 to '40, before the war had got going properly. And Padgett would have gone down with her if it hadn't been for Harry. A lot of her crew had. But not her Captain. Oh no, not

Pelorus's Captain, the Bonny Boy Bonalleck. He'd saved his own skin. There was a story there, but Harry, right then, hadn't wanted to think about that. So all he'd said was, 'Yes, Sir.'

And at that, Clasp had thrust out his hand to be shaken. 'Thank you, Mr Gilmour,' he'd said, 'for saving my friend.'

Harry had shaken his hand and mumbled something about, 'Didn't really know him, Sir. Not for long. To be friends, Sir.'

Clasp had held on to Harry's hand. 'You knew him enough to risk your life to save his, Mr Gilmour. In most people's books, that's best friends.'

Harry had blushed at that, and Clasp had smiled his benign smile and let go of his hand. 'Ted has many friends in the Trade,' he'd said. 'So your name is known now. Carry on, Mr Gilmour.'

Now Clasp had wanted to see him.

'Mr Gilmour,' Clasp said, 'I wonder if you could do me a favour?' as if it were a request and not an order – which, coming from the Captain, it obviously was.

'Of course, Sir,' Harry said, as he was supposed to, as right next to his right ear, the First Lieutenant began issuing orders to blow main ballast tanks, and the Outside ERA began executing them. Beyond the Captain, the men on the dive planes were already planing up as *P413*, pushing through the water at slow ahead, together, began to rise.

Harry, back in the control room of a Royal Navy boat again, at sea and operational.

'Surfacing!' someone said. And Harry, knowing right then that everything really was as it should be, had thought, *God help me, but I actually feel at home!*

'We've spotted a lifeboat through the periscope while doing a routine all-round look,' Clasp explained to Harry, 'bobbing up and down on the usual Mediterranean short chop. It doesn't look in very good nick. Neither did the two heads that suddenly appeared and then disappeared above the boat's gunwale. So, we're going to pick them up.

'So when we surface, be a good chap, Mr Gilmour, and nip upstairs with the Bosun,' the Captain said, 'and haul aboard whoever's in the damn thing before it sinks. They're probably our chaps. I'll send a couple of lads up through the for'ard hatch to give you a hand if you need them.'

It was standard practice in the Trade for the CO to go up first on surfacing but, seeing as they had surfaced in daylight, Clasp opted to stay by his periscope, which fully extended was going to let him see a lot further. Surfacing in daylight within range of enemy aircraft or surface units was, after all, a very risky proposition. So up went Harry, climbing the conning tower ladder behind the officer of the watch, whose name he couldn't remember, and the two lookouts. *P413* had come up slow so there hadn't been that much seawater left sloshing around on the bridge to come splashing down on Harry's head when the officer popped the hatch. But he'd been half-deafened when the officer had called down past him, 'Horizon's clear, Sir . . . but the lifeboat, Sir. There's at least half a dozen of the poor buggers in her bilges.'

And then suddenly Harry was on the bridge, surrounded by the entire azure dome of the Mediterranean sky, studded with high scattered tufts of white, and a turquoise sea empty but for its own little nicks of white froth, stretching out forever. Even the breeze was warm, despite it already being early autumn. It was a beautiful day, until he'd looked down into the lifeboat, already starting to bump against *P413*'s saddle tanks. In it was a scene of some squalor, and in the middle of the squalor there was half a dozen sunburned, beard-grizzled faces looking back up at him, all of them old, gaunt and filthy.

The submarine's crew had moved fast. A couple of ratings up out of the for'ard hatch with a boathook had hauled the lifeboat close aboard *P413*. Harry remembered one of the grizzled faces in the lifeboat struggling to move, fumbling for something and expending a great deal of effort, until he managed to produce a painter from under the prow and hold the end of the flimsy line feebly over the side to be grabbed by one of *P413*'s ratings.

The sailors in the lifeboat had once been merchant seamen, but now they were more like rag dolls, sprawled stupefied, watching everything as if it were happening on a remote screen. One of them, who had actually managed to talk a little, asked for water. A West Country accent, Harry remembered. The Bosun who'd brought a half-gallon can with him, passed it into the boat, and shouted for another one, walking back past *P413*'s deck gun to collect it from the conning tower. Harry recalled issuing orders; telling a rating to tie off the painter to secure the lifeboat; getting the rating on the boathook to drag in the lifeboat's stern, so it could be secured; then telling them to get ready to go aboard the lifeboat and start passing over the survivors; he and the Bosun would lower them down the for'ard hatch. That was when the shout came; right bang on exactly the wrong time.

'Unidentified aircraft off the starboard bow!' a bridge lookout had bellowed. 'Low, closing fast!'

And in the time it would take to draw a breath, Clasp's voice, loud and crisp, 'Clear the casing! Clear the bridge!'

And then two sharp blasts on the klaxon. The 'Dive!' order, so loud you heard it throughout the boat.

On Harry's last Royal Navy boat, *Trebuchet*, her Skipper Andy Trumble could get her down in just sixteen seconds, from klaxon to periscope depth. *P413* was a bigger, more ungainly boat than a T-class, but Harry had been quite confident that a Captain like Clasp would have had his crew trained to such a degree that *P413* wouldn't be that much slower.

The ratings hadn't needed any encouragement: the second one was already disappearing down the for'ard hatch before Harry looked up and could see the tiny dot on the horizon moving with that dedication

21

to purpose you never see in a seagull. When he looked back, the Bosun was standing by the conning tower ladder in the act of slinging down the other half-gallon can. He might as well have been ten miles away.

Harry dropped to his knees. 'Mr Gilmour . . .!' the Bosun shouted. Harry started to tear at the knot in the painter that secured the lifeboat to *P413*'s deck, but his fingers felt like big sausages.

It had been one of those frozen moments when events are moving very fast, and time runs like congealing tar: where you're noticing the small and the irrelevant, when *you* should be moving fast; when your mind steps aside, when it should be racing ahead. When he looked up again, he vividly remembered thinking how the Bosun's huge shoulders stretched the oil-stained blue drill of his overalls until they looked fit to tear; the bushy gouts of grey hair that exploded from his ears and from under his cap; the doughy whiteness of his flesh starting to sag with middle age; how utterly ugly he was, with his jaw slack with horror.

Harry was never going to untie that knot, even as the *P413* went down under him. It was going to stay tied. And it was going to drag down that tattered and frayed wooden lifeboat and all the poor bastards in it, battering it in all the blowing vents against the accelerating steel of a diving submarine, drowning the whole sorry shower. He remembered he'd still been thinking that as he reached for his clasp knife.

'Get down that hatch, Bosun!' he'd yelled.

'Mr Gilmour . . .!'

'That's an order!' This time brooking no argument. Thinking, grinning to himself in one fraction of a second, *Oooh! Hark at little Napoleon there!* And in the next, remembering the words of old Lexie Scrimgeour, the rich man on whose yacht he used to crew, telling him about knives at sea . . . 'Always carry one, Harry,' he'd said. 'Always. Just because you can't imagine now why you'd need it, believe me, when you do, you'll *really* need it.' *How true,* Harry was thinking, as he sawed away at the painter, *how true.*

The sea had been weltering around his knees when he'd finally cut through and launched himself over the lifeboat's gunwale. The top of *P413*'s conning tower was already awash by the time it swept past, with only the periscope stands showing, and then she'd been gone, and the only sound had been the irritating buzzing of the approaching aircraft. When Harry had picked himself off the bottom of the lifeboat, he had been able to see it in all its glory, not that low, maybe at two hundred or two-fifty feet. His first reaction had been to squint closer at the small twin-engined monoplane, with its long sleek fuselage, glass nose and high tail fin, thinking *P413* might have wasted her time – but the aircraft wasn't a Blenheim, wasn't RAF. She was Regia Aeronautica after all. He dredged the name Caproni 314 from his commodious memory for aircraft recognition silhouettes. A shagbat in the vernacular of the Trade; they were all shagbats.

The Caproni circled overhead, and he could see the face of her observer peering down at them. It made two long, low passes over their lifeboat, then lost interest and peeled away to the south-west, flying low and slow; more west than south, he remembered, into the setting sun. Harry had turned to look at his new shipmates. Less than twenty minutes ago, he'd been lying snug on a banquette, reading a book and contemplating lunch.

There had been some kind of discussion going on among the survivors, if their desultory grunts could qualify for such a description. The half-gallon can of water the *P413* boys had passed over first was lying empty on the deck boards, but one of the men was clutching at another – the Bosun must have slung the second half-gallon can as he'd clambered up for the conning tower hatch. The debate had been about whether to drink it now.

And in that moment, Harry had taken in all that had happened; they were all deckhands with tans that had been acquired over decades, not days or even weeks. No officers or Petty Officers among them. They had been sunk, landed in this boat and there had been no attempt to do anything else. From the debris he could see, their survival rations had all been eaten. Obviously their water was gone too – likely in a series of binges with no attempt to spin it out. No attempt had been made to pitch a mast or ship the oars and row. One of them was explaining patiently to the others how they were all saved now; how the submarine would just stooge around until the Eyetie got fed up, ran out of fuel, or it got dark; then the sub would surface and they'd all be bundled aboard and dropped back at Gib.

'How long have you been out here?' Harry had asked. His question had been met with a sea of blank faces. No one knew; no one had been keeping count. 'What was your ship?' he'd then asked.

'The *John Bardine* . . . Liverpool . . . general cargo,' the one clutching the full half-gallon can had muttered. He'd showed no sign of letting it go. Harry had wondered if he knew what Harry knew – that they weren't saved.

Harry had been watching the Caproni, some miles off, orbiting slowly just above the horizon, so that her observer could still see the lifeboat, but a periscope peeking up at wave height would not see it. Which was obviously the idea.

Not long after that, *P413*'s periscope had broken surface no more than twenty yards off their beam, and Harry had found himself looking directly into its single glass eye. He knew why it had appeared; Clasp wanted to know whether it was safe to come up. And, of course, it wasn't. That crafty Eyetie had still been lingering just below *P413*'s line of sight, hoping she would surface so they could scoot right in and drop a bomb down her conning tower hatch before the lookouts had climbed out. Harry had drawn his finger across his throat, and then he'd given a thumbs down just to make sure whoever was looking understood; and he'd finished by jabbing his thumb to the south-west to let them know where the shagbat was circling. There was a long pause, and then the periscope lens started flashing. Someone was sending him Morse code, using a handheld Aldis lamp jammed against the periscope's eyepiece, down there in *P413*'s control room, slowly, to make sure he understood. Which was just as well, as Harry's Morse recognition barely qualified as competent. Then it stopped, and Harry had given a wave and thumbs up to show he had understood; and then the periscope slipped back beneath the waves.

'Are they coming up now?' the sailor clutching the half-gallon can had asked, and Harry had shaken his head. No. The news had taken some moments to sink in through their listlessness, but when it did they'd all done their best to muster something akin to anger, croaking demands for explanations Harry couldn't give them.

P413 hadn't been able to surface again to rescue them because she'd been running to a schedule. As they had thundered through the previous night, going flat out on the surface, Clasp had told him all about it, as they drank coffee in the wardroom. Some six hundred miles ahead of them lay the shallows of the Sicilian Channel – a neck of water the Italians had sown so thick with mines, other submarines had spent weeks probing for a safe route through to Malta. They'd found one, but it involved pinpoint navigation and timing, and began by them having to reach the north side of the Skerki Banks on schedule and running fast on the surface at night to a point ten miles south of Marittimo Island – a point that they had to hit just before sunrise. Because after sunrise, the sky would be full of shagbats on anti-submarine patrol. There, they had to dive deep – 150 feet at least – and then run submerged on a fixed 120 degrees compass bearing for some sixty miles, timing their passage to arrive at twilight ten miles south of Sicily's Cap San Marco, where they'd surface for a night-time dash to Valletta. Everything had to run on a stopwatch, because at the end there'd be one of Malta's precious minesweepers, risking itself to escort them through the island's own defensive mine barrier. And that was why Harry knew *P413* couldn't hang around, waiting for the Caproni to run out of fuel or for it to get dark. But he also knew he couldn't tell this lot that. They might all get picked up by an Italian warship, and blab that there was a British submarine carrying supplies for Malta on its way, and the Italian Navy and the Regia Aeronautica would work out the rest.

Harry had tried to placate them, telling them that the submarine had to leave, because the Caproni was likely calling up every patrolling Eyetie destroyer and sub-chaser in the western Med, but it hadn't stopped the grumbling. If any Eyetie was to turn up, couldn't they torpedo it before it knew they were there? That was the whole point of being a submarine, wasn't it? You saw them before they saw you? But Harry had stopped listening by then, too busy thinking, *Well, this is a right bloody mess.*

And that was when he'd informed them in a seriously forthright manner that he was buggered if he were going to sit about in this tub and wait to die like they'd been doing for God knows how long. First, the remaining water; it was getting rationed from now on, and he'd decide who got what and when. Then he told them to ship the oars, but it hadn't taken long for him to realise that none of them was in a fit state to row, and that he couldn't do it by himself; the lifeboat was too broad in the beam for him to sit on the thwarts and be able to dip both oars in the water at the same time; and anyway, the damn thing had been far too heavy for him to pull on his own. 'So we'll step the mast,' he'd told them, 'and fly something from it that'll be easy to spot.' There'd been no sail aboard – probably stolen out of the boat months or even years before. So Harry had dropped his blue uniform trousers, being made of the only material aboard not bleached by the sun, and up they went. Then they'd sat back again to wait, while the sun rolled inexorably across the cloud-tufted blue.

At first Harry had tried to get some chat going, a bit of let's-look-on-the-bright-side banter, until one of the sailors had started telling him about their lot: how on the outbreak of war they'd all been bound by law to remain in the merchant service for the duration, and how the ship-owners had interpreted that service to their own advantage. And now that they were on the water – the minute, in fact, that they'd abandoned their ship – their pay had been stopped. That had shut Harry up, and left him even more depressed than these poor buggers already were. At least in the Royal Navy, if you got sunk or taken prisoner, the Admiralty continued to pay you, so your wife and children could continue to eat. But not our patriotic British ship-owners. These poor merchant navy bastards were out here risking everything, knowing if their number came up, neither they nor their families would get a brass farthing.

As twilight had approached, and Harry had been looking forward with creeping dread to his first night aboard this wooden hulk, that had been when the Spanish tuna boat had come puttering over the horizon.

Chapter Four

Teniente Coronel Eurico de la Peña was sitting with one buttock perched on the stone balustrade of the balcony, leaning back against one of the pillars, lugubriously savouring one of his cigarillos when Harry stepped out of his office door, followed by a roly-poly figure who went by the name of Mr Wingate. He was the British Consul in Palma. Teniente Coronel de la Peña routinely lent his office to the young, myopic Mr Wingate for his interviews with the interned British officers, it being the polite, courteous thing to do. For, as everybody agreed, Teniente Coronel de la Peña was nothing if not polite and courteous.

'Ah, Eurico!' said Mr Wingate, dithering over the office door, not knowing whether to shut it or hold it open for the Teniente Coronel. Not that anyone ever called the Teniente Coronel anything other than Eurico, as Harry had quickly noticed. 'You are my guests and I am the host,' he would say if they ever tried. 'Ranks are for parade grounds.'

'I have been keeping you from your office,' continued Mr Wingate, still in his dither.

'Not at all, George,' said Eurico, for everyone was on first-name terms in this Spanish Caesar's domain. Eurico slid off his perch with seamless elegance.

'It is this young hero I wish to see, now that you have finished with him.'

Harry, who had been thinking how classical the Spanish officer had looked, poised there like a study of some Roman virtue, was taken aback. What could the great man want with him? And hero? What was that all about?

Eurico stepped forward and took the door, rescuing Mr Wingate from his indecision. Pleasantries were exchanged, and gracious till-we-meet-agains, and Harry and Eurico had each watched in silent amusement as the tubby figure of His Britannic Majesty's representative had waddled away down the veranda, resplendent in his cream linen suit, perching his crisp panama hat on his unruly mop of mousy hair with one hand, and gripping his venerable Gladstone bag with the other.

'So, Harry, you are official now,' said Eurico, turning to him with one of his smiles and ushering him through the door.

'Official?'

'Your story checks out. You are who you say you are. And that, in your eager young fist, if I'm not mistaken, is your letter. For the tailor. Assuring him that if he fits you out with every item of uniform on the consul's list, His Britannic Majesty's consul will pay the bill.'

Harry smiled. 'Yes . . .' he'd been about to add 'Sir', but then remembered and said 'Eurico' instead, which produced a nod and a smile from his host.

'I apologise if you find it difficult to use my first name,' said Eurico.

'Just a bit unusual, you being a senior officer, and me, well . . .' and Harry tailed off, still struggling not to say Sir.

'I know. It is very informal – but I do try to ask first', and a twinkle came into Eurico's eyes, 'especially with you British. Some of your senior officers can be most punctilious.'

'Oh, so you'd use rank if they asked you to?'

Eurico let out a bark of laughter. 'Good grief, no!'

'Then why do you ask?'

'My dear Harry,' he said, with the twinkle going full blast, 'I'd never dream of being irritating, unless it was on purpose. Now, I think we have time for some coffee and a small Soberano before elevenses. How are you enjoying Hotel El Real?'

'Elevenses? So you know about our daily standing orders?'

'Oh yes, Harry,' said Eurico, screwing up his face in thought. 'You English are very accomplished at dressing up anarchy in formal language.'

Harry couldn't be bothered pointing out he wasn't actually English, he'd lived with it for so long – and after all, Eurico was a foreigner . . .

'Correct me if I get it wrong,' Eurico was continuing, 'but there are elevenses, at the time the name suggests, then there's lunchtime aperitifs, then lunch, then digestifs, afternoon tea, sundowners, dinner aperitifs, dinner, digestifs, nightcaps and then – for those who wish – it's time to get drunk. Oh, and not forgetting all the wine and port that attend the various courses of the meals too.'

'Yes,' said Harry, 'it's the RAF's idea, apparently: they find that sort of thing amusing. Although it was Fabrizio who first told me about it, and with great glee.'

'Oh, yes. Your Italian foes have been eager joiners-in.'

'But not the Germans?'

'But not the Germans,' Eurico echoed. Both men paused to contemplate this, and Harry once again found himself wondering exactly how old the Teniente Coronel really was.

'A most unamiable lot, the Germans,' continued Eurico. 'Have you met their senior officer?'

Harry hadn't, but he'd heard of him. 'Herr Oberst Alois Genscher, of the Luftwaffe,' said Eurico and then sighed and rolled his eyes. 'Or *Arse Clencher*, as I believe he is more commonly referred to.'

Harry laughed. 'By the English – you know that too?'

Eurico made a little moue, as if to say, 'Naturally', and then added, 'Oh, the Italians too – they particularly like that one.' He paused then, before going on, 'The Germans are believers. They can't wait to get back to their war. The English and Italians? They are all just young men, young pilots . . . glad to be still alive.'

'And they'd rather stay here,' said Harry, before realising he'd just interrupted the equivalent of a Lieutenant Colonel, and then remembering it didn't matter.

'Have you looked around?' said Eurico, gesturing beyond his office window. 'It's getting a bit cold for the beach now. But when they are not all getting drunk at their governments' expense, they're stuffing their faces on the finest foods, playing games: tennis . . . football . . . *cricket*! And you haven't been here for one of our mess "at-homes" yet. Have you? All the young señoritas of genteel family, and needless to say their chaperones, are invited. It is an event. Their hosts, after all, are officers. And on the night? You cannot imagine. The camellia terrace surrounded by candlelight, the warm evening, the Mediterranean air, and all those young English and Italian fighter pilots, and their guests – young Spanish ladies in the full bloom of their beauty. It is the most romantic, the most intoxicating . . .' and here, even Eurico was lost for words, before collecting himself. 'They are young men enjoying themselves, whose countries might be at war, but who have discovered they are not that much different from each other, and would rather be carousing than killing. It is most reassuring, and amusing, to watch. Your English comrades really do give poor George the runaround when he's trying to organise their repatriation. But he's very patient.'

'Ah,' said Harry, remembering George was Mr Wingate's first name, 'even Group Captain Mahaddie? I can't imagine him giving George the runaround.'

'You've met Jock?' and at that Eurico sighed. 'Of course you have.'

'Another unamiable character,' offered Harry, 'like the Arse Clencher.'

'No,' said Eurico firmly. 'Our Jock might be keen to get back into his war, but it doesn't stop him from enjoying himself. No, Jock is just an oaf. A role he is far too old for. Just time for another little Soberano before they all start getting up.' And Eurico poured him another tiny nip of brandy, Harry thinking if this was the continental way, he could get used to it.

'Thank you for talking with Fabrizio, by the way,' said Eurico. 'I was worried about him.'

Harry looked confused for a moment, but then cottoned on: Fabrizio and his big, glorious gesture against the British battlecruiser. Except all he'd ended up achieving had been to bend his aeroplane. 'It was a very brave thing he did,' said Harry.

'It was a very brave thing *you* did, too,' said Eurico, who then paused while Harry squinted at him. 'I spoke to the men in the lifeboat.'

Harry smiled his lop-sided smile and shrugged.

'You sawing through that little rope while your submarine is diving under your feet. I shut my eyes and what I see is a scene from a Feydeau farce. But you're not depressed by it,' added Eurico.

'I might be,' said Harry, smirking.

'Let me put it this way,' continued Eurico, 'you have more of a sense of the ridiculous than Fabrizio. It is good for a serious boy like him to see that not everyone or everything has to be so . . . do you understand . . . machismo?'

'Yes, Eurico, I understand. And how very wise, Sir,' said Harry deliberately, ignoring Eurico's mock scowl at the word 'Sir'. Harry let a long silence hang as he looked around Eurico's office, with his big tooled-leather desk, and high-backed leather chairs; the glass-fronted bookcase like the façade of a cathedral, and almost as big; the corniced ceiling with space for two chandeliers, and how the gold-and-green striped wallpaper made the room seem darker and cooler than the growing warmth of the morning outside might suggest. 'You're really enjoying all this too, aren't you?' he said, giving an expansive sweep of his arms, as if to include the office, the hotel, all its occupants, the whole island even, and its peace and quiet. 'This is no dead-end posting for you – you're having the time of your life.'

'How very wise of you, Harry,' said Eurico, who allowed his own pause for reflection. 'Indeed, I too have had my war . . .'

Of course you have, thought Harry, *the Spanish Civil War. And you were one of the baddies too.*

'. . . and discovered that it's much more fun to drink and carouse and dally with beautiful women than be involved in the business of killing people.' Another pause, and then a smile. 'Now, your new uniform. I will write you a pass into town for tomorrow. And Fabrizio will accompany you. He knows the way, and as I think he is probably a snappier dresser than you, he will supervise the cut.'

Only after he'd left the office did it dawn on Harry that their entire conversation had been conducted in English. Eurico really was a most accomplished man, thought Harry.

Chapter Five

Her name was Sybilla Cruz Soriano, and Harry first met her on his day out in town with Fabrizio, on his way to be measured for his new uniforms. It was in the old town, in one of the *Calle* that ran down to the harbour, where all Palma's fashionable shops were. She was promenading with her lady's servant, for women of Sybilla's caste did not go a-promenading alone.

It was late morning and the perfect cool for a stroll around the shops. There were a lot of people about, yet she still stood out. She was wearing a dove-grey, two-piece silk suit, with pencil skirt and tailored jacket with high, flamboyant lapels that revealed a shot-silk dark-blue blouse. A cashmere shawl draped her shoulders, and her calves were sheathed in sheer stockings and her feet shod in high-heeled, open-toed shoes cut from the finest chamois. If Harry hadn't been with Fabrizio he would have walked into a lamp post. To have called Sybilla a beauty would have been like saying Michelangelo was quite good at painting ceilings. Her face, her figure, the way she carried herself – where did you begin?

Her skin was translucently pale and peach-soft, taut over high cheekbones, but with a prominent nose that not only did not detract from her looks, but added the dimension of character. Then there were the eyes: feline, and the colour of warm chocolate fondant. And her mouth . . . Oh, but what a mouth! Harry would later hear one of the RAF boys describe it as '. . . lips that could suck-start an Indian . . .' The pilot had, of course, been referring not to any citizen of the subcontinent, but to the 1200cc motorcycle much beloved of dispatch riders. Not a gallant observation by any means, but Harry had instantly known what he was driving at. And then there was the bosom. We have to discuss the bosom, because every other interned belligerent in Eurico's Hotel El Real did. Frequently. When Harry saw it first, taut against the grey silk of her suit, a phrase had shot into his head, completely unbidden, from the rubbish bin of his memory. It had come from a lecture he'd once sat through, from deep in its droning tedium. Some segue into Renaissance ecclesiastical architecture. 'Pseudo-sexpartite vaulting' had been the phrase. Harry hadn't a clue what it meant back then, but the instant he'd clapped eyes on Sybilla's bosom, he knew he was looking at it. As to what was holding that waist, Harry shuddered to think what architectural connivance was going on in there. Finally, but not least, there was her hair. Raven hair, what else, contained by the tiny confection of a hat – hair that radiated all the resting languor of high explosives.

Fabrizio, it quickly transpired, was already acquainted with her, for Sybilla, as he explained, was one of the young ladies of Palma always invited to the Officers' Mess Nights at the Hotel El Real. Harry could see Fabrizio was completely fascinated. And from the moment Fabrizio introduced her, it was apparent to Harry that Sybilla was *more* than acquainted with the effect she had on Fabrizio. Greetings were exchanged with a certain formality, allowing just enough time for one of those timeless little gavottes to ensue: the one where the lady shamelessly flirts with the ardent admirer's best friend – and for all the flashing eyes she directs at the friend, the last flash is always in the direction of the ardent admirer, just to make sure she's having the desired effect.

Yet Harry came away from their first meeting with the sense that for all her conceits and hauteur, Sybilla was probably a nice person.

Why? Because of the way she'd behaved towards her lady's servant. For a start, Sybilla had included her lady in the introductions, by name. It was a small thing, but one Harry had seldom seen before – not from the likes of Sybilla and certainly not from her caste, in any nationality.

Fabrizio's huffiness lasted only until afternoon tea, then it got washed away by a vast vat of *Catalunya rosado*.

Idle days followed. As the days wore on, and the cool of autumn deepened, the sport tended to move inside, card schools being the favourite, and a running chess tournament. The Italians even embraced the joys of dominoes, despite the ever-present threat of crowd trouble. As a result, the only time they ever really saw the Germans was at sundowners, when they were all gathered on the balcony, each man wrestling with his daily quandary: when to escalate from wine to spirits. Meanwhile, the Luftwaffe would be holding their evening parade on the patio below. For the Anglo-Italian contingent, it was always an occasion for the singing of dirty songs, name-calling and ritual bottom-baring – activities that were always met with unflinching Teutonic indifference. Old Arse Clencher himself would march his men up and down. There'd be a lot of stamping and *Heil Hitler!*s, and then a tedious address by the Oberst on how the master race were doing in the war. The whole time Harry was there, no one ever managed to hit old Arse Clencher with a bread roll, though God knows they tried. Then Jerry would march off to an evening of God knows what. And all the time the consuls would come and go, bearing tidings of each man's progress towards repatriation – a process that appeared to advance in geological time. Harry had only ever seen three men actually leave since he'd arrived on the island.

There were two Germans, seen off with parade pomp and Nazi salutes, while the RAF lad was taken in hand the night before the car arrived to take him away, and was fed drink until he was insensible, loaded into a crude coffin with a wilted wreath on his chest and carried off to his bed amid much false, and some not so false wailing and beating of breasts.

'We are a Fascist state, Harry,' said Eurico one afternoon when the card schools were deep in study, others were sleeping off the booze and the Germans were doing callisthenics. Harry and Eurico were speaking French and discussing politics over a pot of exquisite Arabian coffee and Eurico's Havana cigarillos. He was explaining how Spanish bureaucracy worked, or rather, how it was impossible to explain how it worked. 'So we have a Fascist bureaucracy. There's no better way to stamp your power on people than through the dead hand of bureaucracy. In that, we tend to follow the Roman taste in the exercise of power, rather than the Greco, which I feel is the more preferred among *your* democracies. You cannot reason with paperwork.'

Harry so enjoyed their talks on politics, books and Hollywood movies, not to mention their games of chess. Fabrizio played chess too, and was far superior at the game than either of them. 'He lets us win sometimes, you know,' observed Harry one day. 'You noticed,' said Eurico. But they both enjoyed Fabrizio's piano-playing, and that he had put together a trio with two other Italian pilots of a musical bent, who could turn their hands to a variety of strings: viola, violin and the cello. Little afternoon soirées would be convened when the rough boys were off playing cricket and the more refined of their small band stayed back to listen, more of them Italian than English – like the day when Eurico produced a guitar, and they were a quartet. Or the afternoon, with the sun low over the port, with half a dozen of them lying around, rapt with the sound of Boccherini's *La Musica Notturna delle Strade di Madrid*, and then the boys coming back, sweating and charged, shouting up at Harry leaning back against the balustrade, 'Gilmour, you Scotch slacker! You're giving the Group Captain a showing up! And you a Jock like him too!' Followed swiftly by someone pretending to Jock-ness: 'Ah'll jist conduct a wee movement from *How tae pirouette in a French poof's boudoir*, while Ahm still in the mood!' Laughter, interrupted by a more refined tone: 'If we can teach the Tallymen how to play cricket, we can surely teach a haggis-muncher!' Encouraging the less refined,

'Maybe he likes munching more than just haggis!' All just in time for afternoon tea.

They had all signed paroles, swearing never to offend against a lengthy list of prohibited activities including escape, acts of sabotage or subversion, or conduct likely to offend public sensitivities. On the strength of this they would be allowed passes, signed by Eurico and countersigned by the civilian governor, that everyone from the local *policia* to the Guardia Civil, and even the Army, had to recognise. Especially the Army. Not that all of the Spanish Army personnel on the island were so ghastly.

'There is an Engineer Officer called Jaime you must meet,' Eurico had confided in Harry one day, 'and there are a number of Artillery Officers who are quite agreeable. But as for the rest of the Army people,' he said, dismissing his own Army colleagues, 'they all want to go to Russia with Hitler. And like to practise here how they will behave there, while they're waiting.'

Harry's favourite trip was to take the Ferrocarril, a narrow-gauge electric train that ran all the way from the upper part of Palma, through the Serra de Tramuntana to the town of Sóller on the north-west of the island, and then on into its small port. This was where Harry had been unceremoniously dumped by the tuna boat, not that he remembered much about it, being tired and already drunk from all the *fundador* the fishermen had fed him after his rescue.

It was on one of those trips, loaded down with picnic, and looking forward to an assignation with Sybilla – and her lady's servant, and a gaggle of Sybilla's friends, who would be driving up with all their attendant chaperones – that Harry listened to Fabrizio on the subject of the war, and his family.

'My family is very old. We were Roman nobility,' he told Harry as the train rattled along and they both gazed out of the strap window of the little wooden-slatted carriage down into deep, wooded ravines. 'There are *condottieri* and cardinals in my blood line: we are one of the Black families. I hold dual citizenship of Italy and the Vatican City. And now I am expected, nay commanded, to kneel before the son of a blacksmith from the Romagna.'

If you looked up you could see the sunlight dapple the trees and ragged rocks along the mountain's skyline as the little train hugged the opposite ravine wall, and then they plunged into another tunnel, and their faces shone in the pale yellow of the carriage's electric lights. Harry made no reply, but thought, *Ah, so it's all about class.*

'Most politicians make mistakes because they do not know history,' continued Fabrizio. 'Mussolini takes his country to war because he knows too much. Education should be a good thing, no? But this man, he reads a book about socialism and he is a socialist; he reads another about fascism and he is a fascist, and he reads another about Nietzsche and now he is an *Übermensch.* And we are all to follow him down this path of hubris to a new Roman empire, with Il Duce as Caesar. We are good at fighting black tribesmen and Arab rabbles, but now we are fighting you and the Soviets, and soon, as everybody knows, we'll be fighting the Americans and all their industrial might. Does he really think he can win? By throwing in his lot with that failed dauber of canvases? I know he is betting my life on it. *Madre di Dio!* We couldn't even beat the Greeks on our own. "War alone brings up to their highest tension all human energies and imposes the stamp of nobility upon the peoples who have the courage to make it." He said that. He *actually* said that.'

'You sound like my father,' said Harry, thinking, *Ah, so it's not about class, it's about . . . reason.* Then adding quickly, 'Which is not necessarily a bad thing. Not at all.'

'And *my* father,' said Fabrizio, looking now at Harry with a steady stare, 'and his brothers. And their father too. And they're not alone.'

When they met the ladies in their convoy of open-top cars, they motored out to a small promontory beyond the port and spread their picnic. The attention Sybilla directed at Harry meant that he forgot all about his conversation with Fabrizio, and for one glorious afternoon he entertained the fantasy that maybe she just might really hold a genuine interest in a young, bright, articulate, and dare he say it, handsome Highland gentleman of absolutely no estate, wealth or noble line. Poor Harry. He was still not much more than a boy, and God bless him, his head was all too turnable by a pretty face. Certainly turnable far enough for him to completely fail to see the effect all this was having on his friend. The effect was not lost however on Eurico, who spotted Fabrizio's lowering face right away when both young men returned to the Hotel El Real. He filed the insight away as part of his ongoing psychological study.

The days passed.

On one unseasonably warm afternoon, the quartet had set up on the big terrace after lunch's digestifs, and they were listening to some baroque little ditty, joined by several off-duty Spanish airmen and the Spanish Army Engineer, Jaime, who did indeed turn out to be a pleasant fellow and was proving himself quite able to converse with Harry in French. The rough boys had gone off somewhere to be rough, and the Germans to be Teutonic. Harry's mind was wandering with the music when a shadow, the briefest of flits, caught his eye. It came from within one of the little stone-turreted artifices that overlooked the terrace – like toy watchtowers, not very high and not very stout, with vertical windows, decorative rather than genuine arrow slits, through which, at this time of day and this angle of the sun, light should have been spilling through, but for a moment hadn't been.

'Someone's watching us,' Harry said to Jaime, who, along with Armando, another of the Italian pilots, had for the past ten minutes been taunting him on and off about how Britain was a land without music. Jaime, who was an older man than the rest of the Hotel El Real's inmates, tall and square of jaw, and with receding jet-black crinkly hair, had just been telling Harry, 'Writers, you have: Shakespeare, Dickens, Keats. But where are your Mozarts, your Bachs? Albéniz, Vivaldi, Beethoven! How can you have a land without music? How can you live?'

'Don't look, but they're in that little turret,' added Harry, studiously following the music now. Jaime and Armando made faces at each other, and shut up. The piece finished, and it was time for the players' glasses to be refilled, for everyone's glasses to be refilled. Harry stood. 'Follow me,' he said. And the three of them loped off in file as if heading to attend to their toilette. Once through the big French windows, they ran at a clip, through the ballroom, out and downstairs to the long stone corridor that ran inside the hotel's wall. Harry got to the narrow spiral staircase that obviously led back up to the turret, and slowly began climbing, step by step. The other two were right behind him, the young Italian trying not to giggle. Harry was getting ready to declaim, 'Aha!'

But when he turned the final curve, the person he saw stopped him dead. The figure was pressed against the furthest curve of the turret, sitting on its flagstone floor, eyes staring wide at Harry's head in the stairwell. He was a gangly youth, and the first thing Harry was confronted with were feet, without socks, one in a tennis shoe and the other in a loose sandal, the ankle tightly bound in a bandage. Bare, tanned legs disappeared into a pair of sports shorts, and into those was tucked a khaki shirt with a Luftwaffe pilot's wings on the breast, and the rank insignia of a Leutnant. The boy looked barely out of his teens, like most of them. He had blond hair, cropped at the sides and floppy on top, and a smooth tanned face that wore an expression that Harry in his surprise didn't quite read.

Armando's head pushed up now behind him, and when he saw the German, he started to shout, 'What's he doing here?', immediately angry. Then, directly into the German's face, 'What are you doing here? Are you spying on us?', all in Italian, which the German obviously didn't understand. 'So you can go and tell on us? So you can get the Gestapo to tell the OVRA because we drink with Tommies?' And he tried to struggle past Harry, to reach out and lay a hand on the boy.

'Jesus Christ!' said Harry. 'What the hell are you doing?'

'Let's drag him out,' said the Italian pilot. 'Let's parade our prisoner! Fucking spy! Show that bastard Arse Clencher we know what he's up to! He wants our families arrested!'

Harry shot his gaze back at the German, and instantly he read the expression he'd missed a moment before: the boy was terrified, but not of the Italian. And he didn't appear to be frightened of Harry either. Harry shoved the Italian back, telling him in his own language, 'Stop. Wait a minute. Just take it easy here.' But he kept his eyes on the German.

'Sprechen . . . English?' asked Harry, but the German shook his head. So Harry tried, 'Français?'

'Oui, un peu.'

And so they spoke in French.

'What are you doing here?' asked Harry.

'I like the music,' said the German, who risked a wry smile. And right away Harry knew without even having to ask, that if the Arse Clencher ever found out what he was doing, this boy would be in serious trouble. The Arse Clencher didn't care what the Italians did, not really. But his own boy, sneaking off to listen to *verboten* music – that was tantamount to fraternising with the enemy. That's why the young Jerry looked terrified. *Yes*, thought Harry, *you'd be in very serious trouble indeed.*

'I'm Sub-Lieutenant Harry Gilmour, Royal Navy.'

'Leutnant Jürgen Secker, Luftwaffe.' He leaned forward and offered an outstretched hand. Harry shook it.

'So you're not here to spy on us, then, are you?' asked Harry.

'No. Just to listen to the music.'

Harry believed him, and when he said so, his look convinced his two companions they'd better believe him too.

So they came to an arrangement. Leutnant Secker could come and listen to the music any time he liked, and they would keep his secret. Harry would even leave a bottle of something in the turret, bread, stuffed pimentos, chorizo too; they'd even have someone watch the main entrance in case his *Kameraden* should chance to return early from whatever *Kraft durch Freude* activity the Arse Clencher might devise for his *Truppen* that day – activity Leutnant Secker could not for the time being join, because of his sprained ankle.

Armando, the furious Italian pilot, was prevailed upon to calm down, while Harry explained things to him: the perils of dragging poor Jürgen here into the censorious light of day, of having accusations flying back and forth, and the unintended consequences that might arise, which might put an end to Eurico's relatively benign regime.

Even the nice but dim Armando could imagine how the Italian authorities might react to the way in which he and his comrades were fraternising with the British; he could even imagine how the British authorities would react, if it were ever, officially, drawn to their attention. And as for what measures might be taken to assuage an even more outraged German reaction . . . well.

Jaime, the Spanish Army Engineer sagely confirmed this was true. 'They might place you all under Army jurisdiction,' he told the Italian. 'You wouldn't like that.'

Harry and Armando agreed. Everybody knew what the Spanish Army thought of gangs of foreign airmen being allowed to swan around on sacred Spanish soil unchecked.

So they all went back to listening to the music, but not before Jürgen had told Harry that he agreed with the general trend of the discussion taking place just before he'd been discovered. The terrace walls had echoed each word up to him with crystal clarity, and so yes, Britain really was a land without music, and indeed, how did they live with that? *Cheeky bastard*, thought Harry. *I save his arse and that's all the thanks I get.*

Afterwards Harry had asked Armando, 'What's the OVRA?'

The Italian had looked suddenly subdued and almost ashamed. 'Our Gestapo,' he'd said, and refused to elaborate.

Harry's first Officers' Mess 'at home', and Harry was resplendent in his white mess kit, tropical service, for the use of. The tables filled two-thirds of the huge ballroom, each one groaning with food, resplendent with silver and washed by the gently lapping light of a thousand candles, whose reflections danced in the glass of what seemed like as many bottles of wine. A string quartet played at the far end beyond an expanse of open floor, where the couples would soon gather to dance.

When they'd all been summoned to the tables to dine, Harry, his head still turned by Sybilla's flashing smiles, had jostled to get a place close to her, but it was Fabrizio's arm she took to lead her to the table and he stood crestfallen while other guests flocked to grab the best places. Eurico had glided up and steered him away.

'Let me introduce you to . . .' said Eurico, but Harry didn't quite catch the name of yet another temptress. The room was filling with them. Well-bred young women of rich families – they gave him the feeling that it might actually have been against the law for any of them to be plain or unattractive in any way. He was to escort the lady to her seat, but once there, it quickly became apparent he was going to have to share her with an EdA officer, and another Italian.

The food and the dancing came and went in a blaze of light and noise and dazzle, and Harry was sitting at his table again. The girl, Estrella, had been charming, coquettish and everything a young woman should be at a ball like this – and deeply stupid too. Oh well. Not that he had a chance in the first place, or on genuine reflection, even wanted one. He had for a long time watched Fabrizio and Sybilla together: dining, dancing and then taking their stroll upon the terrace, with all the other strolling couples. And he was laughing at himself when Eurico came to join him.

'Another triumph,' said Eurico, beaming from ear to ear, congratulating himself on this, his latest Mess 'at home'. 'I'm going to become a master of ceremonies once this is over. Bugger psychology. Have you enjoyed yourself?'

'A different world, Eurico,' said Harry, returning his beaming smile. 'You have transported me. I am seduced.'

'Not by young Estrella, I hope,' said Eurico with an arching of his brows. 'I'd be obliged to cover up your murder, if her father got to hear.'

'No, not by Estrella,' said Harry, pausing to gaze around the wreckage of the event. 'This *is* a different world for me, Eurico.'

'For us all, Harry. It's called war. None of us would do any of this were the world still sane.'

'I wonder sometimes who I'll be – let alone *where* I'll be when it all ends.'

'Well, let's hope you'll still be alive to wonder,' smiled Eurico, following Harry's line of sight to where Fabrizio and Sybilla were coming in through one of the French windows. 'You have an affection for her?'

Harry looked at her, holding Fabrizio's hand to her cheek and wondered how he could ever, even for a moment, have entertained the notion they might have been together. Sybilla in his parents' kitchen in Dunoon, or even on a Clyde steamer, in the dull grey of a northern day. What part of his life even touched at any point the world she lived in?

'No,' he said. 'No.'

'Why not?' asked Eurico, with that capricious look he had. 'She's a beautiful girl.'

Harry turned to look him square in the face. 'She wouldn't get my jokes,' he said, at length.

And so the days passed.

Eurico and Harry continued to debate the human condition, and Fabrizio forgot all about his embarrassing contretemps with a British battlecruiser, and wanted instead to talk about the wisdom of marriage. Harry even began to strike up a clandestine friendship with Leutnant Jürgen Secker, whose sprained ankle was taking some time to heal and whose presence in the little stone turret was becoming more and more frequent.

'I miss jazz and Hollywood movies,' he told Harry one day in his faltering French, after Harry had sarcastically asked him how he was enjoying the war. 'We don't get them in the Reich any more.'

'Being the master race can't be easy,' Harry had replied, absently, trying to listen to the Bach cello concerto the boys were making a pretty good stab at below.

'You think it witty to be mocking to someone who offers you friendship,' said Jürgen in an even tone. 'Is that the English way?'

'I'm not English,' said Harry.

'Ja, ja, Schotten . . . and I'm not a fucking Prussian, I'm a Mecklenburger. So?', and a deep sigh. 'You know, I really want to visit your country one day and it saddens me . . . breaks my heart . . . that we'll probably have to kill you first . . . because your stupid Prime Minister is too drunk to get in step with the march of history and join us.'

'I'm not talking to you about this again, Jürgen, so just shut up,' said Harry, reaching for the bottle of *fundador* and taking a stiff belt.

But when he looked back at the lad, Jürgen's eyes were tearing up and his face was filled with despair, and in the hole it opened between them, Harry saw how in another time they would have become friends, and he felt the same empty feeling gnawing at him too. 'Any more of your nonsense and I'll get them to play "Hitler Has Only Got One Ball" again,' he said, with his lop-sided grin, 'and you know how the Eyeties love that.' Jürgen wiped his eyes on his sleeve, and then smiled the same tired smile.

It was quite chilly in the mornings now, and Harry had a Spanish great-coat on over his shirt and sweater when he took his coffee out to the terrace to enjoy the view of the port in peace and quiet. The sun was up, and the sky was the usual pure blue, and filled with birdsong that he wouldn't be able to hear once his fellow inmates had risen. He was thinking about home, and about a girl called Shirley there, and how the young ladies of Palma really did come from a different world, when he saw Jürgen leaning out of the turret waving frantically at him. He looked around quickly to see if anyone else were there – this was an amazingly reckless thing for Jürgen to do: if anyone spotted him, if word ever got back to the Arse Clencher . . . Harry hurried over, and Jürgen reached down to pull him up and in through one of the narrow windows. They flopped down on to the flagstone floor and Harry could feel its chill seeping through the folds of the greatcoat.

'What do you think you're doing?' he asked his friend in a hiss.

Jürgen's face looked grim. 'Your friend, Fabrizio. He is a dead man.'

'What?'

'There are two men here,' said Jürgen, holding Harry by the shoulder. 'They say they are from our embassy in Madrid, but they're not. They're from Berlin. They're here to take your friend away. Something his family is involved with. Back in Italy.'

Harry knew it was true when he entered Eurico's office ten minutes later, and found him sitting behind his desk, white-faced, staring into nothing.

'I said they could have my office to talk to Fabrizio,' said Eurico, 'but no. They wanted to take him to the German consulate. More discreet, they said. Ha! More discreet to shut him in a box and put him on that Junkers 52 that's sitting on the runway at Son Bonet. I told them there would be paperwork to complete. They are gone, for the time being.'

Harry eventually found Fabrizio back in his quarters, adjusting his best walking-out uniform in front of a mirror. He was dressed as though he were about to head into town.

'I am going to meet my accusers,' he said. 'I will not skulk from these people.'

One look told Harry there would be no reasoning with him, so he ran downstairs and hunted through the reception area until he found the junior EdA officer of the day.

'Sottotenente de Savelli is intending to break his parole,' Harry told him. Any of the officers in the Hotel El Real could step out for the day, go into town, take the Ferrocarril to Sóller, so long as they had a written pass. There was no note of a written pass issued for Sottotenente de Savelli on the EdA officer's day log. And breaking parole was a serious offence. The officer grabbed two airmen and sped off to detain Fabrizio. Harry went back to Eurico's office, where he found him on the phone. He flopped into one of the huge wing chairs. Eurico finished his call.

'His family. Father, uncles, God knows who else,' said Eurico. 'It appears they have been involved in some sort of plot against Il Duce.'

Harry remembered what Fabrizio had said about Mussolini, the blacksmith's son – and what his father thought. And his uncles.

'They're Black nobility, his family. Do you know that?' said Eurico. 'An ancient Roman baronial family. The "Black" came later though.'

'I know,' said Harry.

Eurico arched his eyebrows.

'You learn Italian as a language, you can't help but pick up a bit of the history too,' said Harry. 'After the House of Savoy entered Rome and unified Italy in 1870, the Pope refused to recognise Victor Emmanuel as King and claimed he was a prisoner in the Vatican. The loyal families locked and draped their palaces in mourning in support, hence the "Black".'

'Indeed,' said Eurico. 'Well done, *mi erudito*. The papacy never forgot that little gesture. So Fabrizio, he is from a *very* respected, very Catholic family. But I doubt even that will save him or his father or uncles from the wrath of Il Duce. Or of the Germans, if they've been plotting.' And there Eurico paused, smiling to himself. 'It would go down well with Señor Soriano, though. He wouldn't demur for a moment at having his Sybilla take the name. But young Fabrizio needs to stay alive for that to happen.'

Harry sat with his head in his hands, then he said, almost as if inspired, 'Your bureaucracy. You can't reason with paperwork. You said it yourself.'

'Fascist bureaucracy,' said Eurico. 'It does what it's told, like everyone else. Surely I don't have to spell it out. El Caudillo is not exactly unsympathetic to Il Duce, or even Der Führer. The Els and the Ils and the Ders of this world do have a habit of sticking together, in case you hadn't noticed.'

'El Caudillo?' asked Harry. 'Is that . . .?'

'Franco? Yes.'

'We have to get Fabrizio off the island,' said Harry, at length.

Eurico stared long and hard at him, his mind working behind his glassy rabbit eyes. Eventually he said, 'I will turn a blind eye. It is the best I can do. Even by my just doing nothing, if you succeed, it will go badly for me. You know that?'

Harry sat back, incredulous. 'If *I* succeed . . .?'

Eurico slammed the desk with the flat of his hand – a rare display of emotion for him. 'Madre de Dios, Harry! What do you want from me? That I lay on a plane for him? Where would it fly to? To the British? Do you want me shot, too? And anyway, do you imagine Fabrizio would get aboard it?'

Harry's stare didn't flinch from Eurico, nor could Eurico meet it. 'Do you think you can morally blackmail me?' said Eurico. 'That I am some child? That you can squeeze some futile gesture from me with your sanctimonious silence?'

'We all wonder, growing up, what kind of men we're going to turn out to be,' said Harry, with a theatrical quiet. 'This is one of those moments where we get to find out.'

It was Eurico's turn to stare at Harry now. Seconds slipped away in the silence, until the noise of the others, emerging from their ignorant slumbers, began to waft into Eurico's office. There was one particular bang: a door, someone falling over?

Harry said, 'Get me a boat. A yacht. There are plenty of them up in Puerto de Sóller. Water. We won't need much food. And a chart . . . No, not a chart . . . A pilot book for the western Med. There must be something in a library somewhere, or on a chandlers' bookshelf. How long can you hold them off?'

'I'm astonished I've held them off at all,' said Eurico, reaching for the telephone and dialling. 'You know he won't go with you voluntarily.'

It only took until lunch for word to spread. Harry was out on the terrace with Russell's *Balearic Pilot*, 1927, in English, which he found in the hotel's own library; he was frantically scribbling while everyone else was inside queuing for aperitifs. A still-pimply RAF type, all pustules and ginger hair, already in his cricketing whites, appeared at Harry's elbow. 'Groupie wants a word in his quarters, quick-time,' said the youth, shallow chest thrust out with the vicarious importance of his mission. 'Follow me.'

Groupie – Group Captain Mahaddie – was standing peering out of his heavily draped windows down into the street, when Harry was unceremoniously thrust into his presence. He turned, gestured with his chin for ginger-pimples to get out, the way real men do, when real business is to be discussed. *Arsehole*, thought Harry, as he routinely thought every time he came into contact with Jock Mahaddie.

Mahaddie, also in his cricket whites, walked deliberately up to Harry until he was invading his space. 'A wee chookie-burdy's been whisperin' in ma lug-hole,' he said into Harry's face. 'Tells me you're plannin' tae jump the dyke wi' yer Wop boyfriend, Luigi the Latin Lover . . .'

'Excuse me, Sir?' said Harry. '"Jump the dyke"?'

'Don't get fly wi' me, laddie. You know what Ah mean. Go over the wall. Escape. 'Cause there's a pair o' Gestapo clowns in town, want tae pull his toenails oot.' Mahaddie stopped, and began to pace around Harry. 'Ah want tae know what yer plannin' . . .'

'Planning, Sir? I've no idea what you're talking about.'

'Good. Then ye'll no mind if I have ye locked up for the next seventy-two hours, will ye.'

Harry did mind. Very much. He said nothing.

'Ahh. Reconsiderin' yer position then, laddie. Wise. 'Cause if you're goin' aff this island, Ahm goin' wi' ye. Or yer no goin'. How's that fer a snooker?'

Harry sighed and looked at the ceiling. Suddenly Mahaddie sat down in one of the room's easy chairs with a flump. He gestured to Harry to sit too. There was a long silence, then Mahaddie, elbows on his knees, and his head looking down into the space between them, said, 'Ye don't like me. Ah assure *you*, the feelin's mutual. But Ah wouldn'a feel victimised if Ah wus you. Ah don't like anybody here, includin' masel'. Look at it from ma point of view. I'm supposed to be oan Malta right now. Deputy Air Officer Commanding. Wi' a gaggle of Wellingtons and Blenheims and Fleet Air Arm Swordfish under my command, wi' orders tae stop aw those Axis convoys shippin' Rommel enough petrol and ordnance to get him tae Cairo. It's the biggest command I've ever worked fer. This is wha' Ah dae. It's ma joab. Ahm no a wee hostilities-only pipsqueak like you, laddie. An' whit am Ah doin'? I'm stuck here. Cause o' a stupid oil leak on a last-aff-the-production-line-oan-a-Friday-night Lockheed Hudson's starboard Wright-fuckin'-useless-Cyclone engine!'

Mahaddie paused to let his fury subside a little. Harry knew better than to interrupt. The man wasn't being your average, everyday professional Jock any more; his true, Glaswegian origins were showing through and any veneer of gentility about him had gone. *Our great contribution to the world,* thought Harry. *Our education system. We Scots really are quite the egalitarians.* He might be an officer now, but Mahaddie probably really had come from up some tenement close. But what had happened to get him from there to here? A bursary to Allan Glen's School, run by the city's corporation for the poor but bright? A school that specialised in engineering and science – and then what could make more sense than an engineering qualification and a career in the Royal Air Force, ever the most egalitarian of the three services?

'How d'ye intend to do it, laddie?' Mahaddie said, eventually, much calmer now, with the veneer returning.

'Steal a yacht, Sir,' said Harry, now convinced prevarication would be counter-productive. 'There's loads of them up the west coast.'

'A yacht? To Malta? Please don't take the mickey, laddie.'

'No, Sir. I'm heading for Gib. It's seven hundred miles, give or take the odd yard or two. A straight, clean run, west-south-west. It can be done. I can do it. It'll take four or five days at the most. Depending on the wind. And the wind is favourable this time of year. Maybe a little too favourable.'

'I thought you were goin' to steal a plane,' said Mahaddie, snorting at the idea. 'Bundle Luigi into the pilot's seat and hold a gun tae his heid, although from what Ah've seen o' the bugger, Ah didn't give much for yer chances on that one. He's a bit too full of himself to be just rollin' over. Thought I could come in handy there.'

'A plane would be a bit too personal for the Spanish air force, I think, Sir.'

'Whit? Too personal?'

'I think they'd be liable to take offence at us for stealing one of their planes, Sir. And come after us. A rich grocer's weekend plaything on the other hand – would they care? Would they bother? Probably think we'd end up drowning ourselves anyway. They might be right. That's what I meant about the wind being too favourable. The tramontane. It's a cold north-westerly. Funnels down between the Pyrenees and the Massif Central in France, and this time of year it can really get going . . . according to my Russell anyway.' Harry brandished his *Balearic Pilot*.

'Well, laddie. Sounds like ye've thought of everythin'. All we need to do now is get Luigi tae the boat wi' out him screamin' murder, polis!'

'. . . three sterrs up!' said Harry, the words of a children's rhyme, heard by Harry the student on a Glasgow street, suddenly flashing into his head.

Mahaddie turned and gave him such a look. '. . . The wummin in the middle hoose hit me wi' a cup . . .' he said experimentally.

'. . . ma heid is bleedin', an' ma face is cut . . .' replied Harry.

'. . . murder polis, three sterrs . . .' added Mahaddie, still looking curious.

'Up!' said Harry, rounding it off with a flourish.

'Ha! Ha!' roared Mahaddie. 'Argyll ye said ye came from! Argyll Street, mair like it . . . the wrang end!'

Harry knocked on Eurico's door and gently pushed a haughty-looking Fabrizio through it before him.

'He wants to ask you something, Eurico,' said Harry. Both he and the young Italian were in their 'stepping-out' best uniforms, having skipped dinner digestifs to do a quick-change act out of their mess ensembles.

'I will not hide from these people,' said Fabrizio, as if daring anyone to challenge him.

'We'd like a pass,' said Harry, by way of clarifying matters. 'Fabrizio and I have taken a notion to go downtown and listen to that dance band that's playing in La Calatrava.'

'You're not afraid, Fabrizio?' said Eurico, leaning back behind his desk.

Christ, you're over-egging the pudding, mate, thought Harry, but he said nothing. Fabrizio's nostrils flared. If there were even the remotest chance he'd be likely to see sense and decide instead to stay home that night, it was gone now. Eurico saw the nostrils flaring, and took that as his answer. He reached for his pass pad and began filling it in. The plan was panning out nicely.

'When the court of inquiry sits on this,' Eurico had told Harry earlier, 'I'm not having any German, or worse, any Army bastard, alleging that any of my men had somehow sneaked him out. Do you understand?'

'Yes,' Harry had said, 'as long as you leave the keys in the J12, and the boot open . . .', referring to the Hispano-Suiza air force staff car that was Eurico's pride and joy, and therefore testimony to the level of sacrifice he was prepared to make.

Walking out of the hotel, Harry couldn't believe there were two men in sharp, double-breasted suits waiting for them on the other side of the street. They fell in behind as he and Fabrizio walked towards the town.

'I don't believe that,' he said, looking behind to convince himself they were actually being followed. The men were pale and northern-looking, hair shorn with geometric precision; they had to be the Germans. But for them to have been waiting there – they couldn't possibly have *known* Fabrizio might be coming out. They must have been hanging around for hours. Playing at being secret agents . . . gumshoes on Sunset Strip. The whole notion was just too ludicrous. Melodrama, except they were playing it for real. *It's just so vulgar*, was the thought that immediately flipped into Harry's mind, followed by *Idiots*. But what he said to his friend was, 'I'm Humphrey Bogart. Who do you want to be? Peter Lorre or Sidney Greenstreet?' before he realised *The Maltese Falcon*, only just out this year, probably hadn't made it to Italy, there being a war and all. But Fabrizio was too incensed by the Germans' audacity to be paying any attention. Harry kept having to tug him by the sleeve to stop him turning around and confronting them, hissing at him, 'If you hit one of them, it's only Eurico you'll get in trouble.'

They walked on down the narrow, winding tenement streets, thronged with people out strolling; cafés spilling out on to the narrow pavements, their tables choked with couples there to see and be seen; and the noise of shouted orders; coffee, beer and wines, brandies, tapas and darting waiters. And everywhere the spill of lights. The civil war had been over for less than two years, and it had left Spain wrecked and impoverished. But not Nationalist Majorca. Its war had lasted barely two months, and that was back in 1936. An assault, aimed at securing the islands for the Republic, had been driven off with help from Fascist Italy. The devastation that had swept across most of the vast European peninsula to its west had never touched here.

Fabrizio and Harry, and the two Germans in pursuit, drew out a little comic daisy chain through the night-time crowds: Fabrizio and Harry stopping twice for coffee, then for wine and tapas, and the Germans all but bumping into them as a kerbside table would appear, and our heroes would plonk themselves down to be served. Fabrizio was by now glowing with the triumph of taunting their two shadows, utterly unaware of where Harry was leading him.

They emerged out of a narrow street on to an open plaza – a small affair, with grass squares and flower beds and benches, with its far end open on to a main road, and beyond that the harbour. A large car, resplendent in EdA markings sat by the roadside, with a bulky big driver, an EdA forage cap perched on his huge domed skull, looking like a pea on a mountain. They could only see the back of his head.

'Oh look,' said Harry, gripping Fabrizio by the elbow, 'It's Eurico. Let's give these goons the slip good and proper.' And before his friend could utter a word, Harry was propelling him towards the Hispano-Suiza's open back door.

The goons had tried to run after them, but the Hispano, door still open and our two heroes scrambling through it, was accelerating away before they'd gone two steps. Fabrizio craned to look out of the back window at them, caught flat-footed, then rolled back on the big leather bench seat, bellowing with laughter. So it took a number of minutes for him to assess this new situation and realise there was no Eurico in the car. That was when he recognised the bull-like head, sitting in the driving seat, and the huge frame, bursting out of a far too small EdA airman's shirt – and his face clouded.

'What is all this about?' he said in a quiet voice.

'And nice tae see ye too,' said Mahaddie over his shoulder, as he gunned the car back through the town heading for the north road. Fabrizio was not to be pacified. Harry tried to explain: they knew the Germans were here to take him away, and they knew why. He wouldn't be going back to Italy, to face his accusers and answer their charges. He was going to Berlin, where they'd want names out of him, where they would expect a list of plotters from him. And they would get a list from him, regardless whether anyone on it was involved or not. Of course, said Harry, he knew he would never willingly betray his country, his uniform or his friends. But this wasn't about duty or honour, or even the war. It was politics. He *would* give them a list – he wouldn't be able not to. Didn't he understand that? Didn't he realise who he was dealing with? What they were capable of? Did Harry have to spell it out for him? You always give people like that what they want in the end. You can't not. No one can. But Fabrizio was having none of it.

'I will not capitulate to you English!' he yelled in Italian. Harry knew Mahaddie didn't speak Italian, but he'd have understood the 'English' bit, and Harry feared for how that might play.

'What about Sybilla?' Harry said, and then instantly regretted it because Fabrizio looked as if he were about to hit him. They were in countryside by this time, the road dark. Mahaddie stood on the brakes, and Harry and Fabrizio cannoned into the seats in front. Fabrizio was still picking himself out of the seat well, when the back door on his side flew open, and a huge fist flew in and knocked Fabrizio senseless. In a moment Mahaddie was on Fabrizio, and had a pair of handcuffs on his wrists, and then another pair on his ankles.

'Where did you get those?' said Harry lamely, but Mahaddie just gave him a withering look as he plucked a roll of heavy tape from the front seat and began gagging Fabrizio's mouth and jaw.

Harry leaned back, catching his breath. 'If you hadn't been going to do that, I was,' he said, making way so as they could stretch Fabrizio out in the seat well.

'Really,' said Mahaddie. 'Well, Ah decided no' tae wait for the pie and Bovril at half-time. Oanywise, if somebody was gonnae huv tae tap him, Ah've got mair psi than you.'

Harry got into the front seat with the big Scotsman, and they drove on into the night, Harry thinking, *Psi – pounds per square inch. Yes. Definitely an engineering background.*

Eurico's directions had been specific: follow the main road from Sóller town to the port, then not far from the head of the inlet on which it sits, you'll see a stone groyne running out from the beach. 'A fisherman who looks like Methuselah, but answers to Pedro, will be waiting,' Eurico had said. 'Do as he tells you.'

Harry, who over the preceding days and weeks, had been learning a little Spanish from his new friend to pass the time, protested that he didn't know whether his grasp of the language was up to that.

'Well, go where he shoves you,' an exasperated Eurico had replied. It really was all slap, dash and flung together, their plan, but there had been no time for it to be otherwise, so no point in either of them pointing this out.

Away from the lights of the town, a half-moon that drifted in and out of the high, scudding clouds – tramontane-driven clouds – delivered a surprising amount of light. They saw their objective clear enough as the road from Sóller town emerged from the gap in the hills, the groyne's black spine obvious on the moon-dappled surface of the water, and when they pulled up, the lump on the end of it they'd taken to be some sort of cairn, rose and came towards them.

Pedro, a small, round figure, dressed all in black with a Catalan beret pulled to a peak low on his forehead, had a face the texture and colour of rotting avocado skin. His little coracle-shaped boat, with two thwarts, all insubstantial and more like a giant baby's bath, was moored in the shadows.

Mahaddie was in the back of the car. He hauled Fabrizio, now fully conscious and looking wild-eyed, on to the seat. It was the early hours, not long until sunup, but the few houses in the distance were all in darkness, and the port was completely shrouded by the black shadow of the massif behind it. Pedro was in his little boat, waiting to cast off and when Harry returned to the car, Mahaddie was sitting on Fabrizio, pinning him to the car seat. Harry waited.

'Right, Luigi,' said Mahaddie in a quiet, affable voice, over his shoulder, his gentility all but returned. 'I'm the senior British officer here and you're my prisoner. And if you think that means that somehow you might be able to appeal to my better nature, then best of fuckin' luck tryin' to find it.'

Harry translated. Fabrizio's eyes never left Mahaddie's half-turned face; he showed no reaction. But Mahaddie wasn't interested; he clambered off the young Italian, stood and bent over to unlock the handcuffs around Fabrizio's ankles and dragged him to his feet. 'Right, we're gettin' in that wee man's excuse for a boat, Luigi,' he said, then frogmarched him out on to the groyne.

'His name's Fabrizio,' said Harry.

'And I'm a Group Captain,' said Mahaddie over his shoulder, 'and his name's what I say it is.'

Mahaddie ordered Harry to retrieve the stuff in the car boot: supplies Harry had asked Eurico to find. There was a military knapsack filled with tinned food, and four half-gallon water cans. Harry lugged them over in two trips. They all managed to squeeze into the flimsy vessel, and Mahaddie and Harry began to row. Pedro, using a third, stunted oar steered, peering into the pitch black like he knew where they were going. Mahaddie warned Fabrizio about struggling. '. . . it won't take much to cowp this tub, laddie . . . How d'ye fancy yer chances at the freestyle with yer hands cuffed behind yer back?' After that, nobody talked.

The yacht was a Bermuda-rigged gaff-sloop, about thirty-five feet long, and Harry could just make out the name *Carmen* picked out on her stern as they came up on her. Pedro, with surprising agility, used his little oar to reach out and lever them in against one of the sloop's deck cleats. He then held them tight, hull to hull, and gestured with his free arm for them to get the hell out of his little boat. Harry leapt up first. Mahaddie unceremoniously, hand on Fabrizio's backside, propelled him on to the yacht, and then began slinging the supplies up, before he too followed. Harry turned to say something, but Pedro was already a dim shape, scooting away and fast disappearing against the black backdrop of the shoreline. They needed to be away too, and out of here before the sun was up and anyone spotted them stealing this boat.

'Stow him in the cabin,' Harry said to Mahaddie, referring to his friend, and went to set about getting ready.

'You're tellin' me what to do?' said Mahaddie, quiet, but belligerent.

Harry stopped in mid-movement and drew himself up, so that in the narrow cockpit, he was face-to-face with the big Scotsman.

'We're on water now,' he said.

And in that moment, and in fairness to Mahaddie, Mahaddie understood. Harry went back about his business, his heart still in his mouth at the temerity of what he'd just done.

'Is there anything I can do tae help?' asked Mahaddie from behind him.

'Don't rock the boat,' said Harry.

It was still dark in the bowl of the harbour, but the sky was light now behind the mountains, as they motored out on the *Carmen*'s small inboard petrol engine. Harry had dipped the tank and it was a quarter-full. He didn't know how much manoeuvring that would give them, but it was certainly more than enough to get them out of the harbour. There was also some paraffin for the small stove, and thank God, but the owner was a lazy enough bastard not to have taken her sails in; they were still bent, the mainsail to the jib, and the headsail to the forestay.

Well, it was going to be a fairly straightforward run. Wind almost permanently abaft the starboard beam, hopefully; steer 250 degrees and keep on going until you raise the coast of Africa, then starboard, thirty and into the funnel of the Straits of Gibraltar and Bob's your uncle – or a piece of cake, as the RAF johnnies were wont to say.

'What happens now?' asked Mahaddie.

'We just need to get out past that big headland there, get the sails up, and then it's turn left for Gibraltar,' said Harry.

'That easy, eh,' said Mahaddie, dubiously. 'How far did you say it was again?

'Ooh – seven hundred miles, give or take. Piece of cake, really,' said Harry, his teeth shining in a smile in the half-light. And Mahaddie, who'd been watching him all the while as Harry had prepared the boat – moving surefooted over its deck, loosening the mainsail's tabs and freeing the halyards, shackling the jib halyard to the head ready for hoisting, running the sheets back into the cockpit, dipping the fuel tank and opening the cock to feed the tiny inboard engine – Mahaddie had found himself actually believing Harry. But then Mahaddie had never seen a fighting sailor about his business before, and certainly not a Royal Navy one.

Chapter Six

Harry was looking at his CO's arse, thinking how big it was, in that sulky way you do when you've finally come to terms with the fact that you don't like someone. Lieutenant Clive Rais's arse wasn't actually that big, because nothing about Rais was that big: it was just because Rais was bent double in front of Harry and the arse was pointed right at him. The other end – the head end – was fixed to an attack periscope, and crouched over the CO was the Chief Petty Officer, not quite in the way, peering at the periscope's bezel, ready to call off the latest bearing. They were at Diving Stations – the Trade didn't use the surface skimmer's 'Action Stations', because if a simple mistake while you were diving or submerging a boat could sink you, calling Diving Stations was alert enough for anyone.

Another enemy convoy was in their CO's sights, the fifth in two days. Harry wondered if everyone else was wondering what he was wondering: was this one going to end any differently from all the others? When he looked around the submarine's control room, the stone-set faces gave nothing away, except to the initiated; each one was flat and expressionless, showing neither enthusiasm nor insolence – just blank, a textbook example of Jack, browned off.

Harry found himself wishing he was back on that gaff-rigged sloop, *Carmen*. How long ago had it been since that particular passage through paradise had ended? Ten days? Less? And now here he was on his new submarine. Not the HMS *Nimuae* he had originally been appointed to, but HMS *Umbrage*. And, judging by the mood of the crew he had come to know over the past week, never had a submarine been better named.

Life with *Carmen*'s crew had been jollier. Not at first, admittedly. But until that RN motor gunboat had intercepted them twenty miles south-east of Marbella, demanding to know since when did Scotland have its own navy, they'd been having quite a jolly time.

The memory of it was making Harry smile even now: how, after they had made it away from the coast of Majorca, he had found the signal flag for the letter 'M' in the yacht's signal locker, and hoisted it as their ensign – the 'M' flag being a perfect saltire.

On *Umbrage* right now, there was no jollity; you could have cut the atmosphere in the control room with a knife. The time was 12.20. They had gone to Diving Stations over half an hour ago, interrupting a puerile harangue by the CO directed at the First Lieutenant. So that, at a time when the CO and the First Lieutenant should have been concentrating on their attack, they were still silently seething at each other. It was a little drama made all the more depressing by the fact that Harry knew one of its actors all too well, from a long time ago.

How much easier life had been on the *Carmen*. Of course Fabrizio had started out beside himself with fury, and the bombastic and deeply irritating Group Captain Mahaddie had done nothing but glower and await an excuse to visit violence on the poor young Italian. But as Harry had noted many times before, from crewing on rich men's yachts, smooth sailing on a long reach can have a soothing effect on even the most troubled soul.

The atmosphere had been further helped by the discovery of wine on board, and by Harry's little talk to them about how they could each have a little shot at sailing if they promised to behave themselves. And how that could be a good idea too, because Harry wasn't going to be able to stay awake for five days on the trot, and if they could each take their turn on the tiller it would make all the difference between them getting to Gib and surviving, and them getting lost and foundering.

Also, the story Harry had concocted about how they'd all happened to be here went a long way towards pacifying Fabrizio. How Harry and Mahaddie had planned their escape all along, but at the last minute they'd been rumbled by this vigilant Italian officer, and so they'd had to overpower him and take him along to prevent discovery – and that was why he was their prisoner. They'd managed to settle down and enjoy their wine and the sunsets after that.

Until the gunboat picked them up and took them into Gib, where Fabrizio had been bundled off by a pair of evil-looking pongoes, with not even a chance for a proper goodbye. And Harry and Mahaddie had been shoved aboard a Malta-bound Sunderland less than ten hours after they'd been put ashore, without even a chance for a drink and a steak in one of the rock's famed hostelries.

And then Harry had been introduced to his new Skipper.

Except no one on HMS *Umbrage* was allowed to call him that. For Rais, 'Skipper' really was an endearment too far.

'Just so as we understand each other from the outset, Mr Gilmour,' had been this CO's first words to Harry, 'I'm not the Skipper. Skipper is what you call the chap on the bridge of the Gosport ferry. I'm the Captain.' And before Harry had even had the chance to say 'Aye aye, Captain', Rais had added, 'And I am an exacting Captain. I know what I want from my crew, officers and men. What might have passed for efficiency on your other submarines won't be good enough on my submarine. Nothing is "good enough" for me. I only accept the best. And you're going to give that to me, at all times. *All* times. Carry on.'

And that was it. Not even a handshake. Was it only last week?

This current 'atmosphere' had been brought on by the First Lieutenant asking Rais if he really thought it was necessary to surface briefly to allow their new Navigator, Harry, to attempt a quick noon shoot and thus confirm their exact position.

The First Lieutenant had doubted the wisdom of such a course of action as it was doubtful whether the sun would even make an appearance, let alone be out long enough for Harry and his sextant to do the business. Then there was the risk of being spotted by the Italians this close to Genoa.

The CO had exploded.

Throughout the harangue, the First Lieutenant had been wearing an expression on his face that some might have taken for a measure of contrition, but Harry knew better – because he knew this First Lieutenant of old. His name was Kit Grainger, and he and Harry had served together before, on HMS *Trebuchet*. Grainger: the man who had come back for Harry, and saved his life.

No, Harry recognised the expression on Grainger's face only too well. It was irritation. Grainger was irritated with himself, that he'd been silly enough to actually offer a suggestion to this new, and obviously inexperienced, CO. If you knew Grainger, you couldn't miss it, not in the tiny, confined space of the control room of a U-class submarine. And that was when Wykham, another impossibly young and daft RNVR Sub-Lieutenant, who was officer of the watch and completing his next regulation all-round look on the periscope, sang out, 'Captain to the control room!', obeying the set-down regulation protocol, even though the Captain was standing barely three feet from him, before announcing, 'Smoke on the horizon, bearing north-west!' Because unlike *Trebuchet*, this submarine, *Umbrage*, was a strictly-by-the-book boat.

Rais had practically shouldered young Wykham off the periscope, if someone so slight could do that to someone so gangly.

'Group up!' Rais had shouted.

No need to shout, Harry had thought at the time. *We're all standing right here.*

'Full ahead, together! Eighty feet!'

At eighty feet, Grainger, on the trim, had levelled them, and Rais had ordered, 'Port, ten!' and away they'd gone, sprinting towards the target. Just like the last time, and the time before, and the time before that – and before that one too.

Then it was up and down, and up and down again, to periscope depth, for Rais to 'have another look'; Rais ordering, 'Group down' to take the way off her, and having the boat plane up to periscope depth – from Group up, to Group down, the motor room crew aft, reconnecting the armatures driving the propeller shafts from 'parallel' for high speed to 'series' for slow.

Harry, standing at the chart table, pencil and ruler in hand, had already begun a plot on the attack, ready to note every manoeuvre *Umbrage* made on the chart. But there was nothing to note. Harry knew how it should be happening: Rais, closing the range to the target, getting their boat into a firing position; Rais, doing it by calling out what he saw – the tactical picture, the range and bearing and estimated speed of the target – for Harry to mark on the chart, and more importantly, for Wykham to dial into their fruit machine. Wykham, who now stood before it – the electromechanical box of tricks tacked by the aft wall that separated the control room from the ASDIC cubby, that crunched all the numbers and then spat out the direction their bows should be pointing in when they fired their torpedoes, so that they had at least some chance of hitting the enemy. But it wasn't happening. Harry had no data for the target, and neither did Wykham. Rais wasn't telling them. No one even knew what the target was. It could've been a gash scow or the battleship *Vittorio Veneto*.

'HE still bearing now red-one-five,' called Tuke, their Leading Telegraphist, who was a dab hand on the ASDIC – just a disembodied voice coming from the cubby next door. 'Still two targets. One, small . . . high-speed diesel . . . slow. The other . . . big marine engine . . . steady one-two-oh revs. She's a rattly one, Sir. Like she was straining herself. Twelve knots, I reckon.'

So it isn't the battleship Vittorio Veneto, thought Harry. HE meant hydrophone effects – the engine noises picked up by their ASDIC set on passive, and as Tuke listened, their bearing was narrowing slightly. So the target was advancing toward them obliquely, from their port bow, and from all the helm orders that were being barked out by Rais, Harry worked out it must still be one hell of a way off.

'Just the numbers, Tuke,' said Rais, taking time off from muttering to himself, one arm linked through the rungs of the conning tower ladder, gripping it like grim death, while he banged at the risers with his other hand in a steady rhythm. 'You're not paid to reckon.'

Officers' callous arrogance towards their crews was nothing new, yet it sounded strange coming from Rais, directed at a sailor old enough to be his father, with not much short of two decades in a blue suit – a highly experienced ASDIC operator and submariner. And Rais, who looked all of fifteen if he were a day, and such an angelic child, with his floppy blond hair, cherub's cheeks and cupid's-bow, bee-sting lips. He could only have been about five foot five or six inches tall. He was even wearing his officer's white short-sleeve shirt, with its epaulettes with the two solid RN Lieutenant's rings on them. And it still even looked clean, all the way from Malta to here in a submarine.

Up and down again they went – Rais taking his 'all-round looks', swivelling round, flicking the up handle, then back again, all the while uttering not a single 'The bearing is that' for the Petty Officer to read off the bezel above his head and sing out. Rais was now cursing all the time, yelling that he needed more speed, draining amps from *Umbrage's* batteries with every bound. Harry shuddered to think about the look that must now be on their Leading Torpedoman's crusty old fizz, back aft in the motor room, as his two darling motors were being flogged flat.

And then there was Grainger, off to the side, attentive to his trim board, making sure *Umbrage* was always under complete control regardless of what wild revolution the CO might order. But like a bystander. Like he wasn't involved. No wonder Jack was browned off, caught between a Skipper with his 'L' plates still up and a Jimmy – as Jack called all First Lieutenants – who is spending the commission just standing around waiting for the Skipper to fall on his arse so he can laugh at him, when he should be presenting his Captain with a boat and crew, ready to go to war.

They were up again, after executing some sharp turns when down at eighty feet. *We should never have to go that deep*, thought Harry, even though he could guess why Rais had ordered it. Here in the Med, the water was sometimes so clear, any patrolling shagbat could spot their shadow down to fifty or sixty feet, especially those little Cant float-planes, with their huge wing areas, that went so slow they could practically hover. But it was winter now, and the patchy cloud and the wind ruffling the surface would have made them invisible even at periscope depth – not much more than twenty feet.

Those were all things Harry knew already, the bits of lore you picked up as a matter of course. But Rais hadn't seemed to. Probably because he wasn't the sort of chap you could tell things to – certainly not if you were just the Navigator. That was the Jimmy's job, ensuring the Captain was up to speed on all the latest tactical ruses, and Grainger would certainly know, yet he hadn't told his Captain. So they'd been going up and down, wasting amps, and time – time that would have put them closer to their target, whatever the bloody thing was.

And then the shout. Rais, like he was hailing the next ship in a squadron, in a North Atlantic gale, 'The bearing is that!'

The Petty Officer practically leapt into the air. He quickly recovered, leaned in to see the bezel that showed the angle Rais was pointing the periscope, and swiftly read it off. Harry heard Wykham pipe up from over his shoulder, repeating it back, and then Harry heard the bearing being dialled in.

'Range . . . is that!' yelled Rais, turning the knob on the little device in the periscope that split the target, showing one image of it super-imposed on top of the other. All you had to do was rotate that knob and it would move one image down until its waterline was touching the mast tops of the lower image, and the bezel above your head would give the angle subtended in minutes for whoever was reading off the bearing data to see.

The Petty Officer called, 'Thirty minutes!'

And now all Rais had to do was guess the target's mast height, divide it by the minutes' reading and then he had . . . 'Range. Four thousand yards!' called Rais.

A mast height of about 120 feet, calculated Harry, so the target must be pretty big-ish.

Wykham called it back and dialled it in. Then nothing. Harry was busy dashing down the new numbers, updating his plot, so he didn't notice right away. Silence. That wasn't right. Rais hadn't called the target's speed. Wykham needed to dial in the speed if he were going to get a director angle out of the bloody machine; the DA which told you . . .

'She's a cargo-passenger job,' Rais was saying smugly, his eyes still glued to the periscope. 'Old, fat and fully laden . . . Seven thousand tons or I'm a Dutchman. More, even . . .'

Two things flew into Harry's mind: *You've had that bloody periscope up too long!* And that, over his shoulder, Wykham was going white and was shaking, waiting to hear Rais call the speed, and it not coming – Wykham, now terrified *he* was fucking it up.

'. . . and I've got us on a near-perfect 95-degree track angle,' continued Rais, oblivious. The control room was getting its tactical picture now, all right. *Well done*, thought Harry, the words laden with sarcasm, for all they were unspoken. A 95-degree track angle. After all his slewing about the ocean, Rais had actually managed to get *Umbrage* into such a position that when she fired her torpedoes, they would cross their seven-thousand-ton quarry's course at almost right angles. Perfect, indeed, but four thousand yards was a hell of a long shot. And unless somebody told Wykham the damn thing's speed, the damn thing could be anywhere when the torpedoes actually got to the target's track.

And then there was another voice in the control room. It was Wykham's again, and there was a quaver in it. 'Shall I make target's speed twelve knots, Sir?'

Harry thought, *Good lad, you've been paying attention*, remembering Tuke's call from the ASDIC cubby, all those hours ago, although Harry knew it had been bare minutes.

'Silence in the control room!' It was another gale-strength bellow, and Rais shot upright at the periscope as if it had electrocuted him, and was glaring, wild-eyed. The noise, in the tiny space, was like a physical slap. Harry took in the tableau: the Petty Officer, big Jonners Roscorla, had had to jerk out of Rais's way.

The PO was a solid Cornishman through and through, his black curly hair greying now, on a head like a cannon ball – an impressive man who, in a past life, looked as if he might have served a 32-pounder on Nelson's *Victory*, and maybe he had; his face, grim and angry. Harry noticed the face of the wiry little Outside Engine Room Artificer too. It had turned inboard at the CO's yell, when it should have been facing the other way, glued to his trim gauges. It was a study in alarm. From the stiffened shoulders of the senior rates on the planes, their backs to him, Harry guessed they were wearing similar expressions. And then there was Grainger, the bastard: that same stone-blank face, just watching, giving nothing away . . . And all the while, *Umbrage* – the boat that it was his duty to keep at the peak of full fighting efficiency – was on the verge of fucking up another attack.

Rais had already sent the periscope down, and Harry was breathing again. A periscope breaking surface too long, leaving its little telltale wake, could be spotted by an eagle-eyed lookout on the cargo ship or on her escort – the source of the other HE and likely an Italian Navy MAS-boat. It didn't matter. A sighted periscope meant the cargo boat would turn and comb *Umbrage*'s torpedoes, run between them as they passed harmlessly down its sides, while the MAS-boat would race towards them, dispensing depth charges. Meanwhile Rais's gaze flicked around the control room. No rage now, but more like a schoolboy caught dozing in class.

'Eight knots,' he said. 'Make the target's speed eight knots. That tub's never done twelve knots in her life.' A silence, as if he were collecting himself; as if he knew it was he who was in error. And then another thing remembered: 'Make ready tubes one and three. Set the depth for fifteen feet.'

The young control room messenger, tucked in for'ard as if he were hiding among the maze of pipework, looked more terrified than alarmed as he repeated the order through the sound-powered telephone to the boat's Chief Torpedo Gunner's Mate in the forward torpedo room.

It's a bit bloody late for that, thought Harry, for those orders should have been given at the start of the attack. But the TGM, a Chief Petty Officer by official rank, was Dinger Bell, an old hand who knew his business. *Umbrage* had only three torpedoes left out of her full load of eight, but Bell would have had their tubes flooded and ready to fire right after *Umbrage* went to Diving Stations. He wouldn't have waited for the call to his station in the torpedo room – this was not the first time he'd gone into an attack under this CO.

The other five torpedoes, fired in their previous attacks, had all missed.

Wykham sang out the director angle, and Rais immediately ordered the periscope back up. *Umbrage* was gliding through the water at dead slow ahead, together, and as the 'scope slid up from its housing, he ordered, 'Turns for three knots', and then he bent and dropped the 'scope's handles and said to the Chief, 'Lay me on the DA, Chief', and big Jonners stepped forward and, reading off the bezel, put his big paws on Rais's hands and steered the periscope on to the right bearing, as though they were performing some baroque minuet.

'Range?' called Rais, and the PO peered and read off, 'Thirty-two minutes!'

Rais called, 'Range is thirty-eight hundred yards.'

Wykham called it back and dialled it in.

Out on the deep blue sea, the wallowing Italian merchantman was puffing and wheezing towards the line that bisected Rais's view through the periscope. When its bows crossed it . . .

'Fire one!' said Rais, managing not to shout. The control room messenger repeated the order in his reedy pipe and a moment later *Umbrage* gave a little bump, like a car hitting a pothole in the road, and they could all hear and almost feel the hiss of the compressed air that had shoved the torpedo out of her tube, venting back into the boat.

Rais had his left hand off the periscope and was counting the seconds as they elapsed with his fingers: one, two . . . At seven, he called, 'Fire two!' then stepped away and sent the periscope back down. 'One hundred feet. Starboard, fifteen, slow ahead, together.'

Tuke called out from the ASDIC cubby, 'Both torpedoes running true.'

They were slinking away as their torpedoes sped at over forty-five knots towards the old, fat merchantman.

'Time to target now?' said Rais to Harry. Harry had already worked out the running time on his slide rule, the instant the first torpedo left its tube: thirty-eight hundred yards, two minutes thirty seconds. He glanced down at the stopwatch to check how many seconds left now: 'One minute twenty, Sir.'

That was a long, long time, because 3,800 yards was a long, long way for a torpedo to run if you were expecting it to be accurate. Time dripped. Over two miles of water to cover, to hit a target that was only a little over four hundred feet long and moving at an estimated eight knots, and no matter what way you calculated the equation, the fact remained that all the figures you'd used to aim it were estimates. Would the target still be doing eight knots? Would it still be on the same course, or would it turn? So they waited.

'First torpedo, thirty seconds to run,' said Harry, and wondered what Rais was thinking. This was the Captain's last chance to hit something on this patrol. If these two missed, he only had one torpedo left, and what did he think he was going to do with that? Rais's previous patrol, his first as part of the Tenth Flotilla, had been a duck too, apparently. Shrimp Simpson, the Captain (S), would be wondering if he had a duck for a Skipper.

Harry looked at his stopwatch, and followed as the second hand swept past the moment, then he gave it another whole five seconds.

Tuke had told the CO, 'Twelve knots' – Tuke, the most experienced ASDIC man aboard. And Rais hadn't listened, had followed what his own inexperienced eyes had told him, and gone with eight.

And their target: she'd still be chugging down that invisible bearing on the water – the one their torpedoes had been fired to cross. If they'd called the target's speed just right, those torpedoes would be crossing it just as their target arrived. But Rais had called, 'Eight knots', which meant the old, fat merchantman would be long gone . . . and their torpedoes just two bubbling streaks bisecting its big fat wake . . . the stupid, arrogant . . .

Harry, still looking at his stopwatch, said, 'First torpedo, miss . . .' and his words were shut off by a loud *budduddum!* that echoed through the boat. Rais's head went back, and he let out a deep sigh. Everyone looked at everybody else. The second torpedo would still be running. Harry started counting aloud, 'One . . . two . . .', but he only got to three, and then the noise of the second detonation filled the boat. 'Both torpedoes hit,' said Harry, grinning now, stating the bleedin' obvious. Everybody was grinning – everybody except Grainger, who merely allowed himself a superior smirk, which Rais, his face wreathed in smiles, didn't see because his head was still tilted back, so that Harry wasn't sure whether he was looking at the deckhead pipe runs or beyond, all the way to heaven.

The merchant ship's escort didn't pursue them, and down at one hundred feet, *Umbrage* tiptoed away from the scene. She hadn't needed to surface to make sure she'd sunk the enemy ship; everybody heard her boilers blowing, and then her bulkheads collapsing; and all the other breaking-up noises a ship makes as she sinks. So *Umbrage* had stayed deep for the rest of the day. Tuke picked up several HE returns, sounds in the water of unknown ships passing, not surprising with a major port like Genoa astern, and off their port beam the naval base at La Spezia. But the returns were all far away, and Rais remained resolutely uncurious as to their identity. Further and further they crept into the Ligurian Sea, on a steady course that Harry estimated would put them fifteen miles north of Capo D'Enfola on the Italian island of Elba after sunset.

Harry was going to have the first watch when they surfaced, which if they were going to let the sun fully set, would be just around 5pm local time. Harry had his head down for most of the day, and when he woke, after making himself a piping-hot mug of coffee with condensed milk, he sat down to encode a signal for Shrimp Simpson, alerting him to their claim to have sunk a seven-thousand-ton general cargo vessel, and to the fact they had one torpedo left and were off on the hunt for a target to use it on. Once fired, they could head back to Malta, and Harry, for one, was looking forward to that. A lot.

Submarines the size of *Umbrage* didn't merit a cook, and their nominated hash-slinger was one of the Stokers, a quiet, diffident Essex lad, who had been in the Navy since he'd graduated from a Barnardo's home in Billericay, and that hadn't been yesterday. He had thinning, swept-back hair the colour of an ashtray, and a submariner's usual pasty skin. The cracks in his rough-hewn hands and the crescents of his fingernails were permanently ingrained with oil and grease, collected over a score or more commissions from Pompey to the China Station, and were beyond scrubbing clean now. But he was a bloody good cook. Everyone agreed, yet that was something he hated to hear. Ken Musgrave was his name, and he was one of those blokes you found yourself liking without ever knowing why.

'Spot o' breakfast, Sir?' said Ken, leaning around the galley partition wall. 'Do you a nice Train Smash, Sir, before we go to red light.'

Like every Royal Navy submarine on patrol, day swapped for night. For each day was spent dived, and it was only during the hours of darkness you came up, the diesels came to life and the work of the boat began, and why breakfast was at 5pm.

Harry was sitting back on his banquette in the wardroom, gazing into space, with Wykham snoring in his fold-down bunk above him, and their CO, Lieutenant Clive Rais, hidden behind the drawn curtains concealing his bunk, a bare two feet opposite him on the other side of the passage. Rais, too, was probably asleep, but with the CO, you never knew. *Umbrage*'s Jimmy, Kit Grainger, was on watch in the control room, all of a dozen feet aft.

Harry, roused from his reverie, smiled. 'Train Smash, Ken? That'd be bloody marvellous. And some buttered toast and more coffee too, please. I'll wake Mr Wykham. He'll have some too.'

Musgrave touched a grubby paw to his cap. 'Aye aye, Sir. Mr Wykham, Sir . . . never been known not to.'

Train Smash: powdered egg, tinned tomatoes and bacon, flung together in a pot, but with Musgrave's little extra somethings. A pinch or so of mustard, Harry reckoned, and maybe even a dash of some of those herbs Lascar Vaizey used to fire in, when he was clashing pans – Vaizey, the curry king from *Trebuchet*, or the *Bucket*, as she was known to the men who'd sailed in her. They'd been a good crew, the Buckets, and she'd been a happy boat. The Umbrages were a good crew too, thought Harry, but there the similarities ended.

Harry prodded the underside of Wykham's bunk. 'Jim,' he said, quietly so as not to wake Rais – if he was sleeping. 'There's grub on the go.'

Two pipe-cleaner legs immediately swung down by Harry's head, and Wykham dropped into the passage, dragging his trousers after him. 'Put that away,' said Harry. 'You'll frighten the children.'

Wykham pulled on his trousers, and dragged his white roll-neck pullover over his head. 'Oh shut up, Harry . . . What is it?'

'Well, if you don't know that, at your age . . .' said Harry.

'To eat, you silly bugger. Grub? What's the grub?' The two young men were both sniggering, but still trying to be quiet. For the same reason.

Umbrage hadn't started life with Clive Rais as her CO; there'd been someone else before him. Another Skipper, and Grainger, as her designated Number One, had stood by her while she was being built by Cammell Laird; sailed her from the Mersey to the Clyde to work her up, and then out down the Bay of Biscay, heading for Gib and then Malta. She'd been a happy boat then, until they'd got as far as Cap Trafalgar, when the Skipper suffered an appendicitis. The poor bastard eventually died from the ensuing peritonitis.

Harry had learned all about the boat's history from Grainger, that first night they'd met again, after Harry had finally made it to Malta, sitting together in the Tenth Flotilla's wardroom, back in Lazaretto. Grainger had told Harry all about how he had brought *Umbrage* into Gib, and how that was when they were all first introduced to Clive Rais. He'd been a spare Skipper on the staff of the Eighth Flotilla, fresh from his Perisher – as the Trade's Commanding Officers' Qualifying Course was universally known – and waiting for just such a chance to assume a command of his own.

Nobody knew anything about him.

'It was a marriage made somewhere,' Grainger had told Harry, 'but not in a million years was it ever in heaven.'

All was quiet as Harry and Wykham fell upon their Train Smash, and their boat crept south, her crew at 'Watch, Dived' – a third of them up and about, and the other two watches racking up zeds: two hours on, four hours off during daylight hours; three hours on, and six off at night.

Umbrage wasn't a big boat, not by *Trebuchet*'s standards; she displaced about 648 tons surfaced, 735 tons dived, and was 196 feet long, with a beam of just eleven feet. So really, if you were one of her twenty-nine-strong crew – including her CO – you knew everything that was going on in her, wherever you were. Right at the back of the boat, in the after ends among the auxiliary machinery, there'd be a mound of sleeping engine-room hands, in hammocks where there was space, or just stretched out on the deck plates – Stokers and Torpedomen. Beyond the bulkhead, in the motor room, there'd be a couple of Torpedomen, the Navy's electricians, on watch, keeping their eyes on the ammeters and voltmeters, making sure their electric motors ran smoothly, and on the battery outputs and temperatures; checking the sumps for any traces of acid that might betray a crack or a leak in the giant beasts, each cell weighing in at over 1,500 pounds.

In the next compartment for'ard, there'd be the engine-room watch on duty: a clutch of Stokers, crawling over their main engines; polishing here, a bit of oil in there; peering in the gaps and spaces, prodding, tightening. Making sure all was just so, ready for the moment they'd surface, and the two 400-horsepower Paxman diesels would be brought back to life with blasts of compressed air to kick-start their huge crankshafts, so they could suck down their own air to feed their combustion, through a now open conning tower hatch.

And on the other side of the engine room for'ard bulkhead, there'd always be a rating on watch in the ASDIC cubby, listening passively to the wide ocean beyond the three-quarter-inch plate that curved above his shoulder; and probably one of the Telegraphists, in the radio room, in case *Umbrage* needed to go up in a hurry and there'd always be someone there to transmit or receive.

And between them and the wardroom, the control room itself, with the two planesmen on duty on *Umbrage*'s hydroplanes off to the side, controlling her miniature wings, two for'ard, two aft, that with a turn on their wheels would point *Umbrage*'s bow either to the surface or the deep.

In front of them, at the helm position from where *Umbrage* was steered, the Coxswain, the boat's most senior rating sat when the boat was at Diving Stations. His name, Chief Petty Officer William Libby, a taciturn south Londoner who had the uncanny ability to exude calm with menaces.

On the trim board, a Gordian knot of pipes, valves, pumps and gauges, would be their Wrecker, the Outside ERA, the engineering senior rate in charge of all that myriad of plumbing that allowed *Umbrage* to control her depth, and in charge of her two periscopes too.

The pencil-thin attack 'scope, slender to avoid detection, and monocular, was aft, while for'ard was the larger-diameter, high-powered periscope, bi-focal and up to x6 magnification, with all the gadgets to help you do everything from calculate range to search for enemy aircraft right above you. Both 'scopes were just under thirty feet long, and recessed into tubes that ran down to the keel of the boat. When raised so the eyepieces were up in the control room where the watch officer could see through them, there was a little over twelve feet of the periscope sticking out above the top of the conning tower, and that was your periscope depth.

Presiding over it right now would be Grainger, with very little to do. For Rais had ordered: no clockwork-mousing up to periscope depth for a quick all-round look, and back down again. So Grainger would just be keeping an eye on the helmsman, and on the gyro compass to make sure he was holding *Umbrage* on her unvarying, unwavering course; with his other eye on her steady, three-knot progress, pricking the chart at every waypoint. And watching the bubble, always watching the bubble, which showed whether *Umbrage* was either pointing up or down. And on the depth gauge, making sure *Umbrage* kept her one hundred feet, because the Med was notorious for thermoclines, sudden changes in water temperature, usually caused here by differing levels of salinity, so that the density of the water around them could change in a blink, playing havoc with a boat's trim, causing them to rapidly sink or rise without warning.

In the wardroom, Harry and Jim Wykham were mopping up the last stains of their Train Smash with buttered toast, when *Umbrage* went to red light. The ordinary low-level lighting went out, and a series of red bulbs came on; it meant there was twenty minutes to go until *Umbrage* surfaced, and it was done to accustom the eyes of the watch keepers about to go up into the dark of another Mediterranean night. In the next compartments for'ard were the ERAs', Petty Officers' and Leading Seamen's messes: tiny spaces, now bestirring with grunts and harrumphs as the men going to Diving Stations for surfacing pulled on whatever few extra clothes they might need, for Mediterranean winter nights could be chilly, even in the boat when the conning tower hatch opened and the diesels starting sucking down the cold sea air. It would be the same in the next space for'ard, in the forward torpedo room, where the ordinary ratings bunked down among the torpedo reload racks and the three-inch gun magazines, where the boat's four twenty-one-inch torpedo tubes were.

And elsewhere in the boat, out of sight, fore and aft, beneath the deck plates, there would be the two Ordinary Seamen, crouched in the pump spaces – there to open and shut yet more banks of valves on the orders of the Jimmy or the Wrecker, the valves that fed and drained the trim tanks and kept *Umbrage* suspended unseen in her dark domain; knowing they would have at least another hour of the First Dog Watch to go before they would be relieved and come up for their breakfasts.

The curtain swished a single, flawless swish, and there was Rais's beatific countenance, fresh, and his eyes darting from Harry to Wykham where they sat opposite him behind the wardroom table.

'Morning, gentlemen!' he said, grinning at his own joke, as he always did, because it wasn't morning, it was evening, and wasn't he a wit. His officer's white shirt had been neatly folded at the foot of his bunk, and laid on top of his folded uniform trousers, and as he reached for them, his eyes focused on Harry's and Wykham's plates.

'Musgrave!' A piercing yell.

The Stoker shot from the tiny galley and stood smartly to attention in the passageway. 'Sir.'

'You have fed these two officers breakfast.' It was a statement, not a question.

'Sir,' said Musgrave.

'Why did you not wake me for breakfast?' The question asked without Rais even affording Musgrave any semblance of attention to what he might say, as he snapped out his folded shirt and began meticulously buttoning himself into it. Harry thinking, *Submariners don't usually get fully undressed while on patrol because clothes take too long to get into if you're in a hurry*, and that Wykham, a new boy, had the excuse that he didn't know any better.

'Why didn't you offer me any breakfast, Musgrave?' said Rais, now busy stepping into his trousers. 'Eh? Speak up!'

'I told him not to,' said Harry, 'Sir.'

Telling a barefaced lie; knowing Musgrave and Wykham would know it; not caring whether Rais, who'd all the time been just the span of two rulers and the width of a curtain away, knew it too; and thinking, *No good sailor is going to get a bollocking for nothing, while I'm on deck.*

Rais, now looking directly at Musgrave, began speaking to Harry. 'And why would you do that, Mr Gilmour?'

And here it comes, said Harry to himself; knowing exactly what was going to happen next; the words that were going to be said, and the full sad, pathetic implications of what Rais was about to do: give one of his officers a dressing-down in front of a member of the crew. Another little morale booster to start the working day.

'I assumed you'd want to . . .' Harry was going to say, *get as much sleep before we surface, Sir*, but Rais interrupted him – in front of a Stoker.

'You assumed, Mr Gilmour? You assumed?'

'Sir.'

'What am I tired of telling you about assuming, Mr Gilmour?'

Rais had never told him anything about assuming, good or bad. Harry was looking directly at him, his face a study in poker blankness, but he was wondering, *What age are you?* Harry had turned twenty-one a bare six months ago. Rais was what? Maybe twenty-five? Not much older, if at all. And he was talking like a pedantic schoolmaster, not the Commanding Officer of one of His Majesty's fighting submarines on operational patrol in wartime.

'Sir,' said Harry.

'Sir, what?' said Rais through gritted teeth.

'Sorry, Sir.'

'Sorry? Sorry?' and as he spoke, Rais's gaze fell back upon Musgrave. 'And why are you still standing there gawping, sailor?' Rais, like all of them, knowing full well that no sailor, standing before his Commanding Officer, can move even an inch without being dismissed.

And that was when the control room messenger arrived. 'Cap'n to the control room, Sir. First Lieutenant's compliments.'

Grainger, on watch, standing on the other side of the aft wardroom partition must have heard it all, and bided his time before deciding to break it up. Harry didn't have to stick his head around the door to know he was probably smirking to himself right now – that sneery, supercilious bloody smirk.

Oh, well, thought Harry to himself. *If you can't take a joke, you shouldn't have joined.*

Chapter Seven

It was the wee small hours, and the night had barely a couple of hours to run before first light. They were close inshore off the eastern end of the island of Elba, between Corsica and the Tuscan coast, trimmed well down so that really only *Umbrage*'s conning tower was showing above the slight chop and anyone looking inshore from the sea would see only the shadow of the cliffs behind them. Occasionally, however, the wedge of a waning moon would appear through the cloud cover to dapple the surface of the offing so that any potential target passing to seaward would be cast in sharp relief.

Harry was on watch again, taking Grainger's stint because the CO wanted him 'rested' for the next day's stalk. Rais had made it clear, using his usual histrionics, that he was determined he wasn't going to miss with his last torpedo, and that was why he wanted his boat under the tightest control when he eventually found a home for it – and that meant his First Lieutenant on the trim board, 'at concert pitch and champing to go', as he put it, in a stage whisper all the boat could hear.

Two lookouts were on the bridge with Harry, and it was bloody cold. *Umbrage* was just drawing enough electrical power to her main motors for steerage way, the rest of the amps from the diesels going into the batteries. Below their feet, Harry and the lookouts could feel the diesels burble away, and up here on the bridge, the noise of them sounded as though it could be heard all the way to Naples, a mere 250 miles over the south-eastern horizon. Harry wasn't all that worried about Elba, even though the loom of its shore off the port beam felt so close you could almost touch it in the dark. No, it had looked like a deserted coast on the approach: not a light, not a glimmer of a settlement, nor even a single house had shown. Harry had the two young Able Seamen facing seaward, covering the starboard bow and quarter, while he kept an occasional eye to make sure nothing unexpected had decided to row out to them from the rock-strewn cliff base that from the surf looked as though he could hit it with a well-lobbed NAAFI scone.

Harry hadn't minded at all being ordered up for another watch. It was quiet with the two young lookouts intent on their work, and far away from the oppressive tedium below. Even when Rais was asleep, his dead hand of command lay across the boat. Take Jack enjoying a gasper, for example. Most boats allowed smoking when on the surface. But even when *Umbrage* was on the surface, her conning tower hatches open and her diesels sucking in fresh air, no one was allowed to smoke. Or Jack's tot? A right that was sanctified, and ancient, under Naval law. Even though *Umbrage* carried her full spirit ration, Captain Rais had ordered that no tots of rum were to be issued or consumed while *Umbrage* was at sea – for although regulations entitled Jack to his daily ration, it remained at the discretion of the Captain when he was allowed to drink it.

That was why, here, in the dead of night, there was at least some peace to be had without having to continually worry about which of Rais's orders, directives or even whims you'd failed to second-guess this time. Even the ratings didn't mind turning up early for their lookout duties, especially if Mr Gilmour was Officer of the Watch, because as everyone knew now, if you did, Mr Gilmour would let you crouch down behind the bridge fairing and have a quick gasper before you did the handover. Three minutes was all you got, but at least there was some bastard aboard who gave a fuck about how Jack was doing. He wasn't a bad lad for a Wavy Navy wonder – or maybe it was because of it.

Then the cloud cover began to thin, and as the escaping slivers of moonlight began to dapple the sea, so the dark shape of a ship appeared. The lookout covering the starboard bow had spotted her first.

'Ship, Sir! Fine on the starboard bow!' he called, and Harry's night glasses were on it. 'Looks like a big one, Sir!' said the lookout, as Harry called down the voice-pipe to the control room, 'Captain to the bridge! Potential target, about ten points off the starboard bow! Diving Stations!' and Harry hit the night alarm twice, sending *Umbrage*'s crew closing up for action. What that action would be, would be up to Rais, but from what Harry could see, at least Rais would have time to decide. Even with his not-so-good night vision Harry could already tell the target was some way off, right on *Umbrage*'s horizon, about five, maybe a bit more, miles away, and it wasn't moving all that fast either.

Rais appeared on the bridge, announcing, 'ASDIC says no HE', as if Harry had called a false alarm. There was no 'Where away?' or any other inquiry as to what might have been spotted. Meanwhile, the target's shape had been rapidly forming and Harry, never removing his eyes from his night glasses now knew why there was no HE. He also knew the lookout had been wrong: she wasn't a big ship, the bulky shadow he had identified wasn't superstructure, it was sails.

'It's a schooner, Sir,' he told Rais. 'A three-master, I think, running south on this north-easter. Probably about three-fifty, four hundred tons and heavily laden. I'd say she's steering 135 degrees, but not making much more than six to eight knots, Sir.'

'Well, Mr Gilmour, let's not just "*say*", shall we,' said Rais, raising his glasses. 'Let's try for "*is*", hmmn?'

The schooner, as her shape filled out looked quite stately, eating up the wind that must have been on one of her best sailing points: not a full tramontane, but strong enough and steady. She was a three-master, and was heading across the mouth of the deep inlet that formed the Mola Gulf, and led into the island harbour at Porto Azzuro. Harry had looked at the chart for the bay before coming on watch, and it was obvious to him what was happening. The schooner would run out on this tack to a point way to starboard of *Umbrage*, where, when she went over on to the opposite tack, she would have a straight run up into Porto Azzuro without a hand having to touch another sheet until she was ready to use her auxiliary engine to motor on to her berth, or drop anchor. *Umbrage* had only to heave to, and wait for the schooner to starboard her helm, and she'd come gliding right across their bows.

Rais called, 'TBT to the bridge' into the voice-pipe. The target-bearing transmitter. Harry had to do a double take. The TBT meant Rais was planning a surface torpedo attack. But no schooner, no matter how tasty a target she might be, would ever merit the expenditure of a torpedo. Torpedoes were too precious, too rare on Malta to waste on a mere sailing ship. Any spare ones that hadn't arrived already on a submarine had to be lugged all the way from Gib or Alexandria, along sea lanes dominated by enemy aircraft and under constant threat from the Italian battlefleet. Blokes were dying to get torpedoes to Malta. Okay, some silly bugger CO might worry about folk thinking he wasn't trying hard enough if he brought a torpedo back from patrol, but surely someone should be on hand to disabuse him, to point out that throwing a perfectly good torpedo away on such a relatively insignificant target as a schooner was unforgivable. He shuddered to think what Shrimp would say if he were standing on the bridge beside them right now.

As Harry looked on, a rating came up, and was passed up the TBT: a bulky device, with a casing like the end of a large mortar, that fitted over a vertical mounting on the bridge front, and on top an elaborate set of binocular sights you aimed with a pair of machine-gun handles, that had all the bearing bezels and a range-finding stadimeter built in. One of *Umbrage*'s Torpedo Gunner's Mates followed it up. Harry couldn't remember the lad's name, but he and the other rating attached it with minimum fuss for such an awkward lump of steel. Rais ignored them.

'Well done,' said Harry, and the TGM touched his cap: 'Sir.' Then he and the rating slipped swiftly back into the tower.

The TBT delivered all the same range and bearing info that the instruments on the periscope did, ready to be dialled into the fruit machine below, so that all the ranges and angles could be calculated to ensure their single remaining torpedo, when fired, would indeed find a home.

And as Rais indeed seemed to be intending to use their last torpedo, here was the TBT to help him do it.

But there was worse to come. Rais ordered 'Starboard, thirty' down the voice-pipe, and Harry almost fell off the conning tower. *Umbrage* was turning *away* from the track Harry had calculated the schooner must surely follow, and Rais was pointing her bows out to sea. What was Rais thinking?

Then it dawned on Harry, what Rais was thinking. Rais had calculated the schooner was going to continue south on her present course, and not turn in for Porto Azzuro. Could he be right? He was the CO, he was supposed to be right, but what if he hadn't been aware of the other possibility? Harry could see now what his CO intended: he was running out to sea to get on to a perfect ninety-degree track angle on a target that would be running sou'-south-east. But if Harry were right, they'd be going the wrong way when the schooner turned in for Porto Azzuro, and too far out to head her off again before she got into the bay. If Rais would only wait, however, until the target reached that point on the sea where, if she was intending to run into port, she must tack, then they would know. If she tacked, they would be in perfect position. If she didn't tack, they would still be able to catch her up before first light.

Umbrage wasn't exactly a greyhound on the surface, but this was a sailing vessel they were tracking; they'd outrun her eventually. No, this didn't make sense. Harry decided to speak up. He wasn't going to be like Grainger. He also knew that with Rais, it would be pointless trying to do it subtly, now orders had been given.

'Sir,' said Harry, 'I believe the target intends to go over on to the port tack in the next few minutes.' Harry kept his voice as low as possible, to at least give some show of not appearing to contradict his CO in front of the lookouts, in the middle of an attack. Harry, still talking, continued, 'And that she is about to head into Porto Azzuro. If she does, and we continue on this course, Sir, I believe we will not be able to get back into an attacking position.'

They had one torpedo left. If Rais was determined to use it, and it was to count, they needed a sitting duck.

Harry and the lookouts all had their white roll-neck pullovers on; Harry, under his watch jacket also wore a preposterously long woollen muffler. The lookouts were huddled in old-fashioned North Atlantic duffel coats, because it really did get cold in the Med at this time of year. But if it had been cold before, the air on the bridge now became downright frigid.

'Is that right, Mr Gilmour,' said Rais; flat speech, his face fixed to his night glasses, trained on the target. 'How interesting. And who do you think is going to win the next Grand National?'

Rais let his sarcasm hang in the space between them. Then he said, 'Get ready to read off my bearings and range,' so that Harry had to *assume* he was talking to him. Rais bent over and spoke into the voice-pipe: 'Prepare tube four for a surface attack. Set the depth at six feet.' Harry put up his glasses for one last look at the target, and as he did so the forward lookout sang out, 'Target changing course, Sir! Turning towards.'

But as Harry looked at her, he could see the schooner was doing more than turning towards; she was turning inside them. She had been running on 135 degrees, as Harry had guessed, and Rais now had Umbrage on one hundred, charging to close the range and get ahead of where he thought his quarry was going to be, so when he got close to her, he could turn on to that ninety-degree track angle and fire his torpedo into her at an impossible-to-miss four or five hundred yards. It was going to be textbook.

Except the schooner was no longer on 135 degrees. As Harry watched, the schooner continued to come about; so that it was now obvious where she was heading. Into Porto Azzuro, as Harry had said. And that her turn would probably put her on a two-eighty heading. She was going to cut behind them, and a long way behind them too. Harry, standing less than two feet from Rais, lowered his glasses and watched as his CO followed through his own glasses, as his target escaped. You could almost feel the rage and fury burn off Rais's diminutive figure, as he leaned out over the bridge's fairing, keeping the retreating schooner in his night glasses. Then he snapped upright, and yelled down the conning tower hatch, so loud his voice was cracking, more in a shriek than a bellow, 'Gun crew close up on the casing! Stand by for Gun Action!' So loud had he been, he needed to take a breath before yelling again, 'And get someone up here right now and get this fucking useless lump of iron off my bridge!'

Harry glanced at the two young lookouts, obviously trying to hide inside their duffel coats; their night glasses firmly stuck to their faces, desperately wishing not to be there and hoping not to be noticed. Harry *assumed* Rais's 'useless lump of iron' was referring to the now redundant TBT – for there was no way he was going to get a torpedo attack in now – and he thought to himself, *Now, that's no way to address a perfectly good item of ship's inventory.*

Rais was at the voice-pipe now, firing down orders for *Umbrage* to reverse her course and begin the pursuit. Harry kept his eye on the schooner, tearing away with the brisk north-easterly on her port beam, heeling her over and filling her gaff-rigged, fore-and-aft sails. He reckoned she must have been four hundred tons, so not *that* bad a target, and she was looking magnificent in the dancing moonlight. And he knew they were never going to catch her before she entered the mouth of Porto Azzuro's bay, and whatever Italian shore defences might await them there.

⌣

It was a beautiful morning, and Harry was watching the dapple of the sunlight dancing on the underside of the undulating chop above. It was a view he never tired of – one of those magical little moments in your grim, grey routine, if you cranked the search periscope's head vertical, so you could look through it as the periscope went up.

It was their first all-round look of the day and his little treat to himself had a practical aspect to it too: checking that there was just enough ruffle on the surface to make you invisible to any passing shagbat, even at periscope depth. There was, and as the 'scope broke surface, Harry did his little 360 dance around the control room as he quickly made sure there were no shagbats passing – crank the head horizontal, and around again: three fishing boats, all at least a mile away, but none of them coming this way.

'All clear,' he announced.

'And still no HE, Sir,' added Tuke from the ASDIC cubby.

The CO was at Harry's elbow, hunched over the tiny fold-down chart table, looking at the approaches to Porto Azzuro, with a set of extended dividers in one hand, and a pencil in the other.

It was a new day, and with it another chance to bag the schooner. Their embarrassing night was over.

Embarrassing, uncomfortable and a waste of time. Rais, his torpedo attack thwarted, had fired off orders in all directions, but in no proper sequence; he'd had the gun crew come up too soon; the helm ordered over, too late. When the gunners had got on to the casing and been ready to open fire in double quick time – nothing for Rais to complain about in that department – they'd been so fast, there had been nothing for them to fire at. The schooner had still been astern, and tearing away in the opposite direction. So when Rais put *Umbrage* under helm, to turn and go after her, he managed to thoroughly drench them. And as he had bashed on in pursuit, it hadn't got any better; the short waves coming over her bow, slap, slap into the gun crew's faces, so that after half an hour of this, the gun crew were barely functional.

Not, in the end, that it was to matter. As they watched, the schooner had slipped into the mouth of the bay to the right of a huge promontory that protected the entrance to Porto Azzuro, and which somewhat unfairly sported a huge Renaissance fortress around its peak, with bastions that lowered over them. Faced with the prospect of trading fire with a huge lump of stone and glacis that looked quite capable of defying siege engines let alone their three-inch popgun, Rais had turned his back. One perfunctory order to withdraw, and he'd gone below without another word. It had been left to Harry to tidy up and get the gun crew back below for steaming mugs of hot condensed milk and cocoa that the service called Ky.

But this was the new day.

Looking through the periscope, Harry could see a range of forested mountains in the background, with the odd jagged edge, rolling down to the top half of a picturesque town, all stucco and red tiles. The rest of the town and the harbour was obscured by the bluff promontory. In the daylight, he now had an even better view of the fortress. San Giacomo, it was called, according to the chart – and it was bigger and more intimidating than it had appeared last night. The walls were constructed of a series of star ramparts, all mossy now, but no less scary, although he couldn't see any obvious gun emplacements. Below it, in the bay, was their schooner: moored fore and aft to a line of buoys, her sails all furled now on their booms, and her decks deserted. Likely no one was up yet despite it being such a beautiful morning. An Italian flag, flapped with some vigour over her transom, having obviously been left out all night, the slack buggers! Harry reported it all, but Rais didn't bother answering, just continued tapping the chart with the dividers, in a manner calculated to irritate.

Harry sent the periscope down.

'Did it occur to you, Mr Gilmour, that I might have wanted to take a look?' said Rais, without looking up.

Jesus H. Christ, Harry seethed to himself, *you know, and I know, and everybody fucking knows, you don't keep a periscope up any longer than you have to, especially when you're this close inshore . . . Did that not occur to you? Sir? . . . 'Oooh! Look! I wonder what that is?' says little Giuseppe to the gun Captain on the six-inch coastal battery! 'Could it be a periscope?'* But all Harry actually said was, 'Do you wish me to call it back up, Sir?'

Rais left a silence before replying, and even then his first words were to the young control room messenger. 'Get me a cup of coffee,' he said, then, turning to Harry, all he said was, 'When I'm ready.'

Rais, coffee in hand, took his look, then issued orders that would take *Umbrage* in a long circle to the south-east, so that she would come up on to the target, bow and torpedo tube pointing directly at her beam. As they motored round, he ordered the torpedo tube made ready to fire, then when *Umbrage* was just six hundred yards from her unsuspecting prey and her bows pointing directly at it, he ordered, 'Stop, together.'

Harry looked at Grainger. When was he going to say something?

The schooner was secured to buoys; *Umbrage* was hove to. The Med was not a tidal sea, but there were currents, some of them notorious. In a normal torpedo attack, you're both under way, both moving through the water, so the action of any current was compensated for. If you were both stopped, it wasn't.

And there was a current.

For Harry as Navigator, it was his job to know. Working from his dead reckoning on the plot, he'd been calculating the difference between where his DR had said they should be, and where his last fix – taken as they'd moved along the coast – said they were. And he'd already advised Rais as to the current, its speed and direction. And he'd been ignored.

Grainger had said nothing.

Suddenly, Rais called, 'Fire one!' and sent the periscope down.

There was a slight lurch as *Umbrage* recoiled from the launch, and everybody waited. At six hundred yards it wouldn't take long.

Nothing.

'Lost the torpedo's HE, Sir,' said Tuke. How was that possible? No torpedo HE meant the torpedo had somehow stopped running, without exploding. How did that happen? Unless it wasn't in the water any more.

'Up periscope!' snapped Rais. He took one look along the bearing, and then another even briefer one, barely two points to port. 'Down periscope! Blow tanks one and six! Surfacing! Close up for Gun Action!'

The gun crew came tumbling into the control room. In a Gun Action, they were always first up, and then the CO.

'Tower clear!' called Grainger from the trim board, standing less than two arms' lengths from where Harry stood at the back of the control room, leaning up again after plotting their manoeuvres on the chart. The gun crew went up, and a cascade of sparkling Tyrrhenian sea came down; and suddenly Harry was hearing some distant whining noise he couldn't fathom. Rais followed the gun crew up, and Harry stepped to call up the periscope, to make sure the noise wasn't being caused by someone sneaking up behind them. A quick 180 look astern and then back on the schooner. Some of her crew were tumbling up, as if woken from their slumbers by some alarm. Maybe even by the mystery noise. Except they weren't looking to seaward, towards where *Umbrage* would have been rising from the deep, as well they might given the bloody racket a submarine blowing main ballast normally makes. No, they were looking up the shore. Harry turned the 'scope two points, and there on the beach, nuzzled underneath a grass bank above the sand was their torpedo, wobbling a little, smoke rising from her mechanism as her motor, still delivering revs for forty-five knots, burnt itself out in a fearsome screaming tantrum.

The current that Harry had calculated, told his CO about, and been ignored, was a well-known one locally. It flowed down the east side of the island, sometimes at several knots, and as it went, it created clockwise vortices in the Mola Gulf; these had swept up *Umbrage*'s torpedo and carried it way off its intended target, leaving it to run up the beach and bury itself in the saw grass.

Harry heard their gun's first round go off, and turned back to see it blow the schooner's transom to matchwood, and the Italian flag, like a flapping shroud, on to the sparkling blue water. The schooner's crew were already diving off, and swimming like torpedoes themselves for the beach, not bothering to launch any lifeboat. The next round went through her side, forward, and was followed by a spectacular *whump* that blew upwards from her guts, launching hatch combings and huge lengths of rigging into the air. The third one hit too, with similar effect, but it was the fourth round that explained why the schooner had moored up outside Porto Azzuro for the night. It turned her into a fireball. Harry and the rest of the control room crew even felt the hot blast of it come down the conning tower hatch. And then they heard the bang.

'That was the schooner,' Harry informed them.

'And we're all going to get a laugh when we see the gun crew's scorched eyebrows,' said Grainger, and everybody laughed. Not because they thought it was that funny, but because Rais was still on the bridge, and they could enjoy the joke.

And the schooner, thought Harry; she must have been carrying a cargo of fuel of some kind – paraffin for the islanders' stoves, probably. And he wondered how much the disrupting of the cooking habits of several hundred Italians had furthered the war effort.

Chapter Eight

Malta. *Umbrage* was tied up alongside the Lazaretto, half a dozen of her crew scouring her out with bottles of Izal disinfectant. Harry was elsewhere. On the other side of Valletta, to be precise, aboard someone else's ship: sitting, grinning to himself like a village idiot, sunk into the enveloping comfort of a floral-patterned easy chair in the Captain's day cabin of the light cruiser HMS *Pelleas*, gazing about, luxuriating in the space a cruiser Captain gets compared to a Navigator on a submarine. He took another sip of the pink gin he was cradling, and it curdled the grin for a moment. The Captain's Steward had handed it to him the minute the Marine who'd escorted him from the gangway had showed him in.

'Captain Dumaresq's orders, Sir,' the steward had said. '"Mr Gilmour is a special guest, so make sure there's enough gin in it to kill a small furry animal." Those was his very words, Sir.' And the glass was handed over with all the beaming hospitality you'd expect from the Royal Navy.

And now he was waiting to see again the officer who had taken him in hand when he was making a mess of everything, and given him a way out before he ended up in front of a court martial. How long ago had it been? Winter 1940? Aboard that old R-class, HMS *Redoubtable* – more gin palace than battleship – where Harry, an RNVR Sub right out of *King Alfred,* had been neither fish nor fowl, either ignored or resented by her hide-bound wardroom. Peter Dumaresq, a Flag Lieutenant then, and older, awaiting his next shove up, had got him out of there.

And into submarines.

Given the chop rate among submariners these days, Harry, when he thought about it, wasn't sure whether it was wise to feel quite so grateful. Which was why he tried *not* to think about it. And now Peter Dumaresq was a Captain, in command of an *Arethusa*-class light cruiser. But then Peter Dumaresq had always been an anointed one – naval aristocracy, who could chart his lineage in the service back to Anson and Hawke. If anyone was going to be on an accelerated promotion ladder, it was Peter Dumaresq. Admiral written all over him was the word among the surface skimmers apparently, one day.

And then the door opened and there he was: tanned, in his tropical whites, looking taller than Harry remembered, and thinner, like a steel hawser now, not an inch of flab. And was that his hair thinning, or was it the cap with the scrambled egg on its brim that he'd just removed, that had been pressing his dark waves too flat? The glint in the eye and the easy smile were still there though – the look that told you all you needed to know about this man's relentless capacity for cheery devilment.

'Harry bloody Gilmour!' he said, his hand outstretched.

'Sir!' said Harry, disentangling himself from the easy chair.

Dumaresq closed the door behind him. 'First names in the cabin, Harry,' he said, pumping his young friend's hand. 'You're looking better than you have a right to.' Then, calling over his shoulder towards the serving hatch, 'Capper! Two more of your special liveners, please!'

'You're one-and-a-half rings heavier since I saw you last . . .' said Harry, trying to say 'Peter' and not 'Sir' . . . and ending up just shaking his head. 'God! I'm becoming a right proper Andrew now,' he laughed. 'Four rings and I'm gobsmacked.'

Dumaresq sat down on his sofa. 'Yes,' he said with that grin, 'but was I born to them, did I achieve them, or were they thrust upon me?' He waved Harry back into the easy chair.

Then he asked, 'Was that you we elbowed aside, coming in?'

Harry nodded. 'Yes . . . Peter,' he said, trying it out. Sub-Lieutenants – being the second-lowest form of marine life after Midshipmen – didn't call Captains by their first names; in fact, they didn't speak to them unless spoken to.

'I saw a white bar and a white star on your Jolly Roger?' said Dumaresq.

Harry, grinning again, too: 'A seven-thousand-ton freighter, torpedoed, and a four-hundred-ton coasting schooner loaded with paraffin, by Gun Action.' Their patrol didn't sound so bad when you described it like that, thought Harry, and he left it that way, not wanting to think any more about Lieutenant Clive Rais. Except he couldn't stop thinking about the expression he'd seen on Rais's face, when he'd been standing next to him on *Umbrage's* bridge, hove to alongside their minesweeper escort a mile off Tigne Point – their return to the submarine base in Marsamxett Harbour blocked as the two cruisers and three destroyers of Force F swept down from the north in front of them, on their way into Valletta's Grand Harbour next door. The ships, running line-astern, had indeed looked magnificent on that blue, blue, blustery morning, but it hadn't been pride that had burned in Rais's steady stare: more like resentment and envy.

Outside, through Dumaresq's day cabin scuttle, were the wharves of French Creek. You could hear the clamour, the shouting and the clanking of cranes. You could imagine the tumult of dockyard workers, climbing over stores, loading the cruisers for their next sortie. And you could crunch the grit and dust in your mouth that had been wafted in through the scuttle. On the next berth up, Harry had passed *Pelleas's* sister ship, HMS *Patroclus*, also being hurriedly re-stored and ammunitioned; and on the other side of Senglea, in Dockyard Creek, was the rest of the squadron, the destroyers *Jocasta, Darter* and *Dimapur.*

'Right, Harry,' said Dumaresq, after Capper had brought them refills of pink gin, 'tell me the secret to how you've managed to stay alive this long.'

Capper had brought them some corned beef sandwiches for lunch, which had helped to soak up all the gin Harry had drunk, but he was still a bit wobbly when he walked to the end of the wharf to hail one of Grand Harbour's *dghaisas* that plied the port like water taxis. He'd taken it to the Customs House Steps, and intended to walk up the full length of the notorious Strait Street – known to Jack and every other service-man who'd ever taken leave on the island as The Gut. A sink of moral turpitude beyond your wildest dreams, Harry had been told. He'd yet to dip his toe in. Then at the other end he'd take another *dghaisa* over Marsamxett Harbour to Manoel Island and the base.

Sitting in the little gondola-like wooden boat being rowed across by a smiling, scruffy-looking Maltese ancient, he felt dwarfed by Grand Harbour. Ahead of him, the sheer walls of Valletta's white limestone bastions were dazzling in the sun, and way over to his left, the citadel of Fort St Elmo at the head of the harbour, looked all too capable of repelling any siege. It was a stunning, glorious sight, and noisy with the sound of caulking hammers from the dockyards. Not too much shipping though – Force F's ships, of course, and two big, fat ten-thou-sand-ton merchantmen, still here from the Operation Halberd convoy apparently, waiting their turn to run back to Gib. And of course there was the minesweeping flotilla, dotted about, moored alongside.

But there were also the carcasses of the ships that, having made it this far, would go no further. Bombed-out twisted hulks, lying half-submerged in the Kalkara Creek, or the ones back up the harbour, under the Corradino Heights. Harry could also see where the bombs had gouged their marks on the walls, and smashed down among the houses on the heights of Floriana. He'd seen them on the way over, all the intimate views of people's wrecked homes, but he'd been in a hurry then to see Peter Dumaresq so he hadn't looked that closely; he certainly didn't need to see any more now.

The submarine base, officially known as HMS *Talbot*, was home to the six remaining U- and N-class submarines of the Tenth Flotilla. Except only *Umbrage* and another boat – another no-namer, just P-something or other, Harry couldn't remember her number – were at home, secured to the floating pontoons jutting out from the old Lazaretto, the island's former fever hospital. The rest were on patrol.

Why the Tenth was here on Malta was on a scrap of paper, pinned to the Flotilla's noticeboard: a scribbled note of the verbal order given to the Tenth's Captain (S), George 'Shrimp' Simpson by the Commander-in-Chief, Mediterranean, Admiral Sir Andrew Cunningham. *Your object is to cut the enemy's sea communications between Europe and Tripoli*, was what it said. Which was typical Cunningham: to the point, no fluff.

The island had been badly bombed, especially between the previous January and the end of April. It had been in all the papers. Hitler had sent an entire Luftwaffe *Fliegerkorps*, a whole air group of over two hundred aircraft, dispatched from its bases in occupied Norway to Sicily to assist the Führer's Italian allies in the Regia Aeronautica in reducing Malta to rubble. But then the Germans had gone, whisked away to take part in the invasion of Russia. Things had been quieter since then, apparently. No more multiple raids every day. And even when the Italians did try to come over, more Hurricanes had been flown in when they weren't looking, and as often as not the Italians had been driven off.

The last convoy had provided a measure of respite, and under it the RAF had built up their force: a couple of squadrons of Blenheim bombers, another two of Beaufighters; there were Wellingtons on the island too. The Fleet Air Arm even had some Swordfish torpedo planes operating out of Hal Far, all attacking the convoys supplying Rommel and his Afrika Korps in Tunisia, who were there with the stated intent of getting to Alexandria and taking the Suez Canal. And now even

Royal Navy surface units had returned to the central Med. Force F had arrived, and another, Force K, was on the way. Yes, in many ways they were still just clinging on, but everyone said things were starting to look up. Harry wasn't so sure, not with the way the war was going in Russia. The Germans were winning, and when they did, the Luftwaffe would be back.

When Harry got to the Custom House Steps, he decided not to depress himself even more by taking the rundown, seedy route. He'd skip The Gut, and all the clubs and the drinking dens sweeping out last night's reek of booze and cigarette smoke and sweat. He'd take the Kingsway, which would lead him past the magnificent façade of the Royal Opera House. Since he'd arrived on the island, a mere few weeks ago, he'd put to sea again almost immediately to go on patrol, and had had no time to explore, but what he had seen during his walk today had stunned him.

He'd known about Malta's history, all the way back to Calypso holding Odysseus as her sex slave; about the arrival of the Phoenicians and the Carthaginians and then the Romans; and of how, at the end of the Dark Ages, the Normans in Sicily had taken the island from the Moors and then how the Knights of St John had defeated the Ottoman Empire's repeated attempts to seize it back again for Islam in the sixteenth century; and how Napoleon had seized it for France, and Nelson had taken it back off him again. The islands had been British ever since. But he'd never imagined this opulence.

The architecture was grand and Italianate: Renaissance, rococo, gothic. Avenues and *strada* lined with high tenements, all in that dazzling Malta limestone, with their wrought-iron balconies and stone verandas, decked with little striped awnings – still trying to look pretty despite the bomb scars. The history, yes, but the wealth of the place, he'd been unprepared for. And as he walked along the crowded pavements, girls in bright dresses and cardigans, some stepping out with a sailor or an airman, he imagined himself hand in hand with Shirley Lamont, sharing it all with her, remembering how she loved all the fine things – anything, really, that had to do with the creation of beauty.

And then he stopped himself. *Maudlin, Harry*, he said to himself, *too easy to fall off that cliff*, and then he thought about the letter she'd written him, the one that had been waiting for him back in Blighty, when he'd reported to HMS *Dolphin*, the Trade's old Fort Blockhouse home in Gosport, after he'd been transferred off *Radegonde*, and that had stayed unopened since. It had travelled a long way, that letter: with him on the Sunderland that had flown him to Gib, then on to HM Submarine *P413*, which was to carry him to Malta and his new posting. And it had remained on *P413* when he was forced to get off, only to be offloaded by Commander Clasp along with all his other kit at the Tenth's Lazaretto base in the hope that one day he might eventually turn up. It was there still, lying in his little stone cabin. He was fed up thinking about it, tired of wondering what it might say, and sick at the thought.

Looking for a distraction, he ducked into a small bookshop, a dusty warren of a place, down two steps and hidden behind caked windows, taped against blast, that hadn't seen a chamois since the days of Jean de Valette. He was barely through the door before Harry knew its shelves contained a veritable treasure trove of leather and even canvas-bound volumes, some practically ancient. Right at the back was an old, round, bald man in a hardware storeman's brown overall coat, sat back on a rickety rocking chair, smoking, with a chipped but elegant cup of piping hot coffee before him, reading the *Times of Malta*.

He looked up and grinned. 'A young British sailor boy,' he said. 'I haven't seen you before. How may I assist?'

'I'm looking for a first edition of Homer's *The Iliad*, and I thought yours looked like a place I might find one,' said Harry. And at that the old man laughed so much he almost fell off his chair.

Chapter Nine

Harry walked into the wardroom gallery at the Lazaretto, and dumped the hessian sack full of books he'd bought by one of the sofas. A cool afternoon breeze was blowing off the water through its open-pillared frontage. Below, on the pontoons, he could see *Umbrage*, some of her crew still fussing about her. Grainger was on her bridge, talking to a man in a gold-braided officer's cap and oil-slathered overalls. Probably Commander Sam MacGregor, the base engineering officer. Harry hadn't met him yet.

Rais had simply walked off the boat after they had come along-side. Off to report to Shrimp, though he hadn't said so. Grainger had watched him go, then sent Harry and Wykham ashore, telling them he'd get *Umbrage* squared away. Not that she needed much doing, just a good clean-out and replenishment.

Harry flopped on to the sofa, and as he watched the Maltese steward come striding down the gallery towards him, a terrible glum weight descended. He should have been in a good mood after his boozy lunch with Peter Dumaresq, and his fascinating chat with the old bookseller and the reassuring trove of books he'd bought, but he wasn't.

'A fifty-gallon oil drum full of pink gin, please, John,' he said. The effects of Dumaresq's hospitality were wearing off, but Harry didn't feel like getting sober again so soon. The steward bowed a little and smiled his customary benign smile; he was used to his young men.

In front of Harry, the harbour water danced in the sun like a scene from a cinema travelogue. At this angle you couldn't see the skein of oil, or make out the rubbish floating in it. Suddenly Harry had never felt so far from home, or far from the boy he used to be. He began scratching at his sandfly bites. The whole base was infested with them, and he'd begun his collection of angry little red blotches the very first night he'd arrived. One more burden on the load.

It felt as though the whole weight of the war was on him. Harry didn't know whether it was the beautiful day that had made the island's scars seem so upsetting, or whether it was seeing Dumaresq that had made him realise how lonely and friendless he felt aboard his new boat. He was usually so good at putting all that stuff in a box, the way he did with fear and with the unavoidable truth of the number of boats and crew they were losing. No point in dwelling on it – nothing you could do.

It even made him remember how happy he had been to see Grainger, of all bloody people, sitting here, the night he'd finally managed to arrive from Gib. And to learn that Grainger, of all people, was going to be his new Number One, aboard his new submarine, *Umbrage*. What a false dawn that had been.

Oh yes, he remembered *that* night well. The Sunderland that had flown him in from Gib had touched down at the seaplane base at Kalafrana just before dusk, and one of the few RAF three-hundred-weight trucks still running – most were up on bricks in a bid to conserve fuel – had dropped him at the Lazaretto's door. He'd lugged his kit up the stairs, and there was Grainger. The friend from *Trebuchet* days that he hadn't seen since they'd managed to coax their battered boat all the way back from Norway's North Cape. Just.

He called Grainger his friend for want of a better description. Grainger, the man who had come back for Harry, after he'd been left lying wounded in the dark, on an enemy deck while a Gun Action with enemy transports raged all around them. Harry, already dead, according to the other sailors from his boarding party. But Grainger hadn't believed them: he had turned their dinghy around and gone to look for his missing man, even though he risked being left behind himself. Apart from that selfless deed, Grainger had always remained a remote figure to him. But then, he'd remained a remote figure to everyone.

And now here was Harry arriving in this strange, new and dangerous posting, and there, waiting for him, completely unexpected, had been Grainger. Harry remembered the grin that had split his face, right up until Grainger had begun telling him his news, that their Gunnery Officer on *Trebuchet*, the Tigger, also wounded in that action, had eventually died of his wounds. Harry couldn't work out how that could be, after the lad had survived so long. But dead he was. And then there was their Skipper, the irrepressible Andy Trumble.

'After the *Bucket*, they gave him one of the new S-boats,' Grainger had said. 'Overdue, presumed lost last month. The word is a mine got them, somewhere in the Skagerrak. No survivors. The *Bucket*'s gone too. Constructive total loss. The dockyard people were amazed she managed to get us back as far as Shetland, apparently. Chopped up for razor blades now, I imagine.'

And that had been before Harry went to report to the base Staff Officer, Operations, known affectionately, or perhaps not, as the SOO – only to learn that HMS *Nimuae*, the N-class sub he was supposed to join, was overdue, presumed lost too, and that he had instead been appointed Navigator on *Umbrage*.

If Harry had arrived on Malta when he was supposed to, instead of ending up in that holiday camp on Majorca, he'd have been on her, and dead now.

Everybody knew the losses had been terrible. Even the newspapers back home had to admit it. But somehow it seemed different when it was people you knew who were filling the lists. Who'd been the first to get it? Sells, of course, his friend from his class at *King Alfred*, blown up by a mine off Mersea Island, wasn't it? He couldn't even remember his face now. Then there'd been Sandeman and McVeigh and all the others who didn't make it out of *Pelorus*. And now the Tigger and Andy Trumble. He was going to die in this war. Why not? Everyone else seemed to be.

John, the steward, was at his side suddenly, handing him a glass of pink gin. 'No clean fifty-gallon drums, Sir,' he said, same smile. 'Can I bring your order in instalments?'

Harry shook himself, and managed a smile back. 'Of course, John. Thank you. But no siphoning off the odd thimbleful, thinking I won't notice,' he said. Laughter.

There had been one bit of good news. Malcolm Carey was also here. *Trebuchet*'s Australian First Lieutenant was in command of another of the Tenth's N-class boats, HMS *Nicobar*. He'd been on patrol when Harry had arrived on Malta, and while Harry had been on patrol, he'd come in and gone out again.

Seeing Malcolm Carey again was at least something to look forward to, assuming he didn't end up overdue, etc., etc., too. Harry took a gulp of his drink and began fishing the books out of his sack, smiling again at last, at the thought of Malcolm Carey: Malcolm and the photograph of his wife Fenella. That Malcolm Carey had been married was exotic enough for Harry, when he'd met him for the first time. Harry had never had a friend who was married. And certainly never one who'd come all the way from Melbourne, with a wife called Fenella left behind. Nor was Carey the usual Aussie. He might have been the typical tall, loosed-limbed, fair-haired picture of rude health, but there was nothing Ocker about him. In fact, when Harry, the young Sub, fresh from his student union had first met Malcolm Carey, he had seemed to embody every notion of sophistication possible. And that was before he had seen the photograph. He still couldn't get it out of his head. 'This is my wife, Fenella,' Carey had said, handing him the little portrait.

And what had he seen? A siren looking out at him from a blustery day by St Kilda Beach. That image had lodged itself ever since – Fenella's mane of fair hair, and the way the wind was pressing the flimsiness of her dress to the curve of her flanks. Being a typical twenty-one-year-old, remembering that photograph cheered him up immensely.

He took a breath, and began ferreting in the bottom of the sack again for his pencil and notebook. Another belt of gin and he began to leaf through the first volume. Working through these books would give him an excuse not to go back to his little cabin, and sit and look at his unopened letter from Shirley.

'What on earth are you doing?'

The voice came from over Harry's left shoulder. The first thing Harry saw when he spun around on the sofa were four gold braid rings on a sleeve. The sight made Harry start to get up, but a firm hand on his shoulder held him in place.

'There's no need to be leaping about in the wardroom. Sit where you are,' said the voice: one of those growls that doesn't need volume to issue commands. Harry looked up, and there was the square, creased face of his Captain (S), Shrimp Simpson.

It was usually tradition in the Andrew that Captains couldn't wander into the wardroom willy-nilly, disturbing the harmony. They had to be invited by the mess president. But this one, Harry had noticed on that first night he'd arrived from Gib, seemed to come and go whenever he felt like it. It was very disconcerting.

'Sir,' was all Harry deemed prudent to respond, as he let his eyes do a discreet check down the length of the gallery. There wasn't another soul in sight to rescue him. Simpson picked up one of the books. 'They're in Italian,' he said.

'Yes, Sir,' said Harry. But when Simpson continued to look down at him, he thought it better to offer further explanation. 'I was studying Italian, Sir . . . when war broke out . . .'

'You speak Italian?' asked Simpson, now mildly more interested, the growl moderating to a grumble.

'Not brilliantly, Sir. A bit. But, the Scottish education system, Sir . . . might not be able to speaka da lingo like a native, but by God, I know the grammar.'

'. . . And what? You're keeping your hand in?'

'No, Sir. Translating.'

Simpson was a short, stocky man, with unruly sandy hair already going salt 'n' pepper not surprising given his immense age – pushing forty, some said. Harry had been warned about his reputation for not suffering fools. So Harry, who could be sensitive to those things when he felt like it, got the message when Simpson's shoulders seemed to sag, as if he were saying, am I going to have to interrogate you?

'Sorry, Sir. I found them in an old bookshop on Kingsway,' said Harry, deciding to start explaining himself. And when Simpson then began nodding, Harry knew he was on safe ground again. He continued, 'It was something that happened on patrol . . .'

'Oh yes,' said Simpson, now definitely interested.

'We missed with a torpedo,' said Harry, but determined not to say more. Knowing when to be loyal to his boat, he only added, 'It was because of currents. And when I saw these, I had an idea.' And Harry held up one of the books. The title page showed a map of Italy imposed on a compass rose, with a Latin title, *Mare Nostrum*, and the author's name, or more likely a pseudonym, printed as a handwritten signature: *Capitano Massimo*. And beneath that, a subheading: *Una guida per la navigazione costiera*.

'They're for yachtsmen. They give descriptions of currents, coastal shoals, points like church towers to aid navigation. A trove, Sir. I thought if I could translate some of them . . . It's a series . . . It covers

from the Ligurian Sea all the way around to the head of the Adriatic . . .
Every port approach, lighthouse . . . everything. First one came out in
1919, but the last one in 1937! It could be very helpful intelligence, for
inshore work. Do you think?'

Simpson took the book from Harry's hand and began flicking
through. 'Line maps . . . and photographs . . . hmmmm.' He handed
the book back. 'You're Gilmour, aren't you?'

Harry nodded.

'Yeeees . . . You were posted to *Nimuae*, but got lost in transit.'

'Yes, Sir.'

'Lucky for you,' said Simpson, turning away. Then over his shoulder, 'Carry on, Mr Gilmour; we'll speak about this later. Meanwhile,
don't mention your books to anyone else yet, please.'

'Sir!' said Harry. 'One more thing, Sir. I've left a note in the mess
president's docket, but just to let you know . . . *Pelleas*'s commanding
officer, Captain Dumaresq . . . I've invited him over for a wardroom
dinner . . .'

'When?' interrupted Simpson.

'Tomorrow night, Sir.'

'He won't be able to make it,' said Simpson.

'Sir?' said Harry, looking utterly crestfallen.

Simpson sighed, and gave him a little consolation twinkle. 'Not
your fault, Gilmour. I've just come from Lascaris . . .', then, seeing
Harry's further confusion, '. . . Lascaris, the joint Ops Room. Captain
Dumaresq is going to be otherwise engaged tomorrow night. Trust me.'
And with that, he was gone, striding down the gallery.

Harry and Wykham went out that night with the Tenth's SOO, an RN
Lieutenant called Hume – a spivvy-looking character with a knowing
look, and, from the shine, what looked like some kind of mechanical

lubricant sealing down his centre parting. There was no one else around. Harry had no idea where Rais had gone, and he'd last seen Grainger's back disappearing out of the front gates, heading off Manoel Island and into Sliema. He seemed to like his own company, or at least that was the impression Harry had got. Grainger certainly didn't seem to associate much with the other Jimmys. Not that there were any other Jimmys about tonight.

The other boat in – that P number – was over in the dry dock, having her pipework welded back together again, and her cable runs rerun. She'd apparently been on the wrong end of a bad shaking at the hands of some Italian escorts, and most of her crew had been packed off to the submarine rest camp in the north of the island at Ghajn Tuffieha Bay, to get over it. Six of them, however, had required more than beer and sunbathing and were in the big naval hospital on the point at Bighi, overlooking the Grand Harbour.

Hume, Harry and Wykham took a *dghaisa* over to Valletta, where Hume had announced he would be their guide to the fleshpots. He then led them up the steps on to the Strada Reale. 'We'll try the Union Club first,' Hume said. 'Don't want to plunge you young virgins into the depths of unspeakable sordidness that are some of The Gut dives. Your mothers would never forgive me.'

Hume had brought a little hooded torch with him to aid their way in the blackout, not that it seemed to be rigorously enforced. Both Harry and Wykham, fresh from bombed-out Britain raised an eyebrow at such slackness, until Hume explained, 'Bit of a bloody waste of time here really, since this is an island and it's the easiest thing to tell land from water from the air. From five thousand feet, they say, Grand Harbour sticks out like that thing you're going to have in your trousers once the chorus girls hit the stage. And anyway, the Eyeties don't tend to venture out much at night, these days. The Brylcreem Boys have a night fighter unit. Keep 'em in a cage up at Takali and force feed 'em carrots all day. They claim they can spot a black cat in a coal cellar.'

The Union Club was on the top floor of some old Venetian-era palace called the *Auberge de Provence*. Harry thought he was walking into a Hollywood set for a Fred Astaire and Ginger Rogers movie. They could hear the music long before the cage lift had clanked them up to the main bar: a band belting out Guy Lombardo's *Penny Serenade*, and they weren't half bad.

He first spotted her talking to the bandleader, by the side of the raised drum kit at the back of the stage. There was a lull in the dancing, so the tight little dance floor, lit from above by a star pattern of guttering faux chandeliers, was all but empty. Only the odd waiter or two, in a tight, white patrol jacket, or folk, table-visiting, were cutting across, so that from where Harry and his two friends were now sitting, on a table with a mob of other Navy officers, you could see down the length of the room.

She was a tall woman, in a sheer, creamy, off-the-shoulder evening gown that hugged her figure to midway down her thighs, and then splayed in creases and ruffles to the floor. Long white gloves sheathed her arms. Even in the suffused light of the place, through the cloud systems of cigarette smoke, he could see her luxuriant hair was the colour of corn, and it didn't look as if it had come out of a bottle. She wore it a bit like a girl he once knew back home. Janis, the local businessman's daughter: a real looker who had very set ideas about what she wanted, and the utter certainty she was going to get it. Except this girl – woman, rather – looked far more dangerous. She had her hair set in two huge bangs, swept off her forehead and pinned, so that it appeared the body of her tresses fell from beneath them, in curls to her shoulder. A bit more Betty Grable than Janis, Harry decided, but not as cheap as Miss Grable. Oh no. Especially when she turned to scan the club room, as if looking for someone, and her face broke into a smile as she raised her arm in a wave, so that it caused a little spasm in Harry's throat. More like Hedy Lamarr, he decided, despite the hair colour. Definitely Hedy Lamarr. Then the band struck up and the lights went down. A man's theatrical voice announced, 'Ladies and gentlemen, Miss Katty Kadzow!' A spotlight came on, and she stepped into it. The band was playing the opening bars to *Begin the Beguine*, and Harry thought, *The last time I heard that was in the wardroom of a Free French submarine . . .* But the memory got chased away in an instant, when Katty started to sing.

The dance floor was quickly jammed, and more people seemed to flood in from vestibules and side doors until the whole club room was heaving. It stayed that way for all of Miss Kadzow's set. Dancers shuffled and glided in a slowly moving eddy around the dance floor, a sea of uniforms from all three services, with the odd colour flash of a woman's dress. On the face of it, it could have been a nightclub in Mayfair – not that Harry had ever been to a nightclub in Mayfair. But it was the noise, and the gleaming excitement in all the faces, sheened with the sweat you work up, dancing two-steps and quicksteps, and from the alcohol. Katty sang, the band played and Harry got up to dance – one thing he'd inherited from his father, how to cut the rug. And he did: with a Wren and a WAAF, and two girls in bright floral dresses who said they were VADs – Voluntary Aid Detachment – nurses. He never quite caught their names, such was the noise, but then they wanted to dance, not talk. And dance, dance, dance they did. Squeezing every last droplet out of it. When he looked, when he wasn't concentrating on dancing, it was as though he were looking into a mirror of the island. There was no frenzy or desperation, but it was as if everything were happening on a precipice. The danger made it feel like fun.

'She's a Pole,' Hume said, when Harry shouted in his ear, asking about the singer. 'Came here in '39 apparently, just as the Hun stopped sabre-rattling over Poland and invaded. After war started here, and they were offering passage to any civvy who wanted to go, she said she wanted to stay. Been the centre of attention ever since.'

Between dance numbers, and in one of those random silences you get in the middle of every racket, the sound of an air-raid siren wafted in – and to Harry's astonishment, there were shrieks of delight, and people started rushing to the stairs. But not to get out, to go up.

'Oh, good-oh!' shouted Hume. 'Fireworks!' and he grabbed Harry and Wykham. 'No. Don't head for those stairs . . . Where's it coming from?' He listened for the siren for a moment. 'From over Sliema. This way', and he pushed them through a set of alcoves to deep, curtained windows. As they went, Harry couldn't help but notice everybody seemed to be heading for the roof. Hume wrenched the drapes back, and before them, spread out, lay the darkened humps of Manoel Island and the west end of Sliema town. Above them, the sky was being stabbed by half a dozen blades of light, pointing vertically into the darkness, and with the windows pulled inwards, and the noise behind all but gone, they could hear the beat of aero engines.

'Hear that?' said Hume. 'Alpha Romeos. You get to tell the difference after a while. Totally different from our Merlins.' Then he noticed Harry and Wykham looking at him in amazement. 'Ah. Your first air raid here. Well, it's nothing like it was when it was Jerry over there in Sicily. The Eyeties, they only come now once a day at the most . . . usually at night . . . and usually only by the handful. We've started looking forward to the show. That's why everybody's rushed to the roof. But you never know what lumps of shite are going to fall out of the sky on your noggin. We're safer in here under the balcony. Watch.'

And as he spoke, two of the searchlights began to move, probing the sky. Then a third. They all gazed up, mesmerised, the noise of the aero engines growing louder. Then, suddenly the beam of one of the searchlights flitted across something, a brief glitter of reflection. Harry had the impression of three shapes, before the beam settled on one and held it: a little flattened silver cross, pinned to the blackness at about fifteen thousand feet or more, Harry reckoned, over the suburb of Msida. Two other beams swung rapidly to join the arc, moving with mechanical efficiency until the aircraft was pinned, and at that moment all the other searchlights, their beams still static, vertical poles in the night, snapped out.

'They've got these tactics,' said Hume in a running commentary. 'It's only sixty miles to Sicily so the RAF boys see them coming with the little radar sets they've got buried up north. They tell the Army searchlight boys where to point, and when they catch one . . . watch.'

Out of nowhere came a string of fairy lights, moving towards the Italian bomber, across the sky from behind.

'Beaufighter,' said Hume. 'They send them up as soon as the radar spots any raid building. Gives 'em time to gain height.'

Another string of lights lazily tracked across the darkness. *Tracer*, said Harry to himself, realising, just as the Italian bomber seemed to give a little lurch and fall several hundred feet. The beams, however, never wavered from it. There was no sound of gunfire, just the steady engine drone. The next shock took only seconds to unfold. There was a series of distant whistling sounds, and then just beyond the Msida sky-line, a line of gouts of earth and debris, and then in the seconds it took for the sound to travel, they heard the rumbling crash of explosions.

'That's the other Eyeties jettisoning their bombs and getting the hell out of it,' said Hume smugly, playing master of ceremonies at the show. When their eyes turned back to the bomber caught in the arc of the searchlights, another surprise awaited, with another set of 'oohs' and 'ahhs' from the mob on the roof above. Three pearl-like blossoms were falling away from the bomber. Parachutes.

'Some more guests at the Takali mess for breakfast tomorrow,' observed Hume, and at that another burst of tracer hit the bomber, and she toppled from level flight into a flaming Catherine wheel and began falling out of the sky. There were cheers now from the roof above.

'Only three 'chutes,' said Hume. 'Oh well. That's one poor bastard didn't make it. More drinks, chaps?'

Looking at the stricken aircraft, Harry was suddenly thinking about Fabrizio: how it could have been him. And he was hit by one of those little waves of silent gratitude that sometimes wash over you, knowing at least that his pal was safe now. A prisoner, yes. He certainly wouldn't be enjoying himself, but Harry, laughing to himself, didn't care about that. If he'd ever done one right thing in his life, it had been to see to it that his friend would at least be going home again, when all this nonsense was over.

Back inside, Katty picked up her set where the air raid had rudely interrupted her, and when she finished, went to join a table on the other side of the dance floor, and a uniformed figure stepped up to escort her to her seat. Although as to what service, or indeed nation's uniform it was, Harry was clueless. Hume noticed him watching, and laughed.

'Ha ha! That's our Chally you're squinting at. Scruff, prima donna, madman and darling of the command. The uniform's RAF, by the way, or it's supposed to be,' said Hume.

From what Harry could see, this Chally fellow was wearing a pair of fawn Oxford bags that did not now, nor ever had formed part of any uniform he'd ever seen. Over them, he had on a lightweight khaki battledress, definitely not regulation RAF. In fact, the only RAF thing about him was a set of pilot's wings on his breast, and the rings on his battledress epaulettes. He also had on the most disreputable pair of suede desert boots. One other thing Harry noticed: beneath the wings were a line of medal ribbons that even from this distance, he could see included the diagonal white and purple stripes of a Distinguished Flying Cross – the gong the RAF gave out when they'd exhausted their monthly quota of VCs.

'Flight Lieutenant Toby Challoner, aka Chally,' added Hume. 'Malta's ace reconnaissance pilot. If we want to know if the Eyeties are on the move, Chally flies in their back window and counts the number of socks they're packing.'

Chally had one hand on Katty's bare back, and the other gripping her forearm, proprietorial, guiding her to the table: directing or controlling her might have been better descriptions. His eyes only for her. And Katty – you could tell she was submitting, but her eyes were elsewhere, as though she were on lookout. Making sure the horizon was clear? wondered Harry. Or checking to see what might be coming over it? Whatever she was doing, watching her, Harry felt as though he were looking through a telescope at someone enjoying a party on the terrace of a palace on a hill.

Harry slept in the next day, and when he ambled into the wardroom gallery, Grainger was sitting on an easy chair, reading a ten-day-old copy of *The Times* with a pot of coffee in front of him. There were some base officers further down who Harry didn't recognise. Grainger waved Harry to join him.

'Seen anything of our . . . Skipper?' he asked, pouring Harry a cup. Harry shook his head. 'Hmmn. Neither have I. He had a very long chat with the S10 apparently, and hasn't been seen since. You have a chat with the S10?'

'I don't think he even knows my name,' said Harry warily, recalling his conversation with the Shrimp.

'I did,' said Grainger. 'He wanted to know all about our patrol. *All* about it.'

'What did you tell him?' asked Harry.

'Oh, I confined myself to the bare facts,' said Grainger. 'Thought it only fair to all concerned. He didn't. I got a lecture from the head-master. Ended with him uttering some puerile rubbish about the Trade being everything to do with teamwork if it were to do with anything, and forgetting that was the quickest way to get you, and everyone else, killed. Most extraordinary.'

Harry said nothing. He especially didn't say he didn't find it extraor-dinary at all. The Shrimp must have put two and two together about what was going on aboard *Umbrage*. For a start, he would certainly have been pissed off at a torpedo being wasted on a schooner, and pissed off at the Jimmy who'd let his CO even think about it, without an argument.

Then there was the implicit deal, the one that applied only to submarines, between the CO and the crew – the deal you didn't find anywhere else in the Navy. Only one man can look through a periscope: the man in charge. The CO. And that means the level of trust a crew must have in that man is a remarkable thing. It's a question of his judgement, how he calculates risk, how he takes his crew into his confidence, so that they can be confident in him. For a CO is never going to be able to exercise effective command if he doesn't have that trust. And to help him, he needs a First Lieutenant who is going to deliver to him a crew, fully trained, competent and ready to do its duty – not one who hides behind smug superiority, and who leaves his crew silent, surly and suspicious.

Sailors raised in the Trade understood that, but Grainger had come from outside, from destroyers. And Harry knew from old, that Grainger had volunteered for submarines, not to learn the Trade, but to get a command faster than was usual in the surface fleet. He'd been like that when he first joined *Trebuchet*, and obviously matters hadn't changed: the Number One, it appeared, was still out for number one. Harry found himself wondering if the words Shrimp must have spoken to Rais would have any more positive an effect than the ones he had just wasted on Grainger.

When Wykham arrived, Harry told him they were going for a swim, and dragged him out via the Leading Writers' office to get directions to the nearest beach that wasn't rolled in barbed wire and planted with mines. They were pointed to a little rocky cove with a patch of sand up the coast near St Julian's Bay. They'd have to walk, they were informed, there and back. And were they mad? The water would be freezing this time of year.

Coming from Argyll, Harry found the water merely bracing. Anyway, it had served its purpose to get him out of Grainger's way.

Wykham, on the other hand, shivered so much Harry thought he would lose his teeth.

Wykham. Harry didn't know what to make of him, if he thought about the poor lad at all. The first thing he'd have to say, was that if you'd asked him right there and then to shut his eyes and give a description of Wykham, he'd have been hard-pressed. *Tall, gangly? Um, yes, I think so. Hair, nondescript. Expression, vacant. Still nineteen. Anything else? Ummm.*

He was only two years younger than Harry, but if you looked at them together, there was a lifetime between them. Yet the lad was coming up the same way Harry had: RNVR, *King Alfred*, then his first sea duty, except for Wykham it had been a six-month sideshow on a minesweeper out of Avonmouth, and not the ordeal suffered by Harry on a battleship based on Scapa. Still, there should have been something.

Umbrage was Wykham's first boat, and Harry kept trying not to think about whether *he* had arrived in the Trade with the same pitiful lack of naval gumption as this bland, utterly inoffensive young officer. As yet, Harry hadn't plucked up the nerve to ask how Wykham had ended up on submarines, dreading to hear some tragic tale of misunderstanding and innocence betrayed. He wondered what Jack made of him – of all of the RNVR hopefuls being churned out into the fleet, children in their first pair of long trousers, being rushed on to ships. But they were needed. Desperately. The Navy needed every one of them. Everybody knew that. The Battle of Britain might've been won, but Britain was still fighting for her life in the North Atlantic, and here in the Med, where her oil supplies were just one more successful offensive away from being overrun by Rommel and his Afrika Korps. And once Jerry had finished with the Russians . . .

When they got back from their swim, Harry ditched Wykham and went off to work on his translations. When he surfaced again, to get a drink and something to eat, there was a full-blown party going on in the wardroom. While Harry had been holed up in his tiny allocated cabin, carved into the limestone behind the Lazaretto and away from all the noise, two boats had returned from patrol. And there were successes to be toasted. The gallery especially, was heaving. Even the CO, the Navigator and the Fourth off the boat over in the dry dock, who'd been recovering up in the rest camp, had come down. Their Jimmy wasn't there though; he was still in hospital. Grainger was there, however, and when Harry went to say hello, he told him one of the boats just in was *Upholder*. 'And that tall, beardy bloke over there,' said Grainger, 'the one who looks like a more hirsute version of Robert Donat about to go on as Mr Chips. That's her Skipper. The Tenth's very own legend, in the flesh. Lieutenant Commander David Wanklyn.'

Grainger rattled off *Upholder*'s patrol score; and the score for the other boat just in, but Harry was only half-listening. More tonnage to go on the wardroom's noticeboard. The official figures were pinned up there: the Tenth had sunk over one hundred enemy ships since the beginning of June, equivalent to well over a quarter of a million tons. But at the same time, five Royal Navy submarines and all their crews had been lost. Common sense and the wardroom by-laws dictated you didn't dwell on the cost in human pain behind those figures. Yours, the enemy's, the folks back home. Even so, Harry, right then, wondered what it would be like if he did – thinking, *Shouldn't someone?* Except, looking at that obviously affable bloke over there, David Wanklyn, a man responsible for more than his fair share of that total, with his self-deprecating stoop and his eagerness to laugh at other people's jokes, and the newspaper pictures he remembered, of his wife and young son back home, from all the morale-boosting stories, all of it . . .

Harry turned away and let common sense and the wardroom by-laws drag him back from that particular abyss.

When he turned, Shrimp's executive officer was there; some amiable old duffer Harry remembered had been called Hubert; first name, Hubert. Remember the days, Harry? When you, in your short trousers and school blazer, would have laughed yourself silly at such a daft English name. Not as silly as Wanklyn though. He certainly remembered the first time he'd heard that name mentioned here in this wardroom, because with it had come with one of those life lessons you were always better to learn before you put your foot in it, while the joke you were going to make that was going to be so funny, is still forming in your head – until you see the flat, boilerplate stares of everyone around you, daring you to say what you're about to say; and you guessing, hopefully, in the nick of time, as sure as instinct, that your entire future in this company now hangs on you not being idiot enough to say it. Anyway, he hadn't said it, hadn't said anything, and so he'd been safe, and now Hubert was smiling benignly at him and offering him a large tumbler of gin.

'It's not a party, Mr Gilmour, unless you have at least one drink,' said old Hubert. 'Now knock it back and come with me. S10 wants a word.'

Shrimp was sitting behind his desk in his day cabin: another limestone monk's cell hewn out of the rock. A desk and chair, a minimal filing cabinet for the minimal paperwork he was reputed for, and a light bulb in a cracked cardboard shade hanging from exposed flex. He had a signal flimsy in one hand and his own gin in the other. He looked very glum.

'Sir,' said Harry, 'you wanted to see me.'

Shrimp looked up as if trying to focus.

It was all quite informal. Neither were wearing caps, so no saluting or any of that stuff. So Harry said, 'Bad news, Sir?' to break the silence.

'A Jerry U-boat's just sunk *Ark Royal*,' said Shrimp. The Royal Navy's last big fleet carrier in the Med. They both looked into space, contemplating the gravity of this development. Then Shrimp said, 'Tragic and serious though that is, it's not why I wanted to see you. How's your translating coming along?'

'I think it could be useful, Sir,' said Harry, eager to get off the subject of the Empire's imminent demise. 'There's a hell of a lot of it though. The entire Italian coastline's there. So I've been pretty selective for my first shot at it. Big ports . . .' Harry stopped as Shrimp pushed a pile of folded papers across his desk.

'Those are Italian railway maps,' said Shrimp. 'Concentrate on the stretches of coastline where the railway lines hug it. From Policastro to Longobardi. It's a bit of a priority, so get as many as you can written up and present yourself here at 09.00. Oh, and your friend Captain Dumaresq. Force F sailed just after dusk for another sortie down to the Tunisian coast. Let's try for a dinner again when they're back. I'd like to meet him. Carry on, and I'll see you in the morning.'

Chapter Ten

Umbrage was barely more than nine hundred yards off the shore, at periscope depth, with Rais's eyes stuck to the big search telescope. They were about six or seven miles south of the small Calabrian coastal town of Diamante. Rais had picked this spot not just because of how close the railway lines ran to the beach, but because Diamante wasn't a port. No fishing boats wandering about, nor any danger of a passing MAS-boat dropping in: those nasty little Italian torpedo gunboats.

'This should suit our purposes admirably,' said Rais, once again being disconcertingly communicative. Then he began calling off bearings to a couple of landmarks, which Harry duly noted on the plot. That all wrapped up, Rais then ordered their withdrawal to deeper water. 'We'll return after 21.00 hours, and see what turns up. A pity that Eyetie holiday guide book of yours didn't come with a train timetable, Gilmour. Anyway, I'm going to get my head down for a bit. Watch, Dived, Number One, and make sure we're squared away to go to Gun Action *before* we head back in. Carry on.'

Grainger left what could only be construed as an insubordinate pause, before he replied, 'Aye aye, Sir.' Then he waited until he heard the swish of Rais's berth curtain closing, and leaning close to Harry, said with his usual irritating matter-of-factness, 'This is all your fault,

Gilmour,' in that way he had, so that Harry never knew whether he was being funny, or whether he wasn't.

There had been lots of little quips on the passage up here, directed at his Eyetie coastal pilot books and his translations: little sneers about how lovely it was, they were all 'going paddling'.

The truth was, the Mediterranean Fleet charts of the Italian inshore waters were notoriously out of date, and closing with the coast always managed to generate a certain frisson in a boat; with everyone hanging on the echo sounder's every ping, as it looked for a bottom or a shoal that should be there, and frequently finding ones that shouldn't. And now along had come Vasco, with that little book written in Eyetie he'd found in a Valletta junk shop, tucked away behind a potted plant and wrapped in a job lot of medieval camiknickers – or so the story went among the for'ard Jacks. What a hoot. But behind all the hilarity, Jack actually approved: an officer who understood foreign and could use his head. Imagine it – going inshore with a Navigator who actually knew where he was going. It was enough to let you sleep tight in your hammock.

Oh, and as for the reference to 'Vasco' – all Navigators got christened that by the Jacks who served with them. It was a nod to Vasco da Gama, the Portuguese sixteenth-century explorer famous for his epic voyages, presumably in the hope that their Navigator would live up to his namesake's formidable reputation.

After Shrimp had ruined the wardroom party for Harry, sending him off to do homework instead, Harry had worked through the night, as ordered. In the morning he presented himself. But Shrimp was busy. Something brewing down in the desert apparently; the Eighth Army was up to its tricks again. So he was handed a note and sent off on his own with his translations, across the harbour to Valletta, then up the steep run of steps to Number Three, Scots Street, where he'd been told the 'crabfats' lived.

Harry walked with a spring in his step, not a trace of resentment at being denied a party *and* his night's sleep, in fact rather full of himself: on a special mission for the Flotilla Captain. Not to mention secret work of operational and tactical significance. Who'd have thought it? The wee lad who used to polish the brass and the deck furniture down at the Sandbank boatyard, involved in secret work. Beat that!

When he got to the RAF HQ, a WAAF had conducted him to a door marked 'Dep. AOC' and inside was Mahaddie, of all people. Much bellowing and handshaking and guff about how old shipmates should stick together, then Mahaddie asked him about Fabrizio. 'Did that Eyetie pal of yours ever let ye know what happened to him? You know, write ye a letter. Promise you a shot at his sister by way o' a ta very much?'

'No,' said Harry, frowning at the crudity. 'I'm not sure they let POWs enter into correspondence with serving officers.'

'Ungrateful wee wop shite,' Mahaddie decided. 'That was a decent thing you did for him back there. God knows why you thought he deserved it.' Then he read the note from Shrimp, and suddenly everything went all serious again.

'Follow me,' Mahaddie had said and led him through the warren to a tiny back office where the Photo-intelligence mob lived. They took two of the books he'd brought off him and spirited them away to photograph the line maps, then his pencil translations were taken off him, and Mahaddie called out, 'Katty!' and Katty Kadzow, in a far more restrained but no less fetching plain grey skirt and white blouse, appeared from a tiny alcove at the back of the room. 'This is Katty,' Mahaddie had said. 'She'll type these up and get them copied and bound with their map photos. Katty, meet that Captain Bligh I told you about.'

So, now here they were, on the Calabrian coast, armed with Harry's translated yachtsman's guide, ready to wreak havoc. The Eighth Army was about to mount an offensive in Libya apparently, or so Shrimp had said. And the more Malta's submarines could choke off the enemy's supplies, the weaker he would be against a British attack. However, sinking his supply ships was just one way to do it. Wrecking the Italian rail network was another.

'Rommel's Afrika Korps and his Italian allies require 100,000 tons of stores a week to keep going,' Shrimp had told Harry. 'You close one of those railway lines carrying Axis army supplies to their ports for just twenty-four hours, and you deny them up to fourteen thousand tons' worth of stuff they need. It's as good as sinking two freighters.'

Up until now, they'd used commando parties to destroy rail lines. Harry had seen quite a few dodgy-looking blokes down in the other Lazaretto building, doing press-ups and arriving back from runs at all hours of the day and night. He'd wondered who they were; now he knew. When ordered, the Tenth's boats had been carrying them and their funny little wood and canvas canoes, called folbots, to within a couple of miles of a shoreline with a railway close by. They'd row ashore and blow it up, and hopefully the submarine would still be there waiting for them when they rowed back, assuming they could find it on the high seas on a dark night, and assuming a passing MAS-boat or shagbat hadn't forced the submarine to dive in the meantime.

But if the submarines could get close into shore, then their gun crews could do the job without any of the risks, either to the commandos, who had to paddle in and out, or to the submarine forced to hang about on the surface off an enemy coast. Enter Harry Gilmour and his fortuitous find among the medieval camiknickers. So Grainger was right, really. It was all Harry's fault.

It was something he contemplated while he played Uckers with Wykham down in *Umbrage*'s wardroom, waiting for night to fall. That and the fact that he had now been personally introduced to the famous, the glamorous, Miss Katty Kadzow, whom he would now be required to meet regularly when ashore because she, the celebrated chanteuse by night, by day was the trusted, efficient typist, secretary and all-round Girl Friday to the RAF Photo-intelligence bods – and now she was also responsible for typing up all Harry's translations. And it had to be Harry doing the translations, Shrimp had said. Yes, there were plenty of others on this island who could read Italian: Maltese in the employ of the British. But the fewer people who knew what they were up to, the happier Shrimp would be.

Musgrave was doing them a kipper and scrambled eggs for breakfast, and Harry had told him to wake the CO when it was ready. So he wasn't surprised when Musgrave, after he'd dumped the cutlery on the wardroom table, turned and rapped the wooden panel by Rais's bunk. 'Cap'n, Sir!' he called in a firm voice. A moment passed and then the curtain was torn back, and Rais's angelic face was staring out at them, contorted with rage. Musgrave instantly went ramrod straight, and Harry, sitting barely two arms' lengths from Rais felt his heart sink. Back to where they'd started.

'Sir,' Harry said, 'I told him to wake you. Breakfast's up.'

Rais's wild eyes shot each one of them in turn, as though he were looking for the slightest sign he was being made sport of, then he fixed on poor Musgrave.

'Do not shout at me again, Sailor,' he said and then swished the curtain shut again, without uttering another word.

Since they'd sailed on this patrol, it had been obvious to Harry that Rais had been trying hard to speak to his crew as if they were human beings, up until now that is.

From the tortured little expressions on Rais's face, and the long pauses sometimes before he could bring himself to speak, it had also been obvious he was finding it a struggle to be nice. On their first night on patrol, he'd even tried to strike up a conversation with Harry on the bridge, as they'd glided along through the night, their diesels pumping charge into the batteries.

'How did you end up in the Trade, Gilmour?' Rais had asked. A personal question. Harry at first wondered whether he'd really heard it.

'Oh, by accident, Sir,' Harry had replied. 'I was the accident. And Captain Dumaresq pointed me in the right direction . . .'

He'd been going to continue, but realised Rais had stopped listening and had been grimacing at one of the lookouts, whose ears had obviously been flapping, desperate to hear the officer chat instead of concentrating on the horizon. Harry waited for the explosion, but it hadn't come. Progress, he had thought at the time.

Now they were surfacing, and Rais was shouting again, this time at a Leading Stoker, who was shadowing the Outside ERA, doing an on-the-job, makee-learnee on the trim board. The Stoker hadn't been executing orders fast enough, apparently.

Umbrage's Outside ERA, her Wrecker, had met Rais's outburst with an uncharacteristic furious glare. Because, as Wrecker, he was in charge, and if the CO had any complaints, he should have addressed them to him. But Rais hadn't been interested enough to notice. Rais was never interested in his crew unless they offered a target to vent his ill-nature on.

The Wrecker was a slight man, who could have been any age between twenty-five and forty-five, known for his nervous fussing about, who seemed at least a size too small for his overalls, with only his ears keeping his cap out of his eyes – those and the springy tangle of ginger hair under it that you could bounce your hand on. He always had a pair of heavy-duty gloves sticking out of one of the bum pockets on his overalls, and a filthy rag out of one of the top ones, which he would use without discrimination to mop either his brow or polish a brass valve wheel. The main thing Harry remembered about him was that he was Welsh and his name was Parry-Jones, except everybody called him 'Cled', which was apparently short for Cledwyn. But not

Rais. If he referred to him at all, he called him Clot, which he thought terribly witty. Especially as Clot looked like the last man on earth to get angry, and certainly not at anyone in authority.

But from what Harry had seen of ERA Parry-Jones, there was nothing at all 'Clottish' about the way he performed his duties.

In fact, the Leading Stoker on the board was a perfect example of his diligence. Mr Parry-Jones frequently rotated a couple of the Leading Stokers through the control room on makee-learn, lest he might find himself indisposed at some time in the indeterminate future when *Umbrage* might urgently require another hand who knew all the right knobs to turn.

But if Rais had bothered to pay attention to his Clot right then, he would have seen a man being pushed too far.

And then they were on the surface, but Rais was still standing by the conning tower ladder, bathed in the red light like some demon, glowering at everyone around the control room, while everybody around the control room wondered why their CO hadn't realised they had surfaced. Grainger waited before he spoke. Deliberately. 'We've surfaced, Sir,' he said.

Rais spun around to see the faces of the two lookouts, standing right next to him and now wide-eyed with fear of him, waiting, ready to go up on to the bridge.

'Well, what are you waiting for!' he hissed, and stepped aside.

It was the CO who was supposed to go up first, was usually already waiting under the hatch, in fact, ready to throw off the clips the moment the conning tower broke surface, to get up there and make sure nothing was waiting for them they didn't want to see. Everybody knew that, as though they knew they'd been on the surface for long, long seconds before their CO had stepped aside to let the lookouts pass, and before he had moved to follow them. And they watched as Grainger's flat, expressionless gaze followed Rais, as he went up into the night, and they read the accusation behind it, just as they were supposed to. Harry took his cap off and swept his hand through his hair, and looked at a deckhead cable run so that he wouldn't have to look at anybody else.

Harry had managed one little victory over Rais before they'd surfaced. The gun crew had been allowed to remain below until a target came into view. Rais had originally wanted them up, pronto, but Harry had cajoled him out of it. If Rais hadn't relented, the crew would be standing by the gun now, down on the casing, with *Umbrage* trimmed down and riding decks awash, and the November Mediterranean sloshing around their freezing ankles, and having to stay like that for however many hours it took for a train to arrive.

Harry, as officer of the watch was on the bridge, but he and the two lookouts were looking to seaward, making sure no baddies were sneaking up. Rais, and an additional lookout, one of the Leading Signalmen from the radio room who had a name for his night vision, were watching up and down the railway line. It was a moonless night, with the usual high, scudding clouds playing their Salome dance with the stars. And with the offshore wind, there wasn't much of a sea running. Good for the gun crew's chances of staying dry when their turn came to take the air, but because it meant next to no surf, it would be a bit of a hindrance when it came to the gun layer being able to register the shoreline.

Following the line of the railway, however, was easy. *Flash Eyeties*, Harry had thought when he'd stuck his head out of the conning tower hatch and saw the rows of pylons disappearing in both directions. *Us? We're still running puffing billys, while the Fascists have modern electric trains.*

The Petty Officer Gun Captain had already been up, him and Rais in a huddle discussing datum lines and ranges, then he had gone back below. Now *Umbrage* just bobbed, hove to, bows pointed inshore, about nine hundred yards off the beach, waiting.

Rais had picked this spot for two reasons; there were no houses anywhere in sight, not even as far inland as they could see, so with no one to hear, *Umbrage*'s twin diesels were still going flat out pumping charge. Also, and it had been Rais who had spotted it as they had burbled at periscope depth, up and down the shore during daylight, there was a small brick structure stuck in the middle of nowhere. And when you cranked up the magnification, you could see all the high-tension cables running in and out of it. It was obviously some kind of switchgear for the power lines. Icing on the cake for the gunners.

And still they waited, Rais continually fretting out loud. Harry had given up worrying about how bad form it was, not because most of it was directed at him – 'How are we going to know if there's one of the damn things coming, until it's on top of us?' . . . 'Bloody electric trains! There'll be no chuff, chuff, bloody chuff.' . . . 'Can you categorically assure me that the gun crew are going to get up in time?' . . . That sort of thing. No, it wasn't because Rais was saying it all to him, although God knows it was hard to imagine anything more undermining of one of your officers, especially as you were about to go into action. It was because Rais was saying it all in front of the crew. The Skipper was supposed to be the strong, silent type in front of his crew before an action, as though he knew exactly what he was doing, supremely confident in manner and deed. And even if, deep down inside he wasn't, the crew had to believe he was. Jesus Christ, it was the number one officer quality they were supposed to surgically implant in your brain before they let you loose on the fleet.

But Harry had already shut down that nagging voice in his head. It was too late now. All that remained to be done was to keep his eyes open, and make sure his lookouts kept theirs open too, to seaward, fixed on the black rim of their horizon, waiting for the slightest break in it, the merest flash of a wake or bow wave, to alert them to something moving out there, when what they needed was nothing to be moving.

Down below, Grainger was standing between the helmsman and the trim board, ready to move *Umbrage* in a hurry; and Wykham was poised over the plot, with his watch and pencil, ready to record the coming action. They waited.

Harry had stopped looking at his watch when he heard Rais's 'Ah-ha!'

He turned as Rais sang out, 'Gun crew close up!' And he saw a single stab of light probing horizontally in the darkness, a good distance up the railway line: a diesel locomotive's headlight.

'How considerate of you Eyeties to have got your plane-spotter books out earlier . . .' crowed Rais, fixing the beam in his night glasses, '. . . just to check there's no Allied bombers within range of your little train set, so you don't have to bother about a blackout . . . but you didn't think to take clever little Clive Rais into account though, did you?'

The gun crew were already tumbling up through the conning tower hatch, and down on to the casing. The first one there yanked the tompion out of the barrel, another undid the clips on the watertight ready-use magazine in the fore end of the conning tower, and pulled out a three-inch shell, arming it and ramming it home into the breech. The gun layer unsecuring the gun was preparing to traverse it, and Rais preparing to direct the fire himself: a task which would require his entire concentration, when as CO he should be concentrating on commanding the boat.

Harry took his eyes from seaward, but not before he made sure his lookouts were attending to their duty even if he wasn't, and he watched the silhouette of the train take shape. Even with his poor vision, the bulk of the loco and of the seemingly never-ending line of freight wagons loomed up, its progress marked by each tiny little red and green trackside signal light it masked as it lumbered onwards at what seemed an ever-increasing speed.

'Range, one thousand yards,' called Rais to the gun layer. 'Make your deflection five right. Commence firing when the target crosses the datum line. Then independent firing. Make every shot count down there, do you hear me?'

Harry sighed. What else was the gun layer going to do?

And then the whole length of the train could be made out, and it was as if the huge loco was beam on to them. Harry could see the little green glow from the driver's cab and even just make out the lattice of its pantograph sucking the power down . . .

BUMMMM! The three-inch had fired.

Almost instantly there was an explosion right in the middle of the locomotive's body. It seemed to arch slightly into the air and then there was a spectacular eruption of blue flashes and sparks along its roof, and on to the top of the first freight wagon; the overhead line coming down, Harry realised. It was like a mini-electrical storm, the sharp cracks of it piercing through the burble of *Umbrage's* diesels. And then came the grinding of metal. The loco must have jumped the tracks and then landed, and although it was still upright, you could see it was derailed. Yet with the momentum of the God knows how many tons of freight behind it – two thousand tons, maybe even more – it was being driven headlong, its bogies gouging up sleepers, twisting rails. The weight of the wagons rolling onwards, broke against the wagons grinding to a halt, and the whole long snake of it began to concertina, grinding the heavy loco further into the ground.

BUMMMM! BUMMMM! BUMMMM! The gun was firing steadily now, its twelve-pound projectiles hitting the freight wagons, ripping shreds of canvas and wood, and boxes of stuff into the night air. And finally, the whole ragged mess ground to a halt. Fires had started in some of the wagons, and suddenly the night air was rent by gunfire: endless, entirely ragged, uncoordinated rattling fire; intense bursts of it, then single and double shots, then the volleys rose again.

Everyone on the bridge had instinctively ducked, except Rais, who sneered down at them. 'Boxes of rifle ammunition, cooking off. No need to hide, girls.'

BUMMMM! BUMMMM! The gun crew were still firing, and more shells were being passed up through the conning tower hatch. When Harry looked again, he could see a tiny figure disentangle itself from the cab of the train's engine, climb down and run away up the track. The driver. Harry smiled to himself, *Poor bastard, you probably didn't expect this when you got up this morning for your bowl of coffee and your* bombalone, *with the wife and* bambini *screaming in the background*. Harry, happy that the driver was getting away: an ordinary working bloke, trying to earn a living, and now he was running for his life. Good luck to him.

The gun layer must have seen the driver too, because he ceased firing momentarily and traversed the gun back up the length of train and trained it on the loco again, whereupon he began to systematically blow it to pieces. Harry, still grinning, found himself wondering if the gun layer had been blasting away at the freight wagons until now just to make sure the driver did get away. It would've been a typical Jack thing to do – giving a bloke a break, one working man to another.

Anyway, Eyetie railways wouldn't be using that locomotive again, he thought, not any more. Its wreckage had, however, managed to shield the brick switching station, so Rais's plan to blow a hole in the line's power grid had been scuppered.

'Check fire!' called Rais. 'Clear the casing', and then into the voice-pipe, 'Half astern, together.' Then he turned to Harry, his face split with a grin, and he performed what could only be described as a little jig, right there on the bridge. 'Now that was bloody good fun, wasn't it, Gilmour!'

Indeed, it had been fun. Jack had thought so too. Harry could see it on the expressions of the gun crew and the spare lookouts as they tumbled down into the hatch. There were few things in life that didn't involve drink or women that Jack could be said to truly enjoy, but a good go at making loud bangs and blowing stuff up, watching the big bits fly off and the wreckage burst into flames – now what wasn't to like about that? And it was all legal too. You could even get a gong for it! It could even put a smile on the face of a twisted little arsehole CO like Rais.

The rest of the night *Umbrage* spent heading west-south-west for the northern coast of Sicily, and two nights later they did it all over again, against the Messina to Palermo line, just where it came out to hug the beach before Santo Stefano di Camastra. They still had eight torpedoes aboard so Rais then headed north again to look for something to fire them at. He'd been in tearing high spirits.

Several days later they encountered a small, escorted convoy coming out of the Golfo di Cagliari at the southern tip of Sardinia. It was straight after first light and they had just dived and were in a perfect position to begin an attack. Three small freighters, each on or under two thousand tons, and a bigger tanker: maybe three thousand or more tons. Tuke, on the ASDIC, had heard them coming first. Unfortunately, they were being escorted by at least three MAS-boats and what Harry identified as an *Achille Papa*-class torpedo boat – basically the equivalent of an RN frigate. Rais didn't put a foot wrong: manoeuvred *Umbrage* on to a 110-degree track angle, and managed to position her so that three of the merchant ships were overlapping in his periscope sights, offering a continuous target almost nine hundred feet long. He couldn't miss, so he ordered a full salvo: all four torpedoes in the forward tubes. But he did miss.

The little convoy had been emerging from the middle of the Golfo into proper open water as the last torpedo left its tube at just over 1,300 yards' range. And that had been when the convoy had executed a very neat 25-degree turn to starboard and began defensive zigzagging.

The first two torpedoes, and the fourth one, went combing down the port side of the convoy, and probably weren't even seen by the merchant ships or their escort. The third torpedo, however, went rogue, its gyro probably failing, and it began circling back. By that time, *Umbrage* was already heading deep – even so, the entire crew were treated to the extremely disconcerting whine of one of their own armed and live torpedoes running over their heads, out of control, twice, before it ran out of fuel and sank to the seabed.

The Italian escorts did spot the rogue torpedo however, and Tuke heard one of the MAS-boats speeding out to where it must've thought the torpedo had been fired. It had begun dropping depth charges. But *Umbrage* had been a long way away by then, and the sound of them was just a distant rumble. Yet it was enough to cause a couple of anxious glances among the younger crew – the ones Harry could see from his position by the plot – crew who had obviously never been on the end of a proper depth charge attack. What a treat they had in store, he thought.

The following day, back off the Golfo di Cagliari, they encountered another small freighter sailing singly: two torpedoes fired, one hit. They didn't hang about very long, watching her sink, because Rais wanted to head back for the Calabrian coast. He'd had an idea.

'You remember that blockhouse thing we saw on the railway line just south of Diamante?' said Rais to Harry and Grainger. They were sitting around the wardroom table, each of them stuffing their faces on huge, freshly caught *lampuki*, with chips that Musgrave had fried up in a pot full of solid lard he'd managed to hoard. They were running on the surface towards the coast, cramming amps into the batteries as they went, with Wykham on watch on the bridge. It was the early hours of the morning and this was dinner. The little deckhead lights, with their chintz shades, reflected off the grease smeared around their mouths and cheeks, in among their ten days' growth. Musgrave had coffee on the go, so that smell all but masked the diesel reek and what was coming from bodies that hadn't been washed over those ten days either.

'The electricity substations?' said Harry. 'The ones with all the switching gear?'

'Wires, cables, those long concertina things . . .' said Rais.

'Insulators,' said Harry.

'Yes, yes, yes,' said Rais. 'Shut up. Electric gizmos for the electric train wires . . . Now, that bloody train outside Diamante, when it came off the tracks it masked that one right in front of us. So we didn't get a shot. But they're important, right? So, what if we go right inshore, anywhere from the instep bit of the toe, up to south of Acquafredda where the railway's practically on the beach, and slowly cruise up and down, looking for every one we can find, and blowing it to buggery? That'd hurt 'em, wouldn't it? Take a bugger of a long time to fix up a row or more of them, eh? Do that at night, withdraw in daylight, to see if we can find a home for our last two kippers, and then Bob's your uncle. Home, James!'

They started inshore the following night. By the time they withdrew at first light, five switching stations and booster transformer buildings had been reduced to piles of smashed brick and tangled metal, each one dispatched in a magical display of sparks and blue flashes. The next night they did it again. And the next night. Until the atmosphere on board was like a school trip at Guy Fawkes. There was a queue of ratings volunteering to get on the shell line, passing up the twelve-pound projectiles – especially for the positions on the bridge and the for'ard casing. Just so as they could see all the bangs and flashes.

On the fourth day, having failed to sight a single ship, *Umbrage* was dived and heading back inshore at a stately three knots on her motors. Wykham had the watch, and Grainger was up in the forward torpedo room with the gunner, checking the remaining shells in the main magazine: getting ready for the night's work.

Harry and the CO were sitting at the wardroom table drinking coffee, with Harry coding the signals they'd be sending back to Lazaretto reporting on progress. His mind wasn't entirely on the job: he was thinking about Rais and his behaviour as his CO was scribbling down what he wanted to send, changing his mind and scribbling again – sitting there, absorbed, like an innocent schoolboy. At first Harry had simply believed he behaved like a martinet because he enjoyed it. But then everything had changed. Whatever Shrimp had said to him back in Malta after their last patrol, Rais had tried to become a different character. He hadn't always managed it, but there had been times on this patrol when Harry had thought his CO was becoming almost human. The changed atmosphere in the boat was testimony to that. That was when he decided to ask.

Nobody knew anything about Rais or where he had come from. It certainly didn't feel as though he were Trade through and through. So what other branch of the service had he arrived from, and why? Now seemed as good a time as any to try and find out.

'How did you end up in this lot, Sir? If you don't mind me asking?'

Rais carried on scribbling, little furrows on his brow, as though he were concentrating and hadn't heard. Then, without looking up, he began speaking as if from a long way away. 'I'm a career officer, Gilmour. I'm doing this because I have to. I doubt you'd understand.'

'Try me, Sir.'

Rais looked up, and his expression had changed. He looked shifty, guilty almost. 'When this is all over, I don't have the luxury of influence. There's no one to intercede on my behalf, to make sure I don't end up with just a cheap suit and a thank you like your kind will. Nor do I have the option of walking back into a cushy number on civvy street. So I intend that my record is going to show the Navy can't afford to let me go. Doing my duty is not enough. I intend to prove to my country that it cannot do without me.' He stopped and looked at Harry, a long appraising gaze, as if trying to work out whether he'd said too much already. And then, almost as a parting shot, he said, 'We're not all handed shortcuts to distinction by virtue of our birth, like your friend Peter Dumaresq.' He pushed the signal pad over to Harry's side of the table. 'Here. The final drafts.'

Harry's probe had been rebuffed. Except that in those final throw-away words, Harry couldn't help but wonder if he'd been given a clue: a pass to a whole new way of looking at Rais, seeing not just a martinet for the sake of it, but a man driven, and frightened that he might not be equal to his ambition.

It was dark now, and they were on the surface. They could see the lights of Acquafredda a few miles up to the north, as they were entering into one of the long shallow bays that scalloped this rocky part of the coast-line. Harry was down below, on the plot this time, and Wykham on the bridge with Rais as they ran inshore. Again, Rais had chosen a remote part of the coast, this time with the railway running along the top of cliffs. Nothing spectacular, forty to fifty feet was the highest escarpment at most, but the line ran in and out of tunnels, and Rais had been day-dreaming all day of catching a train just entering or leaving one of them.

'Block a tunnel too!' he'd been ranting. 'That would really bugger them up!'

Also, deep water ran quite close inshore. Less distance to run if they needed to dive in a hurry. Harry had already traced out on the chart the contours of the band beyond which *Umbrage* would be unable to dive, the S/O zone, surface only, because there the water was too shallow. He had drawn Grainger's attention to it, and he'd merely nodded. Nobody thought much about it after that on the way in, not even Rais, who'd merely given Harry an irritated scowl when he mentioned it to him.

Grainger was leaning against the chart table beside Harry, but they weren't chatting. The control room was in red light, and the gun crew were clustered around its forward bulkhead door waiting for the word.

Rais's voice came down the pipe. 'Give me revs for four knots.'

Grainger leaned over and rang the engine room telegraph. 'Aye aye, Sir. Four knots.'

Harry felt *Umbrage* slow, then Rais was back again. 'Starboard, fifteen. Gun crew close up.'

They were turning parallel with the coast: Rais must have spotted a target. Grainger called back the order, and the gunners filed past and went up the conning tower ladder. The conga line for passing the shells took the gunners' place around the bulkhead door combing; they wouldn't be needed until the ready-use magazine had been exhausted.

Tuke was at his diving station in the ASDIC cubby; the echo sounder was in there too.

'Tuke,' said Grainger, 'what's the depth under our keel now?'

'Shoaling now, Sir,' Tuke replied. 'We had two hundred feet up until ten minutes ago, but we're down to just forty-five feet now.'

BUUMMM!

Harry felt the hull tremble as *Umbrage*'s deck gun commenced firing.

BUUMMM! BUUMMM!

But no sooner had the third round gone off than there were two new sharp bangs, different from the report of their own gun. Explosions, really loud in rapid succession, and close. That you could hear the cascading rush of water falling through the silence that followed told you how close: shells hitting the water beside them. There was a brief silence, then that too was rent by the sound of two blasts from *Umbrage*'s klaxon. And Rais yelling, loud enough to be heard down through the conning tower, 'Clear the casing! Clear the bridge!' The klaxon was the order to dive the boat.

Harry's mouth opened to call out, but no sound came; he saw Grainger's eyes flick to the plot, to where Harry had just marked *Umbrage*'s position, well inside the S/O, and he heard the Number One instantly bellow, 'Shut main vents! Starboard, thirty!' . . . orders that effectively countermanded Rais's order to dive. Grainger reached for the engine room telegraph and rang for full ahead, together. He was making a dash for deeper water.

The Wrecker immediately called back, 'All main vents indicating shut!'

And only then did Grainger stick his mouth to the voice-pipe and yell back, 'Unable to dive, Sir! We're too shallow!'

But bodies were already tumbling down the tower ladder and clearing forward, and Tuke was shouting, 'High-speed HE! Bearing three-two-zero! Closing fast! MAS-boats, Sir! For sure!'

Harry felt *Umbrage* heel into her turn beneath him, and felt her bite into the water as her motors pushed her. The diesels had been immediately shut down on the first klaxon blast, and it would take some minutes to start them up again. Meanwhile, the electric motors weren't going to be able to deliver much more than nine knots, even with the rheostats open to the gate, and MAS-boats were capable of up to forty knots when they got going. These elegant, fast little craft, more motor yacht than warship, could be armed with automatic Breda cannon and sometimes two torpedoes, sometimes as many as six depth charges. Which made them deadly to a submarine, and that was why they had to get to deep water and get down. Submarines weren't designed for gun duels on the surface against gun-armed, high-speed patrol boats. One hit on the pressure hull, and you couldn't dive. And if you couldn't dive, you were sunk.

Two more bangs, close aboard too. Harry felt the concussions through the boat, and water cascaded down the conning tower hatch. Those ones had been close. But somewhere in a back recess of his brain, Harry heard the bangs with relief: they were firing popgun cannons

– old-fashioned single-shot jobs like the one on *Umbrage*'s casing. You load a shell, fire the gun, open the breech, eject the spent casing, load another shell, fire the gun. Time. It all took time: to fire and load and fire again, but time too for *Umbrage* to use – precious seconds that might, just might, let them get away. Because if the Eyeties had been firing a 20mm Breda, or even worse, 40mm Bofors – *bang, bang, bang, bang, bang* – like that: fast, automatic. They'd have been riddled like a sieve by now, and sinking, not diving.

'There are two enemy fast patrol craft closing on us from astern!' Rais yelled down the hatch. Only he was up there now. 'Dive the fucking boat!'

But they couldn't. Not with barely thirty feet under the keel now. And anyway, Harry watching it all unfold, watching Grainger step into the middle of the control room, knew it wasn't Rais's show any more. It was going to be Number One who was going to get them out of this, or no one would, because there was no time any more. And in those flashing fractions of seconds, looking as the red light in the control room picked out every hard, selfish, arrogant and disdainful plane on Grainger's face, you knew that not the slightest notion he might fail had entered the First Lieutenant's mind.

'Wrecker!' called Grainger to the Outside ERA. 'Open four main vents . . . Trim us down . . . 'til the water's coming over the Skipper's boots!' Then to Tuke, 'ASDIC! Water under the keel?'

Tuke called, 'Going through thirty feet now . . . thirty-five feet.'

'Keep singing it out!' said Grainger, staring hard at Harry's plot. Harry, looking at it too, could see what Grainger saw: they weren't going to be able to outrun the MAS-boats to deep water.

Suddenly Grainger called, 'Port thirty!' And as the boat came around, he called a new course for her, heading directly inshore now, instead. 'Group down', and he rang for slow ahead, both on the telegraph.

Bang! Bang! Two more shells went into the water, but it sounded as though they'd missed ahead. Rais was screaming down the hatch, but Harry couldn't make out what he was saying.

Grainger nodded to himself, a little grimace of satisfaction on his face, then he yelled up the tower, 'You must stay on the bridge, Sir! Can you see the enemy?'

He turned to Harry. 'They can't see us,' he said. 'The Eyeties can't see us. They must have been firing on our muzzle flashes. Bloody crappy old ordnance. Fucking Admiralty'll throw nothing away.'

For Harry, leaning over the plot, the physical reality of what was happening had a shape now, he could make sense of it; the MAS-boats must have been in the shadow of the headland to the north of the bay. That was why the lookouts hadn't spotted them as they waited for the enemy submarine to show up, as it had on every previous night, and start attacking the next switching station. And when *Umbrage* had opened fire, they had their target and were now closing on it.

And that, Harry realised, was why Grainger was doing exactly what he shouldn't be doing: heading inshore. As far as the Eyeties on those MAS-boats were concerned, the only sane thing for the enemy to do was to turn and run for it to open water, and dive. But Grainger had known he couldn't escape, so he stopped running for deep water, and was taking them inshore, and into the shadow of the land to hide their silhouette against its loom, just as the MAS-boats had done when they'd set their ambush. And just as *Umbrage* hadn't been able to see the MAS-boats then, Grainger was now hoping the MAS-boats wouldn't be able to see *Umbrage* now.

Grainger called the course change to bring them on a parallel track to the coast. Harry, just by looking at his own plot now, could see they were already deep in the land's shadow, while out there, on the dark water, the MAS-boats were closing fast on where they believed *Umbrage* was heading, while, in fact, she had slunk quietly off to the side. *That was some fancy footwork you just performed there, Mister Grainger*, he thought to himself, with a smile.

Tuke called out, 'The high-speed HE . . . Both targets are coming up fast . . . They're passing us to starboard on heading two-zero-zero degrees. They're both going to pass us, Sir . . .! Still going flat out, Sir.'

But they didn't need Tuke any more. They could all hear the high-speed whine now as it reached them through the water, and through the steel of *Umbrage*'s pressure hull – the same demented sewing-machine sound Harry had heard before, that curdled you like ripping linen. Harry sketched their progress across the plot. Then he marked their own. Their course was already taking them over a looping contour marking the limits of the S/O line. It wouldn't be long now.

Then Tuke called, 'Fifty feet beneath the keel, Sir . . . Sixty feet!'

The noise of the MAS-boats was fading to nothing now. Grainger leaned to the voice-pipe and called, 'Now, Sir! Down the hatch.' Then he turned to the Wrecker: 'Open all main vents, periscope depth.' And he hit the klaxon twice to order the dive.

In the sudden noise of the vents blowing, Rais's voice cut through, a weird echo from the tower, '. . . Two clips on!', and he plunged into the control room, stumbling to his knees on the deck plates.

'Depth?' called Grainger.

'Twenty feet!' came the response from the Wrecker. The conning tower would be under water now, and the periscope stands. *Umbrage* was down at last; down, but far from deep.

Rais's face was eerily calm, as he levered himself up to his feet, and then he turned and leaned over the plot. Looking at it, Rais could pretty well judge where *Umbrage* lay, relative to the shore, and where the MAS-boats were, rushing away. He said nothing. But before Harry could wonder what his silence foretold, Tuke burst in.

'HE! Two high-speed targets closing fast, bearing red-twenty!' he called.

The MAS-boats had reversed their course and were coming back at them. But how could they have seen . . . Of course they hadn't seen! They'd heard. A diving submarine, flooding tanks and venting air makes one hell of a bloody racket. If the MAS-boats were able to fire on their muzzle flashes, they'd certainly be able to charge towards their noise.

The whining started again. They could all hear it, rising to an intense scream, as it went directly over their heads. And as the noise was passing, they heard the deep slap of something very heavy hitting the surface of the water, a mighty splash directly above them, and then the noise had passed, still moving fast, but moving away, out over deep water. And then two sounds together. The first was another splash, further off, ahead. But the other was a bloody great *CLANG!* and everyone in the control room felt it as well as heard it. And right in front of Harry's eyes, the two periscopes, snugged down in their wells, seemed to jump up, and then were dunted downwards again. And almost instantly, the gland packing around them failed and the grease alone that smoothed the running of the periscopes as they moved in and out of the boat could no longer hold back the pressure of the sea. A dozen or more flat, dancing planes of water began jetting down into the control room, drenching the Coxswain, and the planesmen, and the Wrecker on the trim, and Grainger too. And almost instantly there was another reverberating clang, louder this time: the sound metal makes, when it crashes against and bends and twists other metal, and suddenly it was as if a great hand had reached down and slapped *Umbrage's* conning tower sideways, so she wobbled like a bouncy toy.

Every eye looked upwards, towards the scraping on the conning tower.

'Midships,' said Rais, back in command, and just as the words left his lips . . .

BUUDUUDDUMMM!

The noise came through the bow: a shock wave that hit the boat, as if she had been grabbed like a tweaked nose, and shaken. 'A depth charge,' said Harry, stating the bleedin' obvious for the likes of the Wrecker and Grainger, but not for everyone; not for the younger lads in the control room. 'Off the starboard bow, but not that close,' he said, because the sheer terror in some of their eyes told him he needed to. 'Warm-ish you might say, but nowhere near boiling hot. Not yet.'

His words got a few weak smiles, as they were meant to: look at us lads, staring it in the face and laughing. Then the smiles were wiped off.

'We don't need the running commentary,' said Rais, deliberately not looking at Harry. 'Keep your mind on the plot, Mr Gilmour. It was looking a bit raggedy-arsed the last time I tried to read it . . . Where are we now?'

'A little under two hundred yards off the beach, running parallel, course one-seven-zero, speed three knots,' replied Harry, without even referring to his plot.

'Well,' said Rais, ignoring him and looking up instead, addressing the control room, 'I don't think we have to ask who the unwanted guest is upstairs, bumping around in the attic.'

They could all hear something large rolling around above them. The older hands all knew what had happened – one of the Eyetie depth charges had actually landed on their bridge and was still stuck in it.

'What were the chances of that happening, eh?' said Rais, all light-hearted now. 'But not to worry. No, no, no. Depth charges only explode when they reach the depth they're fused to, so as long as we don't go deep, we're all right . . . probably. Ha! Now all we have to do is see it off the premises.'

Rais, all banter. Ho! Ho! Ho! But the mood was gone. He'd killed it with his snapping at Harry, and he couldn't bring it back. Everybody in the control room had realised what the Navigator had been trying to do with his commentary, and understood. And all he'd got in thanks was his nose in a poke. So it was back to business as usual with Rais. What had happened would be all over the boat by change of watch.

Two more distant bangs, but they were heard not felt. Depth charges, but a long way off. MAS-boats didn't carry many depth charges, they must be out, thought Harry. But he didn't say anything. He didn't dare.

'Tuke,' said Rais, 'what are our friends doing?'

'They've moved out off the starboard beam now, Sir,' Tuke replied. 'Bearing zero-nine-five. Seem to be carrying out a search pattern, Sir. Slow speed. They're a bit of a way away.'

Rais issued orders for them to turn now, and head directly away from the coast. It was over.

There was no doubt in Harry's mind that Grainger had saved them.

While Rais had still been on the bridge screaming orders that could not be executed, Grainger had taken command without a moment's hesitation or even word of explanation.

In those vital seconds, he'd countermanded his CO's order to dive the boat. And when he'd realised he'd stood no chance of beating the MAS-boats to the deeper water, that he was in a race *Umbrage* was never going to win, he again without hesitation changed his plan, opting to dodge them, instead of trying to outrun them.

If Grainger had been obeying Rais's orders, they'd all be dead.

But Rais was back in command again. And he was issuing orders. They were going to head further down the coast, staying inshore where he was certain the MAS-boats wouldn't look for them. Then sometime before first light, they would come up, inch by inch, until it was just the conning tower hatch that was above the water. A handful of their burliest Stokers would then go up and manhandle the damn thing over the wall and into the Oggin, that hopefully would be barely deeper than their keel so as not to disturb its pressure fuse and blow them all to kingdom come.

And then they'd head for home, their two unfired torpedoes notwithstanding. You couldn't hunt and sink an enemy with no periscopes to see through, and no one was in any doubt, their periscopes were well and truly buggered.

Just after 05.00 local time, the Stokers went up into the conning tower. There was a bit of a problem at first because of the way the depth charge was lying; it was jamming the tower hatch shut. Rais didn't want to surface completely and send the boys up the torpedo-loading hatch. For some reason, after everything, he'd suddenly become nervous about having sailors clambering all over the casing and conning tower in daylight. Grainger trimmed the boat using main vents so the conning tower was awash, and when she was five degrees down angle aft, he ordered 'Group up!', and they tore off at full ahead, together. The wave coming over the conning tower casing washed the depth charge backwards amid several tearing metal screeches, but at least the damn thing had moved, and the tower hatch was clear. The port ballast tanks were partially flooded to give her a list so the side of the tower hung clear of the casing. The damn thing wasn't that much of a beast as it turned out; the Stokers estimated it at barely more than 350 pounds.

'Don't bloody waste time weighing it,' Rais had hectored them. 'Get it over the side.'

So over it went, on its way into forty-seven feet of water, with the men giving it an extra heave, silently imagining it was something else they were heaving over the side.

The periscopes, when Grainger went up to inspect them with Parry-Jones, were indeed totally unserviceable. The depth charge had hit the stands slap-bang in the middle, putting a huge vertical dent in them, and twisting the tops of each periscope tube outwards, so that depending on the angle you looked at them, they resembled that most English of rude gestures. This was a major dockyard repair job they were looking at. Home, it was going to be.

The conning tower fairing aft, too, was all bent and bashed in.

They dived, and Harry went directly to the chart table, and began plotting a course for the Sicilian Channel. They couldn't risk the more direct route down through the Straits of Messina, with all its shipping, not if they couldn't see what was happening upstairs. Harry decided he needed a cup of coffee, so he went forward, heading for the galley. Wykham was on watch, standing behind the helmsman. God knows what was going through his mind, right now. What a bloody awful patrol it was turning out to be. What was going through Harry's mind was: we should have expected them to come after us, coast crawling, doing the same thing night after night. We might as well have posted a sign. How could I have been so stupid. How could the CO? And why didn't Grainger say something?

But as the kettle boiled, his thoughts were interrupted by the sound of two people entering the wardroom, next door aft. Almost immediately a low conversation started up and quickly became more intense. It was Rais and Grainger. They'd been aft for a confab with the Warrant Engineer, Mr Crabtree, about fuel and repairs. Now they were back. Harry eavesdropped. He couldn't help it, and pretty quickly he wished he hadn't.

'. . . So, perhaps, Mr Grainger,' Rais was saying, 'you'd like to explain to me, why you deliberately refused to dive this boat when directly ordered by me to do so?'

Harry leaned his head into the passage. He could see Grainger who was sitting facing him, and Rais, the back of his shoulder sticking out so close Harry could touch it.

Grainger looked as if he'd been slapped. He wasn't looking at Harry, instead his mouth opened to reply, but Rais interrupted, 'Or under whose orders you decided to assume command of this boat, while I, her Captain, was still on the bridge?'

Grainger and Rais were looking at each other. The unreality of what was happening froze Harry. Everything. Everything was wrong. Again.

'Do not answer those questions now, Mr Grainger,' said Rais, in a thoroughly reasonable voice. 'We will be addressing them at greater length later. In the presence of higher authorities. I will be entering the events and your name in the log. Meanwhile, I expect you to attend to your duties until we have returned to Malta. Carry on.' And then Rais noticed Grainger was looking at something over his shoulder, and he turned. It was Harry, of course. Grainger had finally noticed his head around the galley partition wall. And now Rais was looking at him, with a look of undiluted loathing.

Chapter Eleven

Harry was sitting on his own, propped up on his single cot in his little stone cabin, at the back of the Lazaretto. Shirley's letter was in his hand.

He was a bit drunk. It was what you did, after you'd tied up in front of the entire wardroom, who already had drinks in hand, leaning over the Lazaretto's gallery to admire the mess your conning tower and periscopes were in. You stepped ashore and went up and joined them. At least that was what Harry and Grainger had done. Wykham they left behind, to supervise the half a dozen poor sods and their pails of Izal and their cleaning; along with Parry-Jones, who had to wait to explain why their periscopes were in such a mess to the boys from the periscope workshop, and to help them rig the little derrick mounted in front of the wardroom, to lift them out. There was other damage, too, to repair: from the depth charge that had gone off under their bows, and then from all the other depth charges: all thirty-seven of them that had been dropped during five hours' worth of sustained attack they'd endured off Marittimo Island, two days ago as they'd been limping home.

God, it had been an awful patrol. So, for the initial relief, there had been Scotch. Harry had taken his first one from the concerned hands of another young Sub. 'Welcome back, Jock,' he'd said. 'You look like you really need this . . . and the next five that are standing off, waiting to join.'

After the second, he'd found he didn't mind all the ribbing, about their bent periscopes and their Jolly Roger.

The fact they hadn't even been able to fly their Jolly Roger properly, entering harbour, had caused much hilarity. Because they couldn't raise the bent periscopes to fly it from, they'd had to resort to a clumsy jury-rig from the re-rove aft jumping wire, which had parted when the Eyetie depth charge had hit their periscope stands, to a cleat at the base of the conning tower. Which meant you couldn't properly make out all the little home-designed emblems, cut out of cloth and sewn on by the Bosun. These depicted all the demolition jobs they'd carried out on the Italian railway's electric switch gear: nearly two dozen little red boxes, with little lightning flashes on top, for the electricity they conducted, and a ragged bite out of each, representing the holes *Umbrage* had blown in them; nor their one white silhouette of an electric loco.

Nor the one white bar for a merchant ship sunk by torpedo. There had been a debate about whether they should have sewn that on. But they had.

On their way home, periscopes or no periscopes, Rais had taken them into an attack. Using their ASDIC alone, they had fired their two remaining torpedoes and there had definitely been one detonation, but nobody knew what it was they'd hit, and nobody knew whether they'd sunk it, because that was when the depth-charging had started. What a story that had been.

But they'd made it back, and Harry was here now with the letter he'd so wished he'd read before, because he'd been convinced he was going to die on that last patrol, because as he'd said to himself often these days: *Why not? Everyone else is.*

He'd brought his last scotch with him, so he took a belt, and then slid his fingers along the letter's seal. It had been many places, this letter, following him through the Navy's labyrinthine mail service, posted from Glasgow, all those months ago. A lot had happened since. He'd been halfway around the world and back, and he wondered what had happened to Shirley in that time. He knew she was still alive from his mother's letter, lying open on the bed beside him. And that she was still driving an ambulance in Glasgow. And that she still asked for news of him.

It wasn't much of a letter, he could see that right away – no newsy, chatty ramble like she used to write to him. But then he hadn't been expecting that. Not this time.

On a hill behind the town, he'd been back on leave after that battle in the Russian fjord that officially never happened, back to recover from his wounds, and awash with self-pity that he intended to wallow in. And Shirley too was back for a wee rest, because she too had been through things, driving her ambulance in Glasgow. And she had come looking for him, knowing where to find him, because she needed him. But Harry hadn't been interested in what had happened to her – *Had you, Harry?* asked the little voice in his head.

So when Shirley had sex with you, Harry, there on the hill, it had come as something of a surprise.

You only found out later what she'd been taking a wee rest from. Cleaning up after the Clydebank Blitz. And in need of someone to make her feel alive again, because all the people she'd met there hadn't been.

He waited until the little voice shut up, then he started reading:

> *My dearest Harry, I am sitting down to start this letter, and I don't know how to. But I've been putting it off for too long. What do I want to say to you? The truth, I suppose. Well, as I see it. Then I hope you'll write and tell me if you see it that way too. Wouldn't that be wonderful? You always told me everything and always told me the truth, even when it did not make you look very manly or heroic. So I owe you nothing less. We both know what happened that day, so there is no need for me to spell it out here. But what I want to spell out is why. I needed comforting that day and that*

*was why I came looking for you. Not for your sake, but for
mine and I wasn't prepared to wait. Or ask. You didn't see
that, did you? You weren't paying attention. You were somewhere else. But I took what I needed anyway. And in keeping with the spirit of truth telling, I want to tell you now
that I am not sorry I did. Because I love you. There, another
truth. Now, I want you to tell me the truth. Tell me what
you feel, Harry. I would like to know. It will be better for
me to know. Whatever you tell me, I will understand. And I
will swear to you now, never to take anything from you ever
again that is not freely given.*

    God keep you safe, my darling,
    Your loving Shirley XXX

John, the Maltese steward, was passing by the junior officers' cabins
with a tray full of glasses to be washed when he heard sobbing come
from one of them. He stopped half a step to listen, then carried on. Best
to. If they were sobbing, they were letting it out. Whoever it was would
be all right eventually; he knew his boys.

Two other Tenth Flotilla submarines were in from patrol apart from
Umbrage, and Harry was slumped on one of the wardroom gallery's
easy chairs, wreathed in smiles and sipping pink gins with the CO of
one of them: his old friend and former First Lieutenant on *Trebuchet*,
Malcolm Carey.

'We'll have din-dins here,' said Malcolm, deciding, him being a
Lieutenant and therefore senior. 'Then we'll head over to Sliema to the
ERA Club. I'm not going to the Union Club, Katty Kadzow or no Katty
Kadzow. We won't be able to hear ourselves think in there, and I want
to hear all your news.'

Harry could barely conceal his pleasure at finally catching up with Carey, glad that *Umbrage* had still been in dock when *Nicobar,* Carey's boat, had come in. But then *Umbrage* was going to be laid up for some time. That depth charge, the one that hadn't gone off, had done considerable damage to her periscope hoists and sealing glands; the conning tower hatches needed reseating too, and repairs were not progressing well, or so he'd heard. And, having been temporarily co-opted on to Shrimp's staff, he was in the best place to hear.

Harry had wanted to know about *Nicobar*'s last patrol. 'A peach,' Carey had said. 'We must have shortened the war by at least ten minutes.' He was being modest, of course. *Nicobar* had sunk a total of six thousand tons' worth of Eyetie merchant shipping in just one outing. But what Carey really wanted to talk about was what Harry had been up to, especially with their old friend Grainger. But first Harry told Carey about his wheeze with the bundle of Italian coastal pilot books he'd found, and that Shrimp now had him working on, full-time, translating. Carey had listened and had concluded, 'You know, Andy Trumble always said you were a sneaky little bastard, Harry. And he was right. Thank God you're on our side.'

Now they were talking about *Umbrage*'s last patrol, their voices hushed. The tall, always smiling Aussie's obvious pleasure at seeing Harry again had disappeared, replaced by a very glum face. The long, stretched-out pose had gone too, and he was sitting scrunched up, listening to every word.

Harry did not discuss morale aboard *Umbrage*. He wasn't out to do a hatchet job on his CO, and he knew Malcolm Carey enough to know he wouldn't have wanted to hear one. All Harry would say about Rais and Grainger's relationship was that it was 'difficult'. Carey, who already knew Grainger from his time on *Trebuchet,* filled in the rest for himself.

But the main reason Harry had broached the subject was that he needed to talk to someone about the trip back with no periscope.

'The weather was good to us,' said Harry. 'No overcast, just the usual tramontane streamer stuff, so we were getting lots of good star sights, so we always knew where we were when we surfaced at night. But it was surfacing without an all-round look first. I don't mind telling you, I couldn't believe how much it worked on my nerves, but it did . . .'

Carey let out a small guffaw. 'Really?' And then both of them had a little laugh at that, knowing exactly what the other meant.

'Our ASDIC man, Tuke, he was bloody good,' said Harry, 'probably saved us a few times . . . But without a damn periscope, you can only know so much about what's waiting for you. Your ASDIC man can't hear a shagbat overhead, or a MAS-boat just drifting, so her cook can catch a load of *lampuki* for their tea.

'Anyway, it was daylight, late afternoon, we were off the mouth of the Golfo di Cofaro, waiting for nightfall so we could surface and get down to Marittimo with our diesels getting a full charge on, so we could dive and do our run through the minefield the following day. And what happens? We pick up a lot of HE, coming up behind us. It was the enemy convoy the latest intelligence report was alerting all boats about. And there we were in a perfect attacking position, but we couldn't see. Yet the CO decided he was going to attack anyway, on ASDIC. The two torpedoes were readied. Our ASDIC lad counted five separate contacts. Three, he reckoned were destroyers. One was likely a small merchantman, the other something quite a bit bigger. He explained to Rais it was impossible to know the range – ASDIC doesn't do accurate range – but you know that. Rais didn't seem to, and wouldn't listen. Christ, he shouldn't have needed telling. "Guess," he said, having spent the entire patrol and all previous ones, bawling Tuke out *because* he'd been guessing. So we got on what we thought was the track angle, dialled in Tuke's estimate for target speed, range and bearing into the fruit machine, and we fired a two-shot salvo on the deflection angle that came out. And one minute, twenty-seven seconds into the torpedoes' run, bang! And that's when they turned on us.

'Five hours it lasted,' Harry added. 'It wasn't as bad as what Jerry flung at us off North Cape. But bad enough. And we couldn't go too deep, because no matter how much the Wrecker kept trying to repack the periscope glands, every time we went down, they unpacked themselves and pissed water all over the control room. There were shorts . . . sparks . . . bangs, and not many of the crew had been through a depthcharging before. So you can imagine. Still, no reports of vented bowels or bladders. They were good lads, everyone handled it.

'But even when we thought it was over, and it was dark, we still daren't risk surfacing.'

'Certainly not,' said Carey. 'Your CO got that right. The destroyer's favourite trick. If they lose you, ring all stop and wait and see if you come up to check if the coast is clear. Then they run you over.'

'It got really rank in the boat,' said Harry. 'The air was really bad. And what with all our charging about trying to dodge them, and me not knowing from one moment to the next whether I was going to have to change my nappy, I didn't know exactly where we were. All I knew for certain was that out there were a lot of little islands and a bloody great minefield that stretched all the way to North Africa.'

Carey exhaled, long and loud. 'Bloody hell, chum. But you made it back.'

'We did,' said Harry. 'Thanks to our CO. He's a bastard. He's not interested in his crew and he's reckless, but he sinks ships and he gets away with it. And that's all any of us know about him. I don't even know where he is now.'

Carey considered his drink. Eventually he said, 'I know where he is, and a bit about him too. So does Shrimp', and he paused, as if reflecting how much to confide. Then he decided, 'I'm not sure Shrimp will have approved of your ASDIC attack. He's very strict on how his Skippers calculate their risk. Every boat here is worth its weight in gold. And so are their experienced COs. Horton apparently told him to treat us like Derby winners. Don't go barging in unless you're confident – and that was his exact word, confident – that you're going to get away with it, or the prize isn't really worth the candle.'

Harry nodded, then asked, 'What do you know about Rais?'

'I'm not gossiping, so don't expect me to.'

'Heaven forefend!'

Carey snorted. 'Okay. But mum's the word. He goes and stays with a family up on St Paul's Bay. Some retired diplomat. A civilian cup-bearer to a past HM Governor. Your CO has been here before. Med Fleet. But he has other connections too. When he's in mufti. Big-time connections.'

'He told me he didn't have any connections,' said Harry.

'Really?' said Carey archly. 'Well, maybe not the ones he wants. I'm led to understand, however, that he moves in rarefied circles. So one of the senior pongoes told me. One of the ones with an "Hon." in front of his double-barrelled moniker. But there are complications apparently. It's a matter of Lieutenant Rais not being quite "the thing", if you get my meaning. Apparently some of his fellow "circlers" are not exactly on side. And some are downright sniffy. So I'm told. So a lot of chips on shoulders.'

'I have no idea what you're talking about,' said Harry.

'Jesus Christ, Harry,' Carey sighed. 'I thought you Poms were tuned into all that subtlety stuff. His pedigree on daddy's side is top hole, unfortunately he was born on the wrong side of the sheets.'

Harry's eyebrows shot up. Everything suddenly made sense. *Well, well, well, young Clive,* Harry said to himself. *You must really be out to prove yourself, and then some.* 'How rarefied a circle are we talking about?' he asked.

'How rarefied do you want to go?'

Chapter Twelve

Harry, Wykham, Lieutenant Hume and two other Subs had walked off Manoel Island to have lunch at one of the local cafés on the Sliema seafront. It was one of Hume's favourites, and the owner especially liked him, because, despite it being *really* against the rules, Hume always brought him bags of real coffee, almost impossible to get now for the local Maltese.

It was early afternoon, and although it was another bright, sunny day, there was a chill in the air. The young officers sat round, muffled up, drinking from a large glass jug of sharp-tasting *vino blanca* and tucking into a huge plate of fried sardines and pimentos. Harry was just taking a napkin to his greasy lips when he saw him come on to the far end of the café's patio. Tall, with his hair blowing in the light breeze from beneath that RAF cap that still looked as if it had been slept in, and still wearing the khaki battledress tunic and the Oxford bags and the disreputable suedes.

The patio was mainly full of other officers, a mixture of all three services, the locals being too sensible to sit out in the cold. A waiter emerged, and the new arrival stopped him. Harry wasn't quite close enough to hear what he was asking, but when the waiter pointed in the direction of Harry's table, he heard him say, 'They're the submariners . . . the scruffy ones?' The new arrival walked over. No one but

Harry had noticed or heard, but they were each being scrutinised in turn.

'Is one of you . . .' the RAF officer began, and then his face lighting on Harry's, he said in a voice laden with arrogant presumption, 'You're Harry Gilmour, right?'

Harry, looking back at him with the same candour, thinking, *Cheeky bastard*, replied, 'And you're Twally.'

The RAF officer didn't like that. 'Chally,' he said, 'but only to my friends.'

'Really,' said Harry. 'Well, I had better call you Toby then, Flight Lieutenant Challoner.'

Chally didn't like that either, and Harry got an inkling Chally wasn't used to people talking back to him like *that*. He went back to eating his sardines, leaving Chally just standing there, seemingly at a loss what to say next.

Harry, growing up, would never have been so abrupt with anyone, but Harry, a serving submariner, couldn't be arsed humouring arseholes.

'I wanted to meet this chap my girl is always talking about,' said Chally eventually.

Harry fed himself another forkful of sardine, dabbed his lips with the napkin, then scooped up his wine glass and sat back with an insouciant smile. He could tell Chally expected him to say something, so he didn't. The others around the table were just starting to notice someone else had joined them. When Hume looked up, he recognised Chally immediately, and put down his fork and wine glass to do the introductions.

'Gentlemen,' he said, with an expansive gesture, but not bothering to get off his backside, 'it's the Great Chally-ostro! The D.W. Griffith of photoreconnaissance! Every film an epic!' And while he talked, he pulled a chair out, and Chally sat. 'Do you know that when this man popped over to Taranto last year, to do a last-minute count of the Italian Fleet,' Hume continued, 'just to make sure they'd be in when *Illustrious's*

Swordfish came a-calling, he flew so low so as not to miss any, that they found a ship's aerial wire wrapped around his tail wheel when he landed. Now that was just showing off, oh great Chally-ostro! Admit it!'

Harry turned to look at Chally, expecting him to be embarrassed at all this ham adulation, but what he saw instead was the man lapping it up.

'I met your boyfriend yesterday,' said Harry, as he dropped the past few days' translation on Katty's desk to be typed up. He saw her head go down slightly, like someone preparing to hear bad news, the kind she'd heard before. 'He's invited me along to see your set on Friday night,' Harry added, and she looked up again, a smile, coupled with a wrinkle of perplexity, on her face.

'I'll be nervous, knowing you'll be in the audience,' she said, all faux modesty, 'and I'll be terrible!'

Looking back on it, the days Harry spent on Malta through November 1941 all seemed to run into each other. If it hadn't been for the Italians' half-hearted attempts at air raids most nights, it might have been a holiday.

During the day, he worked his way through Capitano Massimo's remarkably elegant prose, then he delivered the results to Katty who typed and bound them while the RAF photo lab reproduced and appended any relevant illustrations. And then he carried the finished briefings back to the Lazaretto's wardroom, where the Navigators from boats going out on patrol could refer to the particular stretch of coast they were headed for, and update their charts.

Two consequences of the work were that he got to spend numerous hours killing time and idly dallying with the glamorous Katty while she worked, talking away about nothing in particular. That was the good one. The other consequence was that he frequently found himself the butt of endless tedious wardroom jokes about being Shrimp's swot – doing extra homework for teacher: 'Did you get a gold star in your exercise book for that one, Harry, or just a silver?' – and the odd barbed ones, too, about his 'going-inshore-made-easy' guides, and how good was his Italian anyway? One adjectival clause, mistaken for a subordinating conjunction, and some poor bloke could end up killed.

Then on his odd days off he got to borrow a bicycle from one of the base officers, which meant he could go anywhere on the island within the 'get back before dark' radius, but only on the understanding that he filled the saddlebags with any harvestable vegetation, dead birds or animals, or general rotting gash he came across.

'For the pigs,' was the explanation given by Lieutenant Commander Pop Giddings, a former wine merchant and reservist, now turned base Executive Officer: for the Tenth had its very own herd of porkers, and if Harry wanted to continue eating bacon, he'd better start foraging. '*You* don't have to think it's edible, lad,' the elderly Pop had explained, 'as long as the pig does. *You're* not looking for "food", you're looking for what "food" likes to eat.'

It was hard work pedalling up the hills behind Valletta, but the views up the island, when he got there, made it all worthwhile: the barren, white, sun-blasted rock of the place, almost treeless. A landscape of stunted scrub and thin soil, where what there was of it was shielded from being blown into the sea by a vast, interlinking network of thousands of low limestone walls, like a patchwork quilt across the whole island. Sometimes, if he started early, he could get to the small towns of Mdina, Imtarfa, Rabat and back easily in a day. These little white stone hilltop fort settlements, with their church towers and red tile roofs peeking over their bastions – it was beautiful, otherworldly for a lad from the north, almost biblical. Malta: all you got was a mere 120 square miles of it, according to the maps. On paper, it didn't sound much: smaller than the Isle of Wight, almost half the size of the Isle of Man. But it was the views from up in the hill towns that showed you how small that really was.

Or the days when it rained, and he left the bicycle propped up by the pigsty, and took a *dghaisa* over to Valletta to the little bookshop, for long chats with its owner, the little man in the brown overall coat. Louis, his name turned out to be: half-Italian, half-Maltese, and island aristocracy before his fortunes had taken a turn for the worse. How that had occurred was never discussed. Books, music, philosophy, history, yes; even politics and how Louis for years had been pro-Italian, until he was repaid for his loyalty to the maternal side of his family by that bastard Mussolini dropping bombs on him.

It was only after that conversation that Harry decided he'd got to know Louis well enough to risk asking the question he'd longed to ask every islander.

'You must hate us British,' he'd said one afternoon when they were trying a very nice brandy that Louis had been saving.

'Why?' said Louis, puzzled.

'For dragging our war into your lives.'

Louis paused to make sure Harry knew he was taking the idea seriously, before saying, 'Don't be stupid.'

It hadn't been the answer Harry had expected. He was stunned into silence, so that Louis felt obliged to expand. 'Centuries come and centuries go, and so do powers who want to control the Mediterranean. We can't fight geography. We know we live on its pivot, at the centre of the world. Last century it was you British who came. This century you're still here. D'you think we'd rather have the Germans? No! So shut up and start savouring the taste of that brandy before I fall out with you.'

At the end of November, they threw a wardroom 'at home' for Peter Dumaresq. He brought along several of his officers from *Pelleas* at Shrimp's invitation. The evening had been a tearing success, everyone who could still speak agreed. When a dull-looking Shrimp had turned up for work the day after, and his Chief Petty Officer Writer had inquired how it had all gone, the only words he got out of the Captain (S) were, 'Heavy casualties.'

But it was the trips to the RAF HQ and Katty, and the cosy banalities of their inconsequential chit-chat that Harry really enjoyed. He just liked to be with her, to marvel at the many different ways she managed to pin up her hair, the little thrill he'd get every time he made her laugh or even just smile, and the way her skirt would trace the shape of her leg, and how her fair skin took a tan. And then there were the nights listening to her perform at the Union Club. At those moments, he forgot how strange that little world was, stranger still the fact that he had stepped into it. He always sat with Chally and his set. Chally insisted. To any outsider, looking in, it was as if Harry had been adopted as some sort of 'mascot'. And while Miss Kadzow performed, he would lean on the table, chin on palms, and watch enchanted, never noticing how Chally from behind that detached expression of his, would study him.

It was another life, one he'd never expected to live or dreamed might exist, but it stopped him from having to think about Shirley and her letter. All that stuff she had written;, it was far too grown up. He wanted to write back, of course he did. And he wanted what he would write to be mature and honest, but he didn't know how to do it. Every time he tried, emotions crowded in on him – many he wasn't proud of.

November came and went, and all the while that Harry caroused in Malta, five hundred miles to the south-east, the armour and infantry of the Eighth Army were racing across Cyrenaica, relieving Tobruk and its mostly Australian garrison, under siege for over 240 days now; driving back Rommel and his Afrika Korps, and the entire Italian army, then back again. At the RAF HQ in Malta, the chaps in the photoreconnaissance room had their own map on the wall, showing the huge bump of the North African coast, all the way from the Egyptian border, to El Agheila with other place names on it like Sidi Rezegh and Gazala. Little ribbons pinned to it marked each day's advance, always moving in the same direction. West. People were even muttering the word 'victory'.

And each day, while Harry translated, and flirted with Katty, he could hear the RAF Blenheims and Wellingtons taking off from the airfields at Takali and Luqa, and then returning to rearm and go again; pressing home attack after attack against the convoys sailing from the Italian mainland, laden with food and bullets and petrol, trying to keep Rommel's army in the fight. The Fleet Air Arm Swordfish would take the night shift, flying after dusk from Hal Far on the south of the island. And also, each night, while Harry sat listening to Katty sing, Force F now joined by Force K, would head to sea to fall on those same convoy routes under cover of darkness; night actions, fought among the star shells, the piercing searchlights, and the flashes of heavy guns, picking off the Axis merchant ships that had survived Shrimp's U- and N-class submarines, strung out on their patrol lines off the enemy's main ports to the north, where the fighting Tenth were wreaking their own toll with gun and torpedo.

Meanwhile, *Umbrage* was still in dockyard hands, being put back together again. And then, on a quiet Tuesday afternoon at the start of December, the phone rang in the photo-recon office: it was one of Shrimp's Leading Writers, telling Harry that Hubert, the XO, was looking for him and that if Mr Gilmour knew what was good for him, he'd be presenting himself back at the Lazaretto, quick-time. Or words to that effect.

Chapter Thirteen

The chaos below wasn't as bad as it might have been, given the short, pounding seas that buffeted them. *Umbrage*'s crew hadn't had time to load all their clutter back aboard again before they'd been ordered to sea. There were some toolkits and spares bins and even most of her crockery still ashore in the Lazaretto's stores; all hauled off before she'd been handed over to the dockyard workers. They'd never have seen their crockery again otherwise. So on board, there was little to fly about as the boat plunged and rose through the stormy dark night.

On the bridge, it was only the whipped and flying spume off the wave tops blown flat that told Harry he wasn't just staring into nothingness. *Umbrage* was five hours out of Marsamxett Harbour, and halfway to her designated patrol line off Linosa Island. Harry had the watch, while the CO and Grainger sat, or more accurately clung on below, pinning a chart of the Sicilian Channel to the bucking wardroom table, and discussing their tactics for the next forty-eight hours.

There was a gregale blowing – a full north-easterly gale, driving a furious sea that hit *Umbrage* just abaft her beam, lifting, twisting and rolling her 196-foot-long hull off each short, steep, punching wave. The two lookouts, tethered and hunched below the rim of the bridge so only their binoculars showed, scoured the sea ahead, each knowing neither had any chance of seeing anything on a night like this. Harry, braced against the periscope stands – now repaired, and upright again – made no pretence at navigating or trying to con the boat in any way. Like the lookouts, he could see nothing beyond the raging tempest in his face. He concentrated on the only thing he could usefully do, and that was trying to stop the worst of the water going down the conning tower hatch. So he stood staring straight into the seas rolling towards them, watching for the next goffer – Jackspeak for a big one – in the hope that his body would part the wave before it all went down the open conning tower hatch; and maybe be in time to yell, 'Elephant's trunk' to the boys below, so they could quickly swing the canvas trap rigged by the lower lid, to catch whatever deluge would swirl past him. Letting a full column of seawater down the tower and into the boat might short out their electrics or get into their battery acid and fill the boat with chlorine gas.

Anyway, it would be getting light soon and they'd be diving.

Shivering in the cold, and his face numb from the wind and rain blowing straight at it for hours on end, Harry was trying to remember when he had been called to the phone. Had it only been that afternoon? One minute Harry had been teasing Katty about her 'artistic difference' with the Whizz-Bangs, the island's own little cabaret troupe, and why she 'would never work with them', and the next he was back aboard *Umbrage*, with orders to 'get her ready for sea, yesterday'.

Their submarine had been lying around the corner on a pontoon on Lazaretto Creek, with a lot of shore staff on her, finishing up the repairs, doing snagging work. Harry was told nothing, except to round up all the crew billeted in the little private apartments the base had rented in Sliema, and to get aboard. All the dockyard gash had to be bagged and ready to be dumped ashore, and lists made of just the necessaries to get to sea and stay there for two to three days maximum. While Harry went below to do that, Grainger was ordering, 'Cast off, fore and aft', and moving her out into the harbour. 'The torpedo store on Msida Creek,' he'd yelled back, when Harry had yelled up in horror, 'We're not going to sea right now? Are we?'

They went around to the store on motors because there were a couple of big bits off one of the diesels that the Warrant Engineer still hadn't managed to fit back on yet. Wykham had been left in the stores with another handful of ratings to do a smash and grab on anything he could lay his hands on, from twelve-pounder shells to tinned peaches.

It had been well after dark when they'd finally slipped out into this bloody gregale, the crew still trying to stow the last of the supplies they'd just flung down the hatches when the boat started bouncing.

Shrimp hadn't told them what all the rush was about until the very last minute.

'Last night, six large Italian merchant ships with a substantial destroyer escort made a dash from Palermo into the Gulf of Hammamet,' he'd told the officers from *Umbrage*, *Norseman* and *Uttoxeter*, as they stood in a loose gaggle on the wardroom gallery, some of them, like Harry, still breathless from having run there. Outside, they could see *Unleashed* already heading to sea.

'The ships, which are laden with supplies for the retreating German and Italian armies, are now anchored off Sousse, protected by shore batteries and a considerable fighter cap. I have since, however, received a signal from C-in-C informing me that they intend to make a dash for Tripoli tomorrow night or the night after, and that several major units of the Italian fleet are intending to sortie from Palermo to cover this operation. I intend for you gentlemen to set up a patrol line across those warships' path to stop them from doing that. That will leave Force F free to intercept the merchant ships, and stop their supplies from reaching Rommel.'

So that was what all the rush was about. Good old-fashioned Royal Navy 'urry up! His whole time in the Andrew, up until that moment, Harry had never understood the point of it. Well, Jesus Christ! He did now. And why they had to be good at it. To be ready for moments just like this.

'The SOO will give you your rail chits,' said Shrimp, finishing off the briefing. 'I've scribbled out your positions on billet on the backs. Good luck, and good hunting.'

As Harry tore out of the door, he saw Rais and the other two COs gather around Hume.

Hume, the SOO, tearing off chits from his book of railway warrants, stolen off some RTO's desk back in Pompey probably: War Department-issue rail tickets entitling sailors going on leave to free train travel. It was Hume's joke to get Shrimp to write his orders on them: 'Patrol between such and such degrees north, that degrees east, etc., etc.', and the departing CO would sign the stub to show he'd received them. Shrimp obviously wholeheartedly approved of the wheeze. No one ever accused him of not liking a laugh. 'Oh, that Captain (S),' Hume would gleefully confide to any new CO heading out on his first patrol, 'he's a devil for his paperwork.'

Harry had run back to his quarters to collect his charts and Lexie Scrimgeour's precious sextant. And there was that other matter. He had probably just three minutes to do what he should have done ages ago, and then get aboard.

Writing paper, pen, an envelope. There was every chance this might be the last letter he would ever write.

My darling Shirley,

He hadn't time to rehearse excuses why it had taken him so long.

Not a day passes when I don't take out your letter and read your words. I know them by heart. That is where they are burned, anyway. So I ask you to please understand this. I have tried many times to write and tell you

*how I feel, to give you the comfort you deserve. But every
time I sit down to do it, I know it is not in my power to
promise you anything freely. As I write this, I am going
on patrol again. You know what I do and where I serve.
And you must read the newspapers and know what that
means. I worry about you. Shirley v. the Luftwaffe isn't
a fair fight. Take care of yourself, and if there is anything
left of me after this, you will get your answer in person.
Harry XX*

And it went in the postbox as he went past at a run.

Standing on *Umbrage's* bridge, getting beaten in the face by a full gale, seemed a good start for what he deserved for writing that mealy-mouthed scrap of self-pitying, self-serving, overblown, evasive, weaselly . . . and he couldn't come up with any other words sufficiently damning to round off what he thought of himself right now, about what he had written to Shirley; the letter that was now winging its way to her.

Why hadn't he given her an answer? Why had he not just told her how he felt? Or, more to the point, why didn't he know himself? He could have told her that; after all, it was the truth. But no, he *had* to go and write that letter. Just had to. Before he sailed. And that was the best he could come up with. Maybe the damned boat carrying the letter would get torpedoed. But he couldn't wish for that; a whole load of other poor blokes ending up in the water; just so as he wouldn't have to look like the utter shit he obviously was. And how come every time he thought of her, he managed to feel an ache in his chest, and ashamed of himself at the same time?

Another goffer came over, and he stepped in front of the hatch, and yelled, 'Elephant's trunk!'

At twenty-eight feet, periscope depth, *Umbrage* was rolling like a drunken sailor. From the bearing Rais had just sung out for Linosa Island, Harry calculated on the chart that they were as good as dammit, right on the billet scribbled out for them by Shrimp. To port, on a line extending to the Kerkennah Banks, would be *Uttoxeter* and then *Unleashed*, and to starboard, *Norseman*. Together they were throwing a cordon over forty miles long across the neck of the Sicilian Channel. If the Italians were coming this way, one of them would spot them.

'Good enough for you, Navigator?' The first words Rais had spoken to Harry since they'd dived at first light. He had been a right bastard since they had sailed, uncommunicative and snappy.

'Yessir,' said Harry, about to add 'on billet now', when Rais interrupted him.

'Ah-ha! Shagbat on green-fifteen.' He followed it for a few moments, walking the periscope round. 'I think he's lost,' he added, standing up, and closing the handles. 'Anyway, no point in staying up at this depth to get bounced around, I'm going to take her down. Down periscope!'

There was a hiss as it went down, leaving Rais standing in the middle of the control room, feet apart to balance himself against the boat's rolling, arms folded, fingers rapping on elbows and looking very unhappy.

'Why are we still at periscope depth, Clot?' he asked, in a voice all ham weariness.

Harry, like everyone else in the control room, including Grainger, looked up. Here we go again. Cled, not Clot – his full title of address being ERA Cledwyn Parry-Jones – being old in the ways of the Andrew, immediately stood to attention.

'I heard no order, Sir,' he said. He did not point out that he had his most experienced Leading Stoker on the dive board again.

'Really. I distinctly heard myself say "I'm going to take her down", and yet nothing is happening.'

'Sir? You didn't order . . .'

'How about we try pointing downwards first, for which you might find the use of Q tank would be beneficial.' Rais's voice was now dripping with sarcasm. 'I don't know where you trained, but when I say we are going down, I expect Q immediately to be flooded. How does that suit you . . . Clot?'

The Leading Stoker's face had turned white, and his hands on the valves were white-knuckled.

'Aye aye, Sir,' said Mr Parry-Jones. 'Open Q Kingston, flooding Q!'

Harry thought to himself, *Did I really hear that? He's expecting people to be opening valves and operating systems without orders? He's going to get us killed at this rate.*

Grainger, who must have thought the very same thing as he lounged against the chart table next to Harry, drew himself up to assume the job he should have been doing all along. 'I have her, Wrecker. Planesmen, ten degrees down angle.'

. . . and down they went.

Rais left it a long moment before ordering, 'Maintain eighty feet. Mr Grainger, you have her.' And he stepped through the for'ard control room bulkhead and vanished into his bunk for a lie-down.

As they passed through fifty feet, Harry noticed the planesmen seemed to be wrestling with her, as if the boat were bucking under them – nothing a little deft valve-twiddling by Mr Parry-Jones couldn't fix but it jogged something in Harry's brain. Then he remembered the chart notes. Had they just dropped through a thermocline, into water of a different salinity? It would explain why *Umbrage* needed to get heavier to continue her dive, why she needed the extra ballast to overcome the greater buoyancy around her. The First Lieutenant needed to know.

'We're crossing into another current, Kit,' he said in Grainger's ear. The First Lieutenant turned to look at him, with a frown on his face.

'There's a current flows through the Sicilian Channel, from the western Med basin,' said Harry, tapping the notes on his chart. 'We've been motoring against it. But it's a surface current. There's another deeper current runs underneath, going in the opposite direction from east to west. It's more saline, and usually a lot deeper. But there's less than one thousand feet under us right now, so maybe that deeper current has got pushed up around here. Anyway, I think we just bumped through the layer between the two. I'm not sure how fast this deeper current runs. I've got no references on board. But it's going to affect our position. We just need to think about it.'

Grainger smiled, and nodded. 'Do that.'

The day passed.

Then, about an hour before sunset, Rais appeared back in the control room, and without saying a word hit the night alarm twice. 'Diving Stations!'

Musgrave had been in the galley getting his ingredients ready for the crew's breakfast. Harry, by the chart table, could see him through the control room door, having to chuck everything into a big pot and stow the now unusable mess pronto; as the crew thundered through the boat to close up.

'HE?' called Rais.

'No HE,' said Tuke from the ASDIC cubby.

'Twenty-eight feet,' said Rais. Periscope depth. Rais snapped his fingers. Unbelievable, thought Harry. Parry-Jones hit the lever anyway, and the periscope slid up. Rais did his all-round look. Harry could see the sunlight shining out of the eyepieces, reflected on his face as he went round. When Rais sent the periscope back down, he saw Harry looking at him. Harry had no idea what expression he'd had on his face, but Rais looked as if he'd been slapped.

What had he seen? Then it dawned on Harry, and probably on everyone in the control room: he hadn't expected it to be still daylight. If he'd bothered to glance at the chronometer . . . but no. And yet he was committed now.

'Surface, Mr Grainger!' said Rais, pausing before adding, 'That means I want to go up, for all those who need asking twice.'

Orders and responses, and *Umbrage* began to rise. Harry wondered about advising Rais about the currents, and how they might be off billet by now. But his heart sank at the prospect, and it sank even further when he accepted that meant he was becoming as bad as Grainger.

And *Umbrage* was about to surface into broad daylight.

Even though, as everybody knew, that if there were major units of the Italian fleet heading this way anytime soon, there'd be shagbats everywhere, looking for submarines.

'I'm going to take a sighting to make sure we're still on billet, and I'm going to cram as many amps into our batteries as possible before we meet the enemy,' Rais announced to the control room. Rais justifying himself? Had that really happened? Was he apologising for surfacing while the sun was still up? There was no point in thinking about it: Rais would do what he was going to do.

Harry was glad to see Parry-Jones on the trim board for all the little tweaks that might be required to bring her up smoothly, and that he had the Leading Stoker back on the dive board, showing that he trusted him. *Umbrage* began to roll again as she came up into the turbulence being churned up by the still raging gale, and Harry wondered if that was why the poor Leading Stoker was looking slightly ill.

Umbrage was really lurching now: a beam sea. Rais went up the ladder and opened the lower conning tower hatch. His two lookouts had already filed into the cramped space beneath him. While all this had been happening, Grainger, who had made no comment on the wisdom of surfacing in daylight, had stepped into the wardroom and had now re-emerged, buttoning himself into his Ursula suit; he was going up too. Harry wondered why, then it dawned on him. To try and head off any tantrums if it turned out Harry's current had indeed pushed them way off billet.

Grainger looked at the depth gauge. 'Ten feet!' he called up into the tower. The upper hatch would be clear of the surface now. They all heard Rais yell back, 'One clip off, two clips off', and as he did, a deluge of water came down on them. Grainger went up into it, following the CO to the bridge. Harry immediately called the periscope back up. He wanted another look. It wouldn't take a shagbat a moment to pop over the horizon. Handles down, and he had his face slammed against the rubber rests, and he began a low-power scan of the horizon. He saw it almost immediately, no more than a dot as he began turning the periscope, and then, because it was so low, it vanished behind a wave. He leaned back, a quick look at the bearing on the bezel above his head.

'Possible aircraft contact, green-five!' he yelled at the top of his voice, leaning back so he was shouting it up the hatch. Doing it because the control room messenger was still trying to get a bucket up under the bridge voice-pipe, to catch the water that drained out of it when you opened the lower voice-pipe cock. Harry couldn't make out the shout that came back from the bridge – a yell lost in the noise of the wind and sea in the hatch.

Then everything happened at once.

'All main vents indicating open! Flooding Q!' It was the Leading Stoker on the dive board, yelling as he spun the valves. He was diving the boat. Why the hell was he doing that? Harry glanced: the lad looked manic, sweat standing out on his forehead despite the chill in the boat with the hatch open. Harry braced to feel *Umbrage* begin to fall away beneath him, but instead he felt her begin to rise. He didn't understand . . . then she began to lean over. A wave had them. A goffer. A big one. There was another unintelligible scream from the bridge, and suddenly a full bore of sea came down the hatch, everyone instantly knee-deep in water. And flushed down in it was Grainger: a flailing body being blasted on to the control room deck plates, except before he hit them, the water abruptly shut off to a dribble, because Grainger, as he had come through, arms flying, had snagged the hatch stirrup on one of his Ursula suit sleeves and dragged it shut, and the column of water coming down the upper hatch behind him had slammed the hatch against its seals, and was now holding it there.

Harry was instantly up the ladder, dogging the hatch down, water pissing all over him, *Umbrage* falling away beneath him now. Fast, then faster. He could feel fear pulse through the control room.

That wave. It must have swamped them: one of those big bastards that when they broke over you it was like being under water. Was that what Rais had been yelling back at him? A goffer was coming? And Rais? He must still be on the bridge. But he couldn't think about that, nor that the Stoker on the dive board was diving the boat. No one had ordered him to do that. My God! The bloody CO was still on the bridge, the Jimmy had been on his way up. The boat had surfaced. And now it was diving again. And the conning tower above him was filling with water. And they were going down fast, falling like a stone. Harry had to stop the dive.

'Full ahead, together! Full rise on the planes! Shut main vents! Blow Q! Stand by main ballast tank, blow valves!' Harry heard the orders being called; before he realised it was his own voice talking: not yelling, or screaming, like the pressure in his chest made him want to, but cool and firm and clear. 'Mr Parry-Jones!' he called – not Clot, with a sneer, like Rais. Not Wrecker either. 'On the dive board now, please. What's our depth?'

'Going through one-eight-zero feet, Sir, and diving! We are very heavy, Sir!'

'*We are very heavy, Sir!*' The words you never wanted to hear on a submarine. The planesmen's heads turning; the Cox'n, Chief Petty Officer Libby, on the helm, looking back at Harry, his face lined with alarm. And the other Chief in the control room, Big Jonners, alarmed too. Those were sights Harry never wanted to see either. And Harry thinking, *Jesus Christ!*

'Put another puff of air into one and six main ballast! Planesmen, twenty degrees up angle. Mr Parry-Jones, start pumping from M tank,' Harry, hearing his own voice again. His best 'orders' voice. Nobody looking around themselves now, wondering what was happening; doing their jobs instead.

'Two-zero-zero! . . .' Mr Parry-Jones continued to call; another calm voice, and methodical; 'Two-two-zero! . . . Two . . . Zero-zero again, Sir . . . Rising . . . One-seven-zero!'

'Mr Parry-Jones! Bring us up to sixty feet and then hold us at that depth, please. If we need to, cycle one and six main vents to hold her, and please inform me. And when you trim us, remember we have a flooded conning tower.'

'Aye aye, Sir. Maintain sixty feet,' said Parry-Jones, definitely not a Clot now. *Umbrage* rising, planing up; back up, under control again. Harry looked down at Grainger, a sodden heap on the deck plates; something not right in the way his left arm was flung out; the side of his head open, and blood, in swirls through the sloshing seawater. And where was Rais now? He knew the answer before the question formed. Rais was gone. Overboard. A tiny speck, floundering alone for a moment, on a storm-whipped ocean, with no life jacket to support him, only sea boots filling with water and a sodden Ursula suit to drag him down. And that bloody Leading Stoker. Where was he? There he was, ashen, still standing by the dive board. Frozen to the spot.

'Mr Parry-Jones,' said Harry, 'relieve your Leading Stoker, please. Tell him he is to confine himself to the Stokers' mess until I send for him.'

'Aye aye, Sir.'

Then Harry turned to the control room messenger. 'Petty Officer Bell to the control room. And tell him to bring his medicine bag.' Dinger Bell, who treated all the minor gashes, crushed fingers, the runs and fevers, as well as looking after their torpedoes and guns. It looked like he was going to have his work cut out fixing up Grainger. Harry would worry about that later. He turned and called up the for'ard passageway.

'Two ratings to the control room, now!'

Two sailors suddenly appeared, and were promptly told, 'Get Mr Grainger into the wardroom, please, and get all his gear off', and then, leaning back again, 'ASDIC: anybody about up there?'

Suddenly, everything was business as usual in the control room. You could no longer feel the pulse of fear that had run through it, gone now.

Tuke, leaning out of his cubby, said, 'No, Sir. But, Sir?' Something in his voice. Harry turned to look. Tuke was frowning, like he wanted to explain something, but . . .

And the 'but' Harry understood immediately. Serving under Lieutenant Rais had made Tuke reluctant to sing out.

Harry took the three steps to the cubby. 'What is it, Tuke?'

'You know when you were mentioning to Mr Grainger, Sir, about the currents.' Tuke looked apprehensive. Why? Harry was suddenly worried, until again it dawned on him. Tuke wasn't concerned about the currents, he was concerned about speaking out, and was now shitting himself because he was confessing to having eavesdropped.

'Yes,' said Harry, trying a winning smile, 'I'd noticed the planesmen seemed to be wrestling with her, as though the buoyancy had suddenly changed. I thought it might be a thermocline, which was why I mentioned it. Was I right?'

'Oh yes, Sir,' Tuke all grins now. 'It was. I just wanted to say what it means, Sir. The change in water temperature especially, rather than the actual current, Sir. It means you probably don't have to worry about anybody upstairs, Sir. As long as we're still under it. Any Eyetie anti-sub kit, it won't be able to pick us up under the temperature layer.'

'Thank you, Tuke,' said Harry. 'Useful to know.'

'Sixty feet,' sang Parry-Jones.

Chapter Fourteen

It had been a big wave. *Umbrage* had begun to rise on it, and it had broken over them, right at the same time as Harry had been calling out, 'Aircraft!' and not hearing what the CO had been screaming back. The Leading Stoker on the dive board hadn't heard either, but he had heard, 'Aircraft!' And he knew only too well how the CO's wrath fell upon any hapless Jack who didn't jump fast enough, sometimes even before he'd been told to. So he'd asked himself: what normally happens the minute someone shouts, 'Aircraft!' You dive the boat. So he had dived the boat. Harry would worry what to do about him later. Right now he had the Cox'n, Chief Roscorla, Parry-Jones, and the Warrant Engineer, Mr Crabtree, in the control room and they needed to discuss matters.

'Firstly, gentlemen, we have a conning tower full of water above us. I intend to stabilise the boat before any attempt is made to recover the CO,' said Harry, in charge now. He hadn't made any announcement to that effect; he didn't have to. *Umbrage* had only two officers left standing, and Harry was the senior one.

Umbrage's four most senior rates each nodded grimly. Stabilising the boat? Mr Gilmour would get no argument out of them about that. That water had to go. A conning tower full of it made them unstable, especially in that transition from dived to surface. Right now, they were still at sixty feet, steering 110 degrees, and their motors delivering revs for three knots, just enough to counter the deep current trying to wash them into the western basin.

'The conning tower drain valves are working, Sir,' Parry-Jones had told Harry, 'but there's no water coming through the system. It's blocked somewhere.'

Harry took his cap off and rubbed his face, as if trying to rub into it all the coolness and detachment he felt a CO needed to show his crew at a time like this, but struggling. Thinking to himself, *What next?* Mr Crabtree cleared his throat. 'We have a set of separators, Sir. I can prise the hatch off its seal without you having to open it. It'll let the water jet out of the hatch. But it'll take a while.'

Harry looked at them all in turn. 'I don't see what good draining water out of the lower hatch is going to do, if the upper hatch is open to the sea.'

'Actually, Sir,' said Parry-Jones, 'I think there might be some good news . . .' and he trailed off, looking at Big Jonners. And Big Jonners said, 'We don't think the conning tower is full of water, Sir. Me and Mr Parry-Jones, we think the CO shut it before he . . . well, was lost.'

Harry didn't dare ask, he just stared hard, willing the news to justify their optimism.

Parry-Jones spoke first, being the Outside ERA and knowing about trim. 'It doesn't feel as though the tower is actually full, Sir. We've kept a very careful record of how much we've had to pump out from M tanks to get back in trim and it just doesn't equal a conning tower full of water. By our calculations, it's probably not much more than half-full. And that means the upper lid must be shut. If we could just get most of the water out first, we could open the hatch and let what's left flood into the bilges and pump her.'

Poor Rais, thought Harry, for the first time. And he had a momentary vision of the cherubic little face, drenched in spray, clinging as huge cold lumps of Mediterranean sea swirled around him, vanishing into the conning tower of his boat. He would have known the lower hatch had been shut, and would have felt *Umbrage* falling away beneath him. He must have sensed whatever was passing for the line between the surface and the deep on that raging sea, going past him: clinging there, alone and nowhere to go. He must have made the conscious decision then to jump on the upper hatch, and physically slam it down, hoping as the boat dived, the water pressure would effectively seal it shut, and himself off from all hope of saving.

'Do it, Mr Crabtree,' said Harry, trying to look like a CO. 'Mr Roscorla, see if you can rig the elephant's trunk to funnel what comes pissing out more directly into the bilges. I'd rather not have to wear my sou'wester while I'm standing watch.'

'Aye aye, Sir,' said Mr Crabtree, although you couldn't see his mouth move beneath his big, black, full set – beard and 'tache – that sat across his big round head like thatch and climbed like liana up the side and into the line of his oily watch cap, which he touched with an oily fist, and was gone.

'Aye aye, Sir,' said Big Jonners, with his jaw set firm in complete approval of his orders.

'Mr Parry-Jones,' said Harry, 'it is my intention that we hold here. We're not going anywhere until the tower has been drained, on the principle that it's probably better not to rock the boat while she's in this condition, unless it's absolutely necessary. What do you think?'

'Oh, aye aye, Sir! Most definitely. Best not to rock her.'

'Carry on, Mr Parry-Jones.'

Harry turned to Wykham, standing back by the chart table, who was staring at him with his mouth slightly open like some groundling in the Globe Theatre's yard, watching a particularly ripping performance of *Henry V* or *Tamburlaine*. 'Mr Wykham,' he said, trying not to smile, 'you have her. I'm going to see how Number One is doing.'

Three steps and he was in the wardroom. Grainger had been cut out of his Ursula suit, and was lying stripped to the waist, face down on the back banquette, his skin looking fishy-white in the pale glows from the space's two cosy little sidelights. A big torch sat on the deck: they'd obviously needed more light at some point, but it was out now. The table had been unshipped to let Mr Bell get at him. Everything looked surprisingly neat and homely and the air was full of a reassuring antiseptic smell. Bell was kneeling, finishing swathing the First Lieutenant's upper torso in bandages, and was being assisted by a Leading Torpedoman, who was helping prise Grainger up off the table, while Bell did another turn of bandage around him, each movement accompanied by a gurgling grunt from Grainger.

'The noise you heard earlier was Mr Grainger,' said Bell, whose sailor's bashed-about face had none of the sympathy you usually saw when sailors were helping wounded shipmates. Harry hadn't heard any noise. Too distracted, probably. He pushed himself in to kneel beside Grainger's head, trying not to stare too hard into the slice in it, which looked exactly like what it was – two folds of meat held together with cross-hatched gut, and a smear of iodine yellow down the ragged edge.

'You'd've screamed too,' said Grainger wheezily. His face was grey and lined with pain. Harry hadn't heard any screams. Too busy, definitely. Funny what you screen out when you have to. He turned to look at Bell, who was kneeling beside him, his lips tight as he glowered at his patient. Harry was close enough to see beads of sweat in the man's two-day whiskers.

'Mr Grainger has a compound fracture of his left shoulder blade,' said Bell through gritted teeth, 'as well as the head gash. His noise was caused by us having to shove the bone back in place, but mostly because Mr Grainger refused a morphine jag. There's almost definitely a severe concussion as well.'

'What state are we in?' said Grainger to Harry. He wasn't talking about his own shoulder, nor his head. Harry looked back at Bell; he understood now, the glowering. It couldn't have been easy for him and the poor rating, dragged in to help. Hard work, trying to reset a shoulder blade that's sticking out through your patient's back; trying to push and shove it back into place, knowing you are inflicting agony; and the patient is flat refusing a pain-killing blast of morphine that will shut him up and let you concentrate on what you have to do, without the distraction of his cries in your ear. Harry noticed for the first time the blood and gore soaked into Bell's grubby white pullover. When he looked at the Leading Torpedoman, his was covered in blood too.

'Everything is under control,' Harry said to Grainger.

Grainger went to give a nod of his head and Harry thought he was going to pass out. 'Right,' he managed to say eventually, his other cheek still pressed into the banquette cover, 'this is what we have to do.'

Splat! Splat! Another two handfuls of sodden signal flags landed on the control room deck plates. The tower had been drained at last, and the Chief and two ratings were up there inspecting the damage. That was when they'd discovered why, when the tower had filled with water, they couldn't drain it.

The water that had come jetting into the tower had hit their little signal locker – a tiny lattice box, tacked to the tower's steel side, that held the boat's collection of signal flags; kept for tradition mostly. It wasn't often a submarine had call to hoist flags to communicate anything. But the water had blasted the locker full on, and flushed out every single flag in it, and washed them into the tower's drain holes, blocking and choking every one of them. That was why the tower wouldn't drain. Harry ordered them stowed somewhere where they couldn't do any more damage. Bloody things!

It was dark on the surface now, and already close to midnight.

It had been three hours ago when Crabtree had brought his device from the engine room. It looked like a model of some medieval siege engine, or an actual-size torture instrument. They had fitted it under the tower hatch, and prised it up until the water came out in a solid blade into the elephant's trunk, sluicing it into the space made by a lifted deck plate, and on into the bilges – the pumps there going full belt to get it overboard, burning amps and more amps doing it. The battery was going to need another hefty charge, so it was time they went up.

Grainger had passed out again, so Harry didn't consult him. They'd already had their conversation, and he knew the plan. He sent *Umbrage* to Diving Stations, bow into the oncoming seas, and up they went. It was when Harry got on to the bridge, the two lookouts following him, that he began to feel a little more confident. The wind had all but dropped and the seas were definitely abating. And he was away from Grainger. The First Lieutenant might be out for the count at the moment, but he was still propped up in the wardroom and swaddled in blankets, because no jacket would go over that shoulder; his cap stuck on his head, because he'd ordered it. Grainger continued to refuse morphine because he said he'd need his head clear if the Eyeties showed up, but no one looking at him believed he would be in any state to launch an attack.

Umbrage, her CO lost and her First Lieutenant incapacitated, should have been heading back to Malta. But Grainger had been adamant. 'We can't leave a hole in the line,' he'd told Harry. And with a fistful of painkiller pills in him to take the edge off his pain, he'd explained it all: everything Shrimp had told him and Rais, and Rais had said must be kept from the crew.

An Italian squadron was coming their way, probably tonight.

If they left a gap in the patrol line, the Italian warships might slip through and get in among the Force F ships hunting Rommel's supply convoy. Nor could they warn Shrimp to plug the gap. If they surfaced and radioed in what had happened to them, their transmissions would be picked up. The Italians might not know what they were saying because it would be coded, but it would be confirmation that a patrol line was out there, and they would be coming on alerted, the element of surprise lost. They had to stay on the line. And stay quiet. Grainger would command. That was why he was refusing morphine, to keep his head clear, and Harry would be his eyes.

Once on the bridge, Harry had his sextant passed up; through the rat-tails of high scudding cloud he shot Saturn and then Mars rising. Then he got Wykham up to take the watch, and he dropped down to the chart table to work out where they were. They were way east of their billet. He began to plot a course back to where they should be, and worked out how long it would take to get back there. Bugger. He was hoping he would have both diesels pumping in charge right now, hove to, marking time, not having to sprint to get back on the line. So many things going through his head.

'Mr Gilmour to the bridge!' It was Wykham. What now? Harry shot back up the ladder, and there, fine on the bow, and low on the dark horizon, a fireworks display was going on.

Harry raised his night glasses. There were individual searchlights, and tracer in the air, and there, like a fleeting shadow, the silhouette of an aircraft, then out to the right, another. Distinctive, kite-like shapes: biplanes. Darting in and out like mayflies, above the indistinct bulk of a number of ships, he couldn't tell how many from the confusion of shapes, but they were spread across a good thirty degrees of horizon.

'It's the Hal Far Swordfish,' said Harry. 'They're attacking . . . it must be the Italian squadron.' Harry bent to the bridge voice-pipe. 'Stop, together,' he said. And he waited while the thump of their diesels died, and suddenly the distant rumble of anti-aircraft fire came drifting to them over the water. Then he said, 'ASDIC. Any HE?'

Back came a voice out of the pipe: 'Multiple high-speed HE, red five to green-two-zero. But they're a long way off, Sir.'

Umbrage's own racket ceased, had let Tuke pick up what other sounds were in the water.

Harry bent to the voice-pipe again and ordered the diesels back online, thinking to himself, *That's handy, we can really start cramming in the amps while we're hove to.* Then he said, 'Mr Wykham, you have her up here. Keep an eye on that lot and tell me if anything changes', and then he was gone, sliding down the conning tower ladder. When he hit the deck plates, he tapped the control room messenger as he went by: 'Tell Mr Bell, tubes one, two, three and four. Prepare for firing.' Two steps later, and he was squeezing in beside Tuke in the ASDIC cubby. 'Right, Tuke, what have you got?'

'Multiple, Sir. Coming on fast. I'm counting three heavy, and definitely five, maybe six smaller. All high-speed turns, Sir. Easy pushing thirty knots. Smaller ones almost certainly destroyers. The heavy screws, I'd say they were cruisers, Sir. Coming right down our throats, Sir.'

Bloody Norah. Harry stepped out into the control room, and he and Big Jonners' eyes met. Everybody had heard everything, of course; the crew at their stations, waiting. Harry, wondering, *What in God's name do they expect me to do?* Then he saw the look in Big Jonners' eyes and it made his throat tight, and the hairs stand up on his neck. Harry recognised it right away, and knew it: it must've been seen on the decks of every British man-o'-war for the past three hundred years, that look a Royal Navy fighting sailor gets, when he knows he is about to engage the enemy more closely.

'We're starting the attack, Mr Roscorla,' said Harry. *Of course we are*, said the set of Big Jonners' jaw.

Harry lifted the sound-powered phone. 'Mr Crabtree, what's the state of the charge?' Everyone else in the control room saw by Harry's thin smile that he'd liked the answer. He reached for the engine room telegraph and rang for full ahead, together, then he hit the night alarm for Diving Stations, and said, 'Mr Parry-Jones, trim us right down on number four main ballast tank, decks awash.'

Umbrage closed up for action, and Harry stood behind the Coxswain in his seat at the helm, and told him, 'Make your course three-zero-zero, Mr Libby.'

Mr Gilmour in charge now, and wasn't it all a different game from Lieutenant Rais? Harry all 'Mr-this', and 'Please-that'. Okay, so everybody knew what Harry was up to. Saw through it. But then, at least everybody was clear now on what they were supposed to be doing, with orders coming fast but clear, and no having to second-guess. He might be just a one-ring, Wavy Navy wonder boy, with a jawline yet to frighten a razor blade, but here he was taking them into action, and you had to hand it to the lad – he wasn't fluffing it.

Harry took the two steps for'ard to the wardroom. They could still see his bum sticking out into the passage.

'Kit . . . Kit . . . It's Harry, Kit,' Harry said, leaning to speak into Grainger's ear. He could see the First Lieutenant was awake now, but his eyes were glazed. Harry didn't know if it were the concussion, or the constant pain. With a sickening feeling, he knew he was wasting his time before he spoke. 'We are in contact with the Italian surface units, Kit. What do you want me to do?'

'Attack,' wheezed Grainger. 'We must get into position to attack. I am coming to the control room . . .' And Grainger suddenly rose to his full height, physically brushing Harry back on to his haunches, so that as Harry looked up at him, he saw Grainger's eyes roll into the back of his head, and his jaws practically dislocate as they opened to let out a scream so loud, that it felt like a needle go through Harry's ears. And then Grainger fell, like a tree, so that the other side of his wounded head bounced off the passage wall. Harry, up in a moment, pulled Grainger straight in the passage and shoved him into the recovery position.

'Messenger!'

The young rating was there in an instant.

'Go for'ard and get Mr Bell's assistant scab-lifter here, and tell him he's to administer a morphine shot to Mr Grainger. And tell him that is an order. Understand?'

The rating nodded furiously, before remembering to say, 'Aye aye, Sir.' Harry slapped his arm and sent him off with a 'Good man!'

He was alone now. No referring to the Number One. He stepped back into the control room and flipped open the voice-pipe and asked Wykham, what the enemy was doing now.

Harry, standing in the control room, thinking: *This is one of those moments you will remember for the rest of your life*, and then thinking: *However long that might be*. Right now he wouldn't be taking odds on it. He pressed his eyes shut, and told himself: *Get your head into the box, and think it through. The enemy's there, and you're here.*

Wykham told him the fireworks had finished. No more search-lights, no more tracer. The Swordfish must have dropped their torpe-does and turned for home. And no, Wykham said, he'd seen no sign their Fleet Air Arm chums had scored any hits. All he could see was the seemingly solid body of shadow now, thundering onward, heading to pass off their port bow. Just glimmers in the dark.

'ASDIC?' said Harry.

'Still multiple high-speed HE, Sir,' said Tuke, 'bearing red-two-five. Confirm nine targets. Three heavy, six light, Sir. And they are still stick-ing to it. No zigzag yet . . . I'm picking up a lot of echo sounder now, Sir. They're pinging, Sir. Blasting the water ahead of them.'

They're looking for subs, Harry thought to himself, looking for the likes of me.

The control room seemed awfully tight now, all pressed in, in its red light and all the sharp unnatural shadows it threw. And Harry thinking, *You're it now. In command.* Wanting to go and grab Big Jonners and shake him and plead, *What do I do?* All that history, coming all the way down to him, right here, as he stood on these deck plates, aboard this stinky steel pipe called HMS *Umbrage*, on a faraway foreign sea.

'Tuke. Call me back your last three bearings on the target!'

Tuke obliged and Harry scribbled them down on the plot; marked them up and drew a line for each. And as he did, he found himself recit-ing the Royal Navy prayer, just how he'd recited it with all those other spotty hopefuls, all that time ago, stood on the wooden decking over the swimming pool in that Hove leisure centre the Admiralty had taken over, and renamed HMS *King Alfred* . . . '*O Eternal Lord God, who alone spreadest out the heavens, and rulest the raging of the sea . . . Be pleased to receive into thy Almighty and most gracious protection, the persons of us thy servants, and the Fleet in which we serve . . .*'

All the Drakes and the Raleighs and the Nelsons; and now it's your turn, Harry. '. . . *the Fleet in which we serve . . .*' Oh well, there was no one else here to get this done. So he'd better bloody well get on with it.

He worked it out: the target's mean course was 117 degrees. He stepped over and dialled 117 into the fruit machine. Now he needed a range. He called 'Up periscope!' Although they were still surfaced, he wanted to see the enemy himself. As the periscope came out of its well, he reached down to drop the handles and look. There was a Leading Seaman that Grainger liked to use when he was on the periscope – a tall, skinny lad, nimble, who could dance around with him without falling over his own feet and lean far in enough to read the bezel. His name was Low, and his diving station had been in the control room since.

'Low, behind me, please,' said Harry. 'When I call "That!", read off the bearing and range, please.'

Not that the lad needed telling, he'd done it so often. But Harry was being all very formal now: direct orders, so that everybody knew what they were supposed to do, none of that second-guessing lark any more. Which was all right with the crew. Harry, their Vasco, might still be just a lad, but he was doing all right, so far. 'Aye aye, Sir!' said Low.

But it was too bloody dark. He could see nothing. Damn and blast! He stepped to the voice-pipe, telling himself to be calm about it. 'Mr Wykham. What can you see now?'

Wykham's voice echoed back: 'Bugger all, Harry!' Mr Wykham hadn't got used to the fact his old messmate was now his CO. 'But I can hear the buggers! Bearing red-three-zero to red-two-five!'

This was no good. Harry knew he was going to attack submerged. But he needed to get closer in before he dived her. Because he needed a better look at the targets. And since the targets were advancing at over twenty-seven knots, he was going to have to make a decision in a hurry.

Harry left the periscope where it was.

He needed to begin issuing orders now, telling everyone in the control room what he intended to do. He ordered *Umbrage* under helm, turning her in towards the enemy's track, and then he told the control room crew: it was going to be a submerged attack, but they weren't diving yet. And then he shot up the ladder on to the bridge.

Night glasses to his face. Fuck his fucking night vision! What could Wykham see now? Still bugger all. But Harry could hear the Italian ships now as well, even above their own diesel thump.

He was achieving nothing up here. 'Clear the bridge!' The two lookouts shot down the hatch as he hit the klaxon twice to dive the boat.

Harry followed, securing both clips on the upper lid as he went, and slid down on to the deck plates. Wykham was already by the fruit machine, hadn't needed telling. Good lad.

'Maintain sixty feet!' said Harry, then he turned and took another quick look at the plot and then moved to stand behind Libby. 'Cox'n, steer two-seven-zero for four minutes, call it, and then turn us on to zero-four-zero,' he said. It was all starting to shape up in his head.

'Aye aye, Sir.'

But Harry had already gone, back to squeeze himself in beside Tuke again.

'What can you see, Tuke?'

Not 'hear', Tuke notes, with a little grin to himself, but 'see'. Well, well. Mr Gilmour actually understood how it worked. And he wanted to share. Share the picture all the noises were painting inside Tuke's head.

Tuke decides he doesn't mind this officer getting inside his head. Seeing as he isn't that bad a lad, for an officer.

'The three heavies. They're line astern, but a bit ragged. As though they're more concerned about running for it, than keeping station.'

'Of course they are, Tuke,' says Harry, grinning at Tuke now. 'The WAFUs' – Jack's slang for anyone Fleet Air Arm – 'The WAFUs in their Stringbags have just scared the shite out of them. And we like that, don't we?'

'Sir?' says Tuke, scowling.

'If they're running for it, Tuke, they're going to be more interested in putting distance between them and the last attack, than in fannying about zigzagging.'

'Of course they are, Sir,' says Tuke, the penny dropping, and him grinning now, back at Harry. 'The other targets, Sir,' Tuke continues, all serious again now. 'They're destroyers, Sir. For sure. Four of them are running ahead in a screen. The other two are back, on either beam of the heavies. But the bearings are changing fast, Sir, as I'm talking . . . Moving to starboard.'

'I know,' says Harry, nodding, biting his lip, 'we're crossing their track. Now what's all this about their ASDIC kit not being able to ping below a thermocline?'

'Sir. That is correct, Sir,' says Tuke. 'I don't know the exact science, Sir. Just that it's something to do with the temperature difference. The pings bounce off, or get absorbed or something. It's a phenomenon. The Commander S1 on *Medway* knows all about it, he's always going on about it to the First Flotilla lads.'

'Phenomenon,' says Harry with a smile, and gives him a punch on the arm. 'Even the slightest wobble on their bearing, yell. I want to know the instant if they change their minds about zigzagging.'

Harry has lost count of the minutes since the air attack lifted. He curses himself. The range must be closing fast now. He has to get inside that destroyer screen, before he can even think about setting up his attack on the cruisers.

'Good man,' says Harry eventually, slapping Tuke's shoulder and heading back to the control room. 'Carry on.'

They are at sixty feet now. Harry stands over the planesmen, and asks, 'How did she feel going down?'

'Like we suddenly ran on to a squashy floor, Sir,' says one. *Good*, thinks Harry, *we're below the thermocline. They can ping til they're blue in the face now.*

'Multiple heavy high-speed HE, still closing fast now on bearing red-one-five!' calls Tuke.

Then, another voice.

'Helm, turning on to zero-four-zero,' calls the Cox'n. The four minutes have passed. It's too soon to turn. Damn! Harry calls, 'Helm. Make your new course zero-zero-five!'

He marks the plot, and although he is looking at it, he is seeing a big box in his head: where *Umbrage* has gone deep, charging towards the enemy, as the enemy is charging in towards them; and he is imagining the plane of the triangle in the water they make, with the point where *Umbrage's* torpedoes must be, if they are to hit. His mouth is dry and his throat tight.

'Periscope depth!' he calls. And up they rise. He needs ranges now. He needs to know where the screen is, and where the cruisers are, behind it. Before they run over, and past him, and it's too late.

'Periscope depth,' calls Parry-Jones, and Harry calls, 'Up periscope.'

He steps in and drops the handles and Low steps behind. And right away he sees them. Moving the periscope around thirty degrees of angle, small shadows, one to port, others away to starboard, coming on fast. The screen. *You're not interested in them, Harry*, he tells himself. Moving the periscope slower now, he is screwing his eyes to see beyond, and yes: there they are. Bigger shadows.

'The bearing is that!' he calls, and Low calls back, 'Red-two-zero!'

Harry cranks to split image, and brings the top shadow down, but everything is too indistinct. He does it anyway, until what he thinks is the base of something that is just a darker smudge, rests on where he thinks the masthead must be on the smudge below. It will have to do. 'Range!' he calls, and Low calls the minutes back. Harry does the sums in his head. The range is three thousand five hundred yards! He calls it and hears the mechanical ratcheting as Wykham dials it into the fruit machine, and then he calls their track angle, and it's bang on fifty degrees. Wykham's about to call the DA for a shot, but Harry holds his hand to silence him. He's thinking: *Not at this range, or at that track angle.*

Harry slaps the handles shut. 'Down periscope. Make your depth sixty feet!'

And *Umbrage* falls away beneath them. Harry steps back towards his plot, and scribbles briefly; whatever he's drawing must be very rough, and as he does, Parry-Jones is having to make an adjustment to the trim; the outside water density is changing again.

When Wykham turns back to see what's happening, Harry has a stopwatch in his hand.

'They're doing just under a thousand yards a minute down their track,' Harry announces to no one in particular, 'and we're covering two hundred and sixty yards a minute towards it.'

Harry watches the minute hand go round.

Tuke calls out, 'No indication of any target zig, closest escorts are now at green-two-five and red-one-five.'

And then they all hear it: an Italian destroyer's propeller sounds, and her pinging; the noise coming through the hull. But it isn't hitting them; there's no telltale handful of stones rattling the pressure hull the way an echo sounder or an ASDIC beam does when it's bouncing off you. Harry wants to kiss Tuke, and the Commander S1.

Ricka-chicky-Ricka-chicky-Ricka-chicky!

And Tuke calls, 'Escort destroyers abeam now, Sir. Bearing red- and green-zero-nine-zero. Passing now, bearing's drawing aft, Sir!' But they can all hear it for themselves; they are through the screen. The pinging has stopped. They can no longer hear it, and the escorts are charging away astern of them.

'Starboard thirty, steer one-zero-zero!' orders Harry. But he needs to see the cruisers again now; he needs to come up. 'Periscope depth, bring us up fast in the turn.'

And as they rise, he calls, 'Up periscope!' Tuke calls out the latest bearing to the main targets. And Low steps in to begin his dance, holding his hands over Harry's on the handles, placing him on the bearing Tuke's just called out. Harry sees blackness . . . and then there they are again! 'Bearing is that!'

'Bearing, red-one-four degrees, in the swing,' calls Low. They are still turning. Wykham dials it in.

Harry flips the stadimeter down. 'Range!'

Low calls the minutes, Harry does the sums and calls it, 'Eighteen hundred yards!', and Wykham dials it in.

'Estimate target's speed at twenty-seven knots,' calls Harry. He has barely uttered the words, when Tuke calls, 'New HE! High-speed revs, bearing red-two-zero. Closing fast, Sir. It's another destroyer. And he's pinging, Sir!'

It's one of the beam escorts, Harry realises. He has swung the periscope, and there it is. Closer than it should be. Harry can see the bone in its teeth; its huge, creaming bow wave, glimmering pale against the shadow of its hull. Its anti-submarine equipment will acquire them any minute now.

That's a hell of a bloody speed, she's doing, Harry is thinking. He barks, 'Down periscope!' but he doesn't order *Umbrage* down again; no time to dive below the layer now, to try and dodge the enemy A/S, and be back up again to fix the targets for their final firing solution.

Ricka-chicky-Ricka-chicky-Ricka-chicky!

The sound is coming through the hull now, and suddenly it is followed by the first ping. Their depth is twenty-eight feet; well above the layer. They hear the telltale pebbles hitting their hull. They have been acquired, although the destroyer is still too far away to be an imminent threat. But it's closing.

Harry is thinking about Italian destroyer crews. Knowing how everything now depends on how efficient Italian Navy signallers are, how fast they will react. The one on the bridge of that destroyer that has just pinged them – is he paying attention as the yelling starts from the hydrophone cubby; will he understand quickly enough what he's being told, that they have acquired a submarine; and will he have a head cool enough to turn it into a signal, and signal it to the cruiser squadron's flag, and will the flag's signaller, taking it down, get it right, and how quickly will he pass to the flag lieutenant . . . Will he be in time for the flag to order an emergency course change, and turn the squadron to comb his torpedoes, so that they will all miss and run uselessly out into the night to eventually sink and detonate on the seabed. *Time, Harry, you just need time. Don't think about it. Just keep willing them to take their time.*

He consults his stopwatch. It must be close now . . . 'Up periscope!' he orders. Just concentrate on what you're looking at, Harry . . .

And suddenly he is looking at an overlapping target: the lead cruiser's silhouette, which he is sure now is a *Zara*-class, and coming on just beyond her, and behind, with her bows in the shadow of the big cruiser's stern, is the silhouette of an *Abruzzi*-class light cruiser. And they're overlapping. Making not two targets, but one continuous one – 1,700 feet long.

'Steady on course 110,' calls the Cox'n.

He is in an almost perfect position; the track angle is 117. He calls it. Then the bearing is called, and then the range. Target speed is still twenty-seven knots. Wykham has dialled it all in.

'Target track angle is 117!' Wykham calls back, then, 'Director angle is red-three-seven!'

In the periscope, Harry sees that the two ships are going to pull apart now, and become two targets again, with all the space in between for his torpedoes to miss.

'Place me on the DA!' calls Harry, and Low coaxes him round. Mere seconds pass . . . and suddenly he is watching the *Zara*, as her bow crosses the black vertical etched on his periscope eyepiece.

He'd always thought there would have been time for deliberation when this moment approached – the moment when he would fire his first war shot.

'Full salvo, fire on my command!' he hears himself say, so matter-of-fact.

Somewhere off, he is aware of another voice: Tuke, interrupting his train of thought, calling, 'High-speed HE! Now bearing red-seven-five! Still closing fast!'

The other destroyer. Harry can't think about that right now.

He is imagining his own fists with an iron grip on his lungs, so that he only has air enough to call the order, and not scream it like a girl. 'Fire one!' he says. And the control room messenger calls it into the sound-operated telephone, through to Mr Bell in the forward torpedo room. 'Fire two!'

Harry, knowing he has to fire fast, if he's to have any chance of getting two into the big 14,500-ton *Zara*-class; before her two giant steam turbines – made at Wallsend on the Tyne of all places, and sold to the Italian Navy a decade before there was ever any rumour of war – before their 95,000-shaft horsepower drives her out of his torpedoes' run.

Then there are the bumps, quick together, and the hiss of HP air. The first two torpedoes are away in quick succession, and now there is only the drip of seconds. He's counting in his head, thinking, *God, this is too fucking gimcrack*, knowing his torpedoes are running at over fourteen hundred yards a minute, and the target's range is drawing for'ard. He'd launched at nine hundred yards. What is the range now, to the next cruiser, further away and moving further?

How many seconds have passed since he'd fired those last torpedoes? He's forgotten his count. The second target, moving at twenty-seven knots, a thousand yards a minute. The range to that now, what? Twelve hundred? Less? And your torpedoes travelling at forty-five knots.

'Fire three!' he calls. Shutting off the noise in his head. It's too late now to worry. He gives it five more seconds and then calls, 'Fire four!' Then he waits for the bumps to confirm they have gone before he shouts, his voice urgent, but firm and clear. So everybody knows where they're going.

'Group up, full ahead, together! Full dive on the planes. Flood Q! Make your depth 150 feet! Cox'n! Starboard, thirty, when we hit it!'

They're getting out of the way, fast.

Will the second target still be there when his torpedoes arrive? Has he left it too late? He's wondering if he should have made time to check his stopwatch, his slide rule. But what time? From where?

Tuke calls again, 'High-speed HE, still closing fast, going to pass to port . . . passing to port . . .'

But they can all hear the HE for themselves now: the high-speed nagging, *Ricka-chicky-Ricka-chicky-Ricka-chicky!* as a destroyer tears through the water, sounding as if it's right above them. And then the splashes . . .

Meanwhile Low has produced a stopwatch of his own, and he's counting the first torpedo running time, '. . . Ten seconds left to run . . . Five . . .', as he's holding up his hand, counting off on his fingers.

RABUMMDUHDUHDUMMM!

And again.

RABUMMDUHDUHDUMMM!

But the detonations are not any of their torpedoes; they're depth charges.

Umbrage rolls with the shock wave, like a tram passing over a bad set of points. And everyone holds their breath, but the charges aren't close. And there are no other splashes; no more sounds of depth charges entering the water. Even so, no one seems to notice Low's count has gone way beyond his five seconds left; and it is as if everybody has forgotten, until they hear their first torpedo hit.

Harry scrunches his eyes so tight, he misses all the grim grins around the torpedo room, until two more *RABUMMDUHDUHDUMMMS!* brings everybody back to the now. More depth charges, but they're further away, and no one is holding their breath any more, and it's into the depth charges' echoing rumble, as it fades away, that everyone hears their second torpedo find a target.

Chapter Fifteen

There were maybe a thousand people or more lining the path around Tigne Point, on the other side of the harbour entrance, and around below the back walls of Fort St Elmo – all jumping up and down and cheering. Harry, standing on the bridge, bareheaded to feel the weak warmth of the afternoon sun on him, knew what it was for, all right. He'd seen the Maltese people do it before, for the Force F and Force K ships, when they'd come back after blasting their way through another Axis convoy. The Government Information office, aided and abetted by that fierce old biddy who ran the *Times of Malta*, would organise these welcome-home crowds using the Rediffusion service: the loudspeakers on every town and village square and city street corner that used to broadcast what should have been Malta's radio programmes, except the British authorities didn't like broadcasting radio here, on the grounds that the enemy, sixty miles away on Sicily, could hear how you were doing, what news you were listening to and how morale was.

But every time a convoy made it through, or a Royal Navy warship returned with a good account of herself, they'd broadcast it on the Rediffusion, tell the whole island, and everybody would get down to the harbour and line the battlements. Nobody made them do it. And now they were doing it for *Umbrage* and her crew. Well, fancy that.

Out on the casing for'ard, beyond the gun, stood Petty Officer Bell in his Number One jacket and cap, especially for the occasion, and the five ratings in their grubby white pullovers, hands behind their backs, making some pretence of standing at ease in a military fashion – their caps on at all angles, faces wreathed in grins, keeping looking back up at Harry on the bridge, winking. All this while *Umbrage* burbled sedately up the Marsamxett, with her Jolly Roger at the periscope stand.

There had been a big debate aboard, when Shrimp had signalled them. 'Confirmed, serious damage suffered two major Italian Navy surface units.' What were they going to sew on the Jolly Roger? One red block equalled one enemy warship sunk: that was the tradition. However, they hadn't actually sunk anything. But 'serious damage suffered', well, you couldn't let that go unremarked. They'd settled on red blocks, torn half in two. And now, every time another waft of air snapped their little skull and crossbones out, so that it showed their triumphs, a little cheer rippled around the harbour. Harry had got the Cox'n and Jim Wykham up to bask in the glory, and then sent them down to let Mr Parry-Jones, Big Jonners and Warrant Engineer Crabtree up for a look, too. Big smiles all round.

Harry called down, 'Finish with diesels', and they went to motors to come alongside and accept pride of place by mooring right underneath the wardroom gallery, where all the Tenth's officers at home that day were standing above them, waiting, drinks in hand, to hurl abuse, according to ancient tradition.

Another tradition was that the instant the gangway was aboard, the boat's CO was first ashore to report immediately to the Captain (S). But Harry, still the new boy in many ways, still the RNVR boy, wasn't first off. It wasn't that he was consciously being disrespectful or insubordinate even, he just didn't think it was right he should go wandering off until he'd got his wounded First Lieutenant safe into the hands of the base medical staff.

He'd gone below and hung around until they'd got the torpedo loading hatch open, and the doctor and two stretcher-bearers could come down to carry Grainger to the 3cwt ambulance waiting on the shore side of the Lazaretto, and then off to Bighi. Harry had sat with Grainger while they were waiting, telling him about their reception. But Grainger wasn't there most of the time. He was grey and his breathing was shallow, and his eyes seemed to go in and out of focus. He didn't speak at all, and Harry feared it wasn't just the morphine that had put him out of it. When the doctor had come down the hatch and checked him over, Harry had asked him, 'What's the score?' The doctor had replied, 'He needs a blood transfusion', and then had shaken his head. 'We'll look after him now,' he'd said.

Harry went up through the torpedo loading hatch first. His fellow officers were all there, leaning over the gallery a bare ten feet above his head, and the cat calls had started. 'Here he is!' 'Harriet, dahling! Your adoring public is waiting!' 'Stage fright, Gilmour?' But they all shut up when Grainger's stretcher appeared, and while Harry walked behind it across the gangway.

Captain Simpson was in his office, with the Hubert fellow, Commander Marsham, his deputy. They both had their caps on. Harry immediately came to attention and saluted. 'Sub-Lieutenant Gilmour reporting, Sir.'

Both senior officers returned his salute, and Shrimp said, 'How nice of you to join us', before removing his cap and taking his seat behind his desk. Harry wasn't invited to sit. He was, however, invited to make a verbal report.

Harry recited it all, from racing to get on station, to the CO being lost and the First Lieutenant falling down the conning tower hatch; the First Lieutenant ordering Harry to keep *Umbrage* where she was, on billet, no deserting her post; how she had to hold the line. And how the Italian squadron had come over the horizon in a running fight with the Hal Far Swordfish, and how it ended up with just *Umbrage* left to stop the Eyeties disrupting Force F's attack on Rommel's supply ships. And finally how they had ended up firing a full four-torpedo salvo, and scored two hits.

Shrimp listened in silence, and when Harry had finished, he stood and gestured to Commander Marsham, who turned to the filing cabinet.

'So you decided to take it upon yourself to attack?' Shrimp asked. 'No CO. No First Lieutenant. A command team of just you and an even more junior Sub, fresh off the boat from *King Alfred*? Against one heavy and two light cruisers, and six fleet destroyers?'

Harry, standing at ease, stiffened. 'Yes, Sir,' he said.

'Why?' said Shrimp, with an arch of his eyebrows.

Well, if I'm going to have to state the bleedin' obvious, said Harry to himself. Thinking, *If you're going to bollock me, get on with it;* but only saying, 'There was no one else there, Sir. Somebody had to do it.'

Shrimp came around his desk and perched on it. He nodded again to Marsham, then he fixed Harry with a steady eye and said, enunciating his words with deliberate precision, 'That is the most irresponsible . . . reckless . . . downright . . . bloody marvellous . . .' and suddenly his words wouldn't come, and he had grabbed Harry by the hand and was pumping it; and with his left hand had swept Harry's cap off and thrown it on a chair. And when Harry had looked around in alarm, Marsham was standing there by the filing cabinet's open top drawer with three tumblers gripped in one hand and a bottle of Plymouth Gin in the other.

'Bottoms up, young Gilmour!' said Marsham, and he slammed the bottle on the desk and began to pour bumpers.

Harry was sitting on a burst armchair in the corner of one of the photoreconnaissance bods' offices, while Katty typed up his latest inshore pilot translations. They were chatting, drinking fresh coffee from the stash he had purloined out of the Lazaretto stores, when Chally came in and threw a set of photographic prints in Harry's lap, before stepping over to the other burst chair and flopping into it, without saying a word.

It was an overcast, blustery day outside, and cold; and with no glass left in the windows to keep out the wind, the shutters were closed. So it was dark, even though it was lunchtime.

'I thought you were flying today,' said Katty, now concentrating on her typing.

'Uh huh,' said Chally. 'Been flying, flew back. Aren't you going to look at your snaps?' This latter to Harry. 'I risked life and limb to get you those. They're candid studies of the port area of Palermo, as of' – and he archly looked at his watch – 'two hours ago. And I think they're quite dramatic.'

Harry picked them off his lap and began to leaf; there were five of them. Sharp, as if they were shot in a studio – perfect black-and-white studies, but taken at angles far too low for a normal photoreconnaissance shoot, for a non-suicidal one at any rate. Three were of the *Zara*-class cruiser, the *Fabrizio del Dondo*, as Shrimp had later confirmed to him, and she was beached near the entrance, with a huge oil slick around her, and a huge boom, being attended to by a couple of tugs and several more tenders. The others showed the light cruiser, the *Gradisca de Isonzo*. She was in the port, alongside a jetty in the naval base with scaffolding being thrown up over and around her bow, or rather where her bow used to be, because she had lost at least forty feet of it.

Harry stared at the images. Shrimp had given him all the intelligence just this morning. After *Umbrage* had radioed in the action, Shrimp had sent *Unleashed* in pursuit to try and catch up with the retreating Italian force, and *Norseman* racing in the direction of Marittimo Island to try and cut them off. But the U-class boats were notoriously slow, and *Unleashed* hadn't made contact. *Norseman* had, but not until after sunup. And submerged, she couldn't get into an attacking position before the whole sorry caravan had pulled away. The RAF had thrown in several attacks and reckoned they'd got a couple of hits on the *del Dondo*, but it was the damage already done that Shrimp had wanted to tell Harry about.

Umbrage's first torpedo must have hit the *del Dondo* right aft on the port side, in among all her propeller shafts and rudders. The RAF reported she had developed a serious list and had one of the destroyers lashed to her port side, as if to keep her afloat. She was being towed by another destroyer, stern first. The *Gradisca de Isonzo* had been managing under her own steam, but it was precious slow progress with most of her bow blown off.

'They're out of the war,' a cheerful Shrimp had told Harry, 'for the foreseeable future at least.'

And here was the photographic evidence. Harry could hardly believe the state that both ships were in – or that he had done it. Chally, scrutinising him, saw the slack jaw and mistook it for something else.

'Pleased with our handiwork then?' said Chally, winking at Katty and nodding in Harry's direction. 'Gong assured, I'd've thought. Be able to take Mater and Pater to the Palace to see the King stick you with it.'

Harry took a moment to let those comments fully sink in. He knew Chally was mocking him, but he wanted just to soak up that image: of his father arriving at Buckingham Palace to see the King, any King, pin a medal on his son.

'. . . Pater to the Palace . . .'

Harry played with the image in his mind's eye, imagined the noise in his inner ear, the screaming and kicking that would be involved, if it were ever to be made to happen, which it wouldn't. Harry started laughing then, the whole notion of his father at the Palace so hugely, bizarrely, genuinely funny – and then the laughter became a release for all that had happened, and it all poured out of him until he was rolling around on the chair.

Chally hadn't liked that. 'They can treat epileptic fits these days, you know,' he said absently to no one in particular, certainly not to Harry because he was still laughing. While Katty was looking between the two men, having a quiet giggle to herself.

'Get out!' she said at length, but she wasn't angry. 'Both of you! Out! I've got vital war work to do here!'

Harry calmed down, and Chally stood up, all decisive, and said with a thin smile, 'Anyway, we should celebrate Malta's new hero. Assuming you've got any celebrating left in you after your antics on that chair there. Katty has no shows on tonight, so we'll go somewhere away from the in-crowd. Just the three of us. The ERA Club. That's discreet these days. And Katty can lavish her feminine wiles on us. That's settled then.' And with that, he was gone.

Long before the agreed hour for their meeting, Harry had decided he wasn't going to the ERA Club, even though it was only just the other side of the Manoel Island causeway. He was sitting on the wardroom veranda on his own. It was already dark and his only light came from a little torch he had arranged to shine out of the inside pocket of his watch jacket, which he was wearing over his grubby white submariner's pullover to keep out the chill. There was a Scotch and soda on the table beside him, and he was writing a letter to his mother.

The veranda was empty. Although there were four boats in from patrol, all their officers were elsewhere, mainly like the *Umbrage*'s, up at the rest camp at Ghajn Tuffieha. Or they had already headed out to the fleshpots.

He was taking his time between each sentence he wrote, to sip the whisky and gaze out into the night harbour. Thoughts of home;

of what his father would have made of his recent deeds; of Shirley, and of Katty, all passing through his head. That was when John, the wardroom's Maltese steward, came walking down the gallery, his soft footsteps hardly echoing in the long space. When he got to Harry, Harry was already looking up.

'Mr Gilmour, Sir,' said John, 'you have a visitor asking for you at the front gate. A young woman, Sir.'

And when Harry walked up the path, there was Katty. Even in the shadows he could make her out, standing there on the other side of the barbershop barrier in a wonderfully expensive-looking fur coat, chatting away to some local pongo all done up in khaki and a tin hat on guard duty.

'You're not at the ERA Club,' said Harry.

'Neither are you,' said Katty.

'Won't Chally be upset, being left all on his own?' he asked.

And at that she gave a trill of laughter; he loved that laugh of hers.

'What's so funny?'

'The idea of Chally ever being on his own,' she said, and paused to regard him for a moment as if resolving something within herself. 'I'm not feeling very well. Poor me, I had to leave,' she said. 'So I thought I'd come and see what was wrong with you. As friends do.'

Katty, even in the dark, had never looked so well or so utterly beautiful.

They walked up to the café on the Sliema seafront, the one that Hume plied with knocked-off coffee, and as they went, Katty slipped her arm into his.

⌣

'I think you gentlemen are getting ahead of yourselves.' It was Marsham talking, the wise old head trying to exert a bit of calm into the excited babble in the wardroom. 'All Roosevelt said was, "since the unprovoked and dastardly attack by Japan on Sunday, December 7th, 1941, a state of war has existed between the United States and the Japanese Empire". He didn't mention Germany, let alone the Italians.'

It was the ninth of December now, and everyone had gathered to meet *Nicobar*, due in off patrol. She'd been up to the Adriatic and apparently had kills to show on her Jolly Roger, as well as daggers. Special ops stuff, but no staff people were prepared to gossip. Now at least there was the Jap attack on Pearl Harbor to discuss instead, and all the other places the sneaky little bastards had hit at the same time.

'Well it stands to reason the Yanks'll come in . . .' The voice that was arguing from somewhere in the middle of the mob of officers already lining the gallery was quickly drowned out. Harry couldn't see who was doing all the shouting, because he was sitting in his favourite easy chair off to the side, drinking gin and lost in his own little reverie. Then the voice doing the shouting down was drowned out in turn, by another louder and closer fellow, determined to have his say too. 'Who says the Yanks might not be coming in, in Europe? Gawd!'

'Well, they still haven't declared war on Jerry yet . . . or the Eyeties,' said another.

'Don't tell that to the totty plotters in RAF ops! I heard they're expecting the sky to go dark any minute with Flying Fortresses dropping us big Christmas hampers full of nylon stockings and hamburgers!'

'And Coca Cola!' added someone else. 'You can't have hamburgers without Coca Cola. Says so in their constitution!'

Harry tuned out, and returned to thinking about Katty, but the vacant smile splitting his face was starting to arouse suspicion.

'Gilmour, what are you looking so chuffed with yourself about?' *Uttoxeter*'s First Lieutenant barked at him. But someone else had already yelled, 'Steamboat around the bend!' and there through the open veranda could be seen *Nicobar*, coming around Fort Manoel, cutting through the sun-dappled blue of the harbour, looking all very grim and sombre with the bleached white stone of Valletta rising behind her, half a dozen ratings lining her casing, Malcolm Carey on her bridge, and her Jolly Roger fluttering from her periscope standard, sporting its two new white blocks denoting two merchantmen sunk, and two daggers for special ops.

Harry got up to watch them too, knowing full well that only a smarmy shit could think what he was thinking now: that there were no crowds for *Nicobar*. But then two tramp steamers weren't the same as two cruisers, were they? He smirked to himself, then gave a wave just to show how magnanimous he could be, all the while laughing at himself inside, unable to come down from the mood he'd been in since last night.

Nicobar came alongside. Carey came up the gangway and went straight in to see Shrimp, while his officers came into the wardroom, and the party started. There was lots to chew over. War with Japan: the Japs had bombed Hong Kong and Singapore as well as Pearl Harbor, so we were in it with the Yanks, out East. But would the Yanks come in with us in Europe? Then there were *Nicobar*'s two sinkings to be dissected, and the two cloak-and-dagger ops that they weren't supposed to talk about – suffice it to say their passengers had got off without a return ticket, and no, they weren't saying whether they'd been landed in Yugoslavia. Their mission was not necessarily confirmation that Winston was cosying up to Tito. The Nicobars were saying no more, mum's the word. And what about bloody *Umbrage*, eh? Blowing the arse and a nose off half the Eyetie navy! All down to her Vasco too, the Tenth's very own Wavy Navy wonder boy. Damn shame about Rais though. Never liked him, but still. And Grainger? How's he? Flown out to Gib, eh? Sounds serious. Who's going to get *Umbrage*, then?

Harry was half-listening to it all when Carey came out of Shrimp's office and marched directly up to him, taking him by his non-drinking arm and leading him away down the gallery. 'A word,' he said. When they were out of the melee, Carey led him so they could lean out over

Nicobar, where one of the base engineers was just disappearing down the conning tower.

'Now tell me everything that happened on your patrol,' said Carey, face all serious, 'from when you sighted the enemy. What you did, the decisions you made, why, what you were thinking, what you messed up, and what went right. Everything. Go.'

'But you haven't got a drink, Malcolm,' said Harry, still smiling like an idiot.

'At the moment, it's "Sir". And I'll get a drink when you've finished . . . So . . . hurry up . . .' and his words trailed off, and his expression went from serious to curious. He looked Harry in the eye, and then up and down. 'What are you grinning about?' he asked. But before Harry could answer, he said, 'You've been at the counterpane-hurdling, haven't you? You randy little larrikin?'

'Sir!'

'Don't give me that. I'm a married man, I know about these things. She's not a local, is she?'

Harry decided it was too late to look shocked. 'Certainly not, Sir. She's a . . .'

'Thank God!' said Carey, interrupting, his face now trying to suppress a smile. 'Local daddies can cut up rough if they catch you. End up cutting you up rough. And don't tell me who she is, I don't want to know. And don't tell anybody else either. It upsets everyone else who isn't. Now, about what I do want to know about . . .'

So Harry took a belt of gin, wiped the smile off his face once and for all, and started.

⌣

It's early evening now, and the party's starting to break up, but Carey doesn't want to wait until it does before he gets to talk to Shrimp, so he's shoved the Captain (S) back into his little monk's cell to put his plan to him. Carey's talked to Harry, and his mind is made up. Now all he has to do is get the CO's approval.

'He's up to it,' says Carey. 'I know he is. I knew him on *Trebuchet*, and he was a good officer then. And from what he's just told me about what happened out there, I'm not in any doubt now. I know he can do it. And be bloody good at it.'

Shrimp sits back in his chair, knowing he's already had the same thoughts himself, but not saying anything yet.

'Look,' says Carey, starting up again, 'as of ten minutes ago, Bunny Warren was packing his kit for home and his Commanding Officers' Qualifying. So as of ten minutes ago, *Nicobar* doesn't have a Jimmy. I want Harry Gilmour to replace him. I want Harry Gilmour as my First Lieutenant. He's as ready as he's ever going to be. We both know he can do it, because he's just done it. He's got the eye. He can hit things.'

'Oh, I agree,' says Shrimp. 'In fact, I'd go further. I intend to have him on a Perisher as soon as I can justify sending him. But . . . but.'

This Malcolm Carey isn't the one Harry remembers from *Trebuchet*: the young toff from Toorak, Melbourne's toffiest suburb, just off the boat and full of himself. This man sitting deliberating with his commanding officer important command appointments within an operational flotilla in wartime, is a serious and respected submarine CO in his own right now. It is common knowledge that the Royal Australian Navy already have high expectations of him and that his half-ring to Lieutenant Commander will not be far off. And that is why Captain Simpson wants to hear what he has to say.

'Ah,' says Carey, cottoning on to Shrimp's train of thought. 'You're thinking of leaving him on *Umbrage*. Making him up to Number One there. I would suggest you don't do that, Sir. Very strongly.'

'And why is that, Malcolm?'

'You're going to give *Umbrage* to Hume, I take it?' Hume, the Flotilla SOO. Shrimp nods, yes.

'He's certainly hooligan enough. I'm sure he'll be good. But it will be his first operational command. He could probably do with someone more experienced as his Jimmy, Sir.'

'We could all do with people with more experience, Malcolm. Me included. Hume, like the rest of us, will have to *do* with what he's given. But that's not your reason, Malcolm, is it?'

'No, Sir,' says Carey, rubbing his chin, thinking how best to broach the subject on his mind, then deciding. 'Did Harry tell you about how he dealt with the Leading Stoker?'

'You've lost me,' says Shrimp.

'I thought not. The boat's problem: the boat deals with it. He told me though. Something happened. A rating did something he shouldn't. Something serious. They almost lost the boat. They did lose the CO.'

'A rating was responsible for Rais being lost? I rather think that is . . .'

'Sir. Please,' Carey, respectfully raising his hand, interrupts. 'I wasn't there so I don't know, but it appears it wasn't as simple as that. Please, let me finish.'

And Carey tells Shrimp everything Harry has described to him about how Rais had run the boat, how he rode the crew, and about how it had all led to those fateful events in *Umbrage*'s control room. Shrimp listens in silence.

'On their way in, once all the crash, bang, wallop was over, Harry went aft to see the Stoker,' continues Carey. 'The lad was the colour of a sheet apparently, and had been sitting with his head in hands. Harry sat down and spelled out to the Stoker the consequences of what he'd done. That by diving the boat without a direct order to do so, he had killed his CO and critically injured his First Lieutenant. Then he spelled out the consequences that so nearly followed . . . that the boat should have foundered . . . that the Italian squadron would have then been able to slip by, untouched, and as a result, Force F would've been engaged and crippled by a superior Italian force, and a vital Axis convoy would've got through. And how it was only down to pure, dumb luck that it hadn't happened. Then he told him that it wasn't his fault. That he knew exactly what had happened. That instead of doing his duty, he'd been trying to second-guess a madman's whims, because he'd been battered and bullied for too long, and nobody had done a damn thing about it. And if anyone were to blame, it was his officers, because they had let it happen. But, if he promised in future just to stick to obeying orders, and never to listen to a madman again, then he'd hear no more about it.'

Shrimp says nothing.

'It was around the boat in five seconds flat,' says Carey. 'My understanding is *Umbrage* thinks justice was served.'

'You know as well as I do,' says Shrimp, 'what *Umbrage* thinks is neither here nor there.'

'Yes, and no, Sir.'

'It's all right, Malcolm, I understand what you're getting at. He's too close to them now. And they're too close to him. You win. You can have him. Oh, and it never happened.'

Chapter Sixteen

'We lived in Sopot, and my life was a book already written before I was born,' said Katty. She and Harry were sitting at what he had decided would be their table from now on, outside the café on the Sliema shorefront. The owner, Pauli, had even brought them a pair of blankets against the evening chill, to tuck them up while they enjoyed their knocked-off Royal Navy coffee, sold back to them. Harry had just asked the obvious cack-handed question about what she was doing here. He'd at least had the common decency to qualify it by saying sorry, and he could imagine how many times stupid, insensitive people had asked her that, but hey, she was a pretty exotic specimen: a displaced Polish person, on a British colonial outpost in the middle of the Mediterranean, under siege. His curiosity was, he thought, pretty understandable in the circumstances.

She smiled, with good grace. 'Lots,' she said. 'Lots of stupid, insensitive people . . . Lots of times. But I've never been called a specimen before. Or exotic. You are the first. Were you meaning to be charming, or just impertinent? Don't answer that. Since it is you, Harry. And only since it is you. I will grant that your curiosity might be understandable.' Then she began stirring her coffee, not to end the conversation, but to create a little space before beginning her story.

'I am from rural bourgeoisie. My destiny was to be rural bourgeoisie. I would become the lady of a house, with a husband, children. A servant or two. And a cook, obviously.' She smiled to herself, at her oversight. 'For girls like me, from families like mine, it was what happened.'

'Lucky for you it all went wrong,' said Harry helpfully. 'Lucky for me, too.'

She ignored him, blew on her coffee and considered the approaching band of night rising out of the eastern horizon. Then, at length, she said, 'It didn't feel lucky at the time.' Smiling at him, she added, 'But then I didn't know the Germans were coming, or that you'd be waiting for me here. Did I?'

Another silence. Harry stayed shut up this time.

'The husband that should have married me, didn't, so there were no children, and no money for even one servant, let alone a cook.'

Silence, again. Harry knew if he kept asking questions it was going to start sounding like an interrogation, like pulling teeth was the actual analogy that crossed his mind, but he was genuinely curious. He'd never met a real refugee before, and couldn't imagine what it might take to force a person to up and run from everything they'd ever had or known.

But Katty knew what his silence was saying.

'Don't you realise that you are prying, Harry?' she said. There was a flash of irritation in her eyes, but she swiftly covered it with an indulgent smile. Even so, Harry blushed deep red, down into the collar of his white uniform shirt, and his mouth clammed shut in mortification.

Mostly he looked so grown up, she thought, and more than just self-assured: an accomplished man. And then, *pouf!* She was having to comfort and cajole a child. Honestly, why were men such a trial? Oh well. She sighed and continued, if only for the sake of the rest of the evening's harmony. After all, it wasn't as though she were actually going to tell him anything. Certainly not the truth. She'd learned the wisdom of not doing that long ago.

'I'm sorry, my Harry. Sometimes it feels as though my own personal story is the only thing I have left in my life I can keep private.' She paused to take a languorous puff from one of the cigarettes she was always being given by one of her many friends in the RAF and the Army and the Navy, and from the office of the Governor too. Then she smiled again, through the smoke. 'But not from you, *mon cher.*'

Another contemplative puff, but this was the actress in her now.

'Oh, you know how families can do cruel things to each other,' she said, as if she was looking back from far away, 'especially when things don't turn out as planned. Harsh words, slammed doors. Blame and accusation. The innocent tarred as guilty. That was when I discovered what had been just talent for amateur opera in a seaside town could become a meal ticket in the Warsaw nightclubs. And a girl does love an opportunity to flounce, you know. So I flounced. But I hadn't been paying attention to what was happening beyond the front gates. Girls that age seldom do. They rely on their men to keep the world at bay for them instead. Oh, I made it to Warsaw all right, but I didn't really get a chance to put my talents on display for very long, before there was a change of management. In the city, and of the country. The Germans. After that, there was a series of train tickets, mostly going south, mostly just one step ahead of disaster. Then a boat ticket from Constanta. And I got off here.'

'You didn't go all the way to Britain?' asked Harry, leaving the question hanging.

'Why? Just so as I could meet invading Germans, marching up Piccadilly, instead of down the Nowy Swiat in Warsaw?'

'You're more likely to meet the Germans here now,' said Harry.

Which was true; everybody knew it. The mood on the island had been one of relief the day the Luftwaffe had left Sicily and headed for the Eastern front. The threat of imminent invasion had receded, but the Germans were at the gates of Moscow now, even as Katty and Harry chatted away outside their café on the Malta shorefront. If Germany knocked the Soviet Union out of the war, with all those spare planes going a-begging, walking into Malta wouldn't be a problem.

While Harry was thinking this, she was looking frankly into Harry's eyes. 'There's no one to look after me in England,' she said.

When they walked home, Katty wouldn't let him see her all the way back to where she lived in Floriana. She had a cavernous second-floor apartment all to herself there, that she was house-sitting for a French businessman and his Italian wife, now living in Buenos Aires for the duration. So when the two of them reached the Manoel Island cause-way, she said, 'This is your turn-off.'

It would be silly to walk all the way up into Floriana only to have to come all the way back down, wouldn't it? She would see him at the office tomorrow; now, a kiss before you go.

Harry hadn't been totally surprised. There had been a pall over the end of the evening that had left him wondering if it had been anything he'd said, or hadn't said, but should have. He went back to his little hole of a cabin, and hooked back the curtain that served as a door only to discover that he was now apparently sharing it. The other bunk was occupied by a sound-asleep youth, and he could see from the uniform jacket, hung on the hook he normally used, that he was also an RNVR Sub-Lieutenant. He wasn't in the mood to say hello if his new fellow officer awoke, so he quietly picked up his writing case and went back to the wardroom.

It was late and it was empty, and by candlelight he picked up again the letter he'd been writing to his mother. He told her about his new job as First Lieutenant on another submarine, and how that meant he'd been promoted to acting Lieutenant and how it would inevitably mean a second ring, and that she could tell his father that that would mean more pay. He wrote that to be irritating, knowing it would enrage his father, if his mother ever told him. Knowing she probably wouldn't – knowing she always did whatever it took to protect his father, and yet never understanding quite why. Harry didn't tell her any war stuff though, because that was all hush-hush. You didn't discuss operational matters in letters to the folks back home: you never knew who might read it. And anyway, it would have terrified her, and he found himself now always doing whatever it took to protect her. Also, using his letters home to tell war stories would have enraged his father even more.

His mad father, who had fought in the Great War and yet believed every soldier to be a murderer, including his own son now – and who even refused to so much as touch any letter from him, yet interrogated his mother for every detail. His mad father, the gifted language teacher, well known in the town, with his war record that no one talked about – whose name was besmirched by rumours of conscientious objection, yet who'd been awarded a Military Medal: the gong a grateful nation handed out to non-commissioned ranks for bravery on the battlefield.

And now, according to his mother's last letter, there had been a growing number of complaints against him, from parents furious at what he was telling his pupils: the ideas he was apparently trying to drum into them – unsound and un-British, and depending on who you asked, on a scale that ran at best from 'pacifist propaganda' to at worst 'Nazi sympathiser'. Thinking about his father made Harry's heart heavy. He could understand how a soldier could be so traumatised by war. Dear God, especially now, he could understand it. But his father didn't want to be understood. He had become a crucible of ravening fury, driven by the power of his rage and eager to vent it. Ranting in his classroom and in the school's corridors, ranting at people in shops and even on the street, ranting against the very idea of war. This war, all wars. Against all who spoke for it, and even against all who simply found themselves swept up by it, and forced to serve.

It was why Harry never mentioned his father in his letters home these days. Instead, he was telling his mother that he had heard from Shirley, who his mother knew well. Telling her that he had replied, but being careful not to mention what his letter had said, or rather not said.

Nor, how these days he found himself back thinking about Shirley all the time, even when he didn't want to.

He stopped writing and fought an urge to tear up his letter. He was waffling, and if he hated receiving waffly letters, he assumed others did too. He should be writing something more honest. *But,* he told himself, *you don't have time for all that emotional honesty bollocks, not any more. You have a submarine and a crew to get to know; impose your authority on, and deliver, ready to go to sea and ready to fight, to your new CO.* That was what First Lieutenants were supposed to do. And Shirley? She had wanted to know where they stood. Jesus Christ! How many guesses did he get?

Harry, the boy, was too proud to admit that he didn't know his own mind, his own heart even. Too proud to admit he was confused. And firing off such bluff dismissals, even just to himself, made it easier for him to feel he was in control of what was happening between them. So there!

He finished the letter with a 'Love, Harry', and took it to the postbox, blissfully unaware that it wasn't the only dispatch concerning him that went out that night.

Right at the beginning, when Shrimp had assumed command of the Tenth Flotilla, Max Horton, the Flag Officer Submarines, had told him that all recommendations for awards and commendations were to be processed with utmost dispatch. 'Simpson,' he'd said, 'given the rate we're losing them, it's only right that if they've done something that deserves a medal, then they get it, before they get it.'

So a signal went out that night from S10, up the chain of command, recommending that Sub-Lieutenant Harris John Gilmour RNVR, of His Majesty's Submarine *Umbrage* be awarded the Distinguished Service Order for his part in the successful attack on the Italian Navy heavy cruiser *Fabrizio del Dondo*, and the light cruiser, *Gradisca di Isonzo* on the night of the . . . etc., etc.

The next day was overcast and cold. Harry, wrapped in a greatcoat, had marched smartly up Scots Street with his latest translations. He was hoping to grab a quick bite of lunch with Katty before he had to get back down to Lazaretto Creek, where *Nicobar* was trotted up with a U-class. Now he'd been appointed, it was his first priority to get down to her and get to know his new boat.

The N-class were an improved version of the *Unity*- or U-class boats like *Umbrage*, which had originally been designed in the late '20s as target boats, or 'clockwork mice', for training anti-submarine destroyer crews. They were notoriously slow and notoriously under-armed. A U-class going flat out on the surface was lucky to hit ten knots, seven knots submerged, and frequently they were left standing by the fat slug merchant ships they were trying to sink. Their Great War- and some-times Boer War-vintage twelve-pounder deck guns could barely blow a hole in a wet paper bag. And they only had a salvo of four torpedoes for'ard, with single reloads that required the crew's entire messing area to be stripped down to get at them.

But their new diesel-electric power system was a blessing to operate under wartime conditions: it meant U-class boats always ran on their electric motors. Unlike with previous submarine designs, on the surface a U-class boat's diesels acted not as engines, but as generators to deliver power to the motors, while submerged, it was business as usual, with the batteries delivering the power.

The set-up removed the need for big clutches to synchronise one or the other on to the two propeller shafts, and with that, all the maintenance headaches that followed. Also, they were handy little boats for the confined waters of the Med.

With the N-class, they'd just upped the performance. The newer boats were fifteen feet longer and three feet wider in the beam, while their diesels packed an extra one hundred horsepower, giving the boats a top surface speed of thirteen to fourteen knots . . . Some claimed to have beaten even that. They were equipped with a better three-inch gun and they were fitted with two stern tubes, port and starboard, which meant they could go on patrol with ten torpedoes.

Harry should have been keen to get aboard and take a look, and not be set on having lunch with some gorgeous pouting nightclub singer. He should've been on *Nicobar* first thing.

Any half-decent Jimmy would've had a slacker like Harry up on Captain's Report, but this was the last thing on Harry's mind as he rounded the corner and came face to face with the front door of the RAF HQ, and it was even further from it, when he saw who was coming out.

Katty, in her fur coat, had just stepped on to the pavement, and was tucking her hair into a warm woollen scarf she had wrapped about her head. Harry had been on the point of raising his hand and calling, when Chally stepped out behind her, wearing a flying jacket over his usual battledress. He put his usual proprietorial arm around her waist, propelling her off down the street, at a pace that looked just a little too quick for her.

Harry's expression when he got up to the photoreconnaissance office to dump the translations was not a happy one.

'You look like you've heard already, Sir,' said one of the erks who worked as a technician in the photo lab.

'Huh? What?' Harry wondered if his look of shock at what he had just witnessed was so transparent.

'Jerry, Sir,' said the erk. 'He's back on Sicily. Chally was over this morning. All the airfields there, they're chocka with Luftwaffe kites, and more coming over the hill, he says. The film's just being printed up now. Jerry's back. And we all know what that means . . . we're going to start copping it again. Just in time for fucking Christmas. Bastards!'

'Oh,' said Harry, as he placed his bundle on Katty's desk, and caught traces of her scent still lingering, wondering why she had worn it to work that day when she, like every other woman, had so little to waste.

'Oh, if you're looking for Miss Kadzow, Sir,' the erk added as he went out of the door, 'she's just gone, Sir. Went off with Flight Lieutenant Challoner for a spot of lunch . . . I'm sure I heard them say they were going to the Snakepit.'

When Harry got back down to Lazaretto Creek, as he walked out along the pontoon to where *Nicobar* was moored, the slim frame of her Cox'n was leaning over her conning tower. If such a thing didn't constitute a severe breach of naval courtesy, Harry might have suspected he was being appraised by his new boat's most senior rate, and that the appraisal was highly critical. In fact, when he called up for permission to come aboard, he could have sworn as he stepped across the brow that the man's lips had been forming the words, 'And about bloody time too.'

Chapter Seventeen

HMS *Nicobar*'s Cox'n was Chief Petty Officer Bill Sutter, and although he was regular Navy, he was of the new breed: a younger man than most of the CPOs Harry had served with, not as battered by weather or drink, and definitely better educated – more technocrat than swash-buckler. Tallish, slim and verging on the dapper when ashore, with an RAF-quantity application of Brylcreem on his dark waves, and his skills as a dhobeyman and ironer on prominent display. All Harry had heard about him was that he knew his job, which made him downright infuriating when he went all punctilious on you – mainly because he was invariably right, and you knew it.

And, as he was about to learn, the other thing about Bill, as with all Navy men who aspire to inherit the mantle, just getting in step with the service's traditions had never been enough: he embraced them as though they were carved on stone tablets. All things old-fashioned Royal Navy: good. Anything newfangled: bad.

And that was why, when Bill Sutter had been informed his new Jimmy was an RNVR officer, his first reaction had been: no good would come of it. He felt it in his water. And then, when it was revealed the RNVR officer was Harry Gilmour, his worst fears were exceeded. Everybody had heard of Gilmour. The boy who'd hauled Ted Padgett out of *Pelorus*. And now all this bollocks about how he'd blown the arses out of two Wop cruisers. All this told Bill Sutter was that he was about to get dumped with a poster boy with a big head.

And if that weren't bad enough, Wonder Boy had turned up late for his tour of the boat. Well, that was an affront too far. What could a bloke say? Apart from he'd never known his water to be wrong, and the whole bloody Andrew was now gone to buggery. A Wavy Navy Jimmy: it was enough to make you say a bad word – strictly to yourself, of course, and maybe the rest of the Flotilla Chiefs' mess deck.

But that was then. They were at sea now, and time had passed, and this Mr Gilmour had definitely been making his presence felt aboard Bill Sutter's *Nicobar*. To such an extent that, looking at him now, this Wavy Navy Jimmy, trying to take a sight on a coastline that was as flat as a witch's tit, purely for his own amusement, on a night as black as the Earl of Hell's waistcoat – Bill actually found himself quite liking the lad.

Nicobar was working its way west-north-west, close inshore on diesels running charge into the battery, but at barely four knots, with 110 feet under the keel and shoaling. They were looking for a coast-hugging Jerry convoy that their last signal told them was on the way.

Their Navigator Mr Yeo's last sighting had used the port of Ras Lanuf, where the convoy was clearly intending to dash into, so that had probably been accurate. But that was far astern now, and it really was the most damnable coast: no headlands on its one long flat sandy beach, and certainly no handy church steeples – not even a minaret or village or even a goat-herd's dunny. Something you could fix. So the Jimmy was giving Mr Yeo a hand, trying to triangulate their position on something else. The Jimmy's latest estimate was 30 degrees 34 minutes north, 18 degrees 21 minutes east, which wasn't far off the Navigator's, but all they had to corroborate was the frayed nineteenth-century chart that the echo sounder only matched the fathom lines with when it felt like it. Bill was holding the chart for his Jimmy now, below the bridge, with the red torch shining on it.

Acting Lieutenant Gilmour, except you called him Lieutenant. The 'Acting' bit just meant their Lordships hadn't got around to filling in the bumf that would make him 'substantive'. It also meant that, if their Lordships changed their minds, he could be bumped all the way back down again without having to generate any further bumf.

Even after just a few days at sea, you could tell the new Jimmy was one of those 'let's just get on with it' sort of blokes. And at least he'd never called one of those godawful *Address to the Troops* meetings, where you all had to sit and listen to the latest Herbert to be inflicted on you telling you how you were all going to be doing your jobs better, now that he'd arrived.

Harry had been the exact opposite. 'From your reputation, you Nicobars all seem to know what you're about,' the new First Lieutenant had said to Bill after their first walk round, 'so I suppose the best order I can issue is, "Carry on!" and ask you to bear with me while I get in step.'

Bloody hell, had been Bill's first thought, and he remembered having to consciously stop his jaw from hitting the deck plates. He'd said much the same to the Warrant Engineer and the PO 'Guns' and the Torpedo Gunner's Mate over sippers in the mess.

With everybody else the new Jimmy met on his initial wanderings around the boat, right down to the lowest Able Seaman, the story had been the same. A bloke would be polishing a knob or tightening a grommet, or in the mess with a mug of steaming Ky, because it didn't half get chilly in the Med in winter, and the Jimmy'd suddenly appear: 'Hello, don't stop what you're doing. I'm Lieutenant Gilmour, the new Number One. Who are you, and what is it you do?' Every Jack aboard, all twenty-seven of them. If he carried on like that, people might start thinking he gave a stuff.

And now they were off the Libyan coast. Just over a week out and a signal had come through from Captain (S), ordering them off their previous billet in the Gulf of Taranto, and to head south in a hurry.

Of course, by now everybody on board knew they were looking for a convoy. Even though the signal alerting them was marked 'For CO eyes only'. Carey had decoded it himself, then had immediately shown it to Harry. And Harry had told CPO Sutter, and then the Warrant Engineer; and they'd told everybody else. Details corroborated by the wardroom steward, who reported back on every word every officer ever said. So everybody knew the where, the when, the how and the why: only fair, if you were being asked to put your arse on the line. And once you were at sea, on patrol, what was the point in holding stuff back from the crew? Who were they going to tell? That was life in the Trade, the way it should be.

'Well, we might as well be in a fountain in Trafalgar Square, for all I can tell,' said Harry with a grim smile at Bill, 'but don't tell the Captain.'

'Don't tell me what?' said Malcolm Carey, standing right next to them, looking to seaward. They had been told to expect a lot of MAS-boat activity, and even the odd Jerry E-boat prowling up and down.

'The question of my relative utility as a help to our Vasco,' said Harry. 'I think we should ask Grot McGilveray for his assessment. I could do with a laugh.'

'Ah, the wisdom of Leading Seaman McGilveray,' said Carey absently, not removing his glasses – his shape a dark shadow leaning against the bridge. 'He sees everything in terms of competition, of course. So I would imagine it would all come down to the odds for the most useless he'd be offering . . . between you, men's tits and a one-legged man at an arse-kicking contest.'

Harry and Bill grinned at each other, their teeth two little lines of dull glow in the inky night. 'Which I'd win,' said Harry.

'A racing certainty,' said Carey, the smile in his voice, 'but let's not let that stop us from trying, eh, Mr Gilmour?'

'Bridge, control room. Echo sounder shows forty-seven feet under the keel!' came a voice from the bridge voice-pipe. 'Still shoaling, Sir.'

Harry, who was officer of the watch, ordered 'Starboard, fifteen', and *Nicobar* began to swing seaward a little, following the line of the shoal. As she did, Harry matched the depth just called to the markers on the chart, and made another guess as to their position. And so on they went, up the coast. The plan was to keep inshore of whatever was coming their way, to use the shadow of the land to hide their silhouette, and to be where the escorts would never think of looking, when they started firing.

They'd turned into the shallows way back at 17.41 hours local time, not long after the desert sun had set with its usual abruptness, like a light switch going off. The time now was just coming up on 01.40.

'Multiple HE, bearing red-zero-five.' A voice coming up the bridge voice-pipe, from the ASDIC cubby. Carey dropped down the hatch to go and find out more. Harry telegraphed 'All stop, together', and *Nicobar* began coasting to a halt, her diesels still running, but now just pumping amps into the batteries. There was no point him scanning the horizon ahead, not given his night vision, so he covered *Nicobar*'s stern, while the two lookouts searched ahead for the first hint of approaching shadow. Everybody concentrating. Harry told Bill he should go below now; the bridge chart work was probably over for the evening.

'Bloody horizon keeps getting obscured, Sir,' said one of the lookouts. 'There's a load of squalls out there, running inshore.'

This boat wasn't *Umbrage*: everybody was expected to speak up. Your experience was there for the boat to use.

'Ever wonder how the brass hats get to know these things?' Carey asked Harry, as they continued to scan the dark horizon. 'When Jerry gets his sailing orders? And what's in them? D'you think it really is all down to recce pilots the likes of your cobber Challoner? D'you think he really is flying so low he can read through the window their movement orders as they pile up on the signaller's desk?'

Harry sighed, smiling. 'Or maybe somebody among the brass hats is using their brains?' he said.

'Don't be stupid,' said Carey, night glasses still glued to his face. 'Gold braid corrodes brains. It's been empirically proved. And anyway, look at us. Up and down the Med like a whore's drawers. Where's the intelligent design in that. Umm?'

Harry, a vision before his eyes of the big Mediterranean sitrep map on the wall in Scots Street. 'Well, according to the RAF PR maps, General Auchinleck's Operation Crusader has run out of steam about fifty miles back up the coast,' he said. 'It's not a great leap to assume Rommel is sensing he's finally fought Eighth Army to a standstill and has started digging in. But he'll need to get stuff up to his troops fast, and with the Desert Air Force still giving him merry hell all along the roads back to Tripoli, let us assume he needs to move it by other means. And what better means than by night-time dashes by whatever fast cargo ships he has to hand. Along the coast, inshore, and behind his offshore minefields. And who best to put a stopper on his rat run? Us. The ones we don't sink, we drive out to sea. Which would tally with what Shrimp's told you in his signal. That Force F is out there waiting.'

Carey lowered his glasses and looked at him. 'D'you think up stuff like that just to annoy me?' he said.

'You did ask,' said Harry. 'Just trying to rationalise for you how these intelligence johnnies think.'

'Being rational doesn't tell you the time, though, does it?' said Carey, his voice all smug as he put the night glasses back to his eyes. 'It's the timings I'm talking about. How come every time Shrimp sends us a signal telling us what the enemy is up to, he always seems to know the when, as well as the where? Explain that, smarty-pants.'

In truth, Harry had often wondered where all the intelligence came from: how the brass seemed to know so much about what the enemy was up to. How many patrols had he been on when they'd somehow managed to be in the right place at the right time? But where was the fun in admitting that to his CO.

What he said was, in a tone of voice you'd use to deal with a slow child, 'I'd have thought that was obvious.' Then all nonchalant, as if no longer interested, 'You said it yourself a minute ago.'

'I did?'

'Yep. Challoner's flying so low he can look in the window and read the sailing orders off the signal pads. Obvious.'

'Smart alec,' said Carey, glasses down now so Harry could clearly see that mischievous grin on his face. 'If anyone asks you how you knew that, you'd better tell them it was me who told you. That's an order.' And just as the words were spoken, the sky was suddenly full of noise, and straight out of the night flew a shagbat – from the land side, so low you could smell the reek of exhaust fumes from its engine.

Harry, spinning round, astonished, looking up as its dark, djinn-like shape filled his vision. He blinked, and it was almost as if that very action had caused the two bombs to fall from beneath the little aircraft's wings. Two black shapes tumbling free. The first one seemed to be coming right for the end of his nose, and the other – his eyes barely having the time to register – looked as though it were going to go sailing over his right shoulder. The shagbat had gone over his head, so close he had felt the draught of it – a Cant Z.501. Had he really identified it in that flash of a second's glimpse? And the head and shoulders of the little goggled Eyetie perched in its open-nose gun pit, glaring down at him – had he really seen that? And then to his left there was the most God-almighty splash, and when he looked back, the bomb he thought was going to hit his nose had just a gouged a gout of iridescent seawater into the air a bare dozen or so feet beyond their casing. Harry instinctively flinched, but no explosion followed. Then a huge splash from his other side told him the other bomb had also gone directly into the sea.

He wanted to hit the diving klaxon, but that was the CO's job, and anyway, there wasn't much over twenty feet of water under them.

Carey, beside him, pressed the night alarm instead for a collision warning, sending the Nicobars to seal off her watertight compartments so
she might survive if the next bomb hit her – and did go off. And as
he did so, the second bomb detonated. Harry felt the concussion of it
rebound up through his guts, and a draught, as another great gout of
water went up about twenty yards off their starboard beam. While the
blast was still echoing, lumps of water and bomb casing were splashing
and rattling down.

'Shagbat!' said Harry. 'Came out of the shadow of the land. I didn't
see it until it was on top of us. One of those Cant orange crates.'

Carey put his hand lightly on Harry's chest. 'I didn't see it at all.
As you were,' he said, and lifted the voice-pipe. 'Finish with diesels.'

As *Nicobar*'s diesels shut down, they could hear the distant whining now of the little Italian floatplane's single engine, somewhere out
there in the night; it seemed to be moving ahead of them, and out to
sea. Harry could feel the boat wallowing slightly on the waves from the
bomb blast.

'And I bet he didn't see us either,' said Carey. 'At least not until he
was right on top of us. If we don't go charging about, and just stay still,
he'll never find us again.'

Harry suddenly realised he'd been holding his breath. He breathed
out again in a deep sigh. It seemed to really amuse Carey. 'As tension
mounts,' said Carey, arching his eyebrows, his tone like the background
voice on a B-picture melodrama.

They waited in silence. The whine of the little Cant drifted back,
and then drifted away again. ASDIC continued to report multiple HE,
still on the same bearing, getting a little louder with each passing minute, getting closer – the ASDIC man now beginning to identify individual returns: a couple of heavy ones, and a whole scatter of lighter. Then,
on the bridge, they heard it – a little burble rising out of the sound of
the lapping sea, and the wind in the periscope shears; the sound rising a

little, then getting lost, and then coming back again, and then stronger: the low steady thump of marine diesels in the darkness.

Carey lifted the voice-pipe. 'Starboard, twenty.'

Then he rang the telegraphs, slow ahead, port, slow astern, starboard. *Nicobar* started to pivot more than turn, on silent electric power, until her bows were pointing directly seaward.

'Depth?' Carey called into the voice-pipe.

'Two-five feet, Sir,' came back from the ASDIC cubby, then, 'Sir. Target bearing drawing aft . . .'

Now that he had moved the advancing enemy ships to his beam, Carey was expecting a bearing of red-nine-zero or less; he took a deep breath.

'. . . Main HE now bearing red-five-zero, and bearing is drawing for'ard now, Sir,' came up the pipe. The convoy was veering seaward, away from them. Then the voice spoke again: '. . . But there's still two HE contacts on red-eight-five. They're separating . . . Sound like MAS-boats, Sir, but a bit heavier. Still low revolutions. They're creeping, Sir, but closing on us. Dead slow. Main HE now on red-three-zero. Still two heavy engines . . . three, maybe four, smaller contacts. Moving away.'

Carey knew what all that meant, and so did Harry. Their little shagbat friend, not content with dropping two presents on them, had given the game away. Blabbed, telling anyone who was listening, *There's a submarine in your way: two steps to the side, quickly.* As for the two contacts creeping towards them, sounding like MAS-boats, but bigger – they both knew what that meant.

German E-boats.

Bastarding things!

Some MAS-boats were lovely, Italian style written all over them. Strip off the popgun on the foredeck and the racks either side for a torpedo or two, and the racks at the arse end for ditto depth charges, and you'd probably want one yourself: all polished wood, and some even had wheelhouses with nice big glass windows, like a rich man's launch.

German E-boats weren't like that. They weighed in at about one hundred tons and were just over 115 feet long, with low-swept lines and a bridge that looked more like an army pillbox. In their guts they had three huge Daimler-Benz diesels generating almost four-thousand-shaft horsepower. Throttles wide open, they could shift at the speed of a torpedo – over forty-five knots. There were two, and on some types four, torpedo tubes sunk into their streamlined upper works, and they bristled with a 37mm cannon and three 20mm Bofors guns. On their sterns, the ones deployed to the Med all had twin depth charge racks – some carried a dozen charges. If two E-boats were after you, you were in trouble.

'Harry,' said Carey, 'nip down and get Mr Yeo to sort me out the shortest route to deep water. And get a signal ready to send to Force F. No point in radio silence, now they know we're here. I'm not hanging about any longer than we have to with two E-boats about.'

'Aye aye, Sir.' And Harry was gone.

Carey stared into the impenetrable darkness. He could just make out another squall as a shimmering curtain of deeper night, moving from starboard to port. The muted sounds of the enemy's engines in the night came and went beneath the sound of the sea. *Nicobar* was still heading offshore at a steady four knots on her motors and Carey was trying to work out why the Jerries weren't racing down the coast towards where the shagbat must've said there was a submarine. Why were they just pottering along?

The Navigator's voice came up the pipe with a course for the ten-fathom line. Carey ordered full ahead, together on the heading. It was going to take them the best part of ten minutes to get there. ASDIC reported the convoy HE was still heading seaward, moving diagonally across their bows, a long way out. The two likely E-boats were still on the same track, closing on a bearing that would see them pass astern.

Then Sub-Lieutenant John Napier, *Nicobar*'s other RNVR officer, was on the pipe, telling him he'd coded a signal for Flag Officer, Force

F, alerting the cruiser force to likely size, course and current estimated position of the enemy convoy. The minute they transmitted, the Jerry E-boats, a mere few miles away, would know exactly where they were. Not that it mattered. With the convoy's divergent course now, even with the N-class's extra turn of speed on the surface, they were never going to be able to get themselves into an attack position before sunrise, and trying to catch up submerged in daylight was never going to be a runner. Only Force F had a chance now to intercept the enemy, so the sooner *Nicobar* sent her signal the better.

There was a problem, however. They might send their radio trans-mission to Force F, loud and clear, but atmospherics in the central Med were notorious. Your signal might get picked up clear as a bell on first transmission by, say, an E-boat five miles away, or even half a world away in Halifax, Nova Scotia; but the ship just over the horizon you were sending it to might never hear it in a month of Sundays.

Which was why Carey ordered Mr Napier not to transmit right away, but to get the gun crew squared away, and be ready to close up for Gun Action, but to load with star shells only. He had a fallback plan.

Carey let the minutes drip by. The E-boats passed dead astern, still unseen in the night, and now no longer heard; the enemy convoy had long ago passed beyond earshot. Carey ordered Harry to plot the enemy's likely course that would take the convoy to the known inside edge of the enemy's offshore minefield, and where it would then turn, to run parallel with the coast.

'One-five-zero feet under the keel, Sir,' reported the ASDIC cubby.

Carey used the bridge mic to raise Mr Napier, who was in with *Nicobar*'s Leading Telegraphist in the radio cubby. 'Start sending to Flag Officer, Force F now, Mr Napier.'

Harry, leaning against the chart table down in the control room, heard the order, and immediately behind him the wireless operator began to tap out the Morse. But he wasn't really listening to that – he was listening for the ASDIC man to start singing out.

Nicobar's favourite ASDIC man was on the set. A young Eastender called Butler, slight of build and concave of chest, he looked like a specky schoolboy rather than a Leading Seaman – complete with acne, teeth protruding from his mouth at all angles and a brow prematurely furrowed above his thick tortoiseshell-framed spectacles, which he was always losing, and the crew were always helping him to find. He was painfully shy, except when calling out HE, and he always wore a set of overalls with pencils and tiny screwdrivers sticking out of its top pockets.

'Ah! There they go,' said Butler. 'The two E-boats are on the move, Sir. HE gone to high-speed revolutions, turning towards.'

Carey was on the voice-pipe. 'Harry, get on the trim board. We'll be going down pronto any minute now. Tell John, gun crews close up now. Load with star.'

Harry passed on the order, and Napier led his crew up through the conning tower hatch, lugging their illumination rounds.

'Estimated bearing to convoy target, and range, Harry?' called Carey through the pipe. Harry repeated them. Butler began calling out the E-boats' bearings, as they closed from off their starboard quarter. In the radio cubby, they were still waiting for an RT acknowledgement from Force F. And while Harry was trying to do the mental arithmetic on how long it would take the Jerries to be on them, there was a *BANG!* And then another *BANG!* In quick succession. *Nicobar* had fired her first two star shells, sending them up and over in the direction of the convoy: the prearranged signal, if the radios weren't working and somebody had spotted the enemy and wanted everyone else to know where. Then two more. Each round packed with magnesium and a tiny non-flammable parachute, blasting out candlepower by the bucketful as it twirled to the sea, hopefully in a box over the position of the Jerry convoy, and high enough for the British cruisers and destroyers to spot. Then all they'd have to do is turn on their newfangled radar sets and all the merchant ships would suddenly appear as little dancing spikes on their cathode ray oscilloscopes, and then it would just be a matter of flashing 'Enemy In Sight' around the squadron, and they'd all be off in a clamour of Action Stations! gongs and training gun turrets – thundering down their radar beams into the night and right at the enemy's throats!

'Water under the keel?' yelled Carey.

'One six five feet, Sir,' Butler called back after the briefest of pauses.

'Good enough,' Harry heard Carey say through the open pipe, then, 'Wooh! Guy Fawkes!' and a shout, 'Right, John, clear the casing . . . Jesus! Enemy searchlights closing astern!' Then the *buum-buum-buum-buum!* of quick-firing enemy cannon. Instantly, two loud blares on the klaxon and the first of John Napier's gunners came shooting down the conning tower ladder like firemen on twin poles.

Harry was at the trim board with their Wrecker, ERA Bob Mundell. Orders were being shouted and confirmed. 'All main vents indicating open!', and the hands flashing across the diving board, opening valves so that Harry could already hear the air venting out of *Nicobar*'s saddle tanks as the last lookout hit the control room deckplates, and then Carey's voice came echoing down the conning tower trunk: 'One clip on, two clips on . . . One pin in, two pins in!' And he was down too, securing the lower hatch now, and the boat was falling away from them, beneath their feet.

'Depth 120 feet. Group up, full ahead, together,' said Carey in a rush, as he leaned into *Nicobar*'s dive.

'High-speed HE closing fast, astern,' called Butler, and as he finished they could all hear the high-speed HE: the evil whining of the enemy screws rising in intensity.

'Rig for depth charging!' called Carey.

'Inboard one's about to go over the top,' called Butler, not that he had to now. The scream of the Jerry screws was loud and sickening – that tearing linen sound again. Harry looked at the depth gauge; they'd barely passed one hundred feet. And then the thing went over them . . . and nothing. No splash of depth charges. And no click as the detonator fired.

The noise of the E-boat moved away as fast as it had arrived, until the sound of it was there, but only just there, in the water, with only Butler's calls to say which way each E-boat was turning. Then the pinging of an enemy echo sounder started up. But it was quite a bit off to starboard. *Nicobar* was now in water 270 feet deep. Carey slowly took them down to two hundred feet, and rigged for Silent. All non-essential pumps and motors were shut down, and she lay hove to, hanging in the deep while the E-boats seemed to perform an elaborate and noisy search some distance to the east of them.

The control room crew would every now and then fire a quick glance at Carey, leaning beside Harry at the chart table. If he caught their eye, he would smile and shrug, or make a shush sign with his finger on his lips. Jerry didn't look like finding them any time soon, and Carey seemed quite prepared to wait them out. And all the while everyone was thinking, why no depth charges? These E-boats carried them, and who better to drop some on, but a British submarine?

Some time had passed, while Jerry burbled above, and *Nicobar* hung still and silent, when Butler held his arm out of the ASDIC cubby, indicating he wanted to whisper to Carey. The CO bent his head around the thin partition between the two spaces.

'I've got a couple of big explosions in the water,' whispered Butler. 'They're a long way off, to the north-east. There's another . . . and another.'

'Like what, Butler?' Carey whispered back. 'Six-inch salvoes going in?'

Butler shook his head, emphatic. 'No, Sir. No pattern. Random . . . and another. That's five, or is it six . . . pretty big detonations. Almost like torpedo hits, but bigger.'

And then there was nothing. The E-boats performed a flamboyant figure-of-eight high-speed run, the end of one of them going over

Nicobar's starboard bow, never in any danger of making contact, and then they sped off to the east.

Nicobar surfaced later, and almost immediately the radio room began reporting a lot of traffic between Force F and VAM, the Vice Admiral, Malta – an awful lot. There were no signals for them, however. So Carey moved back inshore in case another convoy might be making the run before sunrise. It sounded like their little fireworks display had worked, and had guided Force F right on to Jerry, and that the bangs Butler had heard had been the skimmers sending Rommel's much-needed fuel and ammunition, frankfurters and Lili Marlene records, to the bottom. Nobody wanted to pay any attention to Butler's doubts about what the bangs had been. Between that and them having success-fully dived for cover right under the noses of two E-boats, who never even got a shot in at them, there was a good mood in *Nicobar* as she went back on billet.

And then it was Christmas.

Nicobar was now up in the Gulf of Taranto again, having been sent back by a curt signal from Shrimp; after all, she still had her ten torpedoes left. Now she had eight. On the very day she'd arrived back off Italy, a 1,200-ton steamer with two MAS-boat escorts had come puffing and wheezing over the horizon, with a circling Cant shagbat overhead just to complicate matters. Carey had got them into a favour-able attacking position, but at the point where he guessed the target was going to zag, it zigged, and both his torpedoes had missed. The steamer and her escorts had then scuttled off back towards the horizon, and the Cant had come after them, making two ineffectual passes, dropping two depth charges that landed nowhere near. But it kept them down long enough for the steamer to escape.

So here they were, just after 10.30 hours, on 25th December 1941, heading true north at 120 feet, the motors grouped down, puttering along at a stately two knots, fifteen miles off Capo Colonna. Harry had the watch while the rest of the crew were about to have Christmas dinner. And a particularly festive occasion it was going to be too; Carey had seen to that. For although the Nicobars didn't normally partake of their daily tots while on patrol, the CO had announced he was going to be making an exception for Chrimbo, and 'up spirits' was definitely going to be piped. Yet even this gesture had not won Carey the star of the show – that had gone to Johnny Napier, their Glaswegian Torps and Guns. He said he would cook.

Nicobar, like all Royal Navy submarines, didn't carry a cook: the job went to whichever poor sod couldn't talk himself out of it. *Nicobar*'s poor sod was Able Seaman Empney who, so far as Harry could gather, had never shown any culinary talent since he'd been lumbered with the job way back at the start of *Nicobar*'s commission. *Nicobar* lore had it that he could burn water, but in truth, he wasn't that bad. Frying he could just about cope with, and amazingly he sometimes could conjure up a passable baby's head – Jack's name for a seagoing version of steak and kidney pudding. Anything else, and you took your chances. 'I don't know what you did to this cauliflower, Empney, but it's going to be a vegetable for the rest of its life!' had been Johnny Napier's verdict on one of the hapless rating's dishes.

However, Sub-Lieutenant Napier was in a position to criticise. He had been an assistant hotel manager in civvy street, and the scran he could turn out was fit to grace the table of royalty. Harry, in the control room, could smell Mr Napier's dinner wafting aft from beyond the wardroom, and was transported back to *Radegonde*, the Free French sub he'd served on as a liaison officer, and which had possessed a chef renowned throughout the *Marine Nationale*. The aromas of roasting meat and rich gravy even managed to eclipse the usual submarine reek of diesel, bilge water and young men's sweaty bits.

It had been a bit of a dance to get here, to get Napier laying on the spread. Initially he'd decided to play hard to get – as he always did, before he'd rustle up a treat. He loved all the pleading and begging, and the offers and bribes before he'd reluctantly relent, from gulpers in the PO's mess to once, a beautiful and delicate model of *Nicobar*, machined from a purloined wardroom spoon, filed to a silver brightness and presented by the Stokers' mess.

This time out though, the piglet had been a dead giveaway, so all the begging and pleading was more piss-take than entreaty.

Knowing full well he was going to give in over the matter of Christmas dinner, Napier had gone down to the Tenth's own little menagerie before they'd sailed, and brushing aside all Pop Giddings's assurances that *Nicobar*'s share of the Christmas banquet would be waiting when they returned from patrol, insisted on *Nicobar*'s share now. He'd procured an entire suckling pig, which was promptly dispatched, butchered and secured aboard. You can't hide a suckling pig aboard a boat the size of *Nicobar* for long. He'd also sought across the island for a sack of potatoes from somewhere, and failed. Rumour got out about that too. And then there were the fresh onions that had come aboard, all duly noted by the crew, together with all the ingredients for a huge figgy duff, which of course would be served with custard, because there was always custard. So when the CO let it be known there was the prospect of 'up spirits' on the 25th, it was confirmation. Most of the boat couldn't wait to get on patrol.

The only persuasion Mr Napier had received to cook, however, had come by way of a threat. At the end of the last big exercise before war broke out, with the Fleet back in Valletta, there had been the usual annual competition among the lower decks to applaud the grottiest Jack in the Mediterranean. Grot McGilveray had won it so convincingly that it had been decided to abandon all future 'Most Grottiest' competitions on the grounds that Grot had plumbed a depth so profound that nothing so grotty could ever be conceived of again. If Mr Napier wasn't going to cook Christmas dinner, they were going to get Grot to tell him his winning entry.

'You'll be rendered clinically doolally. You'll have to be tranquillised for the rest of your life, Sir.' . . . 'You'll never get another good night's sleep again, Sir.' . . . 'It's so grotty, Sir, it's grotty-esque!'

'Aren't you intrigued, Johnny?' Harry had asked during the height of the campaign.

'I wrote the book,' Napier had said with a supercilious smirk. 'Nothing Grot McGilveray could come up with scares me. Although he does know a few more dirty songs than me, so I doff my cap to him on that score. I've told them I'll do it, but only if Grot promises to teach me his repertoire.'

Mr Napier, like Grot McGilveray, was a notorious singer, to himself, of dirty ditties, usually while on watch, or lying on his bunk. Mostly, it was quite funny. Leading Seaman McGilveray, on the other hand, sang everywhere he went. He even had a signature tune which you'd hear long before his roly-poly, waddling figure would come flying through a watertight door or up through a hatch. 'Don't be shy, show's yer pie, gie's a gobble!' delivered in an almost impenetrable Geordie accent. Then the doughy face would crack into an almost toothless grin that spoke of a boundless joy of life, and an immaculate imbecility, especially beneath his Henry V haircut, styled by putting a pudding bowl over his head and cutting around the edges. Oh, and he always wore his cap perched on the back of his head, even on parade, to the fury of many a Jaunty. For Grot McGilveray was one of those beings who were obviously bred for the Royal Navy, one of nature's naturally occurring Jacks.

The dinner, when it was served, even looked good, never mind smelled good – no mean feat with twenty-seven men, three officers and a CO to feed from a tiny four-ring electric cooker in a cupboard, with an oven no bigger than a bicycle basket. The pork was thickly sliced and smothered in a rich creamy gravy, and with it went an aromatic pile of fried onions and tinned runner beans, all oily and liberally sprinkled with herbs, and ice cream scoops of dried potatoes, rehydrated and fluffed up into what looked like yellow cumulonimbus, with butter and milk.

A daisy chain of Stokers went past Harry carrying stacked plates of it back to the engine room crew off watch, each one grinning fit to crack his face. The CO and their public schoolboy Navigator, Sub-Lieutenant Giles Yeo RN, had already gone forward, having been invited to eat in the PO's mess.

'Subject to the vagaries of war,' the CO had said to Harry helpfully, as he slipped a bottle of whisky into his jacket before heading for'ard, 'don't feel you have to go up for any all-round looks, at least until we've cleared the dishes, I think.'

So it was just Harry, and the Wrecker's latest protégé on the trim board, two other ratings standing in for the usual POs on the dive planes, and a Leading Seaman on the helm in the control room now; next door, out of sight, was another rating on watch in the ASDIC cubby, headsets on, listening to the sea outside. And as they sat there, bathed in red light, wafting all around them were the luxurious smells of what they could expect to be served when the watch changed.

While they were all lost in expectation of what was to come, Napier appeared in the control room gripping mugs of Ky. 'This'll keep you going, lads,' he said, while craftily nodding Harry towards the wardroom on the other side of the partition wall. Harry stepped out of the control room and into the wardroom after him, all the while listening to Napier hum away to himself the tune for *When the red, red robin comes a bob, bob, bobbin' along, along* . . . Napier turned, and as he started to pour from a half-full bottle of Marsala, began to sing, except Harry couldn't help but notice the words were different. '. . . *A-when the red, red biddy comes a-squirtin' from her diddy, I'll be there, I'll be there* . . .'

'One of Grot's?' said Harry.

'His down payment,' said a grinning Napier. 'Now this might be "enemy" sauce, but I needed it for *my* sauce, and I had to pay for it too, so we don't want what's left going off now, do we, Number One?' And he held a glass out for Harry. 'To all our future Christmases, and may we spend them anywhere else but on a bloody submarine.'

Chapter Eighteen

The weather was terrible. It was dark and cold, with a driving rain and a chop in the water even here inside Marsamxett harbour, so that the three U-class submarines already in, and *Nicobar* now just arrived, were all bobbing and bouncing on it, tied up alongside the corkscrewing and gyrating pontoons.

Harry came into the wardroom, peeling off his soaking watch jacket and shaking his cap. He and the Warrant Engineer, Mr Ridley, had just finished handing *Nicobar* over to the maintenance crew, not that there was much wrong with her, apart from her six unfired torpedoes to be removed for a turnaround overhaul.

The only light inside the inner wardroom – it was too cold and the air too full of driving rain for the gallery – came from a couple of candelabras and some battle lanterns. But there was enough to see everyone was a bit brittle in their jollity. Harry scooped himself a whisky and soda off John, the steward, nodded hello to him, and asked about the lights.

'Jerry's back,' said John, with a resigned shake of the head. 'The power's been off down here for a couple of days now. They've been giving priority to getting it back on at the airfields, and over in the dockyard. We've had a lot of raids since you sailed. The town is in a bit of a mess, the whole island's in a bit of a mess, but you won't have seen it, coming in, in the dark. But we should be all right tonight. Not even Jerry is going to try flying in this.'

Harry had been a bit glum about coming back in. Standing on the bridge being battered by rain seemed to fit his mood. It had been a washout of a patrol. Four torpedoes fired, no hits. Not even a Gun Action. And as for the inshore work, and their failure to 'ambush' the convoy, the least said. But somebody had got lucky that night, if all the bangs in the water they'd heard had been anything to go by. So he'd been hoping that would go a long way to distracting the other crews from taking the mickey out of *Nicobar*'s duck.

Lazaretto had radioed them rendezvous details for a night approach to Marsamxett: signal codes, to be flashed in the dark for the ML – the motor launch – coming out to meet them and escort them in. Everyone knew how hit and miss that could be, especially since the weather was so crap. Then the added alert to look out for mines: how they were to run in on motors, all buttoned up for collision, all watertight doors shut. Still, at least it meant no one would see they were coming home with no Jolly Roger flying. But the ML had arrived at the rendezvous on time, and the right signals were exchanged, and they had come in without managing to hit a mine. And now he was safe in the wardroom.

When he arrived, Harry had spotted Napier and Yeo deep in conversation with one of the other boats' Subs; they were hanging on his every word. He could tell there was news. Something had happened. He'd immediately wanted to go and butt in, but now he had his drink, he sought out Hubert instead. He didn't want to get some flowery interpretation or hearsay comments on whatever event had caused this hubbub, and even new to the job as he was, Harry was well aware that First Lieutenants were supposed to know everything naturally, and that it didn't look good to go jumping around, leg to leg, demanding, 'What's happening? What's happening?'

And that's when he heard; and it wasn't just that the Luftwaffe was indeed back, nor that they'd been stepping up their attacks.

It wasn't that the Luftwaffe's return wasn't big news. It was. They had begun with a couple of hit and run sweeps a few days after *Nicobar* had sailed, and now raids were coming in at a rate of six to seven a day: big coordinated shows with one hundred plus high-level bombers in each attack, with Me 109s on low-level strafing runs, and Stukas sneaking in behind them. They'd been mostly going after the airfields, but Grand Harbour had taken a pounding too. Especially when the remnants of Force F had limped back.

For that was the other news. Just when Carey emerged from making his report to Shrimp, that's when Harry was told. The bangs in the water hadn't been Force F intercepting the convoy, it had been Force F running into enemy mines.

'And we wondered why the E-boats hadn't dropped any depth charges on us,' Carey said to Harry as he too bagged a whisky. 'They hadn't been carrying any. They'd been up to other tricks: them and another half-dozen of the bastards apparently, all buzzing up and down the offing that night. Out laying mines. A whole new field. Beyond the existing one. And Force F charged right into them at twenty-seven knots.'

Apparently *Pelleas* had hit three of the mines in quick succession and gone down in a matter of minutes. Harry closed his eyes, and could see her cleaving through the Mediterranean night, her huge battle ensigns flying; magnificent, until she hit the first mine. Then her four shafts still turning at maximum revs, driving all six thousand, seven hundred tons of her into the ripping, tearing blast of the next one, and the next. Her hull plates being peeled apart by the explosions, and her sheer momentum opening her engine rooms and magazines and ratings' mess decks to a greedy sea.

A fourth mine had sunk the J- and K-class destroyer *Jocasta*. The force's other cruiser, HMS *Patroclus*, had hit another and had limped back, badly damaged. The other two destroyers, *Darter* and *Dimapur* had emerged unscathed and had returned to Grand Harbour laden with survivors. Both had been immediately turned around for a high-speed dash back to Gib. *Patroclus* was now in the dry dock, covered in camouflage netting and surrounded by smoke pots, with the dockyard workers working flat out to patch the hole in her so she too could make a run for it at the earliest opportunity.

'Shrimp says they only picked up seventeen of *Pelleas*'s crew, and your mate wasn't among them,' said Carey, carefully watching Harry's expression. 'They got no one off *Jocasta*,' he added, as if that made any difference. 'Bit of a bloody night all round.'

Harry couldn't think of anything to say. The cruiser had a crew of well over five hundred men; the destroyer, over two hundred. But none of that seemed to matter beside Peter Dumaresq being missing, except he knew what that really meant. He was dead. If the other ships in the squadron hadn't got him, who had? There would have been no other ships around.

It didn't seem possible. Dumaresq had seemed too full of life to allow himself to be killed – with too much promise, too big a career and his whole future beckoning. Somebody had made a mistake. Surely, somebody had made a mistake.

'Bloody night indeed,' said Harry, who could feel his eyes not quite focusing. 'I think we should have another drink, Sir. No point in dwelling on it, eh?'

'Jeez. It didn't take Jerry long to give us a good boot in the cods, did it?' said Carey.

John knew when it was an emergency and had arrived with two tumblers. Harry and Carey swept them up.

'I suppose this is the end of it then, Sir?' asked Harry.

'Not sure I follow,' said Carey frowning.

'Where the attrition rate gets too high, and we pull the plug?' said Harry.

Carey didn't answer for a while, then he said, 'You don't get it, do you, Harry?'

Harry just looked at him blankly.

'Nobody's pulling any plug, Harry,' Carey said patiently. 'Somebody has to be here to stop the Afrika Korps' supplies getting through. And we're it. Because the last time I looked there was nobody else about.'

Harry: he'd used similar words himself, a mere couple of weeks ago: 'nobody else here'. So he raised his glass, and smiled the lop-sided smile Carey remembered from *Trebuchet*.

'Oh well,' said Harry. 'Drink up or crack up!'

The next day the weather was still foul. No raids expected. Harry got up with a splitting headache, not improved by the sudden recollection that he had a crew to see to. But they had all been looked after the night before by Hubert: he'd shipped the lot up to Ghajn Tuffieha.

The Nicobars, being old Malta hands, had nearly all been billeted out in apartments in Sliema, so when they came in, it was usually just a short walk off Manoel Island and up into the town. But three of the blocks had been blown to rubble in the bombing, and nobody knew when the weather was going to change and Jerry would be back again. So Hubert had laid on two of the island's remaining rickety buses, with their windows taken out so their passengers wouldn't get shredded by blast, and had everybody driven up to the rest camp, including all of *Nicobar*'s POs.

So apart from Harry, it was just the CO, Napier and Yeo left in the base, and they all had their little stone cells, except the CO's wasn't that little and like all CO cabins, it opened on to the gallery.

Harry sat down to a breakfast of fried bacon, reconstituted eggs, toast and coffee. There was only powdered milk for the coffee as the goats had got out during a raid and never been seen again. There was no one else about in the wardroom dining area, and as he looked so ill, the other steward, Dommy, a dark-haired, dark-tanned youth who could have been no more than sixteen, decided against annoying him with chit-chat. When Harry'd finished his food, however, he brought him his mail. A letter from his mother, and two other letters, scented, both of which he recognised even before he looked at the handwriting.

There was also a small, flat package, franked and embossed with a Cross of Lorraine and the words *La France Libre* and a London address. He had another gulp of coffee and tore open the package. There was a little leather case inside, and inside that was a small bronze cross with crossed swords, on a green-and-red striped ribbon. In an embossed envelope was a slip of vellum; he slipped it out and started to read. But he didn't get very far before his eyes started to fill. He saw his name, the name *Radegonde*, and that of Lieutenant de Vaisseau Gil Syvret. And that it was a *Croix de Guerre*, and apparently it had been awarded to him by the *Comité national français* for his heroism *en combat avec l'ennemi* while serving alongside officers and men of the *Marine Nationale*.

Hubert, with a cup of coffee was suddenly sitting down opposite. 'I know what that is,' he said, settling himself. 'Yours, I take it.'

Harry looked up with a dumbfounded expression.

'So, it's yours,' said Hubert. 'Well, bloody good show! Well done, young Gilmour. Congratulations. No more than you deserve, I'm sure. But, of course, you know you can't wear it. It's against regulations to wear a foreign decoration on the King's uniform. Sorry. But we'll have to wet it, of course, you realise that.'

They wet it that night with another party: songs around the old upright piano, and lots of Al Bowly and Guy Lombardo records. An attempt to get a game of drawing-room cricket going was vetoed by Hubert on the grounds they'd suffered too many cracked records of late and as there were no more convoys on the board, there'd be no chances soon to make up any further losses. Harry took all the jokes and ribbing in good part, and his fellow officers showed their appreciation that the tab was going on *his* mess bill by not getting too vicious.

Harry grinned through the unreality of it all – the booze flowing and the laughter, and the memories of the people who weren't there any more, and would never be there again. The number of times he'd thought, *I can't wait to tell* . . . so-and-so, or so-and-so . . . *who would love this*, or so-and-so . . . who should be standing over there, the usual indulgent smile all over his face, that he'd never see again. All of them, who never would be there again to tell your story to, or stand there again, waiting to tell theirs. It felt as though the whole world was rollicking along like a runaway train, regardless of who was falling off. And all those left on board had no time to wave goodbye, their time all taken up with just clinging on.

That morning, he'd sat with Hubert after breakfast and been told how things stood: the Luftwaffe top jock Kesselring was back on Sicily with another entire *Fliegerkorps* at his disposal. When Harry had asked how many planes that represented, he'd been told – a lot.

'They're obviously out to smash our offensive capability,' Hubert had said, 'so Luqa, Hal Far and Takali are being plastered, although they're not harassing the seaplane base much. And of course the dockyards. But so far they don't seem to have worked out where we are. You'll have noticed there's no ensign flying above the Lazaretto. We're not advertising ourselves. And all the submarines in port, I've ordered to sit submerged on the bottom of the harbour throughout the daylight hours. Any repair work is being done at night. So we've not been a direct target yet, though the bombs do fly about a lot.'

Valletta, Sliema and Floriana had all suffered damage, he'd said. As well as the areas around the docks, Senglea and Vittoriosa. The gas and electricity supplies had been disrupted, and even one of the island's main bakeries had been destroyed, forcing bread rationing to be introduced for the local population.

'There's a new standing order you need to be aware of, Sir,' one of the base Writers had told him later, when he'd gone into the Flotilla office to fill in some First Lieutenant's paperwork. 'Captain (S) has ordered that all personnel, no matter where they are on the base or anywhere on the island, on hearing an air-raid warning siren, must immediately seek refuge in the nearest air-raid shelter. He says we're all needed for our proper jobs, so he doesn't want to hear of any heroics, or people running about in the bombing trying to save the neighbours' pet cat. Get undercover pronto. And stay there until all the shrapnel's stopped falling. All that anti-aircraft shite we're throwing up at them has to come down sometime, somewhere, and a lump of that on yer noddle, Sir, it'll kill sure as a Jerry five-hundred-pounder.'

Then Harry had gone back to his monk's cell, and lain down to read his letters. He kept his mother's for last.

The first one he'd opened he didn't even have to lift to his nose to smell the perfume. Janis. He almost threw it away then, but curiosity got the better of him. Five pages of typed script, finishing with her first name, signed in a quick inky scrawl between the final endearment . . . *Lots of love* . . . and the kisses . . . *xxx* . . . both typed.

From the letter he learned that his award of the Croix de Guerre had made the local paper, and how proud she was of him and how she couldn't wait to see him wearing it, and how dashing they would look together. Then there was stuff about how hard life was under rationing . . . the lack of nylons and make-up. How the war was dragging on, and the inconvenience. Harry had a sudden vision of her father, Mr Crumley, who ran a county-wide bakers and cake-shop empire, fussing about as his only daughter lay prostrate with distress, presumably from lack of cake. He got to the end of the letter without finding a single mention of the doctor – he was sure the man who'd replaced him as the object of her affections had been a doctor; but nothing, not even a brief aside. Nor was there a mention of the 'Dear John' letter she'd sent, dismissing him as her beau. Just a mild admonition that he hadn't written for a while, and why hadn't he, since he knew how much she missed him?

He rested the letter on his chest and stared up at the hacked-at rock arch of his low ceiling and imagined himself as some latter-day Edmond Dantès, buried deep in the heart of the Château d'If, and he wondered how Edmond would have reacted to receiving a letter such as this from his fiancée Mercédès. He probably wouldn't have bothered escaping, he decided, happy just to stay here instead, safe, deep in the deep, deep rock. In fact, he decided, that would suit Harry just fine too, for ever more.

The perfume on the next letter was not so liberal. Katty couldn't have had that much left and was obviously economising. The note inside was short and to the point: *Where are you?*

'Good question,' Harry said out loud to himself, before folding the note away and reaching for his mother's letter. It confirmed the fact that news of his French medal was out. She told him she didn't want to know how he'd won it, as she probably would never sleep again if she did, and she warned him not to do it again. One medal was quite enough for one war, and now he'd done his bit. So, enough! There was more news about the evacuee children, who were actually settling in – and how the older girl was becoming a real help to her, and how the younger, Aggie, nearly four now, had attached herself like a limpet to his father; and how her presence seemed, against all his irascibility, to be a calming influence. He hadn't even come close, apparently, to the eruption of rage and fury Harry would have bet on when he heard about the medal. And then his mother mentioned Shirley, and how sad she'd been when Shirley had explained she and Harry were no longer writing to each other: how they had each decided to go their own way. She had liked Shirley, but could only assume they knew what they were doing.

Harry rested that letter on his chest too. So Shirley wasn't writing to him any more. Well, that was news. No more than he deserved, though. You tell a chap you love him, and all the chap does is start to waffle. He closed his eyes as he remembered Shirley that day on the Holy Loch, in her duffel coat, the explosion of chestnut hair bursting out from under the hood, there in the winter gloom on Ardnadam Pier, jumping up and down and waving at him in the crew boat, as he was coming ashore for a last few hours before *Trebuchet* sailed again on her last patrol.

Then all the other memories of her began crowding in, until eventually exhaustion saw him drift off into dreamless sleep.

The next day.

Mahaddie started walking back towards the Riley 12, where Harry was sitting in the front passenger seat and Katty in the back. They hadn't said a word to each other since Mahaddie had jumped out to go and talk to the two ground crew standing beside a shattered fuel bowser, whose tyres had been shredded and its cab peppered with bullet holes.

They were on the edge of Takali airfield in the middle of the island, and from where Harry was sitting, all that was left of it were a few free-standing white stone walls surrounded by piles of rubble, and a random series of rock and earth berms stretching out across a flat plain. There were also a dozen or so tents, flapping and bellying in the wind and a few sandbagged enclosures with Bofors barrels sticking up out of them. The only aircraft in Harry's field of vision were wrecks. On the far side of the field, scores of figures in khaki were hacking with picks and shovelling, obviously throwing up even more berms around the perimeter. Blast pens for whatever surviving aircraft were left, he guessed, and for any new ones that one day might arrive.

Mahaddie had one hand holding his side hat on his head against the wind and rain, and the other clutching the front of his greatcoat shut. Harry leaned over and opened the door for him as he came up, and a gust of wind rocked the little car as he climbed in.

'Four Hurricanes operational,' he said to Katty, who dutifully began writing it down, 'and they can't say how many they can bring up before the weather clears at the weekend.' He started the engine, crashed the battered machine into gear and they headed off again, this time towards some tents.

Another rain squall scudded in across the north end of the field – more intense rain falling in rippling sheets and turning the already grey sky even darker. Looking up, Harry doubted the racing cloud base was much above one hundred feet, and probably even less.

'They want permission to cannibalise another Hurricane,' Mahaddie continued, a frustrated growl directed at no one in particular. 'They've got a list of new parts needing casting, except they don't know when they can get the foundry going again, because they don't know when the gas is going to get reconnected, but they want to get a few more kites airworthy now and not have to wait. Jesus Christ, if they go on like this our entire air strength will be in parts bins.'

The big Jock wasn't the same man Harry remembered from Majorca, or even from their little impromptu Mediterranean cruise. He didn't seem quite able to fill a room any more, or even a car, the way he used to, wasn't as loud, or as Scottish. It made Harry smirk to himself to think that maybe this was no bad thing. Especially as the man was actually beginning to communicate like a human being, in English and in a fashion that was understandable. Even the usual intense barrage of insults and abuse had all but abated.

Mahaddie had captured Harry on his way in to see Katty, to ask her, 'Where were *you*?' But once Mahaddie had got in the way, there hadn't been any time for Harry to do that. For Group Captain Mahaddie had got use of the RAF car, the last one left allowed to use petrol, and he'd already corralled Katty as his pencil pusher for the day. 'Come for a ride!' Mahaddie had boomed at Harry. 'Tell me some jokes and cheer me up. Ye can put your hand on Katty's knee when I'm not lookin', if ye like. I'm sure she won't mind if ye tell her it's for the good of the war effort.'

He had obviously wanted the company.

The weather was so bad, not even Jerry could fly in it, but the forecast was predicting clear skies sometime beyond the next forty-eight hours, and everybody knew what that meant. Jerry would be back. So the AOC had ordered his deputy to get out there and see what they would have available to put up against what would be coming in.

On the drive inland, the roads had been totally empty. No buses any more, Mahaddie had explained. 'Can't spare the fuel, and anyway, the 109s shoot them up.' The journey had mostly been taken up in a monologue by Mahaddie: about how nobody at Scots Street knew from one day to the next how many fighter aircraft they had in their order of battle. How one minute the ingenuity and sheer bloody-minded determination of the erks would manage to resurrect one moribund Hurricane and get it back on ops, only for it, or another one, to expire again, the next. Not that the Hurricanes were any good, not against the 109s. They'd see a Jerry raid massing across the straits – courtesy of the island's secret ring of radar stations hidden in collapsed barns or poking out of a ring of Neolithic standing stones – and the fighter controllers in their underground labyrinth, hacked out of Valletta's southern bastions, would scramble whatever was available right away, but even then, the Hurricanes couldn't gain height in time. Jerry was always above them.

As for Malta's offensive capability, the Wellingtons were a liability – too big for a blast pen to completely protect and next to impossible to operate off cratered runways. As for the Blenheims – well, they kept getting shot down now. And shot up. No replacement parts to keep them flying.

And the bastard Germans had only been hitting them for a couple of weeks. What was it going to be like when Jerry settled down to the job, day in, day out. Oh, and another thing: just before the weather had turned bad, they'd started coming over at night too, so that was going to be something else to look forward to.

'What we need here are fuckin' Spitfires,' Mahaddie finally said, with some vehemence. 'There are entire squadrons of the fuckin' things lyin' about all over the south of England, whose sole contribution to the war effort right now is to go swannin' off over northern France shooting up Hun NAAFI trucks. "Our principal role in this campaign is offensive," that's all bloody Hugh Pughe parrots, night and day. "But, Hugh Pughe," says I, "ye cannae stay on the offensive very long if the place yer being offensive from has been reduced tae a smoulderin' pile of rubble!" But does he listen? Naw. Bombers on the brain.'

Hugh Pughe – Air Vice-Marshal Hugh Pughe Lloyd, Air Officer, Commanding, Malta, widely recognised as always being on 'transmit' and never 'receive'.

Mahaddie brooded, and then as he was crunching down the gears, he suddenly asked, 'How's your Eyetie chum doing?'

Harry saw Katty looked confused in the rear-view mirror.

'No idea,' said Harry. 'Situation unchanged since you last asked. Once we'd handed him over to the Army MPs at Gib, I never heard another thing about him. I suspect though he's feeling a lot better than he otherwise might have.'

Mahaddie barked a laugh. Maybe the opportunity for a good moan to someone not in his chain of command was indeed proving therapeutic to him. 'Aye, yer right there, son!' he said, as he pulled the car up at the tents. 'Yon Luigi's got a lot tae thank you for. He's probably a prisoner oot in Canada by noo, workin' fer beer money oot oan the prairie, ridin' the range on one o' they combine harvesters, gettin' a tan and workin' up a sweat fer the Saturday night hootenanny, an' aw them strappin' farm lassies, their farmhand boyfriends away in the soldiers, leavin' them jist dyin' tae fraternise wi' an Eyetie POW. Lucky bastard. Lucky, dirtae bastard, eh?' and he winked at Katty salaciously. Then he turned the engine off and gestured for his briefcase, before lumbering out with a parting 'Wait here', as if they were going to go anywhere in this rain.

Everything was quiet and the only sound in the car was the sound of that rain on the roof, while Harry considered his optimism about war tempering the Groupie might have been a tad premature. The silence dragged on. Katty didn't look as if she were going to say anything, and Harry couldn't think of anything he wanted to say. Until eventually, just to break the monotony, he said, 'It wasn't Luigi.'

Katty didn't respond, so he added, 'His name wasn't Luigi, it was Fabrizio.'

'Ah. The one you kidnapped from Majorca,' Katty said eventually, studying the rain on the windows.

'My prisoner of war,' said Harry, doing likewise. 'To stop him getting . . .'

'Yes, yes,' Katty interrupted testily, '. . . ending up as a guest of the Gestapo. How thoughtful of you.'

She knew the story? Of course. Mahaddie would have told her everything, and then put knobs on it. More silence. Then Harry spoke again. Asked something he'd sworn to himself he wouldn't. 'How's Chally?'

'I've no idea,' said Katty lightly.

'No?' said Harry. 'Well, he never was the chatty type, I suppose, but surely you can tell from his general demeanour . . . the roses on his cheeks . . . any tendencies to flatulence . . .'

'He's in Egypt,' Katty interrupted again. 'Posted there the day you sailed away.'

The silence returned. Then eventually Katty said, 'I heard *Nicobar* had returned, and yet you never came to see me. Where were you?'

And Harry felt a huge fist crush his heart. He turned in his seat and their eyes met and locked, and then the door flew open and Mahaddie dropped himself on to the driver's seat like a felled giant redwood.

'He wusnae pleased, though, your Luigi, wus he?' said Mahaddie, continuing his conversation as though he'd never left off. 'Aw naw. But there ye go. Hoo many o' us always know whit's good fer us, eh? No' a lot. Right, that's us done. We'll no bother wi' Hal Far. It's only your lot, Gilmour, that's doon there, and Ah doot there'll be any volunteers among them, willing to go dogfightin' wi' 109s in a Stringbag.'

He crashed into gear and they were off again, back to Valletta.

Katty was still house-sitting in Floriana, and it was there Mahaddie dropped her and Harry off with, 'Be good and play nice, boys and girls.' Katty gave Harry a blanket to wrap himself in as they sat on the sofa. It was a place with huge vaulted ceilings, striped wallpaper and entire walls filled with art, and some draped in tapestries. Each room had a marble fireplace. The chandeliers were long redundant, and the only lighting came from small gas wall lights and the odd table lamp. Without the gas, the table lamps gave the only light, and the radiators stayed cold. Nor was there anything to burn in the grates. No wood, because there had never been any wood: because there were no trees on wind-scoured Malta. There was no coal either now. Whatever had been left was long commandeered for use in the dockyards. And it was against the law now to own an electric fire – they burned too many amps for the struggling island power stations.

'We've been warned the rationing is going to get even stricter,' Katty had told him, presenting him with a cup of tea brewed over a small spirit stove. 'And the Rediffusion has gone too,' she said with a sigh, 'although the *Times* says it should be back up soon. Meanwhile all I can get on my little crystal set is the same old maudlin rubbish from Italy . . . opera this and aria that . . . not a tune you can tap your toes to.'

They went out to the Union Club that night. She wasn't performing, just a jazz band of RAF erks. The booze was rationed. And there was no point in complaining: it was much worse elsewhere. Apparently they had completely run out down in The Gut, and the drinking dens the length and breadth of it were all now shuttered and closed. They met people she knew, talked and went home. Harry stayed the night. It wasn't discussed, neither asked the other; it was too cold for the layer-by-layer etiquette of seduction. The next day they went shopping for fish, walking all the way to St Julian's, and came home via their café in Sliema, drenched. They went out again that evening, back to the Union.

And all the while Harry was watching her: the way when they were together she always stood close to him. It wasn't clingy, at least it didn't feel like it: it was more like she was making a statement – that she might be here of her own free will, but she was his responsibility. And the more he noticed, the more it seemed that a whole new road was opening up for him, should he choose to take it: the whole panoply of human entanglement laid out along its length, with all the ways on show as to how it would involve, engulf and embrace him, should he choose to take the first step.

Did he love her? Did it matter whether he did or not? There was some indeterminate promise here, that he was being asked to make – one of those woman-understanding things, that men never quite get. Harry, the sensitive boy, was still in there somewhere though: enough of him at least to let him guess that much. So he considered matters.

And that was when he made the decision to cynically take advantage of this woman. He didn't even bother to try dressing it up with fictions, in the way that Harry the young student used to do. This was about sex. He wanted her, and for the first time in his life there was nothing romantic about it. This was all about a man wanting a woman, nothing more. And as for the indeterminate promise? He knew he had no intention of honouring any promise, indeterminate or otherwise;

she could believe what she chose to believe. He didn't care. Harry, the sensitive boy, the knight errant he had always believed himself to be, deep down, had been shown the door. How did that make him feel? Sophisticated? A man of the world? An utter shit? Well, there was a war on, and . . . blah, blah, etc., etc., and all the other excuses he gave himself for not ending up the fellow he'd always thought he'd be. Maybe someday, one day, in the future, he might have the time to reconsider his actions: unless a mine, or a depth charge or a strafing 109 got him first, of course. Right now, he was having Katty Kadzow. She was his woman, now.

Chapter Nineteen

The Bonny Boy had read all about the action off the Hammamet Banks in the newspapers, and the sour expression that hit his face when he read the name of the heroic junior officer involved, who had stepped up to do his duty when all around had fallen, had stayed pasted there for days afterwards.

The story had made quite a splash. An attempt by three Italian cruisers to prevent the Royal Navy intercepting a major Axis convoy carrying vital supplies to Rommel, stopped dead in the water by a lone British submarine. Front-page headlines announced the victory, and the stories filled in the epic details: the small, storm-tossed British submarine, on the surface and alone in the vast Mediterranean Sea, her Skipper washed overboard in the tempest, her First Lieutenant critically injured, leaving her junior officer, just twenty-one years old, to press home the attack. There were photographs of a tiny submarine, and beside it, for effect, two even larger photographs, of the Italian cruisers the plucky sub had crippled – sleek, fast, beautifully-lined: giant floating beasts, bristling with guns. The Bonny Boy couldn't stop himself from reading all about it, especially all about that young junior officer, Sub-Lieutenant Harry Gilmour RNVR, a volunteer, a mere part-time sailor, and his 'cold, calculating courage', and how he had swept the seas clear for the cruisers and destroyers of the Royal Navy's Force F, and let them get in among Rommel's convoy, to sink every damn ship in it.

And now there was that name again, on the pile of signals that had just landed on his desk. That was why the sour expression was back. Funny how you could be sitting safe, buried deep within such an impregnable citadel such as Northways House, concealed inside the vast bland sprawl of a northwest London suburb – the secret home to the Royal Navy's Flag Officer, Submarines – miles from the sea and miles from the war, and yet the past could still reach out and find you.

Sub-Lieutenant Harris John Gilmour RNVR: his name on a recommendation from his Captain (S) for the award of the Distinguished Service Order.

All such recommendations in the submarine service passed across the desk of Captain Charles Bonalleck VC, the Assistant Chief of Operations to the Flag Officer, Submarines. There was a process to be gone through. You didn't just throw out these decorations and gallantry awards willy-nilly on the say-so of so-and-so. You never knew what kind of character, by whatever vagary of fate, might find himself up for a gong. It would be too late, after an award had been Gazetted, to find out your hero, when he took his uniform off, was really called Doris and had worked as a barmaid in Stepney before the war, or was a secret Satanist. Good grief! It was the King's name that went on these citations. No. There had to be checks done. The Bonny Boy wasn't actually responsible for any of the checking himself; he merely allocated the duty. However, he did have a say over what information should be checked.

He didn't even have to think about it, before he was reaching for the typed report he'd written about Sub-Lieutenant Harry Gilmour, that he always kept handy, just in case.

For Captain Charles 'the Bonny Boy' Bonalleck had once been Sub-Lieutenant Gilmour's commanding officer. Way back, when the war was young, and the Bonny Boy had been a drunk. Sub-Lieutenant Gilmour knew too much about the Bonny Boy, and the bitterness burned in him. He'd always sworn there would come a day.

He found the typed report – or rather a mimeographed and de-identified copy of it. It detailed the events leading up to the loss of His Majesty's Submarine *Pelorus* (Commanding Officer, Commander Charles Bonalleck VC) in a collision with a merchant ship at night off the Firth of Forth, back in 1940. Commander Bonalleck had been on watch on the bridge at the time of the collision and had survived. Most of *Pelorus*'s crew, and all her officers, apart from her Fourth Officer, Sub-Lieutenant Harris John Gilmour RNVR, had perished. The report went on to point out that only reason Sub-Lieutenant Gilmour had survived was because he had deserted his station. It wasn't true, of course. The truth about that collision was something else entirely; the Bonny Boy knew that. Unfortunately, so did Sub-Lieutenant Gilmour.

The Bonny Boy folded up the copy and put it in an envelope. He then placed it in a folder along with the medal recommendation, and placed both documents in his out tray. It would do for now. Until the opportunity arose to really destroy the self-righteous little prick. And it would come. Of that he was confident.

Chapter Twenty

Harry didn't like the look of the surf. Yes, the wind had abated quite a bit, and was blowing just a stiff breeze now, none of your tramontane or gregale nonsense, so the flimsy little canoes the pongoes called folbots would have a following sea going ashore. But they'd have to row against it coming back out, with the country in hue and cry behind them; and they'd be a lot lighter and more susceptible to skitter over the waves, going more in the direction the wind wanted them to go, than the one they were paddling.

Carey and the pongo CO were studying the shore through binoculars. They were about three or four miles up the toe of Italy from the little Calabrian coastal town of Bagnara, and not much more than twenty miles away as the crow flies from Villa San Giovanni, where the big railway ferries sailed for Messina and Sicily. Barely two hundred yards from the beach in front of them, the main railway line from the north came out of a tunnel, and five hundred yards further on, went back into it. All the freight, big and small, from oranges for Milan going one way, to vital war supplies destined for North Africa, via Messina or Catania or Palermo, going the other; all heading to or from the huge dock sidings at San Gio, and the big roll-on, roll-off ferries whose cargo decks were floating railway tracks that could each carry half a train across the Straits of Messina and back again.

It was a dark, cloudless night, and bloody cold. But then it would be the first of February tomorrow, so what did you expect. At least the January storms had gone, except that back on Malta that had turned out to be more disguise than blessing. With the clearing skies had come Jerry. It really was the worst joke of the war so far: that you actually felt safer on patrol than back in Lazaretto Creek.

Shrimp had eventually barred Harry from living at Katty's place – not out of any sense of moral outrage, for Shrimp was happier when he knew his boys were able to relax properly when ashore. And even a mature, happily married man like him couldn't imagine a more relaxing spot anywhere on the island for a chap to lay his head than on Katty Kadzow's bosom. It was because the raids now were so intense and relentless: up to nine a day now, and Jerry wasn't caring any more where the bombs fell. Shrimp couldn't have cared less whether Harry was prepared to risk it. He wasn't. Experienced submarine officers were precious commodities on Malta now, especially ones who were First Lieutenants. Shrimp wasn't going to lose one, just because he couldn't get out of his paramour's boudoir in time, and down into a public shelter. Lazaretto's shelters were mere steps away; he could stay there.

As things transpired, however, Harry's domestic arrangements weren't destined to last very long anyway. Three nights after he had been ordered back on to base, a 500-pound bomb went through the roof of the tenement block two doors down from Katty's, and exploded in the basement, shattering the foundations of half the street. The following day, several walls that had survived the night collapsed. Katty's apartment had remained largely intact, but her bathroom had suddenly become open-plan and her bath was left dangling in mid-air. As a result, Katty, being an RAF civilian employee, got the offer of a camp bed in the ladies' section of the basement, below the Lascaris main operations centre.

The thought of it made Harry grimace in sympathy – poor Katty, she wasn't the sort of girl who liked communal living. War is hell, he thought to himself.

'Captain Verney wants to risk it,' said Carey, snapping Harry back from his reverie, which he shouldn't have been indulging in on the bridge, on the surface, less than quarter of a mile off the enemy coast. 'So what do you think, Harry?' Carey asked.

The question was mostly courtesy. Lieutenant Malcolm Carey was *Nicobar*'s commanding officer, and whatever happened on board, or whatever operation it embarked on, was his decision. He might ask for advice, might even take it, but as far as what action they took, as far as their Lordships of the Admiralty were concerned, that was the CO's responsibility, and he alone would answer for it. And anyway, even before Harry had thought what his answer might be, he knew the decision had already been taken: he could tell from that affected relaxed pose his CO liked to strike, when he was about to get up to mischief.

'I think we should get that bloody great rubber thing up first,' said Harry, 'and get an air line on it, before we start wrestling with the folbots.'

Harry could see the glimmer of Carey's toothy grin in the dark. 'I think we're on, Olly,' Carey said to the pongo. 'Down you go and get your boys squared away.' Harry went down on to the casing to make sure the impending mayhem wouldn't get too out of control. He had put the Nicobars through a couple of dry runs on the way up here, but this would be the first time with the full kit and caboodle, troops and all. Still, he had Johnny Napier on traffic duty below, at the for'ard hatch, and Yeo, ably assisted by Bob Mundell in the control room, just in case the battleship *Vittorio Vento* came over the horizon to interrupt play. The Cox'n, Bill Sutter, would be first one up out of the for'ard hatch – there to assist Harry, and on hand to do any actual hitting of people if they didn't do as they were told, and quickly.

Here we go again, Harry: into action against the King's enemies, up and at 'em, one more time.

It was cold and slippery down on the casing. He could feel the slight up and down as *Nicobar*, her bow to the shore in order to present the minimum of silhouette, rode hove to. They were so close in now, Carey wasn't even charging batteries any more in case their diesel thump could be heard on the beach. There was only the sound of lapping waves, and the distant murmur of surf. Until the noise of precision steel being manipulated interrupted the peace, and the hatch lid sprang up before him and he could see the dim red light glowing up. The noise of people shifting equipment below seemed really loud out on the casing.

There wasn't a star in the sky, nor a light from the black smudge of the shoreline: just a thin effervescence in the distance of surf. The waves didn't seem too high any more, not from here anyway, but then here was quite a distance away.

Bill Sutter was up beside him in a flash, followed by a junior rating, Harry couldn't see who – one of the young ABs probably, picked for his brute strength. And then the gnarled, knobbly shape of some black thing appeared, being shoved from below amid a great deal of grunting. All three of them on the casing got a grip of its slimy cold slipperiness, and began to heave too, Harry digging his grip into one of the folds of it. Another heave, and lots more grunting, and then some young voice below saying, 'Sir! You sound like yer havin' sex, Sir!' And Johnny Napier replying, 'You'll be having sex with the toe of my boot in a minute, ya cheeky wee bastard!' And Bill Sutter, hissing low, through his suppressed laughter, 'Quiet below there!' And Harry grinning back at him, and then the thing was up and on the deck. A rubber dinghy, that they now had to inflate.

Harry took the air line from an unseen hand below, as Bill and the AB spread out the flattened dinghy, lumpy shadows moving in the dark. Then it was just a matter of attaching the line to the air valves on each inflatable section, and blasting in low-pressure air from *Nicobar*'s tanks.

Harry left the Cox'n and the AB to finish the job, and waved up two pongoes, both Sergeants with Royal Engineers and Commando flashes on their shoulders. With them came the first two folbots, and Harry guided them aft to either side of the deck gun. The men, just shapes in the dark, their faces blackened, and knitted caps down over their ears, went immediately to work. The folbots were ingenious contraptions made of canvas on a collapsible wooden frame – based on the design of the Eskimo kayak, Captain Verney had told Harry in the wardroom on the way here. The two Sergeants had probably practised themselves silly assembling the things blindfolded, because they certainly knew what they were doing, assembling them in the dark. Harry left them to it, and went to check on the dinghy.

'How're we doing, Mr Sutter?' he said, but he could see they were almost there. Two more folbots were being passed up behind them. When Harry looked up, he was aware of the dim shape of Carey leaning over the bridge, silent, just watching; and he felt a sneaky little pang of pride. The CO, not uttering a word, just letting him get on with it: trusting him to do it right, and not endanger the boat or the mission. Because this was a bloody tricky little caper they were up to here, on a narrow, slippery submarine casing, in the pitch dark, with a lot of bodies working and moving about, right underneath the noses of the enemy. And with a lot more heavy gear still to come up, and a lot more bodies too – pongo bodies – and here was Harry, making it all look easy, and knowing it.

They were working to a plan: Harry's plan. He knew they'd need one if people weren't going to start knocking each other overboard, and kicking kit after them as they got in each other's way. Which had been why Harry had made them listen to his plan, despite all the eye-rolling. The old Harry would never have dreamed he might take pride in such intellectually undemanding, lumpen lifting and laying, but he had to admit, it felt good.

There was something else that felt good too: something he'd learned, that had happened *after* that planning group he'd convened hours before, around the wardroom table.

It had been mid-afternoon, while *Nicobar* moved slowly below, creeping at periscope depth towards the coast at barely two knots, able to do so because the choppy sea above meant any shagbat stupid enough to be flying in this weather would have no chance of seeing them at any depth.

Harry had sat everybody down to a lunch of one of Empney's steak and kidney puddings, stuffed with tinned stew, and served up with tinned carrots, followed by stewed apples and creamed rice. It turned out to be one of the inexpert AB's better efforts. And Carey told him so, much to the lad's obvious delight – so much so that his sticky-out ears positively glowed pink.

Crammed around the wardroom table and into the passageway to hear Harry's plan had been Carey in his usual spot on the corner of the banquette, Johnny Napier, and next to him, the pongo in charge, one Captain Oliver Verney of the Irish Guards, who also wore the dull red eagle, anchor and Thompson gun flash of the Commandos on his shoulder. On an upended carton of tinned peaches had been perched the pongo's deputy and 'blower-up in chief', Lieutenant Colin Cotterell of the Royal Engineers, also the proud sporter of a Combined Operations flash.

They had eaten quickly and in silence, all huddled under the two little deckhead lights that were still glowing sickly white, and casting cosy little conspiratorial shadows. When they'd finished, Empney had cleared the table and brought them their steaming mugs of Ky, because it was going to be very cold up there tonight.

Harry began. In dreary detail. Who would be allowed on deck, and the order they'd come up in; the order the gear would come up and who would stow it in the inflatable; and then . . . and that was when Verney had interrupted. Some carping about how difficult it was going to be with all the gear on deck, to lower the folbots into the water, and for the men to get in them, because the canoes could be tricky little buggers to handle. And then how were they going to secure the inflatable alongside and be able to pass aboard all the crap they had to take ashore, because Harry had seen it all, hadn't he? They had a lot of crap.

Harry had had to force himself to be patient. He hadn't exactly taken to Captain Verney since he'd come aboard, clambering up off the pontoon like he owned the boat. He was a tall, spare, wiry individual, in a crisp battledress with his three pips of dull cloth on each epaulette, and an immaculate peaked cap, with the metal starburst-with-a-sham-rock-in-the-middle Irish Guards' cap badge, dull and ancient-looking, on its brow.

Not that Harry'd had that much to do with Verney since then – just enough to form the opinion that he was a regulation-issue, upper-class twit; and to delegate all responsibility for looking after him and his band of cutthroats to Napier, the hotel manager obviously well versed in dealing with tiresome guests.

So it was only after the meeting had broken up, that Harry found himself talking to the young Guards' officer, and that had been when he'd told him his story.

'You know, you're the person who's responsible for me being here,' Verney had said.

'Not me, mate,' Harry had blithely replied. 'I don't decide who goes on these jaunts . . .'

'No, I don't mean here on this ship, in this . . .'

'Boat,' said Harry, who wasn't normally so pedantic. 'We call them boats.'

But Verney had just smiled and nodded, before continuing. 'In the war is what I meant. Here, in uniform, fighting the war. You don't know me, but I know you. I've seen you before. In action. Or, rather, after being in action. You as good as slapped my face. Accused me.'

Harry had looked at him, much as one might look at a mad man. Verney laughed, 'Oh, we've never actually met. I merely observed you from afar.'

'Is this a joke?' asked Harry, wondering whether he was being mocked, if this bloke had realised what Harry thought about him and was having some sport by way of revenge.

'No,' said Verney, 'I'm thanking you for saving me from being ashamed of myself.'

Harry's rising anger must have shown.

'Shetland,' said Verney quickly. 'Autumn 1940. Your submarine had just come in, looking worse than someone who'd just gone ten rounds with Joe Louis. Lots of wet and fog and wounded sailors being laid out on a stone jetty. I was there. In a Crombie coat and a Homburg hat that made me look like my Uncle Percy, and even more like my liege lord, the Permanent Secretary. Who was there also. And so were you.'

'*Trebuchet*,' said Harry, remembering. 'We'd been up . . . to the Arctic.' Remembering also he was never to talk about what had happened up there, in the Arctic. 'I remember a couple of civvies there in the crowd. Among all the brass.'

'Me in my Homburg, and you in that watch cap that looked as if it had just gone ten rounds with Joe Louis too,' said Verney, grinning now. 'And I'll never forget that pullover you had on that looked like it had been used for elephant tug-o'-war and was the colour of a fifty-year-old face flannel. And the sewn-together jacket so as it would fit over your wound dressing. Oh, and the wellies with the tops turned over. I don't normally make a point of remembering what other chaps are wearing, but you were such a . . . devil for style, that day!'

Harry, grinning too, and shaking his head, said, 'I'm not sure what your point is.'

Verney's expression calmed down. 'You kneeled down to put a cigarette in a wounded sailor's mouth, because he was all bandaged up and couldn't do it himself,' he said. 'And that was how you reminded me there was a war on. That all this wasn't just some theatrical extravaganza to be enjoyed from the privileged seats, and maybe reap a bit of career kudos in the passing. A war that you, you little upstart,' he added, without the trace of a sneer, '*and* your wounded crewman were fighting, while I was carrying some mandarin's pencil case. Made a chap think twice, Lieutenant Gilmour. So here I am. What a coincidence. And I cannot tell you how proud I am to be serving alongside you. I almost feel sorry for the Eyeties.'

'Well, I think that calls for a cup of tea,' said Harry, left wondering about all the things you do, when you don't know you're doing them.

All the folbots and the inflatable were up on the casing now. The two Sergeants, and Bill and the AB were grabbing the boxes packed with Explosive 808, that looked like blocks of green putty and smelled like almonds, and were now being passed up; stowing them in the inflatable where it sat still on the casing. Then came the det. cord and the augers and entrenching tools, followed by the collapsed steel frame, the little petrol motor and the Bergen packs, the Bren guns and spare ammunition and flares, as well as the infrared signalling device. And when the folbots were all assembled and the inflatable packed and its two paddles put aboard, Harry stepped gingerly around it all and climbed back up on to the bridge.

'All set, Sir,' he told Carey. 'When you say go, we're ready.'

Carey leaned over the conning tower hatch and called down, 'Pass the word for Captain Verney.'

Verney was up in a flash. Harry couldn't read his expression – his face was all blacked up too, and his knitted cap pulled down tight. The bandolier of ammo around one shoulder and a big, black Browning 9mm automatic in a shoulder holster slung the other way across his chest made him look like some Barbary pirate. Verney studied the casing below, and his little task force arrayed upon it, then he turned back and grinned, now looking like some desperado Al Jolson.

'Top hole, dear boy!' he said to Harry. 'So we're ready for the off then?'

'Down, Fido,' said Carey. 'Let us just go over the pick-up procedures one more time.'

No one lived along this particular tiny stretch of coast. They perhaps had a good two to three miles of deserted beach and hinterland either way, before you hit people. But behind them, it was a busy sea, and going close inshore was a very dangerous pastime for a submarine. Certainly Shrimp had never been entirely happy that his boats should be used on such perilous enterprises. Nonetheless, here they were, but only on the understanding that the submarine's CO had the last word on whether the operation went ahead or not.

His orders might be to get the landing team ashore, but on no account was he to proceed if it involved any undue risk to the boat. And the same applied when it came time to take the landing team off. People who knew nothing about clandestine sub ops would tell you that how a Skipper managed the risk came down to a matter of fine judgement. It didn't. If a team, particularly if it'd been successful in blowing up whatever it'd been sent to blow up, arrived back at a rendezvous with the enemy hot on their trail, the skies full of shagbats and MAS-boats and destroyers to the left of you, and the right, then you left the landing team and ran for it. Brutal truth number one about these ops was, Commandos were expendable, submarines were not.

And this operation was a particularly complicated one, with lots that could go wrong. But whoever dreamed it up, must have believed it was worth the candle.

Nicobar had been careful on the way in, had made no attempt to sink any targets on her way around the north coast of Sicily, despite the odd juicy merchantman spotted on the horizon. No point in alerting the Eyeties to the presence of another sub in their waters. Then she had pottered up and down the coast for a day, looking for any excessive or unusual naval or air activity. Nothing. Nor, when she turned her periscope on the coast, did she see any military activity either: no sudden appearance of new coastal batteries or beach patrols. Just the steady movement of trains, up and down the line, a dozen or more every day. Big long fat, war materiel-laden trains.

So the plan was that these eight men would go ashore on the first night, opposite a particularly remote and vulnerable section of the line, and set up in the low scrubby hills. They'd lie low over the two tunnel entrances, a soldier out on picket either end, watching. When night two fell, they'd begin work drilling a series of holes into the clay soil above the tunnel entrances, using the little petrol motor to power the augers.

Lieutenant Cotterell would then stuff the holes with the shaped Explosive 808 aimed to blast diagonally into either side of the arch tops and cause the keystones to fail and the tunnel entrances to collapse. They wouldn't fire the charges, however, until a train was passing through – one coming from the north, preferably – and even then they'd wait until the train had re-entered the tunnel, blowing it when the locomotive was at least a score or more yards in beyond the southern entrance. What a mess it would create. All they needed was for no curious Eyetie to turn up, via air, land or sea and stumble on their little civil engineering project, and for the soil to be just as soft and clayey as the geology books said it should be; and for no excessive reinforcement of the tunnel structure to have been undertaken at any time since it was built, and for the petrol motor and the drill bits to work, and the det. cord to work, and the 808 to go off as it was supposed to.

After that they'd drop everything and make a mad dash to the folbots they would have left concealed on the beach. A quick paddle out to *Nicobar* waiting five hundred yards offshore, and Bob's your uncle – they'd all be sitting down for a celebratory tot in a little over twenty-four hours. What could *possibly* go wrong?

'Right then,' said Carey. 'Off you go, and we'll see you tomorrow night.'

'Tally-ho, and all that!' said Verney, and he was down the hatch and gone. Carey looked at Harry and arched his eyebrows. Neither man spoke, because they couldn't think of anything to say. When Harry looked back down on to the casing, the two Sergeants who had come up to assemble the folbots, were already sitting in theirs, where they rested on the casing. Suddenly the next two pongoes appeared, and were guided by Bill Sutter, one into a folbot, and the other on to the inflatable, and the same for the next two. Then came Verney and his oppo. The plan was that the four folbots would tow the inflatable, and the two pongoes in it would use their paddles to help, and to steer the bloody great, cumbersome lump all the way to the shore. On the way back, the two in the inflatable would leave it behind and pile into the spare places on two of the folbots.

As for getting the whole lot actually into the water, Harry had a plan for that too, and it began when he saw Bill and the AB clear the casing and the for'ard hatch shut. Bill's voice came up the voice-pipe announcing it was secure, and Harry leaned over to the voice-pipe and called down, 'Begin cycling main vents.' He was going to take her down to decks awash.

They were almost there, and without any major hitch, not since they'd loaded everybody and all their gear at Lazaretto, and *Nicobar* had cast off. Eight had been a lot of pongoes to carry on a cloak-and-dagger op, but it had turned out a remarkably easy trip from Malta to here on the Calabrian coast. Of course there had been a lot of initial jitters among the soldiers: not about their op, but about being on a sub. But Grot McGilveray had cured all that with his dirty jokes and dirty songs. Carey even remarked on it – how maintaining a generally high level of filth in the forward torpedo room usually worked wonders for curing the sub jitters. That and the food. It was a tradition the Navy fed its sub-mariners like fighting cocks, but as soldiers, even special ones like this lot, they wouldn't have seen a plate of bacon and eggs for at least two years before they boarded *Nicobar*. By the time they were due to get off, they'd had them served up twice. The gratitude was touching and every one of the crew were agreed, the pongoes were a great bunch of blokes. Even though they did often get in the way with all their press-ups and push-ups, and the scary way they were always cleaning and polishing and generally caressing their weapons, and sharpening their knives.

No, all they had to do was get the folbots and the inflatable in the water, and they were away.

Nicobar began gently, and more importantly, quietly, to settle. There was lots of waving from the bridge and back again, everything going swimmingly, until Verney started cursing.

'What's wrong, Olly?' Carey called down to him.

'I'm up to my bally bollocks in water!' Verney hissed back. 'The bloody boat's arse has fallen out!'

Harry's plan: no need to worry about loading the folbots and the inflatable while they bounced around alongside, with the risk of kit falling into the water; load them on deck and just let *Nicobar* sink beneath them until they float free. Except it hadn't occurred to him that the weight of someone sitting in a folbot while it rested on a steel hull, with all the jaggy lumps of steel that stick out of it, might tear the canvas. Bugger! Bugger!

'Any other folbots leaking?' whispered Harry, now at the CO's side. A series of 'No!'s. Which they could see for themselves now, as the other folbots and the inflatable began floating off, bobbing up and down on the waves. Verney's folbot, however, was now all but swamped, and just sliding and tearing itself more across *Nicobar*'s submerged deck. Verney stood up, and stepped out of the wreckage, wading several paces forward, calling and gesturing to the two in the inflatable. They threw him its painter, he caught it first grasp and began pulling the ungainly craft towards him.

The pongo left in Verney's folbot hadn't needed telling what to do: he was up and out of it and climbing up on to the bridge. He hadn't been promoted Corporal without being able to do his sums. With one folbot gone and Verney in the inflatable, the landing party was already one person too many for the trip back, and the Corporal had taken the decision not to make it two too many, especially if the one of them to be left behind was going to be him.

'Slight change of plan!' Verney called back. 'But we'll still see you tomorrow night, even if I have to swim. Cheerio, now!'

Carey didn't say anything. The Corporal was up on the bridge, standing beside him, shivering too much to speak, drenched up to his chest and dripping everywhere. Harry, as he looked into his blackened face, could see he was royally pissed off. 'Go below, and get someone to give you a dry pair of overalls and a mug of Ky,' he said.

Behind him, Carey was speaking into the bridge mic. 'Put a puff of air into one and six main ballast tanks. Group down, slow astern, together.'

When Harry looked over the bridge towards the shore, the black lumps of their little flotilla had already merged into the darkness. They were already reverting to full buoyancy again and now it was time to find that half-sunk folbot before they pushed off. They couldn't leave it to get washed up somewhere – might as well send a telegram saying, 'Hello! We're here!'

⌒

'Multiple HE, bearing red-fifteen,' came the disembodied voice from the ASDIC cubby. 'Low revs . . . target drawing left.'

Carey said absently, 'Uh-huh', as he contemplated his next move; he was playing chess with Yeo in the wardroom. *Nicobar* was as quiet as a Sunday, and he could hear the ASDIC operator's every word all the way from the other side of the control room.

It was mid-afternoon the next day, and this was the umpteenth surface contact of the watch, and the second substantial convoy. They were at Watch, Dived, hanging in the deep pellucid blue at eighty feet, and Napier was Officer of the Watch. Harry was reading a book in French, Stendhal's *The Charterhouse of Parma* – another of the volumes he'd picked up from Louis, the old bookseller in Valletta – the one he passed coffee, cigarettes and rum to.

Napier said, 'Do you wish to take any action, Sir?'

'Nooo,' said Carey, coming to a decision and moving a pawn. 'When's dinner, that's the only action I really want to know about.'

'Don't know, Sir,' said Napier. 'Empney's in the forward torpedo room – Grot's telling dirty jokes.' Said in a voice so that you could tell Napier wished he was up there listening too, instead of watching an endless daisy chain of potential targets pass unmolested. With all the pongoes gone, Jack was obviously celebrating getting the space back. The forward torpedo room had been where they'd stowed all the land-ing party and their gear for the trip. And they'd taken up so much room, there'd been no space for *Nicobar's* seamen ratings *and* her tor-pedo reloads, so *Nicobar* had sailed with just the torpedoes in her four forward tubes. The two stern tubes didn't have the luxury of a reload space. Not that it mattered how many torpedoes they carried right now. Common sense dictated they not stir up the coast while their landing party was still ashore. They wouldn't be firing anything until they had them all back safe on board. Then they could run amok.

Which hopefully wouldn't be too long. They just had to get dinner out of the way, then run inshore and wait for the fireworks display on the coast that would tell them that Verney and his cutthroats had done the job. They'd have their fish-goggled Signalman on the bridge to pick up Verney's infrared flash message confirming they were putting off, and fish-goggles would use his flasher to guide them back to Mama. Mission accomplished.

'He's a nice bloke, your pal Olly,' said Carey, scowling as he lost a rook. 'Although how anyone could ever see you as a role model for the life heroic beats me, mate.'

Carey was talking about Captain Verney's story. His long reminiscence with Harry had of course been overheard and had been all around the boat in ten minutes.

'He's not my pal,' said Harry, mildly exasperated, and not for the first time. He'd been ribbed before. 'I hardly know him.'

Yeo, sitting opposite, had looked confused. 'I haven't heard about this one,' he said.

And Napier, who had heard all the stories about the *Bucket* and what had happened to her, for they were many, said, 'Don't worry about it, I'll tell you when you're older.'

'Ah!' Yeo had said, because he always listened to his new pal.

The waiting continued. They had dinner. Napier said, 'Mmmn. Mince 'n' tatties!' And those were the only words spoken while they cleaned their plates.

They cleared the boat for action after that, then went up to periscope depth and ran down the coast until they spotted the marker points they'd selected to fix the bay. After taking bearings to make sure of exactly where they should be, they went deep again to wait until after sunset.

That had happened just after 5pm, twenty-five minutes ago, and now they were on the surface again, and running in, both diesels charging the batteries with the spare amps that weren't being used to turn the main motors driving them at a steady nine knots through another cold, pitch-black night, with only Harry's translated Italian pilots' notes to help him and Yeo, the Navigator, work out how off their position the various currents and drifts might have left them. At least it was all but flat calm.

From quite far out it was obvious something was wrong. Very wrong. Carey quickly shut down the diesels and they crept on under motors. The sky above where they had calculated the bay to be was suffused with an eerie glow, and as *Nicobar* eased up the coast, not daring to press further towards the shore, the glow settled into a definite light reflecting off the low dense cloud, and back off the scrubby black shadow of the hillside. Carey, Harry, the two lookouts and the Leading Signalman – Dexter was his name, with his IR goggles around his neck – were all on the bridge. Harry warned the lookouts to keep their eyes firmly seaward, in case anything was coming up behind them, not that anyone was going to see too much on a thick night like this.

It started to drizzle. Carey ordered *Nicobar* trimmed down to decks awash, to lessen her profile even more.

Then out of the darkness, from inshore, the bang of a diesel engine bursting into life. The noise was so loud in the deadening rain, it sounded as if it had happened right next door. But it hadn't. The starboard lookout pointed to a shape off their bow as it began to move, a small curve of white water curling from under its stern – a MAS-boat, its propellers beginning to churn the water, getting under way and then heading away from them, down the coast. It had been lying hove to a mere mile away, but no one had seen it against the shadow of the land.

No one spoke. Carey watched it until the pale wake faded to black. They heard its engines rumble on, and then they too abruptly stopped. It was difficult to work out the direction on open water, but it looked like the MAS-boat had stopped quite a bit to seaward of them now, and about two, maybe a bit more miles down towards Bagnara: as if it were standing a sea watch on the eastern approaches to their bay, the direction in which a British submarine might approach.

Carey ordered slow ahead, together, and they edged further inshore.

As they closed, the noises of men at work drifted out to them.

Carey crouched down to steady his binoculars, and he studied the tableau unfolding before him. Harry, even with his crap night vision, put his binoculars to his face, deciding to see what he could anyway. What he saw looked like fairground lights; a serried rank of them, all badly masked the same way travelling folk would tantalisingly surround a circus ring with sheets, making you pay at the gate if you wanted to see the full effect inside.

Every now and again there would be the blue arc of a welding torch flashing above the background glow, and voices, and the chug of a donkey engine pulling something heavy.

'They're fixing the overhead electric line,' said Carey, with the glasses still stuck to his face. 'It's a full maintenance crew. There's some huge track vehicle, like a long railway carriage with a work platform on top, and a diesel loco there to pull it all, I suppose. The carriage has got winches and adjustable ramp things all along the platform. But it's all partially hidden . . . all I'm seeing is through gaps in these huge canvas awnings they've got hoisted up . . . the full length of the carriage, all along it, to mask their work to seaward, I suppose . . . and there's all these floodlights they've got strung out. A whole gang of workmen. Too many to count . . . at least thirty. And they're all over the bloody power lines. Jesus H. Christ. Haven't they got any buxom, *bella* bambolas to bang at night? You'd think there was a fucking war on!'

Harry said, 'What do we do now, Sir?'

And again, without taking his eyes off his glasses, Carey said, 'Well, seeing as you're the boat's resident smart alec, Mr Gilmour, I was hoping you'd tell me.'

Harry smarted at that, and when he turned, he was aware of both lookouts and Leading Signalman Dexter shaking with laughter in the darkness beside him. He turned on the dim white shape of the nearest lookout's face, sticking out of the hood of his Ursula suit, and hissed at him, 'This is no laughing matter, Willoughby!'

'Aw, hell, Mr Gilmour,' said Carey behind him, rising from his now futile survey, with a resigned look on his face, plain to see even in the darkness, 'of course it's a bloody laughing matter. Unless you want to see a grown man cry?'

What *were* they going to do now? Carey's first plan was to wait. So they did, remaining trimmed down, with only *Nicobar*'s conning tower sticking up out of the waves where they wallowed, hove to about seven hundred yards off the beach. Carey had Dexter don his goggles and keep a lookout for any messages from shore, first up the coast from the bay, and then down. One lookout kept his eyes in the direction of the MAS-boat, and the other scanned to seaward. Carey kept the boat at Diving Stations – he wanted to move fast if he had to, even if, right now, he couldn't imagine why. Empney brought them all up steaming hot mugs of Ky. The night dragged on.

In their brief chats, he and Harry wondered at the Eyeties' lack of blackout, but then Malta was the only base the British could launch air raids from, to hit this far up the Italian mainland, and Malta was getting bombed all to hell. As for the sub threat, well, the Eyeties probably thought they'd soon know if there were any British submarines about, because ships would be getting sunk. So, since there weren't, the Eyeties obviously thought they were safe.

But what about Verney and his men? Where the hell were they? There certainly didn't seem to be any evidence of an earlier fight around the tunnels. Maybe they had all just stood up and surrendered when the work train pulled up – unlikely, but was it possible? No, it wasn't. There would be signs: signs of a fight, signs of a surrender too. And there wasn't. No Italian soldiery running about all over the countryside looking for anyone who might have sneaked away; aircraft overhead, ditto; no soldiers guarding the work train. And up and down the coast, no noise of stable doors being slammed shut or any of the usual hue and cry generated by a military caught napping.

With just twenty minutes to go before first light, *Nicobar*'s conning tower silently slipped under the waves and she turned on to a ninety-degree track from the shore, slipping back out to sea. Nothing had been seen or heard from Verney's team the entire night.

The next night they were back. The only difference this time: the weather was worse.

Out of badness, Harry ordered the same two lookouts back up on the bridge for another cold night as punishment for laughing. The old Harry wouldn't have been so petty, but the new Harry was a Jimmy now, and he was buggered if he was going to let the crew think that they were all on some kind of 'All aboard the Skylark!' day out. The odd giggle was good for morale, but Jesus Christ – there were limits!

The same Leading Signalman, Dexter, with the IR goggles was there too. Carey also had the pongo Corporal up, to see if he could spot something they hadn't. During the day, Carey had him in to the wardroom several times, talking over all likely scenarios, then they went through the impossible ones. The Corporal's best bet was that Verney had seen the maintenance train coming in plenty of time and scattered the team to lie low in the rough scrub until they went away.

'The Eyeties must be pretty dim not to spot that mob,' Harry had said.

'It's amazin' what you don't see when you're not looking for it,' the Corporal had replied, and Harry, on reflection, believed him.

So there they were, approaching the bay again, except tonight there was no light reflecting off the low cloud and no maintenance train, all lit up, between the tunnel entrances. It was just dark and drizzly, with a gusty onshore wind coming from the nor'-nor'-east, making the rain sting Harry's left cheek every time it put in another surge of effort. The only thing that told them there was a shoreline ahead was the thin ribbon of phosphorescence where the surf hit the beach.

Then, suddenly, out of the inky black backdrop of the night: *pouf! pouf!* Two sets of floodlights came on, one after the other, and in the sudden splash of their sickly brightness, from *Nicobar*'s bridge the entire gap between the two tunnels was theatrically revealed. They could see the tracks and the power cable pylons, and the scrubby hill rising behind them, and in the immediate halo of each set of lights, each one above the two tunnel mouths, were working parties, moving methodically about their business. The track between was empty however. The maintenance train had gone; so the men on the tunnel roofs must be stay-behinds, thought Harry: there to finish off the job. Although why they hadn't done it in daylight was anybody's guess. Maybe the overtime was better for nightshifts. Harry noticed Carey's back stiffen, and when he looked up along the line of his binoculars, he could see why – the MAS-boat from last night was there again, seen now only because her navigation lights had suddenly been turned on: one at the masthead, and her port red running light. She was about two miles away, close inshore in the lee of the top curve of the bay, hiding again in the shadows. Otherwise she seemed completely asleep, riding at anchor, sheltering from the prevailing wind. A squall could just be made out passing beyond her; it must have helped shroud her up until now.

Harry wondered why Carey didn't dive the boat immediately; there was enough water under them. Or even order a turn away back to sea. But when he took time to lay out the tactical map in his head, he could see *Nicobar* probably wasn't visible from the MAS-boat either, or the shore. Riding decks awash, her conning tower would be lost against the thick, black, shitty wall of weather. Harry wondered, what on earth was Carey up to now?

That was when Dexter sang out, 'Signal from shore, Sir! Bearing green-one-five . . . correct identification code . . . being repeated. The correct landing party ident being sent, Sir.'

There was no point in anyone else looking for the spot the lanky rating was pointing to with his free arm, somewhere ashore, off the starboard bow, because the signal was being sent in infrared, and only Dexter with his silly big IR goggles on could see it.

'Acknowledge,' said Carey.

Wow! thought Harry instantly. That could be a dodgy call. How did he know some Eyetie hadn't nobbled Verney's Signalman, and was getting him to lure *Nicobar* in for a nice surprise?

As the rating flashed his message back to shore, there was a voice behind them. 'Can I get a shot, Sir?' It was the Corporal, at their elbow, his face all anxious and working.

Carey understood immediately and gestured for Dexter to hand over his kit. If the message was kosher, the Corporal would know the sender, and the jokes to tell. Hell, he might even recognise the sender's fist on the lamp. The Corporal began flashing now. There was a pause, and then they saw the Corporal's shoulders momentarily rock. 'It's them all right, Sir. Pansy Potter, Sir.'

'Who?' said Carey.

'Pansy Potter. Captain Verney's Signalman. He says be prepared to take a message.' The Corporal was grinning.

Carey looked at him coldly. 'Something amusing you, Corporal?'

The Corporal shrugged. 'He said some other things too, Sir. Most disrespectful. I'd rather not repeat them.'

'Well, you signal him back, Corporal,' said Carey, 'and tell him you did repeat them. To me. And that I'm going to feed his complimentary Navy tot to the cat in retaliation.'

'You don't have a cat, Sir.'

'Tell him I'm getting one specially.'

They got set up to receive. Dexter mounted his night glasses on the bridge bracket, adjusted his goggles and crouched with his signal pad ready to take it all down. Harry only knew the signal was coming over when Dexter's pencil started scribbling. Then it was done, and Dexter had torn off the message and handed it to Carey, who read it and said, 'Well, bugger me!'

Nicobar was already at Diving Stations. Carey had ordered it hours ago, before they had surfaced and begun their run inshore, so her crew were all closed up and ready to go. Carey stood them down and ordered

Yeo up to take over the bridge watch. When Yeo emerged on to the bridge, Carey grabbed him by the arm and led him right to the front of the bridge.

'That there is an Italian MAS-boat,' he said, getting behind him and pointing it out to Yeo by holding his arm right along the lad's line of sight, just to make sure. Yeo flinched at how close the shadowed shape was, and that it had all its navigation lights on. 'Do not take your eyes off it. Understand?'

'Aye aye, Sir,' said Yeo.

'Dexter, meanwhile, is watching that bit of the coast there, through his goggles' – Carey turned and pointed Yeo towards the black shadow of the coast off their starboard bow – 'in case his pal on the beach, Pansy Potter, decides he wants to chat more. Leave him to that. Now dead ahead . . .' and then he turned Yeo's attention to the pools of insipid light being cast from the floods on top of the two tunnel mouths, maybe seven or eight hundred yards away, right on *Nicobar*'s bow. Carey continued, 'You see all these Italian workers slaving away? Well, they aren't. They're Captain Verney's landing party, pretending to be Italians. And before you say anything . . . Yes, we're all very impressed by their audacity and bravado and all that guff, and won't we all have stuff to tell the grandchildren.' Then he spun Yeo back to face him. 'Now listen very carefully. If the MAS-boat moves or does anything at all, apart from just sit there, dive the boat. Right away. Do you understand?'

Yeo nodded, a solemn nod.

Carey continued, 'Don't call me to the bridge. Just take us down, fast. Anything else happens . . . anything at all . . . get me up here. Got it?'

'Aye aye, Sir!' said Yeo, with the light of battle in his eyes.

'Harry – you too, Corporal – below with me, now.' And Carey went down the hatch.

Round the wardroom table, sitting bathed in the now familiar conspiratorial red light, Napier joined them for their council of war. Right from the very beginning, from when he'd first known Malcolm Carey as First Lieutenant on the old *Bucket*, Harry had often wondered whether it was because he was an Aussie, or whether it was just the man, that Carey had always refused point blank to dodge an issue. He certainly didn't this time.

'Tenth Flotilla standing order one, for boats on cloak-and-dagger ops: you don't mix it with enemy surface craft, on the surface,' said Carey. 'No exceptions. However, Captain Verney has a plan he wants us to go along with.' Carey jabbed the slip of signal pad with Verney's message scribbled on it. 'And it involves us mixing it with that Eyetie MAS-boat. On the surface. Anyone any thoughts?'

He was talking to Harry and Johnny Napier. 'Not until we've heard the plan first, Sir,' said Harry, answering for both of them. Napier gave Harry a look and then smiled and shrugged. They'd just collectively agreed that they were prepared to disobey a direct Flotilla order.

'Good,' said Carey, and he proceeded to outline what the pongoes had in mind. The Corporal sat nodding throughout. When he'd finished, Carey turned to him and asked, 'You think this is a good plan, Corporal?'

The Corporal drew himself up, pleased at being consulted. 'It's as dodgy as hell, Sir. But that's Captain Verney's speciality. He's mad, bad, and dangerous to know, but he's good at gettin' away with it. If you're goin' for surprise, make it a good one. That's his approach. And, as he says . . . no op's any fun unless you get to sneak up behind the buggers at some point.'

'An unimprovable summary of what is being proposed, Corporal, if I say so myself,' said Carey. 'Harry, what about you? Thoughts?'

Harry knew what was happening, he'd been here before: with Malcolm Carey and with their old Skipper, Andy Trumble, now dead at the bottom of the Skagerrak. The decision had already been made. Carey hadn't become a submarine commanding officer without knowing how to make up his mind. And that was fine with Harry. If he'd been in Carey's boots, he'd have already decided too.

'Well,' said Harry, 'no point in faffing about, is there, Sir? Remember what Andy used to say when there'd be half a dozen of us around the table and ten different opinions?'

Carey laughed, and Napier looked confused. '"Good. We're all agreed then",' said Carey, mimicking Trumble's best desperado. '"We're on!"'

The four of them: young men sitting around a table, all in their twenties, all nice lads who in a sane world should have been getting ready for nothing more arduous than taking their girlfriends out dancing or to the cinema. Except they weren't. They were twelve hundred miles from home, one of them a great deal more, sitting bathed in red battle light, preparing to go into action on an enemy coast.

Harry was going to miss seeing the actual fireworks. As Jimmy, his station in the coming action was going to be in the control room. Napier would be up for'ard under the torpedo loading hatch, with his three-inch gun team, and a band of part-time cutthroats. Carey had told his Torps & Guns he needn't bother to clear for torpedo action: MAS-boats were too shallow in draught to torpedo.

Tonight, *Nicobar* was going to fight with her gun, so the magazine had been opened and a shell relay line was in the passageway. But there was also a possibility that *Nicobar* might need people up on the casing too, so behind the shell luggers, two of Napier's torpedo team were waiting, armed with Thompson guns, and several others with Navy service .45 revolvers on their hips. The Corporal, who was with them, had an arsenal all of his own.

Yeo was with Carey on the bridge, along with the two lookouts, and tonight, seeing as Carey had overcome his aversion to having the damn things clutter an already tight space, *Nicobar*'s two Lewis guns had been shipped, and were now swivelling on their bridge wing brackets, manned by two of *Nicobar*'s more steady Leading Seamen. Apart from the clutter, the other reason Carey seldom ordered the Lewis guns up: they took too long to unship and get down the conning tower hatch if *Nicobar* needed to dive in a hurry. However, if tonight was going to go to plan, *Nicobar* wasn't going to be diving. At least not until it was all over.

They waited, mostly in silence. Trimmed down on the surface, back at Diving Stations, the crew closed up for action, but with the watertight doors open, and a clear run through the boat; diesels shut down, and the inside of her all bathed in weak red light. No chat now, everybody waiting for a train.

Yeo had obviously been briefed by Carey to keep the boys below up to date, for every now and again his plummy tones would come down the voice-pipe to Harry. It was now well into the early hours of the morning, and he had already reported two trains – long, rattly lines of goods wagons hauled by shiny electric locos, barrelling through the tunnels, running from the direction of Villa San Giovanni down on the Straits, heading north. Verney's gang had worked on through. But half an hour or so ago, all industry had ceased on top of the tunnel mouths. The floodlights had still glowed, Yeo reported, but there were no figures labouring under them. Then Yeo was back on the voice-pipe, breathlessly announcing, 'Someone's killed the floods!'

Carey's voice came down right after him. 'Righty-ho, Mr Gilmour. Something's afoot. Get everybody on their toes.'

Harry lifted the sound-powered phone and alerted Napier, then the engine room. And then he stood right underneath the hatch, looking up at a flat, black plate of night, with cold drizzle coming down, making a sheen on his face, his ears practically twitching to hear something, anything.

When it did happen, it happened fast. No flashes, barely even what you'd call bangs – just a series of pressure waves, so Harry felt it rather than heard it, through *Nicobar*'s steel skin, in his ears, and in his diaphragm. First, there was the explosive sound of another train, roaring out of a tunnel mouth, and then the rippling clanks in rapid succession of a train covering the gap between the tunnels, and then down an octave, the sound of a heavy loco going into the second tunnel . . . and then the first concussion. It lasted the longest, but only by a second or two, a fraction of one moment – and then the other detonations. Bigger. Lots more oomph. And out of the wake of the pressure waves, the mangling, tearing sounds of two thousand tons of train concertinaing itself into piles of falling masonry, rock and earth.

'Well, that worked,' Harry heard Carey's voice observe casually through the pipe, then, 'What's our friend doing?'

What happened next, Harry had to piece together later. Yeo's attempt at a running description sounded like a BBC racing commentator trying to convey the excitement of the final furlong at the Grand National after injecting himself with an overdose of amphetamines.

Then, through it, Harry heard Carey order 'Slow ahead, together', and the engine room, ringing back, acknowledging. Then the sound of heavy machine gun fire came down the hatch, and the sweep and flash of a searchlight somewhere was reflecting off the tiny circle of black cloud base he could see when he looked up.

Harry learned later, the MAS-boat had woken up immediately: searchlights coming on, turning to sweep the shore and the smashed remnants of the goods wagons still left in the open space between the two tunnel mouths. And as the MAS-boat had got under way, and began curving around to head towards the beach, two machine guns, one either side of its wheelhouse, had opened up on the scrub between the railway line and the high-water mark, spraying it with tracer rounds.

All this, Carey told him, despite the fact there had been no targets for them to shoot at. From where he'd been on *Nicobar*'s bridge, he'd seen no movement on the shore at all: the Italians had been firing wildly.

The MAS-boat had then sped across the head of the bay, right across *Nicobar*'s bows where she still lay, trimmed down, still invisible in the night. The MAS-boat had briefly masked her port machine gun in the process, and so fast had she been racing, her crew preoccupied, they never saw the little curve of white peel back from *Nicobar's* bow as she began to get under way herself.

Then the MAS-boat had slewed again, to starboard this time, to bring both of her machine guns to bear on the shore, before slowing to a crawl, her searchlights continuing to sweep back and forth across the scrub.

While the MAS-boat manoeuvred, Carey was issuing his orders, 'Steer one-zero-zero . . . gun crew close up . . .', and Harry heard the racket of men going up through the for'ard hatch, and then Carey yelling, 'Commence firing!'

And then nothing.

Next came shouts from above that Harry couldn't make out, and the bridge telegraph ringing for 'Full ahead, together', and *Nicobar* surging under his feet, as he heard Carey yelling again, 'Deck party, close up!' The sound of scrabbling feet from for'ard, from the hatch well; men tumbling up in a rush, and then Carey again, 'Port ten! . . . Midships!' And the Cox'n, from a mere few feet away across the control room from Harry, calling it back into his voice-pipe as he touched the helm, only to have his call cut off by the sound of a bloody gun battle breaking out – on the casing, right above their heads! The *Brrrrrp! Brrrrrrp!* of Thompson guns, and shouts. But still no three-inch gun firing. Not even a single bang. And that was when Carey shouted down the voice-pipe for everybody to 'Brace! Brace!' Then *Nicobar* hit something. And Harry thought, *Oh Christ! Don't tell me we've run aground! Not here! Not now!* But they hadn't run aground. Yes, he could feel it as *Nicobar's* way suddenly came off her, but it was as though she'd rammed something, not run on to it. And he knew from his inshore pilot books, there was no reef or bar in this bay. A crunching sound of splintering wood echoing down the conning tower hatch provided the answer. The MAS-boat. They'd rammed the MAS-boat. Next to Harry's ear, the bridge telegraph rang again, 'Stop, together', and with the acknowledgement, the firing fell away too, to just the odd sporadic burst.

'Number One!' It was Carey, calling down the bridge voice-pipe. Harry acknowledged, desperate to ask what the hell was going on! But keeping his mouth shut: Carey would tell him, or they'd all die, one or the other, sooner or later. 'Nip up under the torpedo hatch and prepare to receive the landing party. There'll be a couple of prisoners too. Stow them in the Stokers' mess.'

'Aye aye, Sir!' and then he was running for'ard.

Harry got the shell team organised, told them to push the pongoes forward into the torpedo room when they came in and to get them to stay there. Another pair from the shell team he sent back to help Empney with the flasks of Ky, and he told one of the POs to open the spirit locker and make sure there was a tot in every mug.

The first pair of boots came down the hatch ladder, and in them was a creature caked in mud and filth, still clutching his Thompson gun for dear life. When the AB who helped him off the ladder reached to take it off him, the man's grip was like a madman's, and Harry could see the whites of his eyes – plain murder in them, and fighting fury, staring out of the rimed filth slathered over his face.

'Release the gun and let him stow it,' barked Harry, 'or you'll not get your tot!'

It never ceased to amaze Harry, the effect an order, any order, shouted as loud as possible, had on the military mind. The shivering soldier jerked his head front and himself to attention and presented his gun, which the AB grabbed, and passed it to be stowed back in an empty torpedo reload rack. And down they started coming. Six soldiers, including the Royal Engineers officer, Cotterell. Harry grabbed his arm, and the soldier turned to face him, grinning a huge grin, his face and hair all filthy and matted; more mad than happy, and completely unable to talk. Harry sent him back towards the wardroom.

Harry got up and left Carey, Cotterell and Verney sitting around the wardroom table. The two soldiers had stopped talking now and were stuffing cheese oosh into their faces, specially rustled up for them by Johnny Napier, with some of the contraband he'd liberated from the MAS-boat's galley sprinkled in to give it that extra flavour – lumps of exotic sausage and herbs – and they were mopping up the olive oil it had been cooked in with huge lumps of rustic Italian bread. Neither man had eaten for two days.

Harry was going back to 'interrogate' the prisoners, although every time he said the word to himself he couldn't help laughing. Him, interrogating prisoners. What would his tutorial group have said, or Shirley? What would she have said? He slid around the corner to the galley for a flask of coffee to take with him, and four tin mugs. As he did so, he could see the backside of one of the POs sticking into the passage from their mess, one cabin up, where he knew the Chief had been working on their seriously wounded prisoner. The PO looked like he was mopping up.

Bill Sutter did as *Nicobar*'s medic in the absence of a Surgeon. The boat's senior rating fixed all the bruises, strains and upset tums, and even, if he were pushed, her more serious emergencies. A young Italian sailor from the MAS-boat had been carried aboard drenched in blood, a crimson singlet bundled into his face to try and staunch the bleeding. A .303 bullet had hit him in the head, and smashed his right cheek and blown most of his lower jaw away. They'd got him on a stretcher as far as the senior rate's mess and Bill had said, no further, and gone to work.

Harry had had a glimpse of the mess the bullet had made of the lad as they'd carried him past, and he had looked away, not wanting the image in his head. When he'd gone back to the mess later, Bill had the lower half of the lad's head swaddled like an Egyptian mummy, so that only his eyes showed above the bandages. He'd performed a tracheotomy so the lad could breathe, and out of the gauze a tube had dangled, riffling weakly with every shallow breath. When Harry looked in the lad's eyes, they'd been unfocused, and the forehead above them had that morphine sheen that Harry had seen before.

Harry didn't go back to look again. He knew there was nothing he could do, just as he knew they were lucky this lad was the only serious victim of the mad scramble of an action they'd all just been through. Carey had told him all about it as they had headed back out to sea.

After all the demolition charges had gone off, and the Italian MAS-boat had headed right into the shore, hosing the area indiscriminately, all the while they were doing that, the now legendary Pansy Potter had been flashing away in the direction of *Nicobar's* bridge on his IR device; lying deep in the scrub back up towards the head of the bay, perilously close to where the MAS-boat had been anchored.

His message had been: *We have recovered our folbots, and we are coming off. Right now. Please start distracting the Eyeties.*

Carey had ordered Napier to get his gun crew up and start shooting. But the first round up the spout of *Nicobar's* three-inch gun had jammed. Carey had already demanded to know exactly what had caused that particular timely fuck-up, and was waiting for answers. Meanwhile, the folbots had indeed started coming off the beach, and the Eyeties had already noticed. That's when Carey had ordered the Lewis guns to open up. They sprayed the MAS-boat with their .303 rounds, chipping paintwork, splintering the odd sill, but mainly keeping heads down. That wasn't going to last forever, and Carey – all the while, Carey quite candidly confessed to not being able to take his eyes off the single Breda 20mm anti-aircraft cannon, as yet still unmanned, sitting on the MAS-boat's quarterdeck.

'It was one of those moments, Number One,' Carey had said, with a shake of his head, 'where you know you really have no choice. All the other options have been exhausted, or are going to take too long. You have to do it and do it now . . . and the "it" I was going to have to do, was to have *Nicobar* ram that bloody Eyetie right up the arse. Nothing personal, you understand.'

And that had been what Harry had felt, down below in the control room: the crunch as *Nicobar*'s bows had run right into and through the Italian's transom, so that *Nicobar*'s bows had come to rest in the enemy's engine room, crushing her aft deck frames and half-sinking her. Most of the MAS-boat's crew's immediate reaction had been to dive into the water and start swimming for the beach, almost as if choreographed, Carey recounted. Others, coming up from below were armed, however, and started to make a fight of it. But Napier's lads were already swarming forward along the sub's casing, firing as they went.

'I think it's safe to say it brought out the Glaswegian hooligan in Mr Napier,' Carey had told Harry, with an affectionate grin. 'He was first down off the hydroplanes and on the enemy's deck. It was Nelson and the Glorious First of June all over again. If the damn thing hadn't gone glug, glug, glug on us, he'd have taken her, and we'd all be drinking the prize money by Thursday night.'

The Italian resistance had been token, but the Corporal, who'd been right alongside Napier all the way, had wanted to finish off all those Eyetie sailors who had now decided to follow their shipmates into the water, splashing for shore, by turning their own guns on them. Napier had apparently grabbed him by the throat and explained in easy to understand phrases, that His Britannic Majesty's Royal Navy did not machine-gun shipwrecked mariners in the water, pal!

Harry swung himself through the watertight door into the engine room and squeezed his way past the two diesels, which were going flat out with a noise that seemed to knock his eyes out of focus; through the dense oil and diesel reek, and then aft past the relative cloister of the motor room into the Stokers' mess. It looked like a scene from down a mineshaft instead of at sea; a cramped little domestic nook, with bunks and pin-ups, and a table where two of *Nicobar*'s bigger Stokers were sat, playing cribbage under a little row of yellow deckhead lights, just keeping an eye on things. At one end of the table, perched on a bunk, Bill Sutter was tying off the final suture on an Italian sailor's thigh, the ragged pucker of the wound he'd just sewn up showing what a bloody gash it had been. A large, oil-stained Stoker in his singlet was kneeling beside them with cotton wool and a bottle of alcohol to clean away the remaining blood. Not that the wounded boy was noticing any of this; with his head lolling and a morphine smirk on his face. Propped up against the next bunk was another Italian sailor, another mere adolescent, with a big wad of gauze wrapped against his ribs, and beyond the far end of the table was a third man, in a civilian suit of sorts. He was older, with luxuriant grey hair and an even more luxuriant moustache, seemingly unhurt, sitting with his back against the aft bulkhead, his eyes watchful. His face lit up when he saw Harry come through the door: this officer had spoken fluent Italian to him when he'd first been bundled aboard this steel tube deathtrap – at last someone he could reason with – but his gaze flicked towards the big Stokers and he decided not to break the silence just yet, if silence was what they had in a small compartment surrounded by heavy machinery going hell-for-leather. Harry was pleased to note that the Stokers were no longer carrying the revolvers they'd been issued with earlier. A shoot-out at the OK Corral was all he needed right now. Both Stokers looked up, and one said, 'What's happenin', Sir?'

'We're heading out to get some sea room between us and that bloody mess we've left behind,' Harry said as he sat at the table and plonked the coffee flasks down. 'And shortly, we shall be cruising through the Aeolian Islands. If the weather were better and one was minded to take cocktails on deck, one might see Stromboli's fires light up the night sky.'

The Stokers all grinned. 'Is that Java, Sir?' asked one, nodding at the flasks.

It hadn't taken much interrogation by Harry to establish that the Italian sailors were just boys, both still teenagers – and they knew nothing about anything, including why they were even in the war. One had been the boat's greaser and had been in the MAS-boat's engine space when *Nicobar* had rammed them, and had just got out in time. The other was the boat's cook. Both seemed genuinely amazed and relieved that the Brits had an officer aboard that could speak Italian, and both were almost pathetically grateful for the treatment they had received, each one nodding 'Si' vehemently to every question, as they slurped their piping hot coffee.

Harry explained that they were now prisoners of war, and that they would be well treated. He then remembered what Mahaddie had said about the fate of Axis POWs captured these days by the British, and he told the boys they'd probably end up spending the rest of the war working on some Canadian prairie ranch, going to barn dances at the weekend. And yes, there would be girls at the dances; and yes, the girls would be missing their menfolk who were all away at war. This went down very well. But they must behave themselves while *Nicobar* remained on patrol . . . 'Si! Si!' . . . and make no attempt to interfere with the operation of the boat . . . 'No! No!' Perish the thought. When one of the Stokers came back with bundles of clean slops for them to swap for their tattered and sodden uniforms, both even seemed eager to volunteer to help out while on board. Harry made a note – especially in the case of the cook.

The civilian turned out to be the most interesting of their guests. He said his name was Michaele, and he was an employee of the Ferrovie dello Stato, the Italian state railways. He gave some grand-sounding technical name for his job in Italian, which he himself translated as meaning he was a technical inspector. He said he too was relieved to be able to converse with someone in authority in Italian, but that he wanted to take this opportunity to express his dismay that he, a civilian, should be handled in such a discourteous fashion by the British Royal Navy, of all people. He would have expected more; indeed, he was dismayed *and* astonished; and he asked to be put ashore on Italian soil at the earliest opportunity. His wife and children would be missing him.

Harry, smiling, poured him another cup of coffee, which Michaele accepted gratefully, and then Harry explained. Verney had nabbed him, even though he was a civilian. 'Because I bet he can give us some really damned top-hole gen on how the Eyetie railways work, and how best to bugger them up, what!'

Verney was almost certainly right. Unfortunately, that meant that Michaele would not see his wife and family again until the war was over.

Chapter Twenty-One

Harry stepped into the control room to find Carey on the periscope, cap on the back of his head, two bright circles of light on his face: sunlight from above reflected through the 'scope's eyepieces, as he surveyed the approaches to Malta's Grand Harbour. It was late afternoon on a beautiful flat calm day, and they were at twenty-seven feet, about a mile off Fort St Elmo, at the edge of the swept channel through Malta's own protective minefield.

'The red flag's up,' said Carey, 'but I don't see any air raid in progress.'

There had been a signal the previous day to all boats – *Nicobar* had received it while coming down the Sicilian Channel – air raids were so frequent, all returning submarines must wait submerged at the entrance to the swept channel, and only enter if there were no red flag flying from Fort St Elmo. There would no longer be a minesweeper or ML to escort them in, as any surface ship venturing out from under its camouflage netting in daylight was being subjected to sustained strafing attacks by German 109s. And when they did surface, on no account was anyone to risk coming up on to the conning tower until they were through the boom and under the notional protection of the Bofors gun batteries.

Harry had been aft in the engine room, making sure the fix list was up to date for the base maintenance crew and everything was ready to hand over, so everyone could make a quick getaway when they came alongside. It was always something that miffed *Nicobar*'s notoriously grumpy Warrant Engineer, the dreaded McAndrew: someone checking up on him, as if he didn't know his own job. But Harry didn't care – it was his job, checking up.

'I think I'm going to risk it,' said Carey. 'It'll be dark any minute now and Jerry's probably knocked off for tea—' But his last words were cut short by weird splashy staccato sounds coming through the hull. Everyone in the control room looked up, puzzled, except Carey, his face still stuck to the big periscope. He was transfixed, looking at the sudden blossoming of a row of watery spouts erupting right in front of the periscope head, and then a huge dark shadow swept over everything. He involuntarily stepped back as they all heard a *clunk-clunk-clunk-clunk* hitting the casing above them: the Germans' spent 20mm cannon shells sinking down to bounce off their hull on the way to the seabed.

Carey slammed the periscope handles shut and sent it down. 'Mundell! Eighty feet. Now.' He stood away from the periscope and wiped his brow. 'Bloody hell,' he whispered, 'that was a bloody 109 shooting at us. Where did he come from? The sea's flatter than a witch's tit up there. He must have seen our shadow. Christ. The bastards really are all over us. At least he didn't have a bomb. We'll wait until after dark.'

Everybody was jittery now, the little bounce in the step you get returning from patrol gone.

Nicobar had remained on patrol in the Tyrrhenian Sea for almost three weeks after her action against the railway tunnels north of Bagnara, hunting between the coasts of northern Sicily and Calabria. And she'd collected quite a bag from a series of successful Gun Actions against small trading schooners and other light coastal merchant ships, none of which had been deserving of one of her torpedoes, but each loaded with cargo vital to the enemy's war effort. At least that's what the Nicobars told themselves, and who was to gainsay it?

So the Nicobars had been quite chipper coming in. They would be entering harbour with a lot of new bunting on their Jolly Roger: lots of white stars on it for all her gun sinkings, and a huge dagger for the tunnels op, plus a ram's head for ramming the MAS-boat, and crossed sabres for Napier's foray on to her decks.

But Harry knew Carey was worried the Shrimp might not see it so rosily. They were hauling all their torpedoes back home. And they were doing it because they had avoided any targets deserving of torpedoes: targets with destroyer and torpedo boat escorts, on the grounds that their ASDIC set was buggered. Because Carey had buggered it when he had rammed the MAS-boat. And if you attacked an escorted convoy without having a functioning ASDIC dome, you couldn't tell if the escort was counter-attacking, at least not until the depth charges were raining down around your ears.

All because of Carey's decision to blatantly disregard Shrimp's standing order: not to mix it with surface warships, on the surface.

So, in this case, hauling *all* the torpedoes home wasn't going to be seen as merely prudent. Not by a keen-eyed Captain (S) who was going to take a very dim view of the dented ASDIC. Carey had good reason to suspect there might be squalls ahead.

In the event, he needn't have worried. When they eventually came alongside, it was plain to see that the Shrimp had far more pressing things on his mind. And so had everyone else.

There was no gang on hand to welcome them home, nor even a wardroom to welcome them to. No one around to hear all the stories about Napier's boarding party and the looting of an enemy MAS-boat, and how, all of Napier's gang, coming back aboard, all the ones not carrying the poor Eyeties who'd been shot up, had been loaded down with hams and cheeses and jars of yummy stuff, and butts of wine, from its galley. And that Napier had to be reminded about the other items that might be of interest, such as code books and charts and stuff like that, and that he'd had to go back for them. And how little Carmine, the eighteen-year-old Eyetie with the gash in his ribs, had taken over all Empney's culinary duties – and shown them what a real cook could do, even on a tiny four-ring stove, feeding thirty-eight of them! It was touch and go whether they wanted the patrol to end. The lad had even begged to stay on as *Nicobar*'s cook until the end of the war. And quite a few had begun plotting as to how they could wangle it.

Then there was what they did to keep all the pongoes amused for the rest of the patrol, how Verney had kept them from getting bored by forming them into boarding parties, and how they'd go on to any enemy schooner or coaster they stopped with a shot across its bows, with orders to gather any intelligence they could – but mainly to raid their galleys to keep Carmine's larder stocked – before packing off the crew in their lifeboats and letting Napier's gun crew dispatch the enemy vessel with their three-inch gun, the untimely jamming incident now forgotten.

There'd been no one there to hear about the moving service they'd held on the casing the night the badly wounded Italian sailor had finally died, and how his shipmates and even Michaele had cried, and so had a couple of Nicobars too, when they commended the body, wrapped in a hammock, to the deep.

All the stories left untold.

Because Jerry had finally found the Lazaretto. The gallery that had formed the front on the wardroom was still there, but the back wasn't. It was just a big hole now: no Shrimp's office or CO cabins, the periscope shop and the battery store: all rubble. And the Army barracks, tacked on to the side of the base, where all the Commandos and the cloak-and-dagger johnnies had lived, rubble too.

Miraculously, no one had been killed. But nearly everyone on the base at the time had been cut, gashed, singed or had limbs broken. Even Shrimp and Hubert sported bandages and sticking plasters. And all officers and ratings now messed together in an old, disused, giant underground oil tank, cut by a previous naval generation into the rock face. Shrimp's new office was in a corner, behind a sheet strung up between two scaffold towers. There were rows of camp beds, and against one wall, bunks, a common table with a surviving mismatch of chairs, and on the ceiling, a run of bare cable snaked from hook to hook with naked lamps giving such imperfect light that the whole cavernous space looked under water. And it reeked, with a sometimes throat-gagging stink of oil – puddles of it still here and there, and duck boards laid over the worst of them. But it was safe from the bombs that fell night and day now.

And as for the torpedoes, Hubert told Harry the boss would be quite pleased to see the torpedoes back, and not wasted. The base was running short.

While Carey made his report to Shrimp, Harry was handing over the boat's paperwork.

'You need to detail a couple of POs and an officer to stay behind,' Hubert told him, 'and the rest of you, tonight, off up to Ghajn Tuffieha rest camp.'

'Why?' said Harry. 'Most of the lads have rooms in Sliema.'

'You haven't seen Sliema yet,' said Hubert. He looked really strained in the sickly light. 'Most of it isn't there any more,' he added eventually. 'Whoever you roster on for harbour duty will be staying on the boat. New standing orders. All boats in base have to submerge on one of the buoys out in Marsamxett during daylight hours. They surface at night for any repair or maintenance work. They'll get sunk otherwise. You'll need to draw up a roster before you leave tonight.'

'I'll stay,' said Harry. 'I've business in town.'

'No,' said Hubert. 'No COs or Number Ones to stay behind. You've got to rest. And that means Ghajn Tuffieha. Shrimp's orders. And anyway, who are you going to see sitting at the bottom of the harbour?'

'We'll be needing to go into dry dock,' said Harry. 'Our ASDIC dome needs replacing. I'll stay.'

'Oh,' Hubert sighed, before eventually nodding, because Harry was right: they couldn't leave a dry-docking to a junior officer. 'Jerry got the pigs, by the way,' he added. 'What was left we made into sausages.'

Official business over, Harry went looking for Verney to say cheerio and good luck, and thanks for the fireworks display, and for the professional way his men had taken to pirating Italian Navy galley stores on the high seas. But Verney and his mob had already gone, been marched out of the Lazaretto's gate, and off into some remote gulley in the hills where they could hide during daylight from the marauding Jerries.

Bloody war. You met up, made friends, and the next minute they'd gone, and you didn't know whether you'd ever see them again. Not this side of demob at any rate. Maybe not even this side of the Pearly Gates.

Harry went off to find Bill Sutter and Bob Mundell and informed them they'd be remaining with him on *Nicobar*. Neither looked particularly pleased, so he told them neither was he, but he needed their experience on hand for the dry-docking, and for when work started on the ASDIC dome. It was when you started pulling out the guts of a boat that you started finding things, and he wanted to know what they'd put up with and what they'd say needed fixing. They, in turn, selected four ratings. Along with a base maintenance crew, they conned *Nicobar* around to the Msida Creek torpedo store and unloaded her four forward and two stern tubes. By the time they were finished, it was almost dawn, and a telephone call to Hubert got agreement not to dive in the harbour, but to just throw cam netting over *Nicobar* where she lay alongside the rubble piles that had been used to disguise the arched entrance to the underground store.

Two raids had gone over during the night: high-level bombers that had dropped their loads over Kalkara Creek way. Harry had even watched the searchlights seek out the planes of the first raid from *Nicobar*'s bridge as they'd edged up Marsamxett Harbour. He counted over a dozen Italian Savoias. But the flak Malta's guns had thrown up, had brought no raider down from that raid. He only heard the second raid, being down in the forward torpedo room, helping hump the one-and-a-half-ton beasts up and out of the for'ard hatch. Welcome back from patrol, Harry, he told himself, since no one else was going to welcome him.

Which wasn't strictly true: no person was welcoming him, but the mosquitoes were. And the sandflies. It might only be the end of March, but the temperature was rising, and the buggers were up and about as they laboured to move the torpedoes across the jetty.

When they were finished, and the sun was up, Harry told Bill Sutter to mind the shop; he was off to Lascaris if anyone was looking for him. It sounded like official business, but both men knew it wasn't. Not that it mattered. *Nicobar* would be moving nowhere while it was daylight. But it would take Harry four hours to walk from Msida Creek to Lascaris, the island's combined headquarters and ops room, instead of the half hour it should have.

It was a beautiful, cloudless morning as he stepped out in his whites and dress cap and with his new second ring upon his shirt epaulette, but what he saw distracted him from putting on any swank. As far as he could see, Pieta, Floriana, Corradino Heights – they were all just jumbled mess now, whole streets looking like they'd been stood on, and he could feel the crunch of grit in his mouth, the entire landscape painted with a patina of dust. There wasn't a single living person in sight. He knew it was early, but there should have been someone about.

He'd barely been walking five minutes and he could already see the Upper Barracca Gardens and the Saluting Battery at the extreme south-eastern corner of the Valletta bastion, under which the HQ's tunnels had been carved out of the rock, when the first air-raid siren had sounded, and he'd had to find the nearest shelter.

The moaning wail started echoing out over what was left of the town, and Harry had started running. When he got to the shelter's entrance, he could sense it was already full, even as he dodged through the sandbags, before he even hit the steps, jumping down three at a time. He could smell it.

Coming out from the mote-filled shafts of light into the dark, all he saw were the faces looking up at him: grimy pale women, old people, children; a floating raft of faces, looking to see who was coming down at this hour. They'd obviously all been here all night. There was the smell of unwashed bodies, and the smell of overflowing latrines. Everyone was too tired to get excited about his arrival. An old man who shifted a little to give him a patch of dirt to sit on, had a coat over his pyjamas, a pair of plaid slippers on the end of bony ankles, and a dust-choked, full grey beard – at least Harry thought it was grey: it could have all been dust. The old man eyed Harry's pristine white shorts and shirt, but he was too exhausted to engage in conversation. He just rocked a little with what laughter he could summon, and said, 'Best of luck with that, Jack.'

After the all-clear, Harry had moved on, but had to duck into another shelter for another raid, before he finally made it to Lascaris and Katty.

'We're better than we were,' she said, once all the hugs and kisses and a few tears were over. The two of them sitting with cups of tea in the Lascaris canteen. She hadn't even noticed all the dirt and scuffs on his now filthy uniform. 'Two cargo ships made it in the other day, and they've managed to beach another down in Marsaxlokk Bay. They were all that got through from a convoy from Alex. There was a big sea battle in the Gulf of Sirte. We drove off an Italian battleship.'

Harry thought she looked dazed, like a punch-drunk boxer. She was quiet for a moment, then she frowned. 'But there's a big row going on now,' she said, looking around to see if anyone was listening. There wasn't another soul in the room. 'The ships that made it into Grand Harbour. The bombers got them before they could be unloaded properly. Everyone's blaming one another. And Group Captain Mahaddie has told me all the Spitfires that were flown in while you were on patrol . . . they're all U/S . . . unserviceable. Shot up on the ground, he says. So he's hopping mad too. And no one knows when they're going to be able to try and run another convoy through.'

'You're tired,' said Harry.

'Yes,' she said. 'Everybody's tired. And there's no beer left!'

The days that followed passed in a blur. Harry got his first real view of Grand Harbour in daylight for weeks: the toppled cranes and the wharves with bomb craters like bites out of them. The rising palls of smoke and the tangled wreckage of the crippled merchantmen, both sunk, resting on the bottom with their superstructures and upper decks still showing, crews clambering over them trying to get at any surviving cargo, loading it on to barges. And the light cruiser HMS *Penelope*, still in dry dock from another fateful night in which Force K, this time, had charged into a minefield off the North African coast. HMS *Neptune* had been lost, and *Penelope* was so full of holes she'd been rechristened HMS *Pepperpot* – now festooned with netting and surrounded by smoke pots that they'd ignite to disguise her every time a raid came over, another pall to be added to the ones already smudged across the island's sky; the yard workers labouring beneath it to get her fit to make a run for it to Gib.

And then there were the days of *Nicobar*'s dry-docking, and the yard workers continuing to work on her too, under netting during daylight hours, ignoring the raids; Harry, shamefaced having to run to the shelters, because he was under orders to do so, because sub crews were not expendable. And meeting Captain Clasp again, down on French Creek, his P-boat alongside, discharging cargo after another Magic Carpet run – four of the old minelaying boats now assigned to this emergency lifeline full-time, bringing in essentials such as aviation spirit, anti-aircraft ordnance and baby milk powder. Harry shaking hands with him, the two of them promising each other a drink when there was a drink to be had: Clasp, for Harry cutting free that lifeboat and saving his submarine, and Harry, for Clasp looking after his sextant, and leaving it safe for him on Malta, confident he'd be back to pick it up.

And then there were the three days spent on the bottom of Marsamxett Harbour, listening to the bombs going off above them, playing Uckers or trying to sleep. And four nights with base maintenance crew getting *Nicobar* squared away and ready for her next patrol.

And all the odd hours snatched with Katty, sometimes a whole night, in other people's apartments; at their favourite café on Sliema seafront, dodging in and out of the air-raid shelters when the bombers came over; stepping into the shadows to hide from passing 109s because of the number of people now – civvies as well as servicemen: women, children, any living thing – being strafed by the Germans just for the hell of it. Losing count of the raids. Some days it felt as though Jerry was coming over, dropping what he had, and then just heading back for more.

The electricity was off and the gas, water was intermittent, and the streets were strewn now with the detritus of aerial war: unexploded bombs and cannon shells, lumps of shrapnel from the endless barrages thrown up by the island's anti-aircraft guns, coming down again. There were bodies too – the ones who never made it to the shelters in time, or the ones who did and got blown out again. The only little saving grace that saved you as a passer-by from the full random horror of it: the dust. It coated everything, so that you saw no blood or open wounds, just a bland enclosing sandy patina that blanketed everything until there were only shapes and no colour, so that the newly dead looked like the ancient dead, like a scene from a Pompeii dig.

The Rediffusion was out completely now. Only the *Times of Malta* continued to print, and as well as news, it would run the latest information on the distribution of food. It didn't print the whole truth, of course. Katty had heard the word was around Lascaris that without another convoy they had two months' of supplies left: ten weeks at a pinch, then all the food would be gone. The amount of fuel left and ammunition, the authorities managed to keep closer to their chests.

Then *Nicobar* was ready for sea again, and back she went out on patrol, back to the shallow waters off the North African coast. When she returned at the end of April, there were two more merchantmen and two more schooners on her Jolly Roger. And there was news to digest. Malta had won a medal. The King had written to them, in a personal message: 'To honour her brave people I award the George Cross to the island fortress of Malta to bear witness to a heroism that will long be famous in history.'

The George Cross: the British Empire's highest award for civilian gallantry. To bestow such an award to an entire population was unprecedented, and the news had gone around the world. Everybody was chuffed, even hiding in their holes.

But there was other news too. The Tenth Flotilla's ace and mascot, HMS *Upholder*, was 'overdue, presumed lost'. Her CO, Lieutenant Commander David Wanklyn, VC, DSO and two bars, the submarine service's pin-up boy, and all his crew, gone. Operating out of Malta, they had sunk almost 130,000 tons of Axis shipping in just over a year. The Upholders had been the Flotilla's veterans. The crew who knew every trick, and what a load of nice blokes too. Everybody agreed, they'd done their bit. And they'd been on their last patrol before going home to Blighty for a rest and a refit. If they could get the chop . . . People stopped the conversation right there: no future in going down that road. Not right now, not here, not these days.

There was another matter too, that affected Harry in particular. While they'd been on patrol there had been a scatter of awards Gazetted for *Umbrage*'s crew and their action against the Italian cruisers. No one mentioned it to Harry when he got back. No one had wanted to, for reasons that would become obvious. And since *Umbrage* with her new CO, Hume, had just gone out, no one felt they had to. It had been Shrimp who had called Harry in.

Grainger, who was now back in Blighty apparently, all but recovered from his wounds and pushing pens for the time being in some

Admiralty liaison job, had got a bar to his DSC, and there had been a DSC for young Wykham. The Wrecker, Parry-Jones, and Tuke, *Umbrage*'s ASDIC man, had both got Distinguished Service Medals, and there had been several Mentioned-in-Despatches for others. Harry got nothing.

'It was skilled and determined action that inflicted significant damage on the enemy, and I felt your conduct merited the Distinguished Service Order,' Shrimp had told him.

Harry had been dumbfounded. A DSO. You didn't need to be in the Andrew long to know the old 'Dicky-Shot-Off' usually only went to COs, and even then just to four-ringers and above. For a junior officer to get one, well, that was the next best thing to their Lordships taking out a personal ad in *The Times* announcing you'd just missed getting a VC.

'This matter isn't over, Mr Gilmour,' Shrimp had said. 'Leave it with me.'

What else was he going to do?

Later, when he'd composed himself, he found he wasn't that bothered he'd received no recognition for the action, as if to do so would have been some kind of acceptance that he had signed himself over in his entirety to this life, and that what was important to it, must now be important to him. For some reason, he didn't feel quite comfortable with that. It meant his old tweed jacket and silly scarf days would be gone, and with them all the light, daft days of his life and the luxury of blessed irresponsibility. He decided not to think about it any more, telling himself he didn't have the time to, which seemed as good an excuse as any.

Nicobar was only in for three days, before she was ready to go back on patrol. Carey, having to shout over the noise of another bombing raid going on above him, told Shrimp he felt safer at sea, and so did his crew. Which was true. And Shrimp, well, he knew Malta's only strategic relevance was in being able to attack Rommel's supply lines. Right now, with her airfields looking more like the surface of the moon, the submarines of the fighting Tenth were the only chaps doing the job. And Rommel was stockpiling for another go at the Eighth Army. All the intelligence signals coming in from Northways told him so. So did the photoreconnaissance boys. Chally was still flying, although this time from some flyblown sandpit west of Cairo. So, of course Shrimp said yes, even though the Flotilla's mounting losses were becoming harder for him to take, not easier. Not that Harry knew any of this; he was too busy.

Harry still managed to be with Katty though, twice, before he had to sail.

There was a part of him that used to sit off to the side these days, watching himself with her. Lots of things to see that fascinated him, including the fact of his own fascination. It was as though he were practising some kind of supreme form of detachment: the ultimate selfishness of it, protecting yourself by pretending you weren't actually there, but above it, above everything.

The easy domesticity he slipped into with her amazed him – both of them complicit, and all of it against the most undomestic of backdrops. The two of them, conjuring up an everyday life for each other while the bombs rained down about their ears, and the world fell apart. Blocking out the knowledge that either of them could be killed at any time, for no reason, because it was happening to so many others, and there were no reasons for it not to happen to them.

It made him laugh to himself to think of the Katty of a few months ago, and the Katty now. The glamorous Katty, envied and desired back then; filling her days now, not with nightclub engagements and champagne at the top tables, but with drinking tea with a young Royal Navy Lieutenant with no prospects and nothing to offer beyond his next knocked-off bag of real coffee – and the fun she obviously felt, stepping out with him in the dark, when all the 109s had gone home for the night, for an arm-in-arm stroll to their favourite café, still open, to deliver another bag of that illicit coffee, and trade it for a room to themselves for a few hours, or until the first air-raid siren woke them.

And what was even more fascinating was the number of times he found himself wondering what Shirley would have made of the world he found himself in now. Not about Katty, but about Malta: what it had once been and now was; how the bombs could not quite obliterate the quiet beauty of the place, nor the stoicism of its people. He thought of Shirley walking through a restored island, at some time in a better future, curious about what she would think, curious about who would be with her.

The last snippet of Lascaris gossip Katty had for Harry before he sailed, was that C-in-C, Mediterranean Fleet now considered it too risky to attempt any more relief convoys from Gib, and that the next scheduled convoy from Alex had been cancelled. Oh, and that everyone believed a German invasion was now imminent. And then she'd given him a goodbye kiss, as if none of that had meant anything, and they'd both said they'd see each other in a couple of weeks, and away he went.

Chapter Twenty-Two

Captain Charles Bonalleck VC, Assistant Chief of Operations to Flag Officer, Submarines was absently daydreaming about his next appointment, sitting in his office in the airy spaciousness of Northways. He'd been assured it was going to be an operational command: a Captain (S) appointment. The Blythe flotilla had been mooted, which didn't fill him with the joy he'd hoped for. He'd been envisaging something more tropical – something that would take him away from the cloying presence of Mrs Bonalleck. He was sure, however, that even if it did turn out to be Blythe, he could concoct some plausible scenario that would prohibit her from moving north with him.

That was when the summons arrived: the little light on his bulky Bakelite desktop telephone exchange. It was Max's office.

'Captain Bonalleck. The FOS would like to see you right away, Sir.'

The Bonny Boy wondered if this was the news he'd been waiting for. You might be promised a posting; told, nay assured, it was yours – the orders were going to be cut any day now. And then it never happened. The Andrew was famous for that. Was he about to find out?

He knocked on the door marked 'Vice Admiral M.K. Horton VC' and the PO Writer manning the desk told him to come in and take a seat. Max kept him waiting some considerable time, and when he was summoned into the presence, the face that met him was not welcoming.

Max was seated behind his desk. He did not get up to shake the Bonny Boy's hand, as he usually did; he did not address him by his first name; no 'Charles, dear boy!' this time; nor did he invite him to sit.

On Max's desk, between them, lay a bland, regulation manila folder. Max gestured to it, irritated. 'Look at that and then explain to me why it has landed on my desk,' he said with his crisp, reading-a-grocery-list voice he used to those he was about to destroy. The Bonny Boy felt his guts sag. He leaned over and picked up the dossier.

In it were four separate typewritten documents. The first was a recommendation for the award of the Distinguished Service Order to Acting Lieutenant Harris John Gilmour RNVR, formerly of HM Submarine *Umbrage*, from Captain G.W.G. Simpson, Tenth Flotilla, Malta.

The second slip was from the office of the FOS: an assessment of the officer's fitness to receive the award. Appended to it was a copy of a section of the evidence of Commander C.A.W. Bonalleck RN, VC to the Court of Inquiry into the loss of HM Submarine *Pelorus*. The section concerned the conduct of one Sub-Lieutenant Harris John Gilmour RNVR. The recommendation for the award of the DSO was stamped 'Rejected'.

And the fourth document was a signal from Captain (S) 10, personal to FOS, asking for an explanation.

When Max saw that the Bonny Boy had finished reading, he spoke again.

'I ordered you to make this accusation go away, did I not?' Max said. And indeed he had. Some months ago, the Bonny Boy had been seeking to have Sub-Lieutenant Gilmour put before a court martial for his conduct prior to the loss of *Pelorus*. The accusation was deserting his station. Meanwhile, Sub-Lieutenant Gilmour had been posted to a French submarine as Liaison Officer, where far from being unreliable, his conduct there had led the French to award him the *Croix de Guerre*.

That was why, in the interests of good Anglo-French relations, Max had told the Bonny Boy, 'That accusation of yours, lose it.'

But now it was back, and Max didn't like being disobeyed.

'Yes, Sir,' said the Bonny Boy. He knew never to contradict or argue or dissemble before Max, especially when he was in this mood. He'd served alongside Max in the Great War, both of them in submarines, both winning their Victoria Crosses. He knew him well, and cordially loathed him.

Max had done considerably well for himself since those days, better than the Bonny Boy had.

And that was why the Bonny Boy loathed him, why he'd always kept to hand, lest he needed to rehearse them, the veritable archive in his head of the grievances he had against Max Horton, the conspiracies he knew Max must have fomented to thwart the Bonny Boy's interests and further Max's own.

'Well . . .?' said Max.

'I don't know,' the Bonny Boy lied. 'I have no knowledge of this particular recommendation.'

'Really?' said Max, eyebrows arched. 'The whole country knows the story. You do not read newspapers. Is that what you're telling me?'

'These recommendations come through by the bucketful, Sir. We merely append all the available background. You surely don't expect me to have oversight on every . . .'

'Bucketful? You are telling me what this young officer did qualifies as part of a bucketful?'

'I don't know who . . .'

'I do not care "who". But I know what I smell. Some petty little grudge is going on, doing its little worming worst in your department. The morale of hard-pressed submariners rests on the prompt recognition of their sacrifices. That is why it is vital all such awards are processed and Gazetted with the utmost dispatch. One of your duties is to make it happen, not to sit idly by while your people are indulging in whatever jealousy or spite or other squalid malice moves them.'

Max, his face now a mask of naked authority, while his fingers tapped the desk. When he spoke again, it was in a tone that brooked no discussion: a Vice Admiral issuing his orders. 'I have no intention of soiling my hands getting to the bottom of this. And neither will you. It stops here. Now. Fix this, this day. I expect a report that will meet with my approval when I return from my afternoon round of golf. As for that . . . piece of paper there . . . the contents of which you once drafted . . . it ceases to exist, forthwith. Have I made myself understood this time, Captain Bonalleck?'

The Bonny Boy felt his face burn crimson. That that little shit Gilmour should still be able to reach out and cause this to happen to him. How dare he? He wouldn't forget. Gilmour was on his list. One day, mark my words, you little shit. One day.

'Yes, Sir.'

Chapter Twenty-Three

A tanker, at least nine thousand tons, left crippled and burning after *Nicobar* had put two torpedoes in her, so they had to beach her at the entrance to Tripoli harbour; and an Italian *Spica*-class torpedo boat, a little one-thousand-ton job just like one of the new Royal Navy frigates, sunk with just one torpedo. Not a bad score for their latest patrol. They crept back into Marsamxett Harbour after nightfall, eighteen days from setting out. Bill Sutter had insisted on flying their Jolly Roger even though it was too dark for anyone to see it.

They secured alongside the shell of the Lazaretto. There were no problems to report, the snag list wouldn't have filled a sheet of airmail writing paper and after he'd made his report, Carey assured Shrimp they'd be ready to sail again in the time it took to load more torpedoes, dried spuds and tins of Maconochie's stew. But Carey's optimism and vim failed to put a smile on the Captain (S)'s haggard face. There was news, he said, and none of it good.

He'd skip going into how much more pulverised Malta had been since *Nicobar* had sailed; Carey could see that for himself when the sun came up, always assuming he'd want to stick his head up long enough to look.

There were other things to tell. Last week the Yank aircraft carrier USS *Wasp* had dashed down the Med from Gibraltar, and got close enough to put the 47 Spitfires she was carrying within range of the island's barely functioning airfields. All had made it in, and then within a matter of hours, nearly all had been knocked out by German aircraft, mostly caught refuelling on the ground.

Then there was the matter of the Royal Navy's losses. There was another boat overdue, presumed lost; he didn't want to name her yet, just in case. Call him superstitious. Which brought him to the matter of whether the base was any longer tenable. The unpalatable truth was that Tenth's submarines now no longer had to go out on patrol to get sunk. Christ, when you totted it up; the past few months had seen *P36* get it just after she'd returned from patrol. She was now sitting in eighty feet of water, right under the Lazaretto gallery. Then there had been the Polish boat, *Sokol*, and the Greek, *Glaukos*; both had been operating with the Tenth. Jerry had hit *Sokol* twice, the first time right after she'd come in, and again while that damage was being repaired. *Glaukos*, Jerry had practically blown all the way back to Piraeus from a berth alongside one of their floating pontoons. *Pandora*, one of the Magic Carpet boats, had been too slow unloading supplies from Gib, over at Hamilton Wharf. She'd taken a direct hit that had put her on the bottom and killed twenty-five of her crew. *P39* had been blown in two while being patched up over in Dockyard Creek. And another Magic Carpet boat, *Olympus*, had just sailed for the trip back to Gib, with *Pandora*'s survivors as passengers. She had made it just six miles beyond St Elmo Light before she struck a mine and went down. Barely a dozen of her crew had managed to struggle ashore.

And that mine was one of many now getting dropped by Jerry's bombers in and around Grand Harbour. Hardly surprising, since nearly all the targets on the island had been bombed, and then bombed again. So Jerry had taken to dropping mines, sometimes in the harbour itself, but mainly in the swept channel and further out, way beyond where returning and departing submarine crews would expect them.

Which brought him to his news about *Urge*. She had sailed on patrol yesterday evening, and promptly hit a mine somewhere out in the approaches. 'She was lost with all hands,' said Shrimp. *Urge* had been 'Tommo's' boat: Lieutenant Commander E.P. Tomkinson, the Tenth's top ace after Wanklyn had gone, and also Shrimp's close friend. The most experienced CO with the most experienced crew left in the Flotilla. They should've been bomb-proof, but they weren't.

But Shrimp had nothing to say on that matter, because he was saving the worst news for last. He passed Carey a signal flimsy from Sir Andrew Cunningham, C-in-C, Mediterranean Fleet.

'We're quitting,' said Carey later, not looking at Harry while he gave him the news – staring into space instead. 'Shrimp showed me the signal. All boats to make their way to Alexandria on completion of patrol. The risk to boats returning to Malta to replenish is now officially deemed too great.'

Harry stared into space too. The two young men sat on wood and metal chairs 'rescued' from a bombed-out school, at a metal table in the middle of the cavernous rock-walled oil tank where the Tenth had lived for the past few months; in their shapeless grubby white pullovers and battered caps on the backs of their dishevelled heads; under watery yellow lamps that cast long, strange shadows into the tank's furthest reaches. A Leading Seaman Writer sat way over, by the stretched sheet that cordoned off Shrimp's 'office'. From where they sat, he looked tiny in the vast vaulted space: a little juxtaposition to emphasise the forlornness of everything. From the outside world, there were no sounds of bombs going off right then, just the echoing clack of the Writer's typewriter. And of course, the reek of oil.

'Do the poor bastards out there know yet?' Harry asked. He was talking about the Maltese civilians. Wondering how they would take it.

Having gone through everything, and finding out the Royal Navy was abandoning them. Oh, the two minesweepers might be staying and the couple of MLs. But if the island's main offensive unit was departing, it wouldn't take the people long to work out how it was going to end. Without the submarines continuing to operate, what would be the point in Britain hanging on?

They'd all had conversations with Maltese people about the bombing. Harry didn't know a sailor who didn't feel guilty, or at the very least embarrassed, and he assumed the soldiers and airmen felt the same. Surely everyone on the island must feel the British had brought this down on them: wouldn't it be better if . . .? And the answer was: what would happen to us if you left and the Germans came? We'd be a little people in their way. We'd be moved off our islands, shipped off to camps somewhere. It wouldn't matter where, because they'd be German camps. We all know about German camps. You'd better not be leaving.

But ask any British serviceman and they'd tell you: 'Not a chance, mate. We're not leaving. We're British, we keep buggering on. It's in our blood.' And it was. Nobody had to make a rousing speech to tell you; you were going nowhere. Here we stand, you replied, and you knew it to be true because it was what we British had always done. And that had been all right with Harry, because he was buggered if he was going to stand anywhere else, and certainly not for some fucking Jerry. He didn't know anyone who thought otherwise. And if someone said 'All just jingoistic rubbish!', you just pointed to all the fighter boys who'd taken off to defend the islands' skies and hadn't come back again; all the merchant navy lads who'd set sail in ships loaded with cargo to keep the islands fed and alive, and never made it through; all the submarine crews who had sailed on patrol and ended up overdue, presumed lost; and to Peter Dumaresq and the ships' companies of Force F, and all the New Zealanders off HMS *Neptune* and the other ships' companies of Force K. That was how it was: in it together, since the war started.

Except now they were leaving. Harry felt sick, and when he looked at Carey, he knew he felt sick too.

'It's not right,' said Harry.

'And neither is your port bollock,' said Carey, surprising even himself at how little of the Toorak toff was left in him.

⁓

Harry set off on foot a good hour before first light, to pick his way through the rubble to Lascaris. You cannot imagine his astonishment when, going out of the front gate, or what was left of it, he found himself in step with Leading Seaman Grot McGilveray.

'Off to see yon Katty, are we, Sir?' asked the newly scrubbed sailor; the whole hot water arrangement was still in operation at Lazaretto, and McGilveray had chosen to make use of it before heading off on his run ashore, unlike his First Lieutenant. And of course he'd know about Katty. The whole island knew about the blonde Polish nightclub singer; who else's photograph would they expect to see in the nightlife pages of the *Times of Malta*? And who else would you talk about, but the beaux in her life.

So Harry just said, 'Yes.' What was the point in dissembling? 'How about you, McGilveray? Where are you off to at this godawful hour?'

'Off to make sure our Missus's family is still wi' us.'

'Missus? You're married, McGilveray? Here?'

'Wey' aye. Five year now. Bonny lass. Rosann's her name. Local, like, nice family too.'

'I'd never have taken you for a married man, McGilveray.'

'Well, it's nice to come home ta a wee bit kiss and cuddle and know the lass means it. Better than scatter'n' yer cash up and doon the Gut on floozies ya wouldn'a even ride in ta battle, if ya was sober, like.'

'I hope you find them well then, and still with a roof over their head.'

'Aye. Me too, Sir. They're doon Hamrun way, so it's no' central. No' that that makes much difference these days. Fookin' Jerries.'

And then they took their leave of each other, their faces two pale blurs in the pre-dawn gloom. As he walked away, Harry noticed McGilveray had all along been clutching a bag behind his back – stores being reallocated from Empney's galley probably. Good luck to him and his family, thought Harry. They were going to need it.

Harry turned to head off his own way, and as he did, he heard McGilveray's plangent tones echoing back out of the darkness, obviously singing to himself as he went. 'I'm Popeye the sailor man, I live in a caravan, I sleep wi' ma granny an' tickle her fanny, I'm Popeye the sailor man . . .'

The sun was coming up when Harry made it to the sandbagged entrance to Lascaris and slipped inside, nodding to the sentries. Neither asked to check papers: everybody knew the Royal Navy lad who'd torpedoed two Eyetie cruisers *and* was squeezing that Katty Kadzow in his spare time.

He went down all the stairs into the bowels of the place, then along to the canteen. It was still quite empty; the morning rush hadn't started yet. Just two or three RAF types. One of them was Chally.

Harry collected a huge mug of steaming tea from a still half-asleep Maltese behind the canteen counter, and went and sat opposite him.

'Ah!' said Chally, as Harry sat down. 'Gilchrist! Have a seat, while you've still got time.'

'Fancy meeting you here,' said Harry, ignoring the name nonsense, wondering what he meant by 'still got time'.

'Been here all week, old chap. Back in the saddle, as they say.' He winked an arch wink. 'How about you? Haven't seen you about. Been out to play in Benito's backyard, have we? Just back?'

'Just in a few hours ago.'

'Well, don't get comfy. There are several big fat troopships sitting right now in Palermo. I've been doing portraits of them for the past few days, and call me an amateur, but I think they're about to sail. They were filling them with master race reinforcements at any rate, last time I looked. Off for another shufti this morning.'

Over Chally's shoulder, Harry saw Katty come into the canteen. Her hair was pinned up and wrapped in a scarf and she was wearing an all-in-one siren suit. When she saw them together, she didn't even blink or miss a step, just pressed on, with a wave, to collect her own mug of tea. When she came back to the table, there was no suggestion of an effusive welcome back for Harry, and he was left convinced that this was not the first time she had seen Chally this morning. She sat down beside him and looked at the table, before looking up at Harry opposite, her expression completely opaque.

'All I can say,' said Chally, exuding a presence too vast to register any undertone or nuance from those around him, 'is that you two have let the whole bally dance hall go to hell in a wheelbarrow since I left. Well, it's not bloody good enough.'

'It's all Harry's fault,' said Katty, her eyes level on Harry. 'He keeps going off in his little boat, and he's never here when you need him.'

Harry heard his name being called from somewhere else.

'Is there a Lieutenant Gilmour, Royal Navy, here? A Lieutenant Gilmour?' It was an erk in a tin hat, webbing and a pistol on his hip, head craning around the canteen.

Harry stood up.

'Lieutenant Gilmour? You're ordered back to Lazaretto with immediate effect, Sir. Right away, Sir. Most insistent.'

Chapter Twenty-Four

It was some twenty minutes after nightfall, and *Nicobar* was running on the surface to her billet at the western end of the patrol line, fifteen miles south-west of Marettimo Island. Both diesels running, charging the batteries with the spare amps that weren't being used to turn the main motors. It was a clear night, dark of the moon, so there was a riot of stars out, and getting a fix had been child's play. Yeo, the Navigator, reckoned he had their position down to the very yard. They were well clear of the vast QB 255 mine belt, so no need to worry. They could open her up in these waters. But Carey was still nervous: this close to QB 255, you never knew whether a mine might have slipped loose from its mooring and gone drifting.

It felt good on the bridge. The wind was coming from the south, right off the desert, warm and not kicking up too much of a sea yet. The wait would've been quite pleasant for those on lookout, had they the leisure to enjoy it.

There were three troopships coming their way: the *Lombardia* and the *Toscana*, sister ships, fourteen thousand tons apiece, and the *Sovrana dei Mari*, eighteen thousand tons. And in a line reaching back to five miles off Marsala, were going to be *Nicobar*, *Umbrage* and *Uttoxeter* to meet them.

The three boats were all that Shrimp had left in Malta, but this enemy convoy was a big one. All of them were going out to get it. There would be three other transports with the Italian liners, and an escort of a total of ten destroyers and torpedo boats. As for shagbats, the sky would be black with them.

The other vital piece of intelligence was that because Rommel's next offensive, the one that everyone knew was coming, was so imminent, the troops this convoy would be carrying weren't going to be risked on a long sea crossing. Rommel needed these troops. So they wouldn't be heading down the coast to Tripoli, nearly four hundred miles away, to be landed closer to the front line at El Agheila, just to save them a walk. The intelligence was, said Shrimp, it would be a quick dash out of Palermo and across just 230 miles of intervening sea to Tunis. They could lump the long walk, Rommel needed them ashore and not as bait to Malta's subs.

'Jerry might be pounding us to rubble here,' he had told them at the briefing in the oil tank, 'but our submarines still frighten him.'

And then it had been down to their boats, and the minesweeper HMS *Billericay* had led them out, line astern, during the Luftwaffe's afternoon tea break, while four of the island's remaining Spitfires circled at angels one-eight, ordered to hang about even after the submarines had dived, to give *Billericay* half a chance of getting back in without too many holes in her.

Harry, on the bridge with the CO, wasn't thinking about Katty, or Flight Lieutenant Challoner. If he was brooding about anything, it was the whole tin of cigarettes he'd had to bribe the *dghaisa* man with to take him back across Marsamxett Harbour, the tin he'd brought for Katty and in the end had decided against giving her. And even that hadn't been enough for the *dghaisa* man who had started screaming at him, after the first Jerries had come over, and the batteries on Tigne Point and Fort St Elmo had opened up, and all the shrapnel had begun raining on them: a thousand little gouts of water across the harbour, looking so pretty, except they were chunks of metal coming down at terminal velocity – 120 miles an hour. So that not even wooden boat hulls could stop them, and neither Harry nor the *dghaisa* man had wanted to think about what they could do to mere flesh and bone.

No. No brooding about Katty, because he'd had a little epiphany sitting there in the canteen with her and Chally. A revelation about what it all had meant. With her sitting there, next to her dashing, fearless reconnaissance pilot, in his blue pinstripe shirt and no tie, and his Army battledress jacket with RAF rings around its epaulettes instead of pips, and his wings and DFC ribbons sewn crudely on, and the side cap, with a little Maltese Centaury flower tucked into the badge like a cockade. Flamboyant Chally, larger than life Chally, compared to Harry, the survivor. She'd called Harry that once. A survivor. Was that why she had clung to the little things in life he'd offered: the easy intimacy of their time together, the human-ness, the sheer domesticity? Something she hadn't had to work hard at; something sane, in a world exploding around her; something to concentrate on and take her mind off all the loud bangs?

But now Chally was back, and Chally loved loud bangs – was a loud bang himself. She'd said Chally wasn't a survivor. And looking at him over the canteen table, Harry knew she was right. You just had to look at him to know there was nothing post-war written in his 'to do list'. And how could Harry hope to compete anyway, with such a dazzling light; not the way Chally shone. And did he even want to?

Yes, for a while Harry could see how Katty had liked the easy silence he made for her, and had needed it, just like a trip up to Ghajn Tuffieha rest camp. But in her heart Harry knew she loved the razzle-dazzle more, and how bright Chally's light burned; he could see that. And how, when she was standing in its thrall, it didn't seem to matter that in the end it would burn her.

'Signal from *Umbrage*, Sir. CO to decode.' A disembodied voice coming up the pipe from the control room. Carey gave Harry a quizzical look then disappeared down the conning tower hatch. Five minutes later Napier shot up through it. 'The Captain wants you down in the control room, I've to take the watch,' he said. Harry confirmed their speed and course and went below. It was warm in the tight, red-lit space. Carey was standing by the chart table.

'*Umbrage* has multiple HE coming down the channel between Marettimo and Favigana,' said Carey, 'and there's a lot of depth charging. You know the way the Eyeties throw them about to let you know they're coming.'

It was indeed an Italian Navy practice to send destroyers to drop depth charges ahead of a major convoy or fleet movement. It was a tactic designed to deter any enemy submarine from closing on a convoy, or a battle squadron's track. But up against the Royal Navy, it tended more to attract the RN submarines than scare them off. And that was why *Umbrage* had broken radio silence. She'd heard the troop convoy coming, and was calling *Nicobar* and *Uttoxeter* to the party.

'Are they sure?' asked Harry.

'Am I sure, is what I'm trying to decide,' said Carey, pulling his bottom lip the way their old Skipper used to do. 'Do we go running, and leave our billet?'

And as he said the words, Leading Seaman Butler, sitting in his ASDIC cubby across the passageway, said, 'Sir, I'm picking up HE. It's a long way away. I can't tell how far, but it's far . . . and it's multiple . . . heavy ships . . . and fast. They're to the north of us, just coming out of the shadow of Marettimo, Sir. So they're at least a dozen miles off. Their mean line of advance . . . based on the bearing rate, is west . . . Oh, and there's definitely a lot of them.'

Carey and Harry looked at each other. The targets *Umbrage* had reported were a good twenty miles to the east. 'Start a plot on Butler's targets,' Carey said, and Harry immediately pulled the chart around and grabbed a pencil and parallel rulers.

'They're zigzagging,' said Butler. 'The bearing is red-one-five, and drawing for'ard.'

Harry drew a pencil line across the chart, stretching west from the northernmost tip of the tiny Italian island. 'Whoever it is,' he said, 'I bet they're running out to put a bit more west between them and where they think our subs might be. If it's them, all they'd have to do is a dog leg and drop straight down to Tunis. It could be that the multiple HEs and the depth charging over in the channel is a feint, Sir.'

'Bet I thought that first,' said Carey, with his superior smirk. 'Right. If it is, and our lot are the real target, how far west do you reckon our lot will go before they dogleg? Fifteen miles? Twenty to be safe?'

'Twenty,' said Harry and drew the line. 'And they turn on to . . .' – and he checked with his protractor – '. . . two-two-zero here, and it's a straight run in.'

'Righty-ho. Command decision,' said Carey. 'I say our lot *are* the real target. So I want to get ahead of them. Well ahead.' He slipped the protractor from Harry and placed it on to *Nicobar's* position, and drew his thumbnail down it. Then he took Harry's rulers and drew a line from *Nicobar* running to intersect Harry's projected course for the unknown ships.

Carey called over his shoulder, 'Bring us on to two-four-zero.' Then he turned to the control room messenger by the sound-powered telephone. 'Tell the engine room to give me maximum revs to float the load. Number One, how long until we get there?' he asked, jabbing at the little dot he'd made in the middle of the big blue sea. There was obviously no doubt in Carey's mind now. This was the enemy. Everyone felt the heel of the boat beneath them.

On her builders' trials in 1938, over the measured mile off Arran, *Nicobar* had hit a top speed of fifteen knots on the surface. Right now, with her throttles opened wide, and Warrant Engineer McAndrew kicking her diesels by way of adding more encouragement, Harry reckoned she was doing a bit more than that. They hadn't gone to Diving Stations yet. Carey had the entire crew apart from those on watch, sitting down to a big dinner: broth, veal and ham pie, dehydrated potatoes served as mash with butter, and tinned runner beans followed by sweet rice and tinned peaches. And everybody agreed, Empney had made not a bad stab at it too.

Harry, being the Jimmy, had stood in to take the watch as *Nicobar*, on the surface, was running fast through the night. He was on the bridge with the two lookouts, his face turned into a warm wind coming from a desert that lay just seventy miles dead ahead, blowing warm spray at him beneath a riotous starlit sky. *Nicobar*, rising and plunging as she drove into the oncoming short, choppy seas. He felt a strange kind of marvel at the calm that had settled over him. He was going into action, but he didn't feel frightened. It was more like a kind of elation. And it wasn't just him, he'd felt it through the whole boat. Maybe it was because this was a plum target; Carey had made sure they all knew about that. If they hit this one hard, they'd really hurt the enemy. Maybe it was something to do with them pulling out and leaving the Maltese to their fate. Nobody was happy about that. And since this was their last crack at the enemy before they were being forced to turn tail and run for Alexandria, maybe they all wanted to make this one count. Because in this war, they really did have right on their side. Everybody knew that. It was obvious. Because this fight wasn't about conquest, it was about putting an end to conquest.

Below, Butler, feeling pleasantly replete, was back in the ASDIC cubby with his headphones back on. He was calling the target's bearing every five minutes now. The enemy were zigzagging, but the mean course from the plot was constant now: two-two-zero degrees.

Harry, plotting the arc of the bearings had worked out they were moving fast for a convoy at seventeen knots. But the zigzagging meant their rate of advance was much slower. Carey, studying the plot, realised

Nicobar was going to cross the enemy's track far sooner than he had estimated. Bloody marvellous, he said to himself, triumphant for a change, instead of his usual irony. This was shaping up to be a complicated attack, so every break counted, especially if he was to wreak the maximum havoc he intended. He had a plan. And oh, what a mad, audacious and finely calculated plan it was too.

He checked the almanac for the time for first light again: 05.20 hours; and for nautical twilight – the time when the sun is still below the horizon but is beginning to throw its light into the sky: 04.17 hours. Then he checked his calculations for where *Nicobar* would be at those times, and where the enemy would be. It could work; it was going to work. Now he needed to confer with his First Lieutenant. Number One was going to be crucial to the execution, but hey! What was he worrying about? It was Harry. You could almost feel sorry for the poor Eyeties! He smiled, and did his calculations again.

Yeo was on the bridge now, and Harry was below, leaning over the plot with his CO, explaining what they were looking at.

'Six merchant ships, Butler says,' said Harry. 'From the bearings he's calling from the different contacts, I reckon two divisions.' He stabbed at his scribbles on the plot. 'The first division is the smaller of the two: three ships, not so big. The second is three big ones, which tallies with the liners Shrimp said they'd be. Then there are the escorts. Butler's not sure about them. He thinks at least six destroyers, and a clutch of smaller stuff. MAS-boats probably. But he said they could be Jerry E-boats. They're dashing about all over the place so it's too difficult to pin a number. The two divisions, as you can see from the plot, are advancing in parallel, two destroyers leading . . . two out on their port beam, one sweeping astern. So it must be only one to starboard. You can also see from the plot, there's a bit of a pattern at work . . . When they zig and when they zag, and when and for how long they run true. Which is careless, but then we don't know how experienced their merchant skippers are. Or how scared shitless, or even just how thick and incompetent, and they have to do it by the numbers.'

'Doesn't matter,' said Carey. 'It plays into our plan.'

And then Carey told Harry the plan. And when he'd finished, Harry was grinning from ear to ear. And so were the planesmen, and the Cox'n on the helm, and the Wrecker, and the control room messenger. All of them sitting there, in the otherworld red wash, amid the pipework and the cable runs and the valve handles and the gauges, all woven around them in their tiny little battle cocoon, bouncing and battering its way like a live thing into the head sea and towards the Italian convoy and its ships, laden to the gunnels with German tanks and guns and soldiers.

'Steady on zero-four-zero,' said Carey down the bridge voice-pipe, then, to Harry next to him, 'Ring for half-ahead, together.'

As well as her CO and Number One, *Nicobar* had four lookouts on the bridge, as the boat swung around, practically reversing her course, heading north now, first light still over quarter of an hour away. They'd gone to Diving Stations at 03.30 hours, and the boat was closed up and ready for action. Yeo, below, was on the plot, and Harry had entrusted the Wrecker, Mundell, to take charge of the diving panel, with his top protégé from the Stokers' mess to assist.

Harry had gone through in tedious detail everything that might be expected of him for every eventuality he could imagine, and Mundell, a twenty-year-man, Andrew man and boy, had listened with the best sullen, steel-plate expression he could muster, until Harry had finished by saying, 'And of course I apologise, Mr Mundell, after all that, if I have offended your professional sensibilities, but I am the Jimmy and it's my job to be a compulsive checker-upper, so there.' Mundell couldn't hide his smile at that.

Napier was in the forward torpedo room, with his torpedoes, fingering the firing lever, making sure the pins were out and it would work when he pulled it. He was singing to himself Grot McGilveray's version of 'Popeye the Sailor Man'. Beside him, the Leading Torpedo Gunner's mate was checking the drain valves on all the tubes, making sure they were flooded and ready, and at the same time smirking over his shoulder to the other ratings around the space, and they were smirking back. It was all part of the preparation, their version of a psychological loosening of the limbs, because when the order came to fire, there'd be no room in the plan for any fumbling.

The PO Telegraphist was in the wireless shack, listening in across the frequencies, but picking up nothing of interest to them. He hadn't been called upon to transmit anything himself, to summon the other two boats, strung out back along their patrol line. They were both too far to the east to get here in time, and anyway, Carey didn't want to give away his position by signalling to the enemy and telling them by their radio noise that despite their attempt at a ruse to the east, there was still a sub astride their convoy's course.

Across the passage, Butler was still listening to the HE and calling out the convoy's progress. The enemy were closing fast now.

And in the engine room, McAndrew was pacing up and down between his diesels, oil can in hand, threatening under his breath the two huge, inanimate, thundering beasts of machined and precision steel with all the woe that would betide them if they faltered.

Harry, on the bridge, was polishing the head of the big TBT, the target bearing transmitter, that had already been hauled up and mounted, because Carey's plan called for a surface attack, and the TBT was there to do the job of the *Nicobar*'s fruit machine. It was to be Harry's job to operate it. '*Its* night-vision lenses will compensate for *your* rubbish night vision,' Carey had told him, 'and anyway, who else am I going to trust to remain calm enough to crank the right wheels to the right settings if someone's shooting at us? And being on the surface, they might well be.'

And while Harry was doing all that, Carey, standing right beside him, would be in overall tactical control. 'I'll be keeping an eye on the big picture, Number One,' he'd said, 'telling you who you should be shooting at, while you'll be concentrating on the actual shooting. It'll go like clockwork. Just you wait and see.'

'Of course it will,' said Harry, his voice dripping with irony. 'What could possibly go wrong?' The two men, grinning at each other, knowing the answer.

The sky was beginning to lighten. Butler was reporting the target was on bearing green-ten, drawing left and coming diagonally towards their track. Carey and two of the lookouts were scanning out along the bearing, and Harry had knelt to turn the TBT there too.

Carey's plan was to be in position when the sun came up behind the enemy, silhouetting them, while *Nicobar* lurked just beyond the line of its shadow. They were about to put it to the test. What, indeed, could go wrong? Everything, of course.

'Two aircraft!' called one of the lookouts. 'Two o'clock high, off the starboard bow, green-five, at least ten miles away, heading south. I think they're Savoia-Marchetti 79s, Sir!'

Harry immediately thought, *Sharp eyes, and a lad who studies his recognition charts.* Those were things First Lieutenants had to notice, even when there were other things on their minds.

Carey's binoculars were on the two dots.

Harry's were still on the horizon, looking for the convoy. If *Nicobar* dived now, they would lose speed and lose the convoy. If the S79s bombed them, they'd lose their lives.

Carey stepped to the pipe and called down, 'Slow ahead, together, Mr Mundell! Cycle main vents.' The order would take them down to decks awash.

And as he said it, the tops of the enemy convoy slipped out of the vanishing night, the light of the rising sun at their back. Harry saw them, and at the same time the other lookout called them.

'Two ships, Sir! Superstructures up! Starboard bow!'

Shapes on the horizon now. Right where Carey said they would be. Carey leaned to the voice-pipe again. 'Enemy in sight!' he called down, telling the control room: here we go. The whole crew knowing now. The attack had started. Then he picked up the bridge mic.

'Bridge, torpedo room,' he said. 'Mr Napier. Tubes one to four, make ready. We will fire on command.'

But the tubes were already ready. Back up on the bridge, the lookout watching the aircraft called, 'One aircraft peeling off towards us, Sir.'

'We're a tuna boat,' muttered Carey, still watching the two shadow ships take shape on the horizon. Then he said out loud, night glasses still stuck to his face, 'The power of thought, gentlemen. Everybody think . . . we are a tuna boat!'

If they had to dive now . . .

Seconds passed . . .

'He's blinking at us, Sir!' called the lookout, but everybody on the bridge looking that way didn't need telling; the aircraft was interrogating them with an Aldis lamp.

Nobody breathed. *Nicobar* was easing herself into her attack. The convoy was now well over the horizon. *Nicobar* had to stay on track . . . on the surface . . . but there was an enemy aircraft coming at them . . . They had to dive.

Carey leaned under the bridge parapet and grabbed the signaller's blinker gun, the hand Aldis set, and he deliberately raised it, pointed it directly at the enemy aircraft, and started flashing back at it. And as they all watched, still not breathing, the aircraft turned away, peeling back towards its comrade, already flying cover over the advancing convoy.

'For the record,' said Carey, 'I flashed him, "Waltzing Matilda, your billy's boiling."'

Shoulders rocking, across the bridge. The young lads, the lookouts, they'd loved that. If this was supposed to be war . . . with the Captain cracking jokes and all . . .

And Carey. All he was thinking was, *God knows what that chump in the plane is thinking, except maybe, whoever is flashing at us, isn't hiding; and anyway, they're coming from the wrong side.*

'More ships, Sir!' called the lookout. 'I can see five now, Sir. Two are definitely destroyers, hull up now . . . Big bow waves. The rest are merchantman. Bearing red-ten. They're coming on fast, Sir.'

Harry already had the lead ships on the TBT. 'Range five thousand yards,' he said. Then he called the course, adding, 'Unable to estimate speed. Angle too acute.'

The lookout called, 'Targets zigzagging . . . to their port, Sir!' Harry, glancing down at his watch, said, 'Right on the pattern, Sir!'

Carey smiled at Harry's back, still crouched over the TBT. Then he raised his binoculars and turned his attention to watching the enemy ships, advancing in two columns. Just like the plot had said they would be, coming up on what must have been another waypoint on their course, and now turning in sequence. And as the convoy's columns turned, further to port, swinging wide, another destroyer came into silhouette. And the instant he saw it, Carey saw his opportunity.

This was *Nicobar*'s time, her moment. The port-side destroyer was way out, maybe six thousand yards off the convoy's beam. *Nicobar* had to get inside. But if the destroyer saw her, and opened fire, she'd have to dive. And the convoy would escape.

Carey stepped to the bridge's little binnacle and took a quick bearing. 'Bring us on to two-one-seven,' he said down the pipe, 'full ahead, together. And Mr Mundell, a puff of air in one and six.' And *Nicobar*, came up, her decks just clear, no more washing, turbulent drag of water around her three-inch gun mount and around the base of her conning tower, so she could now surge forward into the widening gap between the turning convoy, and its slower-turning outside escort.

If you looked around you on the bridge, it was still pitch dark, but in the sky rising out of the horizon, the black was turning blue, and lightening all the time.

The three big liners began to blank out the horizon: big slab-sided beasts, towering out of the blackness of the sea, creaming wakes running down their flanks, while beyond lay the three other ships. As their two columns advanced, Harry could see quite clearly the lead cargo vessel beyond the liners, easily two thousand tons of her. But he was aware he was also watching the cargo ship disappear. The leading liner – by her size either the *Lombardia* or the *Toscana* – was pulling ahead. Even though the liners were on the outside of the turn, their more powerful engines were moving them faster, and the convoy was moving out of step. Harry, still bent over the TBT, called the bearing to the lead liner again, then flipped the stadimeter and dropped the top image on to the lower ship's mastheads.

'Range two thousand eight hundred yards,' he said. Then as he watched the white wake along the lead liner's hull diminish, as she slowed to let the cargo ships catch up, he realised he was being handed their speed by this manoeuvre. 'Troopships' speed estimated fifteen knots,' he said.

'Concur,' said Carey, binoculars still stuck to his face. 'There is an enemy destroyer closing on our port bow, Mr Gilmour. Range and bearing, please?'

Harry spun the TBT to the destroyer now. She was now almost bow on to them, and Harry could see clearly the white, foaming bow wave curling from her stem. Harry was sure she was a *Navigatori*-class. These bloody things were practically light cruisers. Over 2,500 tons and 350 feet long, they were armed with six 4.7-inch guns and all the usual depth charge racks and throwers. And they were bloody fast, he remembered that – over thirty-eight knots! He also remembered their draught: eleven feet six inches. And that all *Nicobar*'s torpedoes had been set to run at twelve feet. Which was good, because they weren't after any destroyers. Harry had experience of how handy it could be if you could shoot your torpedoes under an escort. That had been how his first boat, *Pelorus,* had bagged the *Von Zeithen*.

He flipped the stadimeter again. 'Range to enemy destroyer, bearing red-five-zero, is three thousand six hundred yards!'

Carey lowered his binoculars and banged the lip of the bridge with both hands, willing his boat faster. 'Come on, *Nicobar*, old girl!' They were charging into the gap between the destroyer and the liners, and then they were through the screen. Carey said to Harry, 'Start setting up the troopships now, Mr Gilmour. Range and bearing on each one, and let's get a picture set up.'

Harry began taking bearings to the other liners. The *Sovrana dei Mari* was the middle ship; she was so bloody big she was easy to spot. He did the sums in his head for what they were planning. They were now on a track angle of twenty-seven degrees to the liners as they ran out along their zig.

He spun back on to the destroyer. They were inside her turning circle now, between her and the charges she was supposed to be protecting, and still no one had spotted them. He called, 'Enemy destroyer . . . range, two thousand six hundred!'

Then back to the lead troopship, to check. 'Bearing red-fifteen, range one thousand seven hundred!'

It was time. Right now.

Carey flipped open the voice-pipe. 'Starboard, thirty, half ahead, together!' Then he leaned over and picked up the bridge mic and waited, as *Nicobar* began to slow, and to heel in towards her prey. Harry, doing little steps, as though he was shadow-dancing with a midget, taking bearings on all three troopships now, calculating the director angles for a ninety-eight-degree track.

'Midships!' Carey called down the pipe, and then into the mic said, 'Bridge, torpedo room. Open bow caps!'

He'd had to wait until now to order bow caps open. Nobody wanted fifteen knots' worth of water tunnelling into their tubes, spinning the arming props while the torpedoes were still in there, and anyway, they couldn't fire them going at that tilt, without the torpedoes tumbling out of control the instant the compressed air had ejected them into such a torrent of on-rushing sea.

And suddenly they were all bathed in the sodium-hard glare of a searchlight, pointing directly at them.

Harry scrunched his eyes tight shut, but the light had got in. A ship's siren whoop rent the air, so close.

In his ear, Harry heard the order to 'Cycle main vents!' And then two *phwoffs*, a way off . . . Was someone firing starshells or flares? An Eyetie's code for alerting the convoy to the presence of an enemy sub? But they weren't flares. They were the reports of guns firing. Old guns. Then there were two more loud reports. Yes, definitely cannons, but not modern, quick-firing jobs. They must be deck guns on the troopships. He opened his eyes in time to see two pillars of water rise abaft their beam, falling around the *Navigatori* as she was heeling into a high-speed turn, coming around to run them down. And then tracer fire arcing out from the *Sovrana dei Mari*, and when he followed it, he watched the heavy rounds go way wide of them, and then start sparking off the Italian destroyer's superstructure. Two more reports, in quick succession; now the lead troopship was firing. Deck guns. They sounded like three-inchers, and they were aiming at their own destroyer escort too.

What were they thinking? Were they just shooting at anything they could see? They surely couldn't see *Nicobar*, down now, decks awash again and still inside the line of shadow, only her conning tower above the waves. But then nor could they really see the destroyer: she'd just be a dark shape, moving fast in the night. But they were really pouring fire into it anyway – into their own escort! Maybe they thought her dark shape was Force K or F, coming back again from Gib. The Eyetie destroyer was certainly coming from the right direction for that. And every Italian merchant sailor would know by now, what Royal Navy surface units were capable of, if they ever got among your convoy.

Then his astonished reverie was broken.

'You're on, Mr Gilmour,' he heard Carey say. Harry knew immediately what he meant – he needed to start firing their torpedoes now, right now, before the destroyer fired a starshell and showed her charges they were shooting at the wrong target.

He bent back to the TBT; they were now on their track angle of ninety-eight degrees. Perfect. He dialled the range into the TBT; he didn't need to call it, but he did anyway: 'Eight hundred and twenty yards!'

The TBT had calculated the director angle for him and as he laid it on the target's track, he watched the lead troopship's bow edge over the line on his viewfinder, and called, 'Fire one! Commence the turn, Sir!'

'Fire one!' Carey said into the mic, then he leaned to the voice-pipe and said, 'Port, five.'

Nicobar rose, as if upon a steeper wave, and they all saw the telltale torpedo wake stream out from her bows. When Harry watched it go, he knew; he could see: it was going to hit. He could even guess where – just abaft the troopship's bridge.

He began counting the seconds, but before he could call it, Carey did. He could do sums in his head too; the troopship's length, her speed, the time it would take for their torpedo to run.

'Fire two!'

Harry shouldn't have looked up. It took him too many seconds to align the second ship, the *Sovrana dei Mari*. He rushed it as *Nicobar* continued her turn. 'Second target. On deflection angle, red-two-zero . . . Now!'

'Fire three!' Carey called into the mic, and the next bubbling trail shot out towards the enemy. Harry imagining the sums going through

Carey's head; the range to the second target closing to eight-fifty yards; the time taken for a 45-knot torpedo to travel it, and the distance the target would travel in the seconds now counting; and then he called, 'Fire four!' Once their last bow shot had cleared, Carey said into his mic, 'Right, Mr Napier, aft, pronto!' And as he said the words, there was the deafening, reverberating . . .

BUDDUMMMNN!

The detonation of their first torpedo as it tore into the first troop-ship. Harry looked up to see the huge pinnacle of water begin to cascade down again. He'd been wrong, it hadn't hit under her bridge, it had hit right under her fore funnel, right in her forward engine room.

'Port, thirty!' Carey was yelling into the voice-pipe, amid the din: the echoing of their torpedo hit, and the persistent clattering of the machine-gun fire still going on over their heads, and from more deck guns, opening up now, from the *Sovrana dei Mari*, and the other troop-ship astern of her. All battering away at their own escort! When Harry looked back, the big bridge wing signal lamp on the enemy destroyer was flashing furiously back at her assailants, and two coloured flares went up, obviously recognition signals, but the troopships' gunners were too busy, bent to their guns, to recognise that the target they were shooting at was friendly.

More tracer continued to lace the sky above them, and as *Nicobar* turned away from the liners, when Harry looked back he could see the sun was up enough now that the giant troopships were no longer lowering slabs of shadow. Details were beginning to emerge: their lines of boat decks, figures on their gun platforms, fore and aft; figures on the bridge wings. And their immediate victim's name could be picked out on her bows: *Toscana*.

She had fallen out of the line, and behind her, the *Sovrana dei Mari* began turning in to dodge her crippled comrade, turning into the path of the destroyer, which in turn suddenly began to slew away from the giant troopship, and from *Nicobar*.

It was then that their second torpedo struck home.

Harry saw *Toscana*'s stern leap, and a great gout of water rise up under it. But before the noise and the shock wave of the detonation hit them, a terrible rending scream filled the air, like a madman leaning on the whistle of a hurtling steam train, and above the crippled troopship, a jet of roiling white was shooting out of one of the vents on her forward funnel into the sky, its eddies and billows now catching the light from the rising sun.

'One of her boilers has gone,' said Carey, looking back in horror, his voice all but lost in the noise of the escaping steam and the reverberations from their second torpedo detonating, both he and Harry not wanting to imagine what it must be like in her engine room at that moment, and the men cooking in there.

And all the while, torpedoes three and four were still in the water, running toward their target, the *Sovrana dei Mari*.

The mic on the bridge crackled to life. 'Aft torpedo room, bridge. Tubes five and six flooded, stern caps open!'

It was Napier.

This was always going to be the trick shot; firing the stern tubes at the third troopship. Harry couldn't use the TBT; couldn't train it aft far enough for the shot. He was going to have to use the periscope, and he was already in the conning tower hatch, hands on the ladder's uprights, sliding down on to the control room, feet not touching a rung until they hit the deck plates.

Everything speeded up now. Fast, confused. Harry hears the two klaxon blasts, Carey is diving the boat. But then there's a voice: the sound of a lookout yelling, 'Destroyer closing fast! Starboard beam! Red-one-zero-zero!'

It's the convoy's back stop, coming up fast from astern.

Harry has the attack periscope up, and is training aft as the lookouts come tumbling down behind him. *Bang! Bang!* Their feet hitting the plates, and them running, clearing for'ard, first one, then the next and then Carey shouting, 'One clip on, two clips on! Hatch secure! Twenty-seven feet!' Calling periscope depth, as *Nicobar* drops beneath Harry's feet. Yeo is at the fruit machine. Butler's calling, 'High-speed HE, bearing red-one-zero-zero. Closing fast!'

In the back of Harry's mind is a thought: What's happened to their third torpedo? Then they hear and feel it. It's a hit on the *Sovrana dei Mari*, and he calculates: three seconds until the fourth torpedo takes her. But a Leading Seaman is already behind Harry, ready to read the bezel as he searches for the already veering third troopship, the *Lombardia*.

He finds her. 'Bearing is . . . that!' calls Harry, and the rating calls, 'Green-one-sixty!'

As Yeo cranks it in, Harry calls, 'Range is that!' The rating reads the minutes from the periscope, and calls them. Harry does the sums, and says, all calm now, 'Range, one thousand two hundred yards', before his voice gets louder. '. . . She's turning away. Bugger! Speed is twenty knots! Make the speed twenty knots!' He's called it but he doesn't know that for sure, but he has to fire, so he has to guess.

Nicobar is at periscope depth now. Harry, eyes still on the target. He knows the destroyer's coming up fast, but he doesn't know how fast or how close now; but he can't check because he can't afford the seconds it would take to look; and his periscope has been above the choppy surface too long. Where's his bloody director angle?

'Target is turning too tight!' he calls. The solution is unravelling. There's no time for Carey to take over, or to confer. *He* has to act.

He calls over his shoulder to the Cox'n, 'Port, five! Slow ahead, together!' and a beat, and then he takes his big leap in the dark, as *Nicobar*'s stern comes around and the angle becomes ever tighter. He's doing it by eye now, by the seat of his pants, as the submarine and the troopship diverge. He's out of opportunities: either he fires now, or he doesn't. 'Fire five!' but before he can shout 'Fire six!', the whole sky lights up; a huge flash; a supernova of light, just out of the periscope's line of sight, to the south; and then the whole world feels engulfed in the roar of a cataclysmic concussion. They hear it through the hull, and in another beat the whole boat is shaken by a shock wave. He's already called 'Fire six!' without realising it. He has no idea what has happened. He takes his eyes from the periscope, is so shocked he forgets to send it down, but the rating does it for him. Harry's eyes meet Carey's in mutual incomprehension.

'Something close has just blown up,' calls Butler from the ASDIC cubby, and Harry and Carey start to laugh. It's just hearing the bloody obvious being stated again, it just seems so funny, and then the realisation on Carey's face. 'Torpedo four missed the big boy, and hit the tanker in the other column. She must've been carrying aviation spirit or petrol,' he said.

The laughter stops as they contemplate their luck . . .

BARRRUUMMMN!

And that had been the sound of their last torpedo, detonating. The *Lombardia.* They'd hit her.

Then, amid all the crashing noise in the sea around them; the tearing metal and the noise of secondary explosions, timid things now by comparison to what had gone before, comes an all too familiar sound . . .

Ricka-chicky-Ricka-chicky-Ricka-chicky-Ricka-chicky! . . . and the destroyer goes down their port side, mere tens of feet away, so close, they hear the splashes as the depth charges are rolled into the water.

'Two hundred feet!' yells Carey. 'Everybody hold on!'

Six depth charges caught *Nicobar* as she dived, three of them came very close indeed. The boat was hit as if by a series of express trains; every item of crockery in the galley shattered and nearly every light in the boat too; they were plunged into total darkness that lasted over a minute before the first emergency light appeared. All the glass facings on the gauges had disintegrated and deck plates jumped out of their seatings. High-pressure air lines sheered, as did the hydraulic lines to the bow planes, and most of the valves on the trim board were sprung.

Where the closest charge had gone off, mere feet from the senior rates' mess, several rivets on the pressure hull sheered, and a severe leak had opened where one of the hull plates had sprung.

When the concussions stopped, and the boat stopped jumping, nobody could hear for the screaming of ruptured air lines; but they could all feel *Nicobar* falling away beneath their feet. Harry and Yeo, and Mundell's Stoker began hanging emergency lights, and an eerie coven glow came into the control room, where the air was already thick with cork dust.

Carey, right away, could see no gauge was functioning. He didn't know what depth they were at, but he knew they were rapidly going deeper. He grabbed a sound-powered phone: 'Captain, engine room. Full ahead, together!' Then he bent and yelled in the planesmen's ears, 'Planes on maximum rise!', only to be told the bow planes were not responding. 'Aft planes, then, please,' he said with arch calmness. Then he turned to Mundell. 'Blow all main ballast tanks. And then get someone for'ard to hand-turn the bow planes. Maximum rise. Now. And...' And Mr Mundell interrupted, '... and shut off these HP lines!' He didn't need telling.

The *Nicobar*'s crew were moving, shutting valves, kicking deck plates back into place, hanging more emergency lights. The scream of escaping air was silenced, but only to be replaced instantly by a more terrifying sound – the sound of a hull breaking up. At first everyone thought it was them, but it was too big, and out there. One of the troopships; it must be.

They felt *Nicobar* start to rise again.

Carey started calling for damage reports. Butler was first: his ASDIC set was in bits, and God knows what that charge that went off for'ard did to the ASDIC dome.

McAndrew had sent a Stoker for'ard with his list: water was pouring in through the starboard propeller shaft gland, the main switchboard was in danger of flooding, and water was lapping around the starboard main motor casing. He was checking the battery cells right now for cracks. It was bad, but it would be brought under control.

A damage control party ran through from aft, heading for the big leak; carrying wooden battens and hammocks.

Nicobar was going up fast now, and Carey still didn't know what depth they were at. He thought a moment then ordered up the main periscope, and as it rose, he grabbed the handles and rolled it back as if for an aerial survey. Kneeling in the shattered glass, he could see the surface above; the sun dappling the slight chop. It was difficult to say what depth they were at; maybe forty feet, not much more. He fought the urge to look around, not daring to wonder where the destroyer was and why she wasn't coming back to finish the job.

Harry was on the trim board behind him, trying to control their depth using the main vents; it was proving to be an imprecise science. The boat's rise had slowed, but she wasn't stopping.

'It would be good if you could put the brakes on now, Number One,' said Carey.

'Aye aye, Sir,' said Harry, but it wasn't working.

Oh well, thought Carey, if they were going to broach, he might as well have a look. The periscope broke the surface, and Carey turned to look to port. There was a lot to take in. Six torpedoes fired; five hits.

Closest was the *Lombardia*. She was well down by the stern, with an impressive list to starboard. Her entire upper works were crawling with soldiers; on her decks, in her lifeboats; and the lifeboats were being lowered. The *Sovrana dei Mari* was under way, and further off, but down by her bows, and listing too; and she appeared to be under tow by another *Navigatori*-class destroyer, or maybe it was the same one she'd tried to sink earlier? They were steaming north, very slowly, with two cargo ships steaming ahead of them, going faster. Of the *Toscana*, there was no sight – just a lot of lifeboats and rafts bobbing on the surface, carpeting the surface, each crammed with soldiers in the sand-coloured uniforms of the Afrika Korps. It wasn't hundreds of them; it seemed more like thousands. And he could see why their attacker hadn't come back, why none of the escorts were hunting *Nicobar* any more; they were all busy picking up survivors, on a sea dark with them. Carey called Harry to take a look.

Nicobar began going down again, the waters lapped over the periscope, but she didn't go deep; Harry had already got her back under control before he stepped to the periscope.

Chapter Twenty-Five

Harry could make out the unmistakable outline of Shrimp, standing alone in the dark at the end of the quay, waiting on them, as they limped around the corner from the main harbour into Dockyard Creek. Apart from a group of local dockyard workers, there to throw the piles of camouflage netting over her, Shrimp Simpson made up *Nicobar's* entire welcoming committee. They couldn't take her directly into the dry dock; its gates had been damaged in the last air raid – or was it the one before? They all seemed to run together now.

In the background was the glow of a welding torch, flashing from underneath a canvas canopy strung out to shield its light from the air. Everything else was black shadow. You could still smell the reek of fire and high explosives in the air.

Carey was bringing them in, and for that Harry was grateful. He watched a docker throw a heaving line to one of *Nicobar's* ratings out on the casing, for'ard. Concentrating on it, to try and block out the gnawing in his guts.

It was fear. There was nothing else to call it. It had been there, eating at him since halfway through the afternoon watch. It had hit him when he had sat down, for the first time in thirty hours, to drink a mug of coffee, and his mind had started doing sums again, like a gramophone needle stuck in a groove. He'd been doing sums since before they'd gone into action; speeds against distance; bearings, track angles, director angles, ranges. And he'd still been doing them as they had worked flat out to repair the damage done to the boat by the Eyetie's departing depth charge attack.

Especially to their fuel tanks. One of the depth charges had smashed the sub-pressure system, the pipe network that reduced the pressure in the tanks to below the outside sea pressure, so the oil would stay in the tank if it were ruptured. And one of their tanks had been ruptured, so he had to work out the time it would take to pump it out and flood it with seawater so they wouldn't leave a telltale slick of oil for any passing shagbat to follow. Then he had to work out if they had enough fuel in the other remaining tanks to get back to Malta. Then he had to check all Yeo's navigation calculations: thought it best to, since they had to get them past the QB 255 mine belt without straying into it; then their speed and the timings to their waypoints; the course changes and the currents to factor in, knowing they could never surface to take sightings with a sky full of enemy aircraft hunting them. The charge left in their cracked battery cells, that McAndrew's team were frantically strapping to get every last amp out of them – would it be enough to get them back to Malta? The air left in the boat – would there be enough of it for them to breathe?

And then there'd been the sum his brain had wandered backwards into, when he'd finally sat on his arse, shattered. How long ago had it been since he'd last slept? Even a catnap? It took a long time to count back, trying to work his brain as if he were cranking a machine with a cracked sump. The foul air he was breathing wasn't helping. Three days – he hadn't slept in three days. And that was when it had started – the fear.

It wouldn't go away. Still hadn't gone away, even now they were surfaced, were back in harbour, coming alongside. For all he was trying, standing there on the bridge in the warm night, he couldn't block it out. The fear in his guts.

He'd tried at first thinking back to all his past ruminating on this thing called fear: its nature and corrosiveness, who it touched and who it passed by, seeing himself like some sort of scientific observer monitoring an experiment. Using all that as a device to push the fear away. And look where it had got him. Picking away at what made it tick, and now, suddenly, out of the blue, while he was tired and not looking, it had turned around and started picking away at him.

How had it started? He'd been sitting minding his own business and an empty hole had opened in him and his throat had closed, and he'd felt his skin sheen with cold sweat; and he'd started yawning and couldn't stop. And his hands had started shaking.

All he'd done was stop being busy, and the fear had taken it as an invitation.

Sitting there, down in the wardroom, falling apart inside, abstractly wondering if he was going to crack up, and if he was, how was it going to manifest itself. He'd never actually seen anyone crack up yet, except that young rating in *Pelorus*'s escape trunk. But then he'd felt a bit like yelling for his mum too, right then, until the big Chief Petty Officer – what had his name been? Gault; yes, of course. Until Gault had calmed the rating down, calmed everybody down. Thinking about Gault again had calmed Harry a bit, even if it hadn't quite made the fear go away. At least his hands had stopped shaking.

After the attack on the convoy, they had remained submerged all that day, the crew working to fix their damaged boat as they sneaked away. Their ASDIC set wrecked, they were unable to listen for the approach of any enemy ship. They hadn't even risked a look through the periscope. Not in daylight. But when night fell, they had gone to periscope depth three times, and on each occasion they had sighted an enemy warship looking for them, and had to dive again. Fast.

As the hours passed, the air had started to become increasingly foul, and Harry had ordered everyone not on watch to lie down and limit all movement. Soda trays were laid out in an attempt to soak up the excess carbon dioxide; Harry had no idea if they were working or not.

The following day, they again didn't bother to look around. Everybody was breathing in short gasps. Harry had felt he was thinking through treacle. The fear didn't help; and it didn't help the fear, sitting around, limiting all his movements too. But come nightfall, they risked raising the periscope again, and brought the north tip of Gozo in sight. Carey had ordered them to the surface, and when Harry had gone up on to the bridge behind him, both of them had been sick. The two lookouts who followed them had been sick too. Carey sent a signal to Shrimp: *Nicobar* was returning to Malta. She was too damaged to make it to Alex. She'd be in the next night.

How many hours ago had that been? Despite being on the surface again, in the good clean air, the effort to try and count back now was too great. The fear continued to wash over him like Canute's incoming tide, indifferent to all his ploys to order it, halt!

Suddenly, he heard Carey shouting, right next to his ear.

'Good evening, Sir!' Carey was calling to someone on the quay. 'Bet you didn't expect to see us back so soon.'

Harry looked down, and saw it was Shrimp. He'd forgotten all about Shrimp.

'Just glad to see you back at all, Malcolm,' Shrimp called back. 'Very glad indeed. Is that Mr Gilmour next to you?'

'Yes, Sir,' Carey replied, looking at Harry as if to say, *You can't answer for yourself?*

But Harry couldn't.

'Mr Gilmour!' called Shrimp. 'Go below and get all your kit, and report to me the minute the gangway comes aboard.'

Harry's brow furrowed. Everyone was going to have to get their kit off the boat. She was going into dry dock. Why was he being told . . .?

'Well,' Carey hissed under his breath, 'get a fucking move on. The Captain (S) is talking to you.'

Harry jumped, and vanished down the conning tower. Busy again, noticing in passing, as his feet hit the control room deck plates, that the hole in his guts had suddenly gone.

When Harry came down the gangway, in a press of sailors, Carey was standing talking to Shrimp by a pile of rubble, opposite *Nicobar*'s aft end. Somehow Harry knew they were talking about him.

The hole in his guts might have gone, but now it was replaced by another dread. It made him remember how Carey had left him alone once all the repairs were done and they'd cleared QB 255, hadn't issued even so much as an order in his direction for the whole final run down to Valletta.

Had he seen? Did Carey know what had been happening to his First Lieutenant? Did he recognise the symptoms? The flutter inside that Harry thought he had hidden so well. And was that him now, telling the Captain (S)? Officially? Gilmour had been about to flunk it.

Oh well, better he got spotted now, before he did any damage. The thought that even just one of his crew might suffer because he'd been found wanting, or that someone might actually get killed, that the boat might be lost . . . He'd take the shame any day before he'd let that happen, without a second's regret. Better they found him out now.

He squeezed by Bill Sutter, who was at the end of the gangway counting everyone coming off, getting ready to march them around to the Lazaretto. Nobody was going to Alexandria any time soon, and certainly not in *Nicobar*.

Harry, with his kitbag over one shoulder, and the Bergen he'd purloined off Olly Verney to hold his sextant on the other, marched up to his Flotilla Captain. Prepared for it.

'Lieutenant Gilmour, reporting, Sir,' he said, and saluted. Shrimp returned his salute, but Harry missed it; he was looking instead at one of the island's remaining MLs burbling up, coming alongside the quay behind him, a rating on her bow, with his boathook in both hands.

'Captain Simpson says the photoreconnaissance boys have reported the big one, the *Sovrana dei Mari,* beached at the entrance to Cagliari,' said Carey, all smiles. 'Neither she nor her troops made it to Tunis. There's no sign of the other two. We must have sunk them. How about that then? We did it. We're the boys, are we not, Harry?'

Harry was too tired to say anything.

'You might as well shake your CO's hand now, Mr Gilmour,' said Shrimp. 'You're being relieved.'

'Sir?' said Harry, realising he was too tired to speak. He just stood there, feeling sick, beaten, crushed. To have come so far and to have failed his crew, his Captain, himself. Wondering whether he had enough fortitude left to ask, even if just for form's sake, why. What the hell. If he was going to get cashiered and transferred to the infantry, he might as well know the reason. Hear the terrible truth.

'Permission to ask why, Sir?'

'Permission granted, Mr Gilmour. You've become too good at your job. There's a Sunderland leaving for Gib tonight and you're going to be on it. The ML is going to take you round to Kalafrana.' Shrimp put his hand out to be shaken.

Harry shook it. 'Sir?' he said.

Shrimp smiled. 'I've had this going through channels for a while. You were due to leave from Alex, when you got there. But leaving from here's just as good. You're on the next Commanding Officers' Qualifying Course, Mr Gilmour. You're going home to do your Perisher.'

Afterword

THE ROYAL NAVY SUBMARINE SERVICE

At the beginning of the twentieth century, the idea of submarine warfare was considered by senior Royal Navy officers to be 'Underhand, unfair and damned un-English' – that particular quote being attributed to Admiral Sir Arthur Wilson VC, who went on to call on the Royal Navy to 'Treat all submarines as pirates in wartime . . . and hang all crews.'

However, those in favour of experimenting with submarine technology eventually won the argument, and the Royal Navy launched its first submarine, *Holland 1*, in 1901.

For anyone interested in finding out more about the service in which Harry Gilmour, the hero of this story, would find himself in 1941 to 1942, there is the Royal Navy Submarine Museum, situated adjacent to the site of HMS *Dolphin*, the submarine service's first shore establishment on the Gosport side of Portsmouth Harbour, Hampshire.

It is Europe's only dedicated submarine museum and houses exhibitions covering the history of submarine warfare in general, and the role of the Royal Navy in particular.

The centrepiece is HMS *Alliance,* the UK's only surviving Second World War-era submarine, which has been preserved as an operational boat of the day, and is fully accessible to visitors, with frequent walk-through tours conducted by former RN submariners. HMS *Alliance* is also the Royal Navy's memorial to the 5,300 British submariners who lost their lives in the service.

Among other displays are a series of interactive exhibits including a working periscope, and a collection of thousands of personal items, photos and documents detailing the everyday lives of those in 'the silent service'. The other submarines in the collection include the original *Holland 1*, and *X24*, the only surviving Second World War midget submarine, similar to the boats that crippled the German battleship *Tirpitz*.

Acknowledgments

I would once again like to thank Captain Iain D. Arthur OBE RN, the former Captain (S) of the Devonport Flotilla, for his technical guidance in writing this novel. The accuracy of my portrayal of submarine warfare is entirely down to him.

About the Author

David Black is a former Fleet Street journalist and television documentary producer. He spent much of his childhood a short walk from the Royal Navy Submarine Memorial at Lazaretto Point on the Firth of Clyde, and he grew up watching the passage of both US and Royal Navy submarines in and out of the Firth's bases at Holy Loch and Faslane. As a boy, the lives of those underwater warriors captured his imagination. When he grew up, he discovered the truth was even more epic, and so followed the inspiration for his fictional submariner, Harry Gilmour, and a series of novels about his adventures across the Second World War. David Black is also the author of a non-fiction book, *Triad Takeover: A Terrifying Account of the Spread of Triad Crime in the West*. He lives in Argyll.

About the Author